BAREFOOT IN THE DARK

COPYRIGHT

NYLA Publishing
121 W 27th St., Suite 1201, New York, NY 10001
http://www.nyliterary.com

BAREFOOT IN THE DARK

SUZANNE ENOCH

DEDICATION

To every single person who ever read about Samantha Jellicoe and Rick Addison and wished, privately or aloud, that someone (ie, me) would sit down and write another one, for crying out loud. You're the reason this story exists. Thank you for being so very, very, very patient.
And thank you for encouraging me to jump back into this crazy world. It's really fun in here.

1

Tuesday, 1:02 p.m.

Samantha Jellicoe paused, her back plastered to the warm, rough-surfaced stone wall, then edged closer to the barred gate just beyond her. A thin line of sweat trickled down the side of her face, but she ignored it. That was rule number three in the thieves' handbook; when any movement can get you noticed, don't move.

The mutter of conversation just on the other side of the gate was mostly about filing times for stories, the legality of drones "accidentally" straying over private property, and something about shoes. It might have amused her, except that her name kept edging into the discussions. Her name. Her actual, real name. "Dammit," she muttered under her breath. This was not good, especially when all the people who knew her name also knew exactly where to find her and had surrounded the place so she couldn't leave without being seen. Well, *most* people wouldn't be able to leave without being seen.

The phone in her back pocket vibrated in three short bursts.

Refusing to jump, she tapped her earpiece against the wall. "What?" she breathed.

"You can see them from the security room, you know," the cultured male British accent noted.

She stepped back a few feet from the gate. "Any sap could do that. And stop spying on me."

"I will, if you'll stop spying on them."

Finally turning her head, she sent a glare up at the security camera hidden inconspicuously among the palm trees. "I don't like being stuck in here. I want to go for a run."

She could almost hear the man on the other end of the phone sitting forward. "Samantha, if you want to go for a run, have Ben drive you out somewhere. Do not hop the fence."

"Sorry, Rick, you're breaking up. I can't...hear... Oops – lost you."

"I can still see you standing there, dammit," Richard Addison retorted, his voice dropping and his accent intensifying. "And I don't want to see your arse disappearing over the wall on the evening news. Come back inside."

Because she wasn't an idiot, she left the line open, but she didn't bother to answer him. Yes, she could have seen them from the security room. She already had. She'd been glaring at them for the past twelve days, as a matter of fact. But she'd wanted information, and she couldn't get that from the non-stop, indecipherable buzz of overlapping voices echoing in the security room. So now she knew, and it did *not* make her feel any better.

"Samantha, get away from the wall before someone sees you."

She shot an affronted look at the camera. "Who do you think you're talking to, bud?"

"I didn't mean to insult you. Just come inside."

"You're the one who had to go and tell Frank Castillo we're engaged, so this zombie horde of press vultures is all your fault. If you can't think of another way for me to get out of here without

2

people snapping photos and shouting questions at me, I'm going over the back wall. You have two minutes."

"I had no idea Frank would type up our conversation in his police report, or that that bloody *Backstage Pass* show trolled the damned things. It's not entirely my fault, anyway; I was only attempting to explain why I'd put a Samurai sword through a man's shoulder and left him stuck to a shelf in my library."

"Ah, good times." And to think that had only been two weeks ago. Since then, the press and paparazzi and half the girls from the "Rick's Chicks" fan club had been staking out Rick's Solano Dorado estate. Stupid West Palm Beach was supposed to be used to shit like rich, gorgeous Brits getting engaged to mysterious nobodies, but they apparently hadn't gotten the memo about that this time.

"Yes, good times," he echoed. "Except for the bits about you nearly getting killed and me ruining a perfectly good Samurai sword. Get back in the house."

She continued away from the front gates, heading for the east side of the property. "Ninety seconds," she breathed.

"Why do you have to be so bloody stubborn?" Rick's hiss came in her ear as she changed course, moving in a direct line toward the back of the estate once she'd gotten beyond the line of sight from the front gate. "And why does part of me think you're trying to escape because of our conversation this morning?"

"Sorry, 'conversation'? I don't recall."

"You recall everything. And I only asked you if you like the *idea* of a spring wedding. Not that the ceremony had to take place then."

Because he was still watching her, Samantha kept moving, didn't clench her fists, and didn't let the stark terror running down her spine show at all. "I told you I'd marry you, Rick. Don't I have to look at bridal magazines and shit before I decide on what season I prefer?"

"It's not a requirement, no," he returned.

"Fine. But this is about me being a prisoner in here. Not about a wedding date." It was mostly about that, anyway.

"I don't like this scrutiny either, but I'm not planning the Great Escape."

"That's because you're used to people looking at you and taking your picture. I nearly shit myself the last time I ended up in that clip on *Nightly Dish*. People aren't supposed to know who I am."

"People aren't supposed to know who you *were*," he amended, that smooth, seductive whisper touching his voice. "The person you *are* has nothing to hide."

"Bullshit. The person I am still has nearly six years of statutes of limitations to wait out. I'm going for a run, or I'm going to end up looney tunes crazy and taking off all my clothes while I go screaming through the house."

Silence. "I might enjoy that," Rick said after a moment. "Come in and give it a go."

Samantha slowed as she reached the midway section of the east-facing wall of the large estate. This side bordered the Newton property, which didn't have nearly as many cameras and sensors as Solano Dorado boasted. From there it would be just one more wall jump to the road that meandered through the plethora of multi-million-dollar homes that littered this part of Palm Beach. Then she could even boost a car and get the hell out of Dodge until things calmed down a little – the point being, she would have some options.

She took a run at the wall, digging the toes of her running shoes into the uneven stone, and gripped the ridged top with her fingers. "I'll see you in an hour or two," she said, levering herself up to a crouch at the narrow top of the wall. "Or maybe I'll check into some cheap hotel in Orlando and pretend I'm a tourist."

"Devon," he said.

Pausing, Samantha looked over her shoulder to face the nearest security camera. "What?"

4

"You asked for an alternative to this break-out. I'm suggesting Devon."

"Could you be more specific? Because as I recall from an earlier conversation, you were planning on spending the entire month of September roasting in Florida while I wiggle around like a butterfly on a pin."

It wasn't the middle of nowhere, but it did have the benefit of being not Palm Beach. Plus, it had an even stonier wall around the house and gardens than the one on which she currently perched. "You're not lying just to get me back in the house, are you? Because you wouldn't like me when I'm angry."

"I'm not lying. But I'm not discussing it any further while you're perched like a damned owl on my wall."

"I'm perched like Batman. Not an owl." She'd likely pushed him far enough, though. Honestly, she didn't want to see her arse on the evening news, either – or spend the night in a crappy hotel. Shifting, Samantha dropped back into the garden, bending her knees to absorb the jolt. "Okay, but we're leaving tonight."

"I'll make arrangements as soon as I hang up with you." He paused. "Meet me in the kitchen, will you?"

"Fine."

Though she was perfectly capable of getting into the house completely unseen and undetected, there was an almost equal thrill in simply walking up and pulling open a door. Just like she belonged there. Rick, of course, would say that she did, but even after a year with him it still felt...like a very expensive outfit that didn't quite fit. Or maybe it did fit, and she was just worried about getting mustard on the front.

It was all so...weird. She'd pretended to be a wealthy, sophisti-cated gal on more occasions than she had fingers to count them on. She spoke a couple of languages and knew more about art and antiques than some museum curators. But when she drank cham-pagne with men – and women – in order to case their estates and then steal their treasures, that was an act. That was just her fitting in to go mostly unnoticed.

But now one of the wealthiest, most eligible bachelors in the world had decided he liked the scrapes and scars beneath her act. That made going unnoticed much more problematic. For her, at least – Rick seemed to think she was just being paranoid. In fact, he insisted that she had nothing at all to worry about as long as she stayed retired. Yeah, right. She'd believe that…well, never, probably. And since he knew more about the jobs she'd pulled as an art thief than just about anybody else, he probably didn't believe it, either.

As she opened the house's side door, she pulled her phone from her pocket and dialed. After two rings the line picked up. "Jellicoe Security," the smooth, Southern drawl announced.

"Hey, Aubrey," she returned, jabbing a finger in Rick's direction as he emerged from the hallway and the security room beyond. While he didn't mind her – them – being seen in public, anyone overhearing an argument ticked him off. "Please tell me I have some business."

"What you have, my dear," the sometime professional date for the elderly ladies of Palm Beach and her self-appointed office manager said, "is reporters. They're even trying to talk to me, and you know it's against my nature to refrain from chatting with people. I'm feeling positively frazzled."

"I've never even seen you sweat, Aubrey. Which is quite a thing, being that it's ten thousand degrees and four hundred percent humidity here right now."

"Precisely."

She made a face at the phone. "Just keep refraining, please. Shit. I don't suppose anybody cares if no privacy-minded client is going to hire me for a damn thing as long as all those cameras are circling me."

"Well, you could always just get it over with and give them an interview."

"Keep making jokes, funny man. I may be making myself scarce, but I'll check in later and let you know the details."

"No hurry, Miss Samantha. I'm teaching myself a new photoshopping program. I thought it might come in handy if we ever have to analyze photo evidence."

She hung up, turning to face the tall, black-haired Brit who'd literally exploded into her life just over a year ago. Bomb makers didn't advertise the romantic potential of their products, but she'd certainly come to appreciate it. "Aubrey's learning how to doctor photos, and tumbleweeds are blowing through my office."

Caribbean blue eyes took her in, from her auburn-colored ponytail to her scuffed white running shoes. "This will die down, you know," he commented, leaning a hip against the small kitchen table. "Someone will cheat on someone or start showing a baby bump, and the tabloids will charge back to the West Coast and forget about us."

"Then they should fuckin' get on with it," she retorted, opening the fridge and pulling out a diet Coke. "I can't even get to my own damn office."

"You could, if you weren't determined to remain invisible. We could control the circumstances of an interview."

He tilted his head at her, a lock of his black hair falling across one eye. The man could have been a model, or more likely one of those gorgeous athletes selling energy drinks or soda or mysteriously seductive colognes. He could have any girl he wanted even without the billions in his bank account. Being the complete package made him way too noticeable, as far as she was concerned. The exact wrong man for her ever to fall for, really. But fall she had, and hard.

"My profession – both of them – requires discretion." There. That sounded logical.

Rick straightened, approaching to lean around her for a bottle of water. "Your one profession," he corrected. "You are not a thief any longer."

"And I still don't want my face plastered all over the damn world. You know there's got to be that one security guard somewhere who happened to see me at a distance four years ago when I heisted a Monet." When he frowned, she squinted at him. "That hypothetical guard and that hypothetical Monet," she amended, "but you know what I mean." She elbowed him. "So, have you called the airport yet to gas up the jet?"

A slow smile touched his mouth. "Perhaps we should pack rucksacks and hike into the wilderness. Live off the land."

She snorted. "Sam don't live off the land. I mean, I could, but it would have to be guys with badges and guns chasing me. Not guys with cameras."

"Nice to see you put it into perspective. If we're going to be away for a time, I need to go see Tom." He dipped a finger into the neck of her T-shirt, hooked the material, and drew her up against him. Dropping a hot kiss on her mouth, Rick lifted his head again to look down at her. "Don't disappear anywhere."

Samantha reached up to tuck the straying strand of his hair back behind one ear. "I'm not missing that flight."

"Mm hm. We're leaving for the airport at seven."

"'K. I just have a couple more phone calls to make."

Rick paused halfway out the kitchen door. "Walter Barstone and Aubrey Pendleton are not coming with us. We're going on holiday. This is not going to become one of your capers."

"Huh," she returned, folding her arms across her chest. "You sure that's how you want to word that?"

He walked back up to her, his steps measured. "If either of them appears anywhere in the U.K. while we're there, I'm going to fly Tom Donner in to stay with us. That's how I'm wording it."

Well, that was the kind of bluff she didn't want to call. Samantha scowled. "I do not want stupid Tom Donner, attorney at law, everywhere I turn around."

With a smile, Rick brushed his thumb along her lips. "I know. Hence the effectiveness of the threat." For a long moment he gazed at her, those blue eyes of his practically melting her insides. "I know Walter is your family," he finally said, leaning in to kiss the corner of her mouth. "I also know that when you have him about as back-up, you tend to take more risks." He kissed the other corner of her mouth. "We're going on holiday. To escape from the press. Not to jump off buildings or break into museums."

"Very funny." Weighing her alternatives, Sam stuck out her hand. "No Stoney and no Aubrey, and no Tom Donner."

He shook her hand. "Agreed."

She pulled her hand free, then put a finger into his breastbone. "And you will relax, too. You talk a good game, but I know you're pissed off, too. Holiday. Vacation. Whatever you call it. That's what this is. Just you and me."

Richard continued gazing at her, but she knew it was more to let her know he was serious than anything else. Just like she knew he didn't like any of this, either. Anything obstructing the way he lived, the way he conducted his business, didn't get tolerated. Generally. She had a good hunch that the only reason he'd restrained himself from bellowing and flinging people about for the past two weeks was because he was trying to set an example for her. "I'll see you by seven."

Before he could turn around again, Samantha grabbed his shirt. "Not so fast, Brit," she muttered, and plastered her mouth against his. Whatever it was about this guy, and however bad she probably was for him and his massive business empire, she was supremely glad that he'd asked her to marry him. Because she didn't think she'd ever be able to shake him out of her system. He kissed her back, pressing her up against the kitchen counter in that possessive way of his that made her all shivery inside.

Just when she was ready to start ripping the buttons off his very expensive blue dress shirt, he stepped backward. "Seven o'clock," he said, his voice a little rough, and with a cocky grin he left the kitchen.

Dammit, he did that on purpose. The damned Brit totally got

off on her not getting off, or he wouldn't wind her up and walk away like that. Cursing under her breath, Samantha made her way upstairs to call Walter "Stoney" Barstone and tell him to hold down the Jellicoe Security fort because she was going on vacation.

"Good," Stoney said when he picked up his phone and she told him about England. "I can't even watch the local news anymore without needing a valium. You're way too in the spotlight, honey."

"It's not my fault," she returned, scowling at the vase of orchids resting on the end table. "Castillo blabbed after Rick blabbed. You'd think cops and billionaires would be more discreet."

"No, it *is* your fault, because you're hanging out with cops and billionaires."

She sighed. "Just be glad I'm not engaged to the cop."

"Christ, Sam, I think I just had a seizure. Go to England. Have a vacation. If this is the life you think you want, you'd better get a good taste of it before it's too late to change your mind."

"I'm not changing my mind, Stoney. Besides, wasn't it you who told me I'd live longer if I hung up my cat burglar suit?"

"That was before half the reporters in Florida started hanging out twenty feet from where you sleep. Go. I'll keep Aubrey in line."

More likely it would be the other way around. "Thanks. I'll call you."

"Be safe or be smart, honey."

Samantha smiled at the phone. Some things never changed. "Will do."

She updated Aubrey next, and at least he didn't snipe at her for falling in love with Rick. She hadn't actually ever hired Aubrey to be the Jellicoe Security office manager, but since he'd shown up six months ago and kept all her crap way more organized than she had any interest in doing, and because he seemed to have some idea about what her past was like and had never called her on it, she had no objection to him sticking around.

Once her two bases were covered, she trotted down the

hallway to the humongous bedroom she shared with Rick and went to find a suitcase to pack for a trip to England. In the past she would have pulled out her emergency backpack filled with all the essentials a girl needed if she had to leave somewhere in a hurry, added a couple of shirts and pairs of pants, and been good to go. But Rick had shredded her pack and tossed it into the pool, so she had to start from scratch. With one of *his* monogrammed suitcases. That only seemed fair.

○

"PARKING GARAGE OR OUT FRONT?" Ben asked from behind the wheel.

"Out front," Richard returned, eyeing his phone and its streaming live coverage of his Mercedes heading into Palm Beach proper. Bloody drones. "More direct flight line. I'll be about an hour. Be close by; when I leave, it's going to be fast."

"No problem, boss."

At that, Rick stifled a grin. Previous to Sam coming to live at Solano Dorado his personal employees had been more...formal. God, his life had upended over the past year. While he hadn't loved every bit of it, neither would he have changed any of it. "And don't bother to get out, since that'll just give the press more time to catch up."

Samantha would have suggested they just slow down and have him jump out the window so that Ben could lead the press cars on a merry chase, but he settled for a quick exit and a determined walk up from the curb. Refusing to hurry his steps as doom raced up behind him, he walked to the rotating doors of the building which housed the Donner, Christensen and Rhodes law firm and entered the glass-enclosed lobby. Doom was very loud and had a great many questions about who Samantha would be wearing at their wedding. All he cared about was that on their wedding night she would be wearing *him*, but he wasn't about to say that aloud.

"Mr. Addison," the security guard said with a nod, and pushed a button to unlock the nearest of the elevators.

"I believe I'm being followed, Joe."

"Not for long, Mr. Addison."

Rick stepped into the elevator and punched the button for the top floor. "You're a good man, Joe."

Tom Donner, for once in a suit and tie, was waiting by the elevator when the doors opened again. "Why is it that the private guy with the publicity-shy girlfriend always has a parade following him now?" he drawled, offering his hand.

"Because they want a story I won't give them."

"Well, at least I know when you're coming by, these days. I just keep a computer streaming the local news."

"If you're finished pointing out the obvious, I could use a bloody beer," Rick commented, returning the handshake and then leading the way into the well-appointed offices. While the other partners had a select few clients, he was the one who funded the tasteful paneling and the posh address. In fact, he was Tom Donner's only client. That was the way they both liked it.

"Did Jellicoe chase you off Solano Dorado?" Tom pursued, closing them inside his office and pulling a pair of beers from the refrigerator set beneath a credenza. "She's been calling Katie, you know. Nearly every morning. They're like little hens, except one's a scary, fanged, cat burglar hen."

"Ex-cat burglar hen," Rick amended. "I'm glad she likes Katie. Your wife's a good influence on her."

"Too bad I can't say the same thing about Jellicoe."

With a short frown Rick dropped into one of the two chairs facing Tom's big steel desk. "That's not what I hear. Wasn't there something about a little surveillance the two of them did a few weeks ago, and the resulting—"

"No, you do not get to talk about that. Dammit." The big former Texan flushed a bright red as he stalked to the window and back. Finally, his empty fist balled, he sat behind his desk. "She didn't really tell you about that, did she?"

"She only mentioned that she'd taken Katie somewhere with her and that your significant other had seemed...excited afterward. And frankly, Tom, I know the benefits of having an adrenaline junkie about after they've had a rush."

Over the past two weeks he'd also been learning what it was like to have a *caged* cat burglar about. It was not a happy experience. As agile-minded as she was, with nothing to occupy her but thoughts of ways she could escape the house without being seen, he was at least as ready for a holiday as she was.

"Suddenly some things make sense," Tom muttered, taking a long swig of beer. "No wonder you want to marry her."

"No wonder I'm going to marry her. Speaking of which, I had to agree to take her to England this evening."

"I thought you weren't going till late next week. Is everything ready?"

"No, not quite. I'll need to make a few calls while I'm here." He sat forward. "And as far as she knows, we're going to Rawley Park to look at some art and work on the museum."

Finally, Tom grinned. "Man, I wish I could be there when she realizes you're going to the middle-of-nowhere Scotland."

"You have no idea how difficult it is to keep secrets from her. But she'll enjoy Castle Canniebrae, I'm certain."

"Sure. A big, old, moldy castle ten miles away from anything resembling a city? Nowhere to burgle, no one to grift, none of her cronies around, and your relatives to meet? She'll love it." Tom snorted. "The two of you'll be back here in under a week. Probably separately."

It was a distinct possibility that Sam would detest that life, and the idea that he'd sprung his aunt and uncle and cousin on her without warning would piss her off so much that she *would* leave without him. But she enjoyed history, and Canniebrae had that in spades. Aside from that, he hadn't seen the old castle since he'd been fifteen, and back then it had held a certain kind of...magic for him. A magic he wanted to share with her. But warning her in advance that he meant to spring his relatives on her would ensure that she would, as she put it, freak out. "She doesn't grift," he said aloud. "Don't be lumping more sins on her head. Besides, if she's listening this'll come back to bite you."

"'Listening'? What, you think she bugged my office?" Tom started to laugh, then choked into silence. "Christ. I'm never going to sleep again, you know."

"Serves you right for calling her a grifter. Anyway, let's get to it, shall we? Pull up my calendar so we can take this in order."

Over the next hour they rescheduled appointments and paper signings, arranged for Tom to be his signing proxy for the new Tokyo deal they'd polished off yesterday, and had two contracts forwarded from London so he could make some revisions on the flight over and email them back. Depending on how long they stayed in Scotland he would have to fly down to London once or twice, but since he'd been working on this surprise for the past two weeks, much of the rest of it was already taken care of.

Finally, Tom sat back. Swirling the remains of his beer lazily in the bottle, he eyed Rick. "So, what are you going to do if she doesn't like the quiet country life or the relatives? Or if, God forbid, the relatives don't like her? Sam Jellicoe ain't precisely old English aristocracy."

"I've done for the past year without their paths crossing, so I imagine I can do it indefinitely if need be." As for the quiet life, he did like the down time on occasion, but he could live without it. The caged version of Sam hopefully differed from the idle-ish version, but he honestly didn't know that for certain. She did tend to create her own excitement – for the both of them. "*You* don't like her, and I've still managed to keep both of you around."

"Yeah, well, it's not that I don't... I mean, she's good in a pinch, but she seems to get you into trouble at least as often as she gets you out of it. Unpredictability and arrest warrants don't mix well with power and wealth."

"Says you. There aren't any arrest warrants. None with her name written on them, anyway." No, they were all blank and waiting for someone, somewhere to find that one piece of evidence linking her to some of the most daring and lucrative burglaries in the world. That could not be allowed to happen. Luckily those few law enforcement officials who suspected who she was – Frank Castillo here in Palm Beach and Sam Gorstein in New York – had already been both thoroughly charmed by her *and* put somewhat in her debt. Still, he didn't think he would rest easy for another six years, at which time the last of the statutes of limitation would expire. As long as she didn't pull off any new jobs, that was.

"Okay. I know I'm not going to win this fight."

"No, you're not." Richard finished off his beer and pulled out his iPhone to dial Ben. "I'm heading downstairs," he told his driver.

"I'll be waiting for you, boss. Do you want me to hold the door?"

"No, I'll be diving in."

As both men stood, Tom shook his head. "Until this past year I never doubted your sanity, Rick. Have a good trip. I hope it goes as well as you hope it will."

"Thanks. I'll be in touch."

2

Wednesday, 8:15 a.m.

Samantha sent a sideways glance at Rick. He sat in one of the comfy leather chairs by a window, the slide half closed to keep the glare of the sun off the paper he was marking up. Another contract, from the look of it. Probably that timber recla-mation thing she'd been bugging him about, though he wouldn't admit that he'd taken up the cause. Evidently, he found it amusing that she cared about the environment – as if a cat burglar couldn't watch *Blue Planet* or *Cosmos* or something.

When he didn't do more than flip to the next page and continue jotting notes, she slid her phone out of her pocket and checked her GPS. It kept fritzing out, but it at least confirmed what she'd been suspicious about for the past ninety minutes or so: They weren't on their way to Devonshire. Or to London. They were too far north for that.

"GPS doesn't work in the air," he muttered in his heart-thud-ding British accent, though he didn't lift his head or pause in his writing.

"Why are we going to Scotland?" Counter attacking seemed a

better tactic than admitting that she'd been checking up on him. Not that she had a reason to do so, except it seemed like they'd been flying for an hour or two too long.

"Fuel," he answered, and turned another page.

"Liar."

At that, he looked up at her. Caribbean blue, she always thought, gazing at those pretty eyes of his. Hot, sweaty, awesome sex and cool boat drinks. That was Rick Addison. Or the part she had hold of, anyway. There was also the son-of-a-bitch business shark that had made his family's millions into billions, and she liked that aspect of him, too. She could understand the idea of doing whatever it took to attain a goal or a prize, whether it was a company or a Matisse painting.

"What makes you so certain I'm lying?" he asked, lifting an eyebrow.

"Because we could have been in London already, and we're still flying. And because we've never stopped in Scotland for fuel before. And because you answered right away, like you had the answer ready for me."

"I'm always ready for you," he murmured, a half-smile touching his lean face. He slanted an annoyed glance toward the flight attendant currently brewing him another pot of tea at the front of the cabin. "But you're correct."

"I know I'm correct. But why are we going to Scotland? And why didn't you mention that to me when you said we were, hmm, what was it, oh yeah – 'going to Devonshire'?" She took up his Oxford-educated accent for that last part, mimicking him.

"It's a surprise."

"Don't think for a second that I won't jump out of this plane, Brit. I know where the parachutes are."

Sighing, he stacked the papers in front of him and set them and his pen aside. "Very well. We're going to a place along the River Dee, about midway between Inver and Keiloch. It's a place that's been in my family for a time."

Samantha did some swift calculations. Aside from the fact that for English aristocrats the idea of "a time" could be anywhere between a hundred and a thousand years, she'd heard the River Dee mentioned before. Not by him, but on the news. "Isn't that where Balmoral Castle is? You know, the Queen of England's place?"

"Yes, I know what Balmoral is. Canniebrae is approximately four miles southwest of it."

"Ah." She folded her arms, trying to decide if she was annoyed or grudgingly interested. "And why are we going to an estate in the Scottish Highlands?"

"Because I haven't been there in eighteen years, which makes me think the press won't expect to find us there."

She continued to eye him, looking for any of his rare tells. "Okay, that makes sense," she said grudgingly. "Which makes me ask why you bothered to keep it a secret, Brit."

Rick stood up. "Amber, that will be all," he said, not bothering to look at the flight attendant. Which was good, because Amber -- or whatever her name really was – had rolled up the waist of her skirt until her ass showed every time she bent over. It was amazing how many vital snacks seemed to have been stored in bottom drawers for this flight.

"Of course, Mr. Addison." With a quick flutter of her eyelashes she went into the forward cabin and closed the door behind her.

"Who hired her?" Samantha asked, as Rick walked up to hold either arm of her chair and lean over her.

"What?"

"The girl with the balloons stuffed down the front of her blouse." When he continued to frown at her, she gave up and grinned. "Okay. Point taken. You only have eyes for me."

Rick smiled back at her, which had the effect of making her insides feel all mushy. "Precisely. Aside from that, anyone who shows her arse that readily must not have much else to offer."

Of course he'd noticed; the flight attendant's ass had been

pretty hard to miss. But being gorgeous, rich, and divorced he'd no doubt had more than his share of asses and boobs flashed at him. "Back to Scotland, then," she said aloud. "What's the secret? Or rather, why the secret?"

He leaned closer, touching his mouth to hers. Goose bumps lifted on her arms. They'd joined the mile-high club a year ago, but hell, if he wanted to re-up their membership, she wasn't about to complain. Unless he was just trying to keep her from asking questions. That wasn't allowed.

When he pulled the pony tail holder from her hair and drew his fingers through her shoulder-length mess, she took a deep breath and then shoved at him. "Not so fast, Prince Charming. What's going on?"

"I'll tell you once we land. I'd rather be doing something else right now."

Samantha stood, having to maneuver around his tall, rock-solid form to do so, and headed for the rear of the plane. "I'm getting a parachute."

Rick made a motion like he wanted to grab her arm, but she had to give him props when he settled for making a fist instead. "We both know you're not going to jump, so sit down and I'll attempt to explain how difficult it is to surprise you with anything, and why I wanted to do so this time."

He didn't look happy, but neither would she if some big secret she'd tried to keep had thrown up all over her. As she gazed at him, though, part of her wanted to give in, have some awesome airborne sex, and let him play out his secret surprise however he wanted to. Most people liked to be surprised, after all. Most people appreciated when their significant other went to lots of trouble to arrange something special. But she wasn't most people.

She didn't exactly want to jump out of an airplane, either. Not when she'd never done it before, and not when she was in a jet. Another time, in a plane made for jumping out of, sure. In fact, it sounded fun. Keeping a wary eye on him, she sat down again. "Talk."

"I wanted to see your genuine reaction to Canniebrae," he said after a moment, sinking into the seat directly beside hers. "I didn't want you to look it up online or call any of your nefarious business contacts to see whether anyone had cased the joint or anything."

Samantha grinned. "'Cased the joint'? Who are you, Dick Tracy?"

"You know what I mean."

"So, you think something about Canniebrae will be unexpected," she mused, half to herself, and caught the swift narrowing of his blue eyes. "Is it haunted?"

Rick snorted. "I thought so eighteen years ago. There were certainly tales told 'round the dining room table. It was built in 1291, after all."

Wow. Anything that old was automatically interesting to her, and he would know that. Which begged a couple of questions. "Why have you never mentioned it before?"

"I've been saving it, I suppose. As I said, I haven't been there in quite a while. I don't spend a great deal of time thinking about it."

"Just how oldy moldy is this place?"

He stretched, slipping one arm around her shoulder as he settled again. "I suppose we'll find out."

Leaning in, he nibbled at her ear, and her eyes rolled back in her head. It might be that he was attempting to distract her from asking any more questions, or it could be that they hadn't had sex in nearly forty-eight hours. Whatever it was, he was good at the kissing thing. And the sex thing. She settled into the curve of his arm, kissing him back, sliding a palm beneath his T-shirt and up his warm, flat abdomen.

"Mr. Addison," the overhead speaker burped into life with Amber's perky voice, "we'll be landing in ten minutes. May I come in and clean away the drinks?"

"Fuck," he muttered, then leaned across Samantha to tap the intercom button. "Come in, Amber."

"Non-fuck," Samantha whispered into his ear, chuckling despite the fact that she was a little annoyed, herself.

While Amber wiggled her ass around the cabin, clearing away the remains of their breakfast and a tea cup and two sodas, Samantha buckled herself into her seat. Rick did likewise beside her, curling his fingers around hers. Even after a year he still looked for opportunities to hold her hand, and she'd gotten well past the suspicion that he was holding her to keep her from escaping. He liked touching her. She liked when he touched her. It didn't have to mean anything more than that.

Samantha sent him a sideways look, to find a slight grin on his face. Okay, she'd missed something. "Did you tell Donner where we were going, or did he suggest we might try getting away to Scotland?"

Damnation, she was clever. That was what Richard loved about her, of course, but sometimes he wondered what sort of business tycoon she would have become all on her own if her proclivities and upbringing hadn't led her to a life of high-end crime. "I mentioned that I wanted to take you somewhere with a guarantee of some privacy, but where you wouldn't feel trapped. He might have mentioned Canniebrae first, or I might have. I don't remember."

Samantha shifted to face him more directly. "So, he suggested an seven-hundred-year-old castle in the middle of the Scottish Highlands, a place you haven't been for eighteen years, one that you didn't even remember you owned. He thinks I'll be bored to tears, doesn't he?"

"I don't care what he thinks. I think–"

"Does it have electricity?"

"They answered the telephone when I called, so I assume so."

She narrowed her eyes. "So, what, you guys think that just because I like city life that I can't hack it in the boonies?"

Richard stilled his responding smile. "Boonies" didn't even begin to describe Canniebrae. "I never said that."

"He did though, didn't he? Donner?"

"You are paranoid."

"Damn straight. That's what he said, wasn't it? That I'd hate it here. That manly man Rick would go for hikes and shoot elk with a bow and arrow and live off the land, and I would be stealing a car within an hour when I couldn't find a hair dryer."

"He didn't call me 'manly man Rick'." Richard didn't bother trying to hide his amusement this time; she would see it anyway. Aside from that, the lady loved a challenge. If climbing the walls kept her from climbing the walls, so to speak, then so much the better. If that had been the end of it, he would have counted the conversation as a victory. But she'd made it plainer than ever that she didn't appreciate surprises. And he had another one.

"Well, you can call Lawyer Man right now and tell him that I'm loving Scotland," she announced, settling back into her seat again. "Nessie could chew off my leg and I'd still be loving Scotland."

"I'll pass that along," he said, trying to decide whether now would be better than after they landed. Now made more sense, because the plane was too low for parachuting. "There's one more thing."

She turned her head to look at him, clever green eyes searching his expression. "What?" she asked dubiously.

"Since you're joining the Addison family, it's time you met them. The rest of them."

For a long moment she stared at him, a hundred different emotions flitting across her face. Samantha Jellicoe had been raised by her father – if one could call it being raised as opposed to being unleashed. These days Walter Barstone, the towering, male version of Diana Ross, was as close to family as she had. Except for him, of course, and an assortment of other nefarious characters she seemed to charm and collect. He, on the other hand, was *not* a hanger-on; he was the one riding the whirlwind.

"You have an uncle." She narrowed her eyes. "Rowland, isn't it?"

Richard blinked himself free from wayward metaphors. "Yes. My father's younger brother. And his wife, Mercia. And their son, Reginald."

"They live at Canniebrae?"

"No. They're coming to visit. To meet you."

He waited silently, the muscles down his back tense as he readied himself to react to whatever she might do. Punching him in the head seemed the most likely, closely followed by silence and then an attempt to flee once they touched down. She didn't move either, her gaze blank as she no doubt ran a dozen or so possible scenarios through her agile mind.

"Well, you met my so-called dad," she finally said, furrowing her brow. "I suppose it's only fair."

That had not been what he expected. "You're all right with it, then?"

"Depends. What are you going to tell them about me? Or do they already know something?"

"I'm in occasional contact with Reginald. When the photos of our first outing came out he emailed me. You were 'hot', as I recall, and he wanted to know if you had a sister. I called my uncle after our engagement news leaked, an—"

"You mean, after you blabbed about it," she broke in.

"Yes, after I unintentionally cooperated with the police department after impaling a man in my library." He frowned at her; reminding her that Gabriel Toombs had been in the Solana Dorado library because of the lunatic's obsession with her would only gain him more barbs. "Anyway, Reg suggested that the family be introduced to you. The rest was my idea." Richard took a breath. "As to what I'll tell them about you, you are a retrieval expert hired by some of the most prestigious institutions and collectors in the world."

Her scowl flipped into a grin. "Ooh, I sound awesome. Just

don't mention how I've also stolen from most of those same places."

"I won't. Neither will you."

Thank God. The weight on his shoulders for the past few weeks, the worry over how she would react to all this, melted away. It had made his typical tensions over business dealings feel like so much fiddle-faddle. This mattered. She mattered. Nothing else came close.

The jet bumped, followed by the unmistakable sensation of deceleration. Samantha gripped his fingers. He knew quite well that she wasn't frightened. She liked the feeling of going too fast, of being not quite in control of circumstances. Of course she would have preferred it if the jet had been a convertible, so her hair could blow in the wind. Whatever he was getting himself into with her, however mad she drove him, he was never letting her go. No matter what.

"Don't tell me what to do," she said, squeezing his hand and then with swift fingers unfastening the seatbelt and standing. "But duh, I'm not going to tell anybody how I make a living."

"How you used to make a living."

She used the present tense just because she knew it would provoke a response from him, but reminding her on occasion that she'd elected to travel the relatively straight and narrow couldn't hurt. Standing, he watched as she collected her handbag, which she'd likely chosen because she could sling it across one shoulder to leave both hands and arms free. It wasn't an escape back pack, but she would consider it the next best thing.

"We'll take the helicopter to Canniebrae," he announced. "That'll get us there by midmorning."

"Awesome. Is there a landing pad, or do we rappel to the ground?"

"There's a clearing. By the loch. And Canniebrae is accessible by car, or at least four-wheel drive vehicle."

He couldn't quite shake the suspicion that she was being too agreeable. Yes, it would be amusing to see a consummate suburbanite like Samantha Jellicoe dealing with the relatively few amenities and amusements of country life, but he also wanted her to enjoy herself. He also wanted her to like his relatives, as little as he generally had to do with them. As to whether they would like her... If they didn't, they were simply foolish. Her zest for life and everything in it had torn into his heart months ago, and if Reg and his aunt and uncle couldn't see her the same way, he could only pity them.

British customs and half a dozen airport workers hurried up to the plane as he descended the stairs to the tarmac, and the helicopter next to the nearest hangar started its engine. He flashed passports and identifications at the customs agent while he gave instructions for their luggage to be loaded on the helicopter, with anything that wouldn't fit to be trucked up after them. His jet needed to leave again for London as soon as possible, before anyone could confirm where he and Sam had actually gone.

Her shoulder-length auburn hair kicked up in the downdraft, and she grinned over at him. "Do you think they'll let me pilot the copter?" she asked, leaning up to shout in his ear.

"Good God, I hope not."

They clambered aboard, and the moment they were both belted in, the helicopter rose into the cloudy sky above Inverness. Sam was already wearing a headset and deep in conversation with the pilot. She'd temporarily taken over the controls of a helicopter once in Florida, but there they'd at least been over water. Now she had a taste for it.

"So, what do you think, Blakely?" she was asking, as he donned his own headset. "Just once around Loch Ness?"

"I could lose my license, ye ken. And if we crash, I—"

"If we crash, I'm sure we can make it look like Samantha's fault," Rick broke in. "Otherwise, no one's going to say anything. You have my word."

"And mine," Samantha seconded.

"We'll be passin' over a few hills where ye couldn't do much damage, then. If ye're certain, Mr. Addison."

No, Mr. Addison wasn't certain, but he didn't want to look like he had a stick up his arse. "Just try not to do the crash thing."

"I make no promises," she returned, and climbed into the front co-pilot's seat.

By the time the River Dee came into sight, Richard was regretting the omelet he'd eaten on the plane. He wasn't certain whether Blakely had invented the rule that a helicopter couldn't fly below a thousand feet except during landing and take-off, but if the pilot was lying, Richard was giving him a generous Christmas bonus. Generally he liked flying, and he specifically enjoyed flying by helicopter, but he had the suspicion that the light-fingered Samantha was being intentionally ham-fisted. Her revenge for him keeping a secret from her, most likely. That was why he gripped the handhold and kept his mouth shut as they lurched across the Highland skies.

"We're coming close to Balmoral air space," Blakely finally said, and took the controls back. "Don't want the Royal Air Force shooting us down, now."

"No, that would be bad," Sam agreed, climbing out of the co-pilot's seat and dropping down next to Richard again. "How was it?"

"Lovely."

She grinned at him. "Did you barf?"

"Nearly." If the pilot hadn't also been on the intercom he would have said more, but any revenge he had in mind for Samantha could wait until they were somewhere more private. From the way she looked back at him she knew it, so he glanced out the window. "Look over there. That's Balmoral."

She leaned across his legs to look down the valley. "Man, that place is huge! It would be awesome to...visit after dark."

"It's haunted, ye know," Blakely put in, following the River Dee around the bend, continuing deeper into the Highlands. "Every old castle in the Highlands is haunted."

They were right up against the Cairngorm Mountains, where the low grasses and windswept hills made way for deep ravines and old pine and elm forests, and endless, sweeping moors. It might well have been the most beautiful country in the world. Of course, those poetical thoughts paled when compared to the sensation of Sam doing more intentional wriggling across his thighs.

"Stop that," he muttered, his jaw clenched, as he resolutely kept his gaze up and away from her squirming arse. He was damned Richard Addison, and he was not going to exit his private helicopter with a stiffy in his jeans.

With a chuckle he could feel, she sat up again. "Every castle?" she repeated, facing Richard. "Who's Canniebrae's specter, then?"

Curiosity might kill cats, but she was one former cat burglar who'd found her life saved more than once simply because of her curiosity. Well, that and her exceptional skill and intelligence. Shrugging, he took her hand and twined his fingers around hers. The fact that she'd allowed herself to be captured still stunned him, sometimes. "I don't know, specifically. I heard noises once or twice that I couldn't explain, but I was very young, then. It's generally some ancestor or other, if you believe that sort of thing."

"Mm hm."

Richard looked out the window again. "Just over the rise ahead. Your holiday from civilization and the paparazzi."

Immediately she leaned forward, her hands on the back of the seats in front of them. A moment later it came into view through the mist – a gray, sprawling behemoth of centuries-old stone and wrought iron, ivy climbing the north-facing walls all the way up to the pitched roof of the third floor.

"It's Dracula's castle," she announced, lifting both eyebrows. "You're going to murder me here."

"If I were Dracula, we would have flown up here at night," he

27

countered smoothly. "And I wouldn't spend most of my time in – what do you Yanks call it? – the Sunshine State."

She snorted. "Sounds like a perfect disguise to me." Leaning over, she kissed his temple. "Except you're James Bond, not Dracula," she murmured, then straightened to look forward again. "Well, part of it's still standing," she commented after a moment. "Blakely, how close is the nearest inn?"

"Orrisey is down the hill about a mile. It was voted the second bonniest village in the Highlands last year. It's on Canniebrae land, actual—"

"We're not staying at an inn, Samantha. We're staying at Canniebrae," Richard interrupted. "It has very gothic turrets. And a widow's walk."

"You're serious. You didn't just rent this place to scare the shit out of me or something."

In truth she looked more baffled than alarmed, as if she thought him too...well-pressed to own anything remotely ramshackle. Richard gazed down at Canniebrae as they circled it a second time. Broken windows and holes in the roof of the west wing, which actually sagged now in the middle, at least one tumbled wall around the remains of the garden – yes, it was definitely ramshackle. It was also his. While he'd expected her to be surprised and out of her element, unlike Tom he hadn't thought she would hate it. "That bad, is it?" he commented aloud.

Narrowing her light green eyes, she continued studying his ancestral pile. "How much did Donner bet that I'd run?"

"A hundred dollars." That wasn't true, but if he'd mentioned it, Tom would certainly have put a sawbuck on Sam running away to civilization.

She took another long look before she turned away from the window to face him again. "Okay, then. I'll play along. Why does it have a widow's walk? You can't see the ocean from here."

"No, but from the roof you can see across the loch and all the way down the length of the valley. A lady would want to know if her laird was returning from battle."

"Or if she needed to gather her wee bairns and flee because the Sassenach lobster backs were coming," she countered in a pitch-perfect Inverness accent. Even Blakely turned his head to glance back at her.

"Nicely done," Richard said, taking hold of her hips to pull her back down to her seat.

She shrugged. "What? I saw *Braveheart* and *Outlander*."

He kept his mouth shut. Whatever he wished to say to her could wait until they were alone. In fact, he now had several reasons to want to be alone with her. "What do you think, then?" he asked again, mostly to distract himself.

"Too early to tell." Samantha spoke almost absently, her gaze still on the castle as they crossed over the loch and set down on the large, sloping lawn to the east side of the main building. "You're sure there aren't any vampires?"

"Reasonably sure."

"And the roof isn't going to fall in and smash us into pancakes?"

"I put our odds at fifty-fifty. The west wing's been closed for years, so the being pancaked odds increase there."

By this time, he had no idea whether she was looking for ways to gain illegal entry or if she'd already moved on to categorizing the various time periods when his ancestors had added rooms or done renovations over the years. He certainly hadn't done anything to the place. Eighteen years. Had it truly been that long since he'd last set eyes on Canniebrae? Growing up, this had been where he spent a good part of nearly every summer, at least until his fifteenth year. Richard shook himself. This was about Samantha and him and their future. Not about the past.

"Thanks, Blakely," Samantha said, shedding the headphones and unlatching the door to hop out of the helicopter.

Richard joined her on the lawn, the stirred-up chill digging through his light jacket and reminding him that autumn in the Highlands was far different than autumn in southern Florida. A pair of men in matching black waistcoats and black and green kilts emerged from the house to unload their luggage. With some bobbing and greetings that he couldn't quite hear over the rotor noise, they moved well away from the copter.

The helicopter lifted off again, and in less than a minute was out of sight behind the hills and trees. The sound lasted for another handful of seconds, then faded into silence.

"Wow," Samantha whispered, stepping sideways to take his hand and lean into his shoulder. "It's really creepy now that I see it from ground level."

"Samantha, y—"

"Easy, Brit. Nobody's asking me if we've set a date, where I get my hair cut, who my favorite designer is. It'll do."

Kissing her pretty, autumn-colored hair and more relieved than he cared to admit, Richard smiled. "Then we can go in the front door, I assume, rather than scaling the walls?"

"Sure. This time."

3

Wednesday, 10:31 a.m.

Rick owned a lot of antiques, but he was careful with them. He appreciated their rarity and their beauty. Even if the west wing of Canniebrae had started falling apart a long time ago, it wasn't like him not to have repaired it. That left Samantha with the hanging question of "why". Before she asked that out loud, though, she needed to look around a little. She was one mostly former cat burglar who preferred to know where the alarms were before she started stomping around willy-nilly.

She kept an eye on Rick as the butler, Yule, welcomed them and showed them up the mahogany-railed grand staircase, down a long, high-ceilinged hallway right out of *Beauty and the Beast*, and out to the end of the castle's east wing where the master bedchamber had been aired out and made ready for them. There were no cobwebs in the corners here, but Cannibrae didn't feel at all like any other place he owned.

Even with the broken windows and the holes she'd seen in the roof, the place did ooze with power. The old, inherited kind of power. The stone walls practically hummed with it. For a few minutes she felt like Elizabeth Bennet in *Pride and Prejudice*, except that her Mr. Darcy made way more than ten thousand pounds a year. It was times like this, though, when he stood looking out the open bedroom – bedchamber – window, the wind ruffling his wavy black hair, that she remembered he *was* Mr. Darcy. Or Richard Addison, the Marquis of Rawley, rather. He came from an old, old line, with bazillions of years of history and pomp and shit. She, on the other hand, couldn't even remember for certain what her mom's maiden name had been.

"What?" Rick asked, turning around as Yule deposited the last of the luggage and left the room.

"What, what?"

"You're staring at me."

"I'm always staring at you. You're gorgeous."

Rick grinned, walking over to casually latch the bedchamber door – it actually had one of those old, oversized brass keys stuck in the keyhole – and shed his light jacket. "Thank you, but your expression was more contemplative than lustful."

Sam shook herself. "I just forget sometimes how oldy, moldy – I mean pedigreed – you and your family are."

"Mm hm." With the same smooth motion, he pulled the black T-shirt over his head and dropped it onto the floor. "I am not oldy. Nor am I moldy."

No, at thirty-three he wasn't at all oldy. With everything he'd already accomplished it seemed like he should be older, but he had her beat by only seven years. As for being moldy, uh uh. Six pack abs and a light dusting of chest hair that narrowed as it traveled down his flat abdomen to disappear beneath the line of his jeans – an arrow pointing to the very nice package below, an athlete's lean, graceful lines... Yummy. "Your heritage is."

"So is yours. Everyone's heritage is old. Mine just happens to be better documented."

"Well, that's very non-snobbish of you to say."

The loose grin with which he favored her spoke more of heat

and sin than humor. "Yes, well, I might have avoided mentioning that I'm an aristocrat from a long line of them. We can't all come from peasant stock."

"Jerk."

"You'd be just as happy to be staying at the Roadside Burger and Dentistry Inn in Duluth, Minnesota, then?" he mused, approaching her with a slow, steady step. "Us being in the master bedchamber of a seven-hundred-year-old castle larger than the Queen's doesn't affect you in the slightest?"

"Burger and Dentistry?" she repeated. "Do you get to choose which side you stay on?"

"Samantha."

"Okay, yeah. I'm a snob, too. But only because Dentistry. Staying there sounds risky."

Stopping in front of her, he hooked a finger around the neck of her blouse and unbuttoned the top button. Heat spooled down her spine, and she lifted on her tiptoes to kiss him. *Mm, Rick Addison sex.* In some ways, it was more addictive than that adrenaline punch during a good B and E.

"Hey," she murmured, running a thumb along his lower lip as she kissed him again.

"Hey," Rick returned, finishing the rest of her buttons and then opening her blouse to run his palms up her ribs and beneath her frilly pink bra to cup her breasts. "I want you to enjoy yourself here. My stuff is your stuff. My house is your house. Oldy and moldy or otherwise." His mouth took hers in a hot, open-mouthed, tongue-tangling chocolate sundae with a cherry on top. "My heart is your heart."

For a second she couldn't breathe, much less talk. This was the Rick who'd caught her – the sexy, warm, generous one, not the hard-assed, cutthroat guy who bought and sold companies like kids did baseball cards. "Well, if it's all the same," she finally managed, reaching down to yank his belt off and undo his jeans buttons, "you can keep this part, as long as you share." With a grin she slid her fingers down between warm skin and denim to stroke his hard cock.

"That's a deal, Samantha," he rumbled, his Oxford-educated accent deepening. Bending, he scooped her up in his arms and walked over to dump her on the high bed.

"Hey, careful!" she cautioned, shedding her top and bra as she scooted backward, wincing a little at the squeaking sounds emitting from the frame. "This is a seventeenth century bed, hoss."

"Yes, I know. I can hear it. Tell me why my ancestors thought it was prestigious to own a bed so high off the ground they needed a stepladder to use it." Taking a step back, he hopped up to join her on the heavy, elegantly-quilted coverlet.

"I would, but it might spoil the mood," she returned once the creaking subsided, unzipping her own jeans and squirming out of them. "Something about vermin." Another thought occurred to her, and she eyed him as he pulled off his hiking boots and dropped them to the floor next to her Nikes. "You weren't...conceived in this bed, were you?"

Rick laughed. "It's entirely possible, I suppose, but I promise it's a new mattress." Yanking off his jeans, he turned onto his hands and knees and crawled up over her.

"Not a new frame, though." Samantha wrapped her ankles around the back of his thighs, pulling him closer.

With a deep sigh he canted his hips forward and entered her, hot and hard. "Welcome to Scotland, Sam Jellicoe," he growled, pumping into her deep and fast.

Christ. He felt so good, and the way he always wanted her was...amazing. Sam lifted her hands to tangle her fingers into his black, thick hair, drawing his face down for another deep kiss. Whoever said the British were reserved had never had sex with Rick Addison. She moaned, drawing tight and coming around him, shifting her grip to his shoulders so she wouldn't yank his hair out.

"I'm afraid this is going to be a quickie," he grunted with a half grin, increasing his pace.

"That's good," she gasped, tilting her head back, panting in time with his thrusts and the responding rhythmic squeaking of the old frame. "Not sure how long the bed will last."

A moment later he came, groaning as he emptied himself into her. Rick lowered his head against her shoulder, sinking his weight along her body. "Traveling with you plays the devil with me," he murmured, "seeing you so close and all those pesky pilots and drivers about."

"And busty flight attendants," she agreed, kissing his ear.

A low-pitched howl came through the window, distant and mournful, rising and falling with the light wind. If she hadn't been so relaxed, it would have made her shiver. She kept listening, but the sound faded away and didn't repeat.

"Tell me that was the Hound of the Baskervilles," she finally whispered.

"We're in the Highlands, not the moors," he commented, his voice muffled and still breathless. "And the Hound signaled the lord and master's untimely death, so I do hope it's not him."

"And you're a Rawley and not a Baskerville." Which was a good thing, since the idea of him being torn limb from limb by a hellhound wasn't anything she wanted to contemplate. "Maybe it was a ghost, then."

He lifted his head to look down at her. "And maybe it was someone's hunting dog. This is an old house in an old land. Isn't that intriguing enough?"

She held his gaze. "That depends."

"We're still not moving into the local inn."

"That's not what I mean." Samantha took a slow breath. "You said your stuff is my stuff, but do I really get to have the run of the place, or are you going to try to keep tabs on me every minute?"

Putting his arms around her, he rolled them so that she was on top, looking down at his deep blue eyes. "I meant what I said."

Samantha grinned. "Yes, but that was during sex. I don't think it's binding."

He visibly relaxed. "It's binding. And by all means, explore anywhere you want. Just keep in mind that after seven hundred years there may be some loose stones, and the west wing is rubbish. For the sake of my heart be careful."

"Security system?"

"None but the butler and other servants and some ancient weaponry. No cameras here to capture your arse doing anything suspicious."

Sitting up, putting her hands on his chest for balance, she rocked forward and back. "This arse? It's busy right now."

"So I've no—"

The light beside the bed flickered and went out. "Ghost," she said, looking down at him, a very kiddish feeling of excitement trilling down her spine. Yes, this castle was really, really old, and probably not in as good shape as it could or should have been, but whatever Tom Donner thought she would or wouldn't like, this was swiftly becoming her kind of place.

A moment later faint echoes of "power's oot again" began sounding through the house. So evidently this kind of thing happened a lot. For her, used to the precise timing of locks and the challenge of avoiding cameras and alarms, the idea of a place where the power seemed to be…iffy, was kind of cool. But then Rick grabbed her shoulders and tossed her onto her stomach. Figuring out Canniebrae could wait.

"WHAT DO YOU MEAN, 'it happens all the time'?" Richard asked, holding back a scowl only because his life with Samantha had shown him quite clearly that there were several layers of trouble and that a power outage was barely a blip on the newly-reconfigured Addison radar.

"Well, just that it does, m'laird," Yule said in his soft Scottish brogue, shrugging. "I'm verra sorry, but when the wind comes up, the pines play hell with the power lines."

"Don't you have a generator?"

"Aye, a grand monster of one. When Freddie comes back from the village with Agnes the cook, he'll bring the petrol to start 'er up."

Out at the edge of his peripheral vision Samantha strolled past the office doorway. Then she walked back in the other direction. On her third pass she finally stopped, leaning into the room. "Do you have candles, Yule?" she asked. "I want to look in the attic."

"Candles? We're nae so primitive, Miss Sam. We have torches aplenty. The power—"

"Goes out a lot. I heard." With a grin, she straightened. "I'll be in the drawing room, when you're finished here."

Yule lifted a bushy red eyebrow. "The drawing room? Alone?"

She paused halfway out the door. "Yes. Why?"

"I..." The butler glanced at Richard. "No reason, Miss Sam. Please keep in mind, though, that this house is quite old."

The glance she sent Richard was full of amusement and, unless he was mistaken, excitement. But then she'd been trying to get him to admit that he believed the house was haunted from the moment she'd found out where they were going. Having the damned power out didn't help his denials.

"Do your best," he said aloud, clapping Yule on the shoulder. Before the big and rather startled Scotsman could reply, Rick left the office for the drawing room at the far end of the hall.

At this time of year six o'clock was definitely evening, the sun less than a rosy memory in the western sky. Dim hardly described the long, wood-paneled hallway, and even if he refused to rush his steps, he was quite happy when the wall sconces flickered into yellow light. The orange glow of the fireplace as he neared the drawing room was brighter than the questionable electricity, and he slowed to see Samantha squatting to one side of the hearth, an open book in her hands.

"What's that you have?" he asked, dropping into the chair closest to her.

She looked up. "You look so lord of the manor," she said, grinning up at him. "All you need is a pipe and a hound at your feet."

"I *am* lord of the manor," he returned. "You found that old copy of *Haunted Balmoral*, didn't you?"

She nodded, settling onto her backside and folding her long legs beneath the book. "This ghost somebody drew on the inside of the cover has a word bubble saying 'Boo'." She opened it, flipping the book around to show him. "Your handiwork?"

"Good God. Yes. I must have been six years old. My mother caught me at it and informed me that I was too young to be reading ghost stories, and that one did not mark up first editions of *any* books. Even rubbish tourist books."

Samantha snorted. "When I was six, my dad told me not to bother snatching any book that wasn't a first edition."

That made him frown. For God's sake, she'd had a different upbringing than he had. How did someone raised to believe that she had every right to walk away with anything as long as it wasn't nailed down, come up with her own sense of morality, and more importantly, have such a good heart?

"Uh oh," she muttered, and knocked him in the knee with the book. "Don't give me that look."

"What look?" he responded.

"I grew up inside my life, Rick. Not looking at it from some enlightened, elevated height. I thought it was cool. By the time I was twelve I'd been to twenty different countries, all without a passport. I could trick anybody into doing anything, pretty much. People were saps." She grimaced. "Realizing the world wasn't my personal jewel-encrusted platter took some time."

"But you did realize that. That, my dear, is why I find you so remarkable."

"I realized it *mostly*," she amended. "Remember, just a year ago I was after a stone tablet that belonged to you. Maybe I got more selective as I got older, but the rush of it all never goes away."

Richard tilted his head at her. Samantha was frequently reflective and thoughtful, but she deigned to talk about her thought process and her past much more rarely. "Why did you stop, then? Truly?"

Making a face, she flipped through a few more pages of the book. "Because you're a whole different kind of rush," she muttered after a moment, keeping her head down. "I had to choose. I chose you."

He slid onto the floor to sit cross-legged in front of her, their knees bumping. Perhaps she'd merely exchanged one addiction for another, or perhaps that was simply how she chose to describe it. Either way, and however uncomfortable she felt admitting that she needed him, she was here. "Samantha," he murmured, reaching out to tilt up her chin, to gaze into her bottomless green eyes, "I love you more than you love Godzilla."

Her burst of laughter sounded surprised and delighted – two things he most prized being able to give her. "Even the new Godzilla?" she asked him, leaning in to give him a kiss that ended with her nibbling on his bottom lip.

"I love you quadruple the amount you love the new Godzilla."

"Wow. That's a lot."

"Shut up and kiss me again, Yank."

She shifted up to her knees, stretching forward and draping herself down his chest as she wrapped her arms around his shoulders and sank against his mouth. Her trust, her admission that she'd willingly given up her old, lucrative life to stay with him – taken all together, it meant that this might well have been his favorite kiss. And they had shared some rather spectacular kisses previous to this one.

Richard sank backward, freeing one hand to shove the old, overstuffed chair out of the way so he could lie flat on his back, drawing her up along his body as he did so. No, she wasn't anyone he *should* have ended up with. She wasn't anyone he even should have met. But they had met, and she was never, ever, getting away from him.

"Miss Sam, I have the torches ye... Oh, I beg yer pardon, m'laird." Yule came to an almost comical halt in the doorway.

With her typical grace Samantha rolled to her feet and walked up to the butler. "No pardon to beg, Yule," she said smoothly, taking a flashlight and experimentally flipping it on. "The door was open."

Because he didn't wish to remain lying flat on his back in the drawing room, Richard hauled himself upright, as well. If nothing else, Sam Jellicoe was a damned good reason for him to stay in shape. "What she said," he echoed. "Though I did just notice some smoke stains on the ceiling. Do we have a flu problem?"

"Aye. I'll have Freddie look at the fireplace again in the morning. We've had mice lodging in there; could be they've made another nest."

Samantha scowled. "So that's not roast venison I'm smelling?"

The butler grinned, then swiftly cleared his throat and flattened his expression again. "That is indeed roast venison. His lairdship said we're to serve at seven o'clock, if that's acceptable."

"Very acceptable."

So once again she'd begun winning over his staff, leaving him a distant second, and more or less at her mercy. By now, Richard was accustomed to it. "Do you want company in the attic, or do you prefer to prowl alone?" he asked her.

"Alone, m'laird?" Yule took up, looking uncomfortable again.

"You'll find that Miss Sam can more or less take care of herself, Yule," he returned, and faced Samantha again. "You have your phone?"

She patted the back pocket of her jeans. "Yep. And you're number one on my speed dial."

"I'd better be. I'll be in the downstairs office, checking on the internet connection."

"Internet?" Yule repeated, falling in behind him. "We have a fax machine. I'm afraid cellular service is questionable, though. We think it's interference from Balmoral."

Resisting the urge to send a glance back at his adrenaline-junkie betrothed, he edged sideways to let the butler draw even with him. "Why the trepidation about her going anywhere alone?"

"I... Canniebrae is an old pile, m'laird. It's only a matter of time until the west wing slides down into the loch. Part of a chimney in one of the east wing bedchambers collapsed just last month. As ye know, this place is something of a labyrinth, anyway."

Splendid. Samantha had already called the place Dracula's castle, and that was without any of the old stories to clutter things up. "More than likely Miss Sam will be asking you to regale her with the old ghost stories."

"I understand. She'll hear nothing of spirits from me, m'laird. I'll tell the rest of the staff, as well."

That would work – for about five minutes. Richard shook his head. "No, if she asks, tell her. Just please make clear to her which parts of the house are supposedly haunted, and which parts are actually dangerous."

"Aye, m'laird. I'll see to it."

He'd decided on the largest of the castle's three offices, and the light switch on the wall actually worked. After taking an emergency torch from Yule, Richard sent the butler on his way. Warning Samantha of danger likely wouldn't dissuade her from going anywhere, but she could at least take some precautions. It made sense she'd want to begin with the attic, since the staff had moved all the west wing's valuables there once the structure became unsafe. The artworks and antiques would keep her interest, and all told the house boasted an obscene number of them scattered throughout the house.

He also meant to take her out hiking and riding, and to introduce her to fly fishing. That was what one did in the Highlands, after all. Yes, he might have preferred a location with wi-fi and more access to...well, to the world, but this would be the first time they had really had any time just to be together. No murders, no thefts, no cat burgling. Just fly fishing, seeing the sights, and long, uninterrupted nights of sex.

The lights flickered and went out again. Taking his seat at the desk, Richard turned on the torch and rested it on its butt so that it lit up the ceiling. Sex and ghosties, he amended to himself, taking a piece of paper from what had once been his father's desk and beginning a list of what Canniebrae required to bring the old pile into the twenty-first century. Or at least the twentieth.

4

Rain batted against the roof a few feet above Samantha's head. It wasn't like Florida rain, which tended to be torrential and generally brief. Rather, it pattered and hesitated, roaring and then whispering as it meandered its way down the long valley. She sat back in the Louis the Fifteenth chair she'd discovered, just listening.

Footsteps thudded up the narrow, unadorned stairs that led to the Canniebrae attic. With a short smile she reached over and flicked off her flashlight. Gray edged in from the small, square window at the front of the long, low-ceilinged room, but here against the wall she knew quite well that she was cloaked in gloom and shadow.

The footsteps stopped at the top of the stairs. From where she sat she could see him quite clearly – or his silhouette, anyway – lean and tall, his black hair caressing the collar of his brown leather jacket, and his jeans stuffed into the tops of his old hiking boots. Six-foot two of brilliant, witty, toe-curling English aristocrat. And all of him belonged to her.

Of course the whole ownership thing was a two-way street, and that was what she'd been having the hardest time with. As a cat burglar she succeeded by never becoming entangled in anything – and that included both traps and relationships. But as Rick kept reminding her, she wasn't a cat burglar any longer. She'd gone directly from free as the wind to becoming engaged. Or it felt that way, at least. The past year had been a whirlwind of blowing debris she'd never seen coming.

"I think you should be aware that if you jump out at me from the dark you may get clocked," Rick commented.

She snorted. "You aren't spooked, are you?"

He turned his light in her direction, making her squint as it flashed across her eyes. "My girl lurking in the dark in an old attic with a storm thundering outside? What's spooky about that?"

"Lower the light, will you?" she returned. "I don't like being blinded like that. Yes, I know I'm safe here. Not being able to see just makes me jumpy."

Immediately he lowered the light to her knees and picked his way through centuries of clutter to squat beside her. "I thought you were going to do a floor plan study before you started exploring."

Evidently Rick was getting to know her methods pretty well. "I was going to, but when I took a peek up here last night I discovered that Rick Addison's ancestors owned some furniture worth a couple of grand, a painting that looks to be a Joshua Reynolds, and a first edition of *Treasure Island*. That's just in the ten square feet around me right now. Aside from that, you brought me up here to meet your family. I'm meeting them. I'm just starting back in the thirteenth century and working my way forward."

He panned his flashlight around them. "A Joshua Reynolds? Where?"

Not surprised he would focus in on the artwork, she flicked on her own light and pointed it at the opposite wall. "There. Behind the pianoforte."

As he walked over, tucking his light beneath his chin to free both his hands, he sent her another glance. "There's a portrait gallery in the long hallway, and a couple of journals from a great-great or two in the library. The attic is where the staff moved the valuables from the west wing back when I was a kid, but it's mostly for discards." Carefully he lifted the wrapped canvas from behind the old pianoforte. "With the occasional treasure thrown in, apparently, because I don't remember this one."

Untying the twine over the blanket, he peeled back the material. Samantha had already looked, but any opportunity to view a Reynolds painting, especially one that hadn't seen the light of day in a hundred or more years, was welcome. For a long moment the two of them gazed at the pretty, rosy-cheeked young woman standing in a room draped in deep reds and greens.

"It does look like a Reynolds," he agreed, shooting an annoyed glance toward the ceiling. "Isn't there any electricity up here?"

"Nope. We're living the way your ancestors lived when they were in the attic."

Rick snorted. "As if my ancestors ever deigned to climb into the attic. Will you help me get this downstairs so we can take a better look at it?"

"Sure. And you might want to mount an expedition in here. It looks like your great-greats collected some nice stuff without realizing what they were doing. There are some damn treasures in here, Brit. And those *are* the discards."

They each took an end of the four-foot painting and carried it gingerly down the steep, narrow stairs and into the main part of the house. The power seemed to be out again, and the light wasn't much better than it had been in the attic. As they reached an upstairs sitting room and set the painting down on a table, a dull grinding roar reverberated through the sprawling building, and then the lights flickered dimly on.

"That generator's an antique too," she said, pulling open

curtains. Thanks to the gloom outside, it didn't make much of a difference illumination-wise, but the room felt less closed in.

"Evidently they don't even bother firing it up unless a guest is here or it's snowing." Rick took a seat, wiping his hands on his jeans. "I don't expect you to catalog all my possessions, you know," he said after a moment. "That isn't why we're here. It isn't why *you're* here."

Samantha leaned back against the wall beside the window. "I know. I like looking through things. I'll stop if it makes you uncomfortable or something, but you know I'll always pick digging through somebody's attic over a trip to Disneyland."

Deep blue eyes gazed at her. "I do know that, and no, it doesn't make me uncomfortable. I'm aware that there are likely more uncatalogued objects at Canniebrae than any other place I own. This place...isn't just its monetary value, though."

Rick hesitating over words was unusual enough that she left the window to sit down beside him. "You haven't been here in almost twenty years. What's kept you away?"

"It's..." He frowned. "It's slower here, I think," he said, his gaze wandering the knickknacks on the mantel. "My life has gotten progressively more hurried."

She leaned against his shoulder. "Am I making you more contemplative? That's kind of scary."

That made him smile again. "You make me need to catch my breath. So just give the house as a whole and the land around it at least a once-over, and then you can spend the rest of your time digging through seven centuries of rubbish."

"Well, considering that we found a diamond necklace in the stable wall at Rawley Park, your ancestors and I clearly have different views of what rubbish is." Taking his hand, she twined her fingers with his. "Thank you for getting me away from Palm Beach. I will get used to having cameras pointed at me. Just give me a little more time."

"I don't particularly like seeing my picture everywhere, either,"

Rick admitted, though she wasn't at all surprised to hear it. "It's more a balancing act. We give them a little view of us in order to get a little privacy. We'll figure it out, Samantha. I'm not in any hurry."

"You, my dear," she said, leaning in to kiss him and adopting his very suave English accent, "are a very patient man."

Somebody knocked at the open door, and she looked past Rick to see Yule standing uncomfortably in the doorway. "M'laird, ye have a phone call."

Rick gave a very quiet sigh. "Did they give a name?"

"Aye. Oh. Tom Donner, m'laird."

"He probably wants to know if I've fled the countryside yet or not," Samantha commented. "Make sure you tell him I'm having a grand time."

Pushing to his feet, Rick tugged on her ponytail. "You *are* having a grand time." He slowed at the doorway. "I'll take it in the small office, Yule."

"Aye, but… Well, the phone cord only reaches as far as the kitchen, m'laird."

Samantha was fairly certain the veins in Rick's forehead were standing out about now. "There's a phone in the office," he said crisply.

"The wee buttons don't work."

"I see. I'll add that to my list, then."

Richard was fairly certain he could hear Samantha snickering behind him, but he pretended to ignore it. Considering that this holiday had been his idea, he wasn't likely to receive any sympathy from her. Moving ahead of the lumbering butler he made his way downstairs into the servants' hallway and picked up the phone where it rested beside the cradle on a small side table.

"Tom?"

The line crackled as thunder rumbled up the hallway. "Rick? I can barely hear you."

"Call me back on my cell, then."

47

"Wait! Don't hang up," Tom's Texas drawl returned, a note of frustration in his tone. "I've been trying your cell for three hours. It keeps saying you're out of the service area."

With a scowl Richard pulled the iPhone from his pocket. It was on, and fully charged, but where the service bars generally were wherever he traveled in the world, a small red X blinked balefully at him. "Dammit," he muttered, pocketing it again. "I've been told Balmoral likes to block the cellular signals."

"Damn royals."

"You're not allowed to say that. Only Brits are," Richard informed him. "What did you need, anyway? I have no idea how long the connection will last."

"Right. Two things. First, I have the Chicago small press numbers you wanted, though I have no idea why you think being a vanity publisher is so interesting."

"It's not for vanity publishing. I told you, print-on-demand is the future of the book industry. If I can find a way to make it both cost effective and profitable, everyone will have to emulate my plan. That will cost them. What's the second thing?"

"No cell signal, iffy phone lines? How's Jellicoe? Is she on her way to London yet?"

"There's also iffy power and no internet. She actually seems quite happy with it so far. It's only been a day, but she hasn't tried to reach anyone from her Hole-in-the-Wall gang yet."

"No internet? Do you want me to fax you the figures?"

That would be nice, if he had a phone line in the office for the existing fax machine. "Hold onto them for another day or two. I'm putting in an order through the London office for some updated equipment. It's amazing how technology has changed everywhere but here in the last eighteen years."

"Will do. Let me know when she starts to crack."

Informing Tom that Samantha had guessed about the lawyer's dubious predictions and would never admit publicly to disliking it here would only wound the poor lad. "I will. Take care. I'll call you tomorrow with an update."

As he hung up, he caught sight of Mrs. Agnes Yule, the house's cook and wife of the butler, hurrying back to stand over the old wood stove in the adjoining kitchen. Only one working phone and no privacy to boot. This was one situation that was going to have to alter – and quickly.

Before he went to find Samantha again he detoured to the big office to add phone lines and updated phones to his growing list of basic necessities. At his other residences he referred to the place where he conducted most of his business as *his* office. Even Rawley, where he'd spent most of his child- and adulthood. Not here, though. Perhaps it was because the last time he'd been here, the office had been his father's. He'd still been in school, not even close to becoming who he was now.

Well, he was Richard damned Addison now, and Richard damned Addison needed internet. Grabbing up the torch, he crawled beneath the old mahogany monstrosity of a desk to see if there were any actual electrical outlets. At the same moment, a low, heavy crash echoed from further down the hallway.

With a frown he backed out from under the desk and got to his feet, then headed in the direction of the sound. A section of rooms on the north side of the castle were long emptied and longer abandoned. If they'd lost part of the roof or a wall, they would have to close that wing, in addition to the already-condemned west wing. This had once been a glorious place. He'd let it go for too long. It was past time to either raze it or repair it.

A door ahead of him thudded closed, and he sped into a run. He pushed the handle down as he reached it, but the heavy oak didn't budge. Frowning, he put a shoulder against the door and shoved. It gave an inch or so, something very heavy clearly behind it. Taking a few steps back he launched all his weight forward and shoved again. With a heavy scraping sound, the door bumped open and he half fell inside the dark room.

An open window with flapping, tattered curtains let blowing rain spray halfway across the remains of a large bedchamber. The bedframe itself remained, sagging on the window side, while thankfully the mattress was long gone. On the floor, face down, a heavy wardrobe rested against the back of the half-open door.

He sent torchlight into the dim corners and, with some embarrassment, beneath the skeletal bed. Empty. The wind might have blown over the wardrobe, he supposed, especially if the front legs had rotted in the damp weather. Previous to meeting Samantha, that answer likely would have satisfied him. Now, though, he took a moment to estimate where the heavy thing had been before he'd shoved it sideways to get into the room. As best he could tell, it had been up against the wall beside the door.

Well, that didn't make sense, then. Richard squatted to grab onto the behemoth and haul it onto its side. The front legs were intact. Logically, then, there was no reason he could figure that the wardrobe would have toppled over, and even less why it would have ended up behind the door. The multi-company owner part of him, the businessman who wanted and needed to know how and why everything worked, didn't like not having an explanation.

"Hmm."

He whipped to his feet, the torch raised like a weapon. Directly behind him Samantha stepped back, dodging his elbow with that easy fluidity of hers. "Christ," he muttered. "I forget how quiet you are."

She sent him a crooked grin. "I'll try to remember to wear my clompy shoes next time." She nudged the toe of her Nikes against the wardrobe. "What happened in here? I heard it crash from all the way up in the attic."

For a moment he debated whether to say he'd knocked it over himself. She delighted in teasing him about supernatural happenings – and honestly since meeting her there had been one or two things that logic couldn't quite explain. But a wardrobe toppling hardly ranked with the Amityville horror, and she would be all over it like a dog with a bone. Finally, he shrugged. "I figure the wind blew it over. It looks like the pine tree out there broke the window."

Samantha glanced from the window to the side wall and down to the upended wardrobe. "We should probably board the window up, then," she said after a moment. "That wardrobe's nearly three hundred years old." She stepped around it and crouched. "Let's get it out of the rain, shall we?"

On the count of three they heaved it back upright and shoved it against the wall. Richard seriously doubted that she was convinced by his interpretation, but even given her tendency to jest about ghosties, an actual thing happening needed a more logical explanation.

Once it was back in place she nudged it experimentally. It didn't budge. Then she pulled open the double doors – and a mouse jumped out, ran down her leg, over her shoe, and into the shadows beneath the bed. "Hmm," she said again, not even flinching.

Richard folded his arms over his chest and leaned back against the doorframe. "A mouse just ran down your pants, you know."

"I know." She gave another loose grin as she finished exam-ining the wardrobe and then closed it up again. "Once I waited in an air duct for so long a rat pooped on my hand. When you have to be still, you have to be still."

"And here I thought you were all glitter and diamonds."

She faced him, pulling his arms apart and stepping into the open circle. "That's the payoff," she murmured, and leaned up along his body to kiss him. "And the wind didn't do that."

For a long moment he occupied himself with kissing her back. She tasted faintly of chocolate; evidently, she'd found the kitchen. "Then what's your explanation? Your genuine, logical explanation."

She moved back a little, so she could look him in the eyes. "Logically, I think I don't know. Yet."

"I didn't expect that," he returned, deciding that today, in Scotland and with the rain outside, her eyes were the color of new leaves. Tilting her chin up with his fingers, he kissed her again, still relishing in the way she now sought him out. For a time, he'd thought he was the only one doing the pursuing.

"Yeah, well, once is an aberration. If it happens again, I'm going straight to blaming the ghost of your old great Grandpa Bob."

"That would be great Grandpa Macrath," he corrected. "And he collected fine furniture. I don't think he would risk scratching it, even in death."

Something unreadable crossed her expression for a moment, and then she grabbed her fingers into his hair to pull his face down for another kiss. "Let's go find some more bedchambers to explore," she whispered.

His cock jumped, even with the mice and dust and cold, flinging drops of rainwater. "I think the master bedchamber is mouse free," he returned, digging his fingers into the waistband of her jeans. Not putting cameras throughout this big, old castle was quite possibly the most brilliant thing he'd done – not that he'd ever given it much thought in the first place.

"Chicken."

Richard lifted an eyebrow. "You want your naked arse rolling about in the damp and dust, then?"

She licked his throat in a way that had his eyes rolling back in his head. "I figured it would be *your* arse on the floor. The…" Samantha trailed off, her muscles beneath his hands tensing as she turned toward the window.

A moment later he heard it as well, the low, rhythmic thrum of blades cutting through the wet air. He started to curse, until he remembered that he'd invited the helicopter's occupants to join them here. "I am getting tired of people interrupting us before we can even do anything worth interrupting," he muttered anyway, changing his grip to her hand.

"We can still hide in the attic," she suggested, and he wasn't entirely certain she was joking. "I made a clean spot."

He leaned his forehead against hers. "Fuck." Then, before she could invent some reason to vanish into the hundred-room castle, he tightened his grip and towed her toward the hallway. "Let's go meet my family."

ŏ

FOR SOME REASON the old movie *The Haunting of Hill House* kept running through Samantha's mind as she and Rick descended the stairs to the main floor of Canniebrae. In particular she recalled the part where Dr. Markway's wife vanished into the bowels of the house for the duration of the movie. She could totally do that too, pop her head down from the attic once in a while, sneak down to the kitchen in the middle of the night for snacks.

In fact, there was only one problem with that scenario. First, she'd become accustomed to spending her nights in bed with Rick – both for sex and for the way he made her feel not precisely safe, but…connected. To him, and to the world. That was important to her. It was easy for someone who slipped into places solo, who lived by night, to become disconnected from the world. To see people as nothing more than marks or targets. Her father had fallen into that trap, and the world had become about nothing but what it could give him. The next score, the false feeling of being the only human with a brain in his head, and in the end, it had gotten him caught.

She wrenched her thoughts back to the present, to her reasons for *not* wanting to meet Rick's uncle and aunt and cousin. To the reason she was tempted to slip behind the walls and vanish. Because they might not like her. Sure, she could be charming, and she could carry on a conversation with the best of them, and in several languages. But Rick would want her to be herself. *She* wanted to be herself. Very few people in the world had ever met the real Samantha Elizabeth Jellicoe. She could count them on two fingers, in fact: Rick, and Stoney.

Rick had told them she was an art restorer and now a security and art retrieval expert. All of that was true; she'd been working at an art museum when Stoney had signed her up for the break-in job at Solano Dorado. She *was* out of the game now. Hell, in a few months she would be getting married. But parts of her still didn't quite accept that this was anything more than a really awesome dream, even after a year in Rick's company.

"How long has it been since you've met them face-to-face?" she asked, as half a dozen footmen gathered in the foyer, ready for a dash through the rain to the helicopter for luggage.

"Five or six years for my aunt and uncle. Not since my wedding, anyway."

"Well, it's nice that you get together whenever you get married, then," she returned, squinting one eye.

"Samantha," he said, his tone saying that he didn't like the comparison.

"What? They'll be comparing *me* to Patricia at her best. You know, when her clothes had names and she employed a hair stylist and never carried her own shopping bags."

"Reggie tried to throw me a divorce party, if that makes you feel any better." He took a breath. "And no, I didn't attend. I wasn't in the mood."

"Was he being thoughtful, or did he want to throw a party?"

Rick shook his finger at her. "No, you don't. You figure them out for yourself. Other than a handful of third and fourth cousins, they are my only relations. You decide how you wish to view them."

"And they'll be deciding how to view me." Had she said that out loud? *Crap.* "I mean, I've been a lot of people. Some of them are better than I am."

"I don't care which face you decide to show them, my dear," he said, surprising her to her bones.

"You don't?"

"No. Just make it one you're comfortable with, because you'll have to bring it out and wear it at holidays."

While she was still digesting that particular morsel, Yule threw open the front door, popped open his black umbrella – brolly – and led the charge out to the helicopter pad. The footmen followed in ragged, kilt-wearing unison. Samantha started forward, reaching for one of the half-dozen brollies left in the coat rack, but Rick held her back.

"We'll wait here," he said.

"Strategy?"

"Everything means something," he returned, echoing one of her favorite sayings. "But this morning, I'd just prefer to stay dry. Plus, they interrupted sex. That does not make me happy."

She smiled. "I'm cool with that."

In truth, she *was* perfectly happy to give herself another few seconds. Hell, she'd begun break-ins that made her less nervous than meeting Rick's family. This wasn't the anticipatory kind of tension, either, where the payoff was a great big adrenaline rush and a million dollars. This was just having to be on her best behavior for God knew how long and hoping she survived. And more importantly, that this...thing between her and Rick survived. Because she was pretty sure she wasn't ready to go back to navigating the world without him.

"Ready?"

Through the open doorway the herd of umbrellas closed on them like angry bats. Samantha squared her shoulders. "Bring it."

5

Wednesday, 4:38 p.m.

Rick hated being without wi-fi. If he hadn't been so obviously pissed off, Samantha would have thought he might have picked Canniebrae for his family reunion just so she couldn't look up his relatives online. Of course, she'd had a year to do just that and hadn't bothered. That, even though in her first dig for information about him she'd read that he had some. She could say it was because *she* didn't have any – none that she cared to become reacquainted with, anyway – but now it seemed lazy. And she was about to pay for her ignorance.

The lead umbrellas tilted up to spit out a quartet of heavily-coated people into the foyer. As they shrugged out of their rain gear she let Rick take a step forward without her, using the seconds to do a quick visual assessment. Aunt and uncle, with Rowland at first glance bearing a passing resemblance in the chin and mouth to Rick. Reginald seemed to have wedged himself behind Yule, but that left her with a good look at the Nordic statue shaking her blonde locks from a wool hat. Unless Rick had a secret, adopted female cousin who hailed from Valhalla, Reggie had a girlfriend.

"I have to say, that *All Access* show didn't do you justice."

Samantha nodded, stepping up beside Rick again as his cousin moved out from behind the butler. "It was the telephoto lens. You'd be Reginald, then, I assume," she said, and stuck out her hand. Whoever she ultimately decided to be for clan Addison's holidays and get-togethers, it would be someone they liked. Hopefully.

In a sense she was grateful that Reginald Addison mentioned the stupid television piece first off. It set her back up, which calmed her nerves. Now that he'd made himself visible, she took a look at him. Dark hair, shorter and straighter than Rick's, handsome in that smooth, slightly-too-pretty way that British aristocracy seemed to have, and a little less slender than his lean, hard cousin. New shoes, freshly-shaven, and a heavy blue sweater – or jumper, rather, according to Bridget Jones – that nicely brought out the color of his eyes. It likely wasn't fair to Reginald, but the thought that immediately came to her mind was that he was Rick-light.

He shook her hand, inclining his head in that almost unconscious aristocratic way that said he was being a good sport by chatting with her. Then he stepped aside, gesturing at the towering goddess who swayed into the circle of his arm. "My special friend, Eerika Nyland. Eerika, Samantha Jellicoe and my cousin, Richard Addison."

"Reginald talks about you all the time, my lord," Norway said in a smooth English accent. "It's a pleasure to meet you." She offered her hand. "And you as well, Miss Jellicoe."

Rick shook her hand. "Miss Nyland."

"Oh, Eerika, please." She chuckled, tucking a strand of Thor-colored hair behind one ear. "We're practically family, after all."

Rick was taller than the Viking, though not by much. Samantha in her deck shoes barely weighed in a five-foot-five.

Eerika of course wore three-inch red heels, the spikes now muddy brown with bits of grass hanging on them. But hey, they'd probably looked great on the shelf.

While the Viking hand-wrestled Rick, Samantha looked over to see Reginald gazing at her. "So, you're the one who landed my cousin," he mused, taking her hand again. "Reggie."

"Sam. It was mutual." Yeah, she could be charming as fuck, but if this was going to turn into a "look at the grabby, gauche American", she was going to stop being nice.

"Art retrieval, eh? You'll have to tell me about it." Reggie gestured toward the older couple standing behind them. "My mum and dad, Lady Mercia and Lord Rowland Addison. Mum, dad, Samantha Jellicoe."

"I believe you're stepping on my lines, Reg," Rick said, moving in smoothly to take her hand in his again. He leaned down to peck his diminutive aunt on the cheek, then held out his free right hand. "Uncle Rowland. It's good to see you. Thank you for joining us up here. All four of you."

The tall, broad-shouldered man with the close-cropped black and gray hair smiled as he shook Rick's hand with both of his. At second look she could see the similarities around the eyes, too. As the younger brother to the former Marquis of Rawley, Rowland would carry the courtesy title of "lord", and he could lend it to his wife, but nobody else in that line of the family could be lorded. Unless Rick died without an heir, that was. Then Rowland would become the Marquis of Rawley, himself, with the title and properties then going to Reggie.

It was all weird, and the disposition of noble titles had no doubt led to more patri-, fratri-, and matricide than anything else she could think of but the plague. All she'd ever done was steal some rocks and scribbles and shit. Okay, precious gems and priceless paintings, but still.

"It's lovely to finally meet you, Samantha," Lady Mercia said in a fairy godmother voice right out of *Cinderella*. She was heavier-set than her husband, expensively dressed, but a little dowdy even so. She had golden-blonde hair in a modified "Princess Di" bob, but Samantha would have been willing to bet serious cash that blonde hadn't been Mercia's natural hair color even before she'd begun dyeing it to hide the gray.

"I'm glad you could come," Samantha said when Rick squeezed her hand. Dammit, she knew better than to stare. Especially when a mark – or a future in-law, rather – was looking right back at her. "I think Rick's ready to move into the inn down the road, though."

"Nonsense," he countered, the barest thread of annoyance in his voice. "All Canniebrae needs is some more reliable electricity and internet. And a bit of patching."

And some mouse traps, Samantha thought to herself, but kept her mouth shut. Clearly this wasn't one of those families who could joke about each other's weaknesses or failings. Not in the foyer after five years apart, anyway. Not with Norway and the thief there to overhear. Hell, she didn't know that much about family dynamics to begin with.

"Where are you stashing us?" Reggie asked, stepping sideways as the footmen charged back in, handing umbrellas over to Yule and then trotting up the stairs with a great deal of luggage in tow. She was kind of surprised the helicopter had been able to carry it all. "Not in the haunted wing, I hope. I'll never be able to sleep with your great aunt Sophia walking up and down the hallway all night crying for her wee bairns."

"Oh, tell me more," Samantha said, slipping free of Rick and wrapping her arm around Reggie's. Whether she believed in spooks other than the government ones or not, any tales about Rick's ancestors intrigued her.

"I don't even think I had a great aunt Sophia," Rick commented from behind her. Valhalla had confiscated *his* arm, she noticed. Floozy.

"Oh, don't listen to him," Reggie countered, grinning at her as they ascended the grand staircase behind the luggage. "He has no imagination."

That made her smile. "I don't know about that."

"Thank you, Samantha."

Reggie clearly had a good share of the Addison line's charm. Behind Rick and Eerika, his aunt and uncle were talking about the state of the castle, focusing their commentary on the fine mahogany railings and the antique side table in the foyer. Despite the rundown state of Canniebrae, then, they weren't going to criticize it, or their nephew. Were they being British and polite, or did Rick's money and position have them bowing and scraping?

"How old is this bloody wallpaper?" Reggie asked, tapping it with one finger as they reached the landing. "I swear I remember it from the last time we were here."

"Did you summer here with Rick and his parents, then?" Samantha jumped in. She wasn't certain whether she was being herself or not, but she did want to know how these family dynamics played out before she stepped where she shouldn't.

"Yes, you must tell us. Samantha and I are horribly curious," the Norway added, her heels muffled on the carpet runner that went up the length of the staircase.

"We generally came up in what, early August?" Lord Rowland commented.

"Yes, dear. And stayed through the middle of September. I remember returning to London just as the leaves were beginning to turn, like they are now. It'll be pleasant to see them in all their splendor."

Wow. That sounded so...English. It was kind of endearing, really. Honestly, endearing was the last thing Samantha expected from anybody Rick had kept away from her for the entire length of their acquaintance. Hell, if she hadn't read up on him, yesterday would have been the first time she'd even heard that he had living relatives. Or maybe he'd kept her away from them. Hmm. She didn't much like that thought. Sure, he didn't like her past, but did it...embarrass him? Did *she* embarrass him?

"We've set up rooms in the east wing for you," Rick said from directly behind her. "You're sleeping in your old room, Reg."

With her arm still around his, Reggie Addison headed to the right as they topped the stairs. He knew at least the basic layout of the castle, then, but that didn't surprise her. In fact, she didn't know that it mattered one way or the other, except that she'd long ago developed the habit of learning about people from what they did, how they acted, rather than by what they said. Because people lied.

"I remember this place being old," he said conversationally, reaching over to run a finger across the surface of an old oak hall table, "and the west wing sagging, but it's definitely taken on a shabby sheen."

"I've neglected it," Rick returned, a sharper edge touching his voice. But then he didn't like being criticized. "I've already begun taking steps to make some repairs."

"Honestly, Richard," his uncle took up, "I don't know that Canniebrae is salvageable. You might consider turning it over to the National Trust and letting them sink their funds into the place."

She didn't need to see Rick's face to know how that had gone over. Receiving unasked-for advice came in just above criticism in his book or irritants. "I asked him if I could take a look at it, first," she cut in smoothly. "Restoring old classics is kind of my thing." There. She was an asset. Not a disorderly bump to his proper Britishness.

"Well, you've worked wonders with Ricky," Reggie offered, grinning. "Turning the stable at Rawley Park into a museum? For the public? I nearly fainted when I read about it."

"It's a lovely idea," his mother countered. "The Addisons have such a long line of collectors in the family, it's a shame to leave Gainsboroughs in the attic when they could be displayed."

"Thank you, Aunt Mercia. I much prefer being referred to as a collector than a hoarder."

Reggie snorted. "I don't think you'd qualify as a hoarder – can you have too many Rembrandts, for example?"

"You'd have to ask Mrs. Rembrandt about that." Samantha smiled, gesturing Reggie into the room on her right. "This is yours, Reggie." She leaned a breath closer. "Will Eerika need her own?"

"No," he whispered back. "I remember this room being bigger," he continued in a normal voice.

Rick came up beside them to grip her free hand. He'd managed to extricate himself from the Viking, who swirled into the room ahead of the rest of them. "We have no wi-fi, at least until Thursday, but the phone in the kitchen and the one in my office both work, except for the hold buttons. There's a torch in the lavatory and another one in the nightstand, because the power hasn't been reliable. I'm working on that, as well."

"Oh, a rustic holiday," Eerika chirped. "How delightful!"

They showed Reggie's parents to the room across the hallway, and then invited the lot of them down to the morning room when they'd settled in. With that Rick practically dragged her back to the stairs and the ground floor. Samantha put up with it mainly because he looked genuinely unsettled, and partly because she wanted to ask him a few more questions to help with her assessment of the people who were on the verge of – cripes almighty – becoming her in-laws.

"They seem nice," she ventured, when he finally released her in the morning room doorway.

"'A rustic holiday,'" he echoed, doing a fair impression of the Viking's smooth, honey-dripping voice. "'How delightful.'"

"What did you expect?" she asked, dropping into a chair that gave her a view out the front of the house and the rain outside. "You're the rich relation. Reggie's probably trying to show off for his girlfriend. They were hoping for opulence. Or at least a telly that receives the BBC."

"It does, when the wind is southerly." With a sigh, Rick sat on the arm of the chair beside her. "Don't think I dislike them. We all used to be fairly close." Standing again, he wandered over to the hearth and squatted to toss another piece of wood onto the fire. "I could do without a stranger."

"The Viking goddess? Norway?"

He snorted. "She has a handshake like a rag doll, if that makes a difference."

It did, though she didn't exactly want to admit that. She didn't like jealousy, in herself or anyone else. It wasn't as if Rick would be smitten by Eerika's Scandinavian blue eyes and run off with her. Before she'd broken into his house in Florida, he'd dated actresses, reporters, all sorts of professionally gorgeous women, and he'd become bored by the succession of pretty faces and empty heads.

"You charm strangers all the time, Mr. Bond. What's different about this?"

"Because this is my place," he said, then sighed. "No, that's not it. I don't know. We should have had them over to the flat in London. One evening, dinner and drinks, and done with."

Rick Addison, uncertain of himself. Just the idea of him not knowing what he wanted to say or how he felt fascinated her. The guy had bought a local Florida cable television station just so they would show monster movies for her. The fact that it had since become the highest-rated non-syndicated station in the Southeast had only been a happy coincidence. God, she hoped it wasn't about her. She could adopt a blue-blood heritage, but it wouldn't fool the one guy who mattered.

"We'll manage," she said, wrapping her arm around his waist. "I'll give you plenty of things to worry over, and you'll hardly remember they're here."

"Thanks for that."

Great. She'd wanted a bit of reassurance. Either he was focused on his own thing, though, or whatever bothered him wasn't anywhere near her torches and pitchfork thinking. She hoped it was that. "You're welcome."

A gust of wind sent the lights flickering, and rain spattering against the window before them. "When my father died," he said into the silence, "Uncle Rowland decided he should become my advisor in all things financial, spiritual, and personal. I was still at Oxford, but I did not appreciate the interference. I'm certain he was only trying to help, but…"

"You didn't want anyone dictating where your life should go?" she suggested, trying not to put any additional meaning into the words – even though that was precisely what he continued to try with her.

He shot her a glance, one eyebrow lifting. "I didn't want to live his life," he countered. "And certainly not so he could live mine vicariously."

"I get that. Nobody wants to walk out of one shadow and into another."

"Precisely."

Straightening again, he made his way over to the window. Once he'd shoved open the heavy forest-green curtains as far as they would go, Samantha went to join him. Maybe she was being shallow, but she was really glad this was about his issues, and not hers. Rain-streaked glass gave way to a gray haze beyond, a pine tree branch here or there emerging like crooked, creepy hands. So far Scotland was pretty damn awesome.

"And I'm not trying to dictate where your life should go, Samantha," he continued. "I'm trying to ensure that you remain in *my* life. I don't want you absent for five to ten."

"More likely fifty to life," she countered. "That's a worst-case scenario, of course." It was pretty accurate, too. Rick knew about a lot of the jobs she'd pulled, but she hadn't told him everything. Not yet, anyway.

After all, she'd been stealing shit from people since she'd turned six, and had pulled her first solo million-dollar cat burglary at fifteen. Yeah, she'd slowed down beginning about four years ago, and had stopped completely when she'd met Rick, but for those six years between fifteen and twenty-one she'd been freakin' notorious. And obscenely successful.

Rick faced her. "How often do prisons allow conjugal visits?"

"Not often enough for you. I can pretty much guarantee that."

He stuck a finger into the belt of her jeans and tugged her closer. "Then let's avoid that, shall we?"

"That's the plan, man." With a smile she leaned up along his chest and gave him a peck on the lips. "This was your idea. If you don't want 'em here, make up a trip to London or something."

"I wanted you to meet them," he repeated. "And honestly, you'd make mincemeat of them over one dinner. I'm forcing you to run a marathon."

"And you forgot you'd have to run it right along with me? So, this is all about making me pick a persona?"

His shoulders tensed. "Nonsense. Well, partly nonsense. I separated myself from them. You've been without family for a very long time. I thought…what's mine is yours. I suppose we can all be more honest in private, out in the middle of the Highlands." Slowly he relaxed again. "I didn't plan on sharing this with someone I don't know. Especially with some rough water that isn't quite under the bridge, yet."

Samantha nodded. "I'll be good. I'm not even crossing my fingers." She held up one hand, demonstrating the Vulcan salute. "See?"

Rick elbowed her in the ribs. "I'm not worried about you. Except for your opinion. I do want you to like them, though I'm not entirely certain why. Keep in mind that where my uncle is concerned I'm still nineteen," he said, throwing an arm around her shoulders, "but don't let that sway your opinion."

It already had, but she nodded. "Gotcha. I mean, hell, you've met my dad and you're still here, so fair is fair."

Of course where Rick's Uncle Rowland was too handsy-onnie, her dad was a convicted cat burglar who had nearly gotten her killed a few months ago in New York, was presumed dead by law enforcement in general, and was now apparently working with Interpol. Or letting Interpol think he was working with them, more likely. Compared to that, Uncle Rowland could be a poo-throwing circus monkey and would still be a few rungs above Martin Jellicoe in a humanity contest.

"What's fair?" Reggie's voice came from the doorway.

"*All's* fair, in love and war," Samantha said promptly, sliding gracefully from beneath Richard's arm to claim a corner of the long sofa at one end of the room.

So far Samantha had more or less been herself, which Richard decided to take as a good sign. She'd only spent fifteen minutes with his relations, of course, but he knew very well that six or seven months ago she would never have stuck around long enough even to meet them. Entanglements. That was what she called relationships. Even some friendships. Luckily for him, she'd evidently cast most of the pages of her rulebook aside where he was concerned.

Reg started toward the couch. For a bare second Richard weighed moving in to take the seat beside Samantha before his cousin could do so. He wanted to. He treasured his possessions, and Samantha Jellicoe was the rarest and most precious of them all. As he'd said, though, he'd arranged all of this, and better to see them acquainted here, where there were both plenty of places for her to hide out, and where he was the undisputed master of his realm.

"Where's your Miss Nyland?" he asked, because it never hurt to remind someone of obligations they had elsewhere.

"Hanging up clothes. She'll be down shortly, I imagine."

Richard damned well hoped so, but he settled for nodding. He wanted more information about Norway the Viking, as Samantha called her; like Sam, the nuances of what drove people interested him. For her it was more about truth and a genuine curiosity and occasionally looking for a good mark to fleece, while he tended to look for vulnerability, chinks in the armor. A side effect of being in the business of businesses, he supposed. No one could argue that it hadn't served him bloody well.

"So, you restore paintings?" his cousin asked, sitting a breath too close to Samantha and flinging an arm across the back of the couch behind her.

"I did. Not so much, anymore. I recover artwork, mostly. I also advise on security for exhibits and museums, and help track down things that go missing."

Rather than edge away from him, she turned in, putting on her brightest smile. Richard knew that to be a warning, even if Reginald didn't recognize it as such. Samantha didn't like being caged in. Hmm. This might be amusing, after all. He moved over to the chair she'd vacated by the fire and turned it to face his cousin and fiancée.

"That's a bit of a leap, isn't it?" Reg pursued, now wearing *his* famously charming smile. Good God, it was a pleasantry contest. "From artist to...what, bounty hunter?"

"Not really a leap at all," she said smoothly, shrugging. "I like puzzles. Taking them apart and putting them together." Samantha settled in a little closer to Reg. "I didn't get a chance to ask Rick: What do you do?"

"My dear, aristocrats don't *do* anything. Don't you know that?" Reg returned, chuckling at his own humor.

"I knew that during *Pride and Prejudice*. That's a long time, though, for a family not to have a job. Rick works."

"I have to disagree. Ricky *commands*. There's a difference."

They'd had this argument before. As long as Samantha remained cool, though, Richard would attempt to do so, as well. "You're changing the subject," she noted.

Reg's smile deepened. "Am I?"

This conversation was a bit like watching a fencing match. Slick as Reg was, he was in *way* over his head, and he had no idea. "If I command, then I command you to tell her what you do for a living. Or I can tell her."

Reg flipped his free hand at the air. "Heaven forfend. You'll say something gauche, like 'he sells cars'. What I do, my dear Sam, is match a particular driver with the perfect car. It takes skill, patience, and sometimes a great deal of flattery."

"Love connections between man and Mercedes?" she queried, real amusement touching her voice.

"Or between man and Porsche. Or man and Maserati. Or woman and Jaguar. You get the picture."

"Ah. I do."

"I'm very good at it, too." He half-lidded his eyes, studying her closely. "For instance, I would say you're a...Lamborghini Aventador woman. In red. Or custom pink. Am I right?"

Richard snorted, then tried to turn the sound into a cough. In England Samantha drove a blue Mini-Cooper. In Florida, she generally used his yellow '67 Mustang – unless she was on a job. Then it was the '15 Honda Civic he'd bought her. He knew her motto as well as she did: Never stand out. A pink Lamborghini was about as far away from Sam's style as it was possible to get.

"Something amusing, Ricky?"

"He's just laughing because I keep trying to borrow his Lambo, and he won't let me. I actually drive a Tesla, these days."

"Ah. Environmentally conscious, are you?"

Samantha's smiled deepened, though Richard wasn't certain how she managed that. And now he was going to have to buy her a Tesla. "I'm on the S.P.E.R.M. committee," she said smoothly. "I have to be environmentally aware."

Reginald's cheeks darkened. "I beg your pardon?"

"S.P.E.R.M.," she repeated. "The Society for the Protection of the Environment and Range of Manatees. Manatees are very big in Florida."

"Well. Thank goodness. I wasn't certain what you were about to say." Reg laughed, putting his free hand on Samantha's knee as he did so.

That, as far as Richard was concerned, was poaching. He stood, walked over, and pulled Samantha to her feet. The odds were about fifty-fifty that she would be angry at him for stepping in, but since she was already beginning to spin tales about automobiles, he decided to risk it. "Don't let Reg charm you," he drawled, pasting a smile on his own face. "He's notorious for that."

She sent him a quick frown as if to say, "please, dude". The fact that she was puzzled by his concern reassured him to a ridiculous degree – and left him annoyed at his own lack of restraint. They were engaged. Samantha had agreed that marrying him was what she wanted. He knew damned well it was what he wanted. The sight of his charming cousin putting a hand on her leg was… Hell, Reggie had brought someone with him, as well. The fact that the gesture had troubled him was, as Sam would say, so *Pride and Prejudice* of him.

When he released her hand, she leaned up to catch him with a quick kiss. "If you thick-blooded Brits don't mind, I'm going to go find a jacket. This is *not* Florida weather."

Hmm. Was that her, fleeing? More likely it was him, unable to help reading significance into every damned second right now, because he'd introduced her to the three people in the world he couldn't dismiss from his life – his relatives. "My blood's thinned a bit, as well," he said to her back. "I think my jacket's over the bedpost."

Samantha nodded without turning around. "Ten-four."

"Where in God's green Earth did you find her?" Reg asked the moment she left the room, sitting back and crossing one ankle over the other.

"A museum event," Richard returned. That was what he and

Samantha had agreed on, since neither of them was about to admit that she'd tried to rob him and then ended up saving him from a bomb. "Then when my house was burglarized, I brought her in to help with the investigation. I asked her to stay, and she stayed." The negotiations had been far more complicated than that, but Reg didn't need to know that. He paused. "Why?"

Reg cracked a grin. "That's the Ricky Addison I know. 'My word is law.' Does she always do what you tell her to? Patricia did. Until she didn't, of course."

"So, this is the segment of the conversation where you remind me that my ex-wife slept with my college roommate? I do remember, so I suppose it's meant to make *you* feel better. It's very gauche, you know, to have your sense of self-esteem based on the misfortunes of others." Richard opened his mouth to continue; God knew he'd had both sides of this conversation memorized for weeks. What was the point of it, though? He had Samantha. He was happy. Damned happy. Grinding Reg into paste didn't serve any purpose. He took a breath. "Tell me about yours. Eerika, yes?"

"Yes. She's a professional shopper." Reggie sent him a sideways glance, chuckling. "I was waiting for that expression. She purchases for some of those 'I'm secretly shagging my flatmate's partner' reality shows. She's even been talking to a producer about getting her own show. They're still working on a concept."

Ah, reality shows. He'd never been a fan, but Samantha liked to study some of the so-called "real" housewives. Apparently Eerika Nyland didn't shy away from publicity, and that set his teeth on edge. Thank God for no cell service, after all.

"How did you meet?" Richard asked.

"She contacted me four months ago about a car. Ended up passing on it, but here we are." He uncrossed his legs. "She confessed last week that she'd seen me about and asked me to find her a car as an excuse to meet me. Best sale I ever lost."

The meet was so stereotypically cute that Richard almost expected his cousin to finish his sentence with, "the saucy minx".

Perhaps he had no right to sarcasm or cynicism where the meet-cute was concerned, because while he remained fairly certain very few people could match a bomb or Samantha dropping in through his skylight, he could also never tell anyone else about it.

"Mum and dad seem to like her, which puts her several rungs above the previous three girls I brought home."

Shaking himself free of the considerable tangles of his life, Richard glanced toward the open door. "Your first mistake might have been referring to them as 'girls'," he commented. If his aunt and uncle liked the Viking, perhaps she wasn't all that bad.

"A figure of speech between cousins," Reg said dismissively. "At least I'm not dating my own employee."

And this was one of the bloody lies he would have to live with. "Contracted consultant," he amended, anyway. "And another crack like that might make me reconsider chatting with you about the new Bentley EXP 10 Speed 6."

His cousin blinked. "You are aware that's just a concept car at this point."

"And?" Richard prompted. He'd bought cars through Reggie before – not out of necessity, but because it would look bad if a man who bought as many cars as he did, didn't deal with his cousin who brokered them.

"If you're serious, I'll see what I can do. Don't mention it to Dad, though, if you don't mind. He sees you coming to me as charity."

No, Uncle Rowland didn't like charity. He preferred to make his money the old-fashioned way – by inheriting it. *That* was perfectly acceptable. "No worries."

"By the way, he's going to ask you about investing in his leatherworks company. Again."

Ah, finely-tooled leather wallets, purses, boots, and jackets. A nineteenth-century business in a twenty-first-century world. The very fact that it was old-fashioned made it acceptable for an aristocrat to own it. Stifling a sigh, Richard nodded. "Thank you for the warning."

"You're welcome." Reggie stood to give a mock bow, then strolled over to the liquor table in the corner. "Tell me you have the good Scotch."

"This is Scotland. Of course I have the good Scotch. Pour me one, will you?"

A moment later his cousin handed over a brimming glass of amber and settled into the chair opposite him across the hearth. "Is the west wing really that bad off? I'd love to go exploring through our old haunts. There may be some antiques in there that should be moved to safety."

"Don't worry about the antiques. It didn't just begin falling apart yesterday. We should never have been allowed to play in there as children, in fact." The entire wing needed to be surveyed – and he knew who was best suited to do it, even if he preferred that she remain well away from any rotted ceiling beams and crumbling mortar. Apparently he needed to secure some hard hats.

"If you say so. I'd still like to see it."

"Why?"

Reg downed half his Scotch. "Memories, my dear cousin. I'm certain I hid away a handful of those old lead soldiers. They're worth their weight in gold, these days."

Scavenging. He was accustomed to it. There was an entire industry of scavengers who followed him about in business, picking up his leftovers and remains and rejects. For as long as he'd known him, Reg had been...an opportunist, he supposed it was. That characteristic made him a perfect car salesman – or broker, as Reg preferred – but it made him feel a bit greasy at parties.

"I'll see what I can arrange," he said aloud. "Are your parents going to join us?"

"I doubt it. That helicopter flight had Mum clutching her

handbag hard enough to leave claw marks. They'll make an appearance for dinner. You'd best tell your American girl that we Addisons dress for dinner with the family. Eerika already knows – hence the mountain of luggage."

"Samantha's not even distantly related to hillbillies, Reg." At least he didn't think she was. "And West Palm Beach isn't exactly Blackpool in the summer."

His cousin laughed. "I saw her, Ricky. That girl has got some class. And ass."

Well, that was enough of that. "Leave rhyming to the poets, Reg. Do try to keep in mind that I'm marrying Samantha."

"Right. I keep forgetting she's not one of your Victoria's Secret girls."

For God's sake. Ask one – or three – models out to charity events, and suddenly no one remembered that he'd ever dated anyone else. No one remembered but Samantha, that was, since she had a nearly photographic memory and delighted in googling him. "She's like no one you've ever met, Reg. And when you fall in love with her – which you will, despite Eerika – just keep in mind that she's mine. She's more than you could handle, anyway."

Reg lifted both eyebrows. "That almost sounds like a challenge." He finished off the Scotch and stood. "But considering that I know what you did to Patricia and Peter when you caught them shagging, I'll decline. Now if you don't mind, I'm going to go find *my* girlfriend and occupy myself until dinner."

"*Mi casa, su casa,* as they say in Florida."

"God, you've been away for too damned long, Ricky."

Once he was alone again, Richard finished off his own Scotch and then rang for Yule to request a half dozen hard hats, portable lights, and generators to power them. This would have been an easier holiday if the castle wasn't practically begging to be dug through, but it had been his bloody idea to come here. Hopefully Samantha would decide that mice and rot wasn't her style after all, and they would have an excuse to go to London before long. Fingers crossed.

Because as well and thoroughly as he generally planned, he'd begun to realize that he'd overlooked a few rather important things. Things he didn't want anyone digging through. Not even Samantha. Especially not Samantha, because she would likely figure them out.

6

S amantha reached out to push the curtain open a little, then sank back down again with a shivering sigh. "The sun's up," she panted, lifting and lowering herself over Rick again.

He continued playing with her boobs, pinching her nipples in a way that had her on the verge of coming for the second time that morning. "Breakfast will wait," he returned, his own voice more of a hard grunt than his usual smooth British tones.

"I mean, it's not raining." Sinking down, she favored him with a hot, openmouthed kiss and sped her pace. She usually preferred it when he was on top, but so did he. A little loss of control was good for him. It felt damned good for her, too.

Rick shifted his hands to her hips, lifting up beneath her and holding her down hard against him. "Hold, please," he rasped, growling as he came.

That sent her over the edge again, and with a keening sigh she flopped down over him. Good gravy. A year after they'd first done it – in the back of one of his cars, as she recalled – and it only got better. He knew damned well what set her off, and vice versa. "That was my line," she mumbled against his ear, tugging her hair out of her eyes.

She could feel his laugh all the way inside her. "You broke my brain there for a moment," he breathed, wrapping his arms around her back. "I vote we stay here in bed all day."

"Dude, what would your relatives say?" Samantha nipped at his ear. "It's weird enough trying to imagine that Aunt Mercia and Uncle Rowland had sex at least once to end up with Reggie. I'm pretty sure they think no one else does it at all."

"I am not having this conversation. Ever."

Chuckling, she shifted to kiss him again. His warm mouth molded with hers, familiar and comforting and arousing and exotic all at the same time. This guy, the one that hundreds of women wanted, wanted her. For keeps. And hell, she certainly didn't have a better plan than that – because there wasn't one.

That, though, was what worried her a little. Okay, a lot. Good stuff, luck, she had in spades with her chosen profession. It was her personal life that was messed up. No attachments, no strings, no one knowing enough about her to get her in trouble when she left. This guy, though, knew it all. Well, most of it, anyway. Eventually he'd know everything about her. Just as she knew almost everything about him. Every so often, though, he surprised her. Like he had with Canniebrae Castle. She'd known he had property in Scotland, but this place was stunning. Rough, more than a little crumbly and creaky in places, but amazing.

"I have someone flying in from Inverness to run wire and give me an internet connection, by the way," Rick commented, rolling her onto her back and running his fingers through her hair while he kissed her.

"Good luck with that," she returned, reaching over her head to grip the wooden headboard. Rick's kisses trailed down her neck to her tits, and she let out a breath in a shivery moan. God, he felt good.

"No luck required," he said, his voice a little muffled. "Just the proper application of money."

"Snob."

He lifted his head again, resting his chin on her sternum. "That reminds me. Reg and Uncle Rowland will likely want to go shooting."

Ugh. "Shooting what? Pheasants? Deer? Rabbits?"

"Grouse, pheasants, partridges. Birds, for certain."

"Are you going?"

"That depends. Are you going to make that face if I do?"

"I promise nothing." She shrugged as best she could with her arms over her head and his hands on her breasts. "I get the whole cultural heritage blue-blood thing, Brit. But it would be more fair if the birds were armed, too."

"That would change the circumstances a bit, wouldn't it?"

She grinned up at him. "Yep."

"I'll go with them," Rick said slowly. "I won't kill any birds – unless they are armed and shoot first."

"Deal." Tugging his arm to bring him up over her, she kissed him again, in that feathery way he claimed drove him crazy. "And I appreciate it, Rick. Really."

"Well, we can't have it getting out that one of the board members of S.P.E.R.M. advocated pheasant shooting."

It wasn't a big deal, really. No, she didn't like the idea of anyone shooting something they didn't require for food, but if he really wanted to participate, she wouldn't have given him a hard time about it. Probably. But he'd known she didn't approve, and rather than countering her argument by pointing out some wackiness about how he didn't approve of someone breaking into other peoples' homes and taking their shit, either, he grinned and gave in.

"You're kind of a nice guy," she said aloud, brushing his black hair out of his eyes. "Have I mentioned that lately?"

Running his hands up along her arms to grip her fingers with his, he kissed her back, slow and deep. "I'm not a nice guy. While I'm out shooting, you'll have to entertain my aunt and Miss Nyland."

"Well, sh—"

The door rattled as someone thumped at it.

"Fuck," Rick muttered. "We're asleep!"

"M'laird, ye wanted to know... That is, I... I require a word with ye."

Rick buried his face between her tits, then scooted backward off the bed. Snagging a robe off a chair, he pulled it around his shoulders and walked to the door. "What is it, Yule?" he asked, then to Samantha's surprise slipped into the hallway and closed the door behind him.

She lay spread-eagled where she was for a moment, then sat up and made her way into the tiny shower. It was barely big enough to turn around in, and halfway through the shower the hot water vanished. Yelping, she reached for the handle – which came off in her hand. Samantha hit the door with her haunch and sprang out of the stall.

Yep, that was her, using all her awesome cat burglar skills to escape a cold shower. "Dammit," she said aloud, shivering, and with a breath stuck her head back in to finish washing shampoo out of her hair.

Whatever Rick hadn't wanted to discuss in front of her had best not have been about the lack of hot water, or somebody was going to get their ass kicked for not telling her. On the other hand, she was definitely wide awake now. After she wrapped herself up in the other bathrobe she crawled under the sink and turned off the water to the room. The shower spit and farted in protest, but slowed to a bare trickle.

What *had* Rick not wanted her to overhear? Something stupid, probably, like the west wing collapsing entirely and he didn't want to be embarrassed by admitting in front of her that the castle truly was a wreck. On the other hand it could be a surprise, the last one of which had ended with her staying in an old Scottish castle instead of a much warmer and more modern estate in Devon.

Dammit, she couldn't help being curious. It was in her nature. On the other hand, Rick's business was Rick's. She wasn't a hoverer or a prier, unless she figured the secret somehow involved her – or their safety. But she had no reason to think there was anything nefarious going on behind her back.

After she dressed in a loose sweater, jeans, and some Nikes, she trotted downstairs to the breakfast room. Yule was the only one there, so she helped herself to some scrambled eggs and an English muffin-looking thing and took a seat where she could look out the window toward the white-shouldered mountains. "Yule, I just wanted to let you know that the hot water went out earlier," she said conversationally. She wasn't his boss, and he wasn't her servant, so she'd decided on friendly ease. To most of the staff at Rick's estates in both England and Palm Beach she'd become simply Miss Sam, and while she could have done without the "Miss" part, it seemed to make them all nervous not to use it.

"Just the hot?" he asked in his warm brogue.

"Yes. The cold water's fine."

"Bloody hell. The laird and his ladyship will be rising soon, and I'll damned well nae hear the end of it from Mr. Reginald, either. Will ye excuse me, bonny lass?"

"Sure. Oh, and I shut the water off in my bathroom, because the shower handle came loose."

"Och, this poor old pile doesnae remember how to behave with guests," he muttered, slapping the doorframe in apparent rebuke as he hurried out toward the kitchen.

Once she was alone, Samantha stretched her hand across the corner of the table for the *London Times*, which had been placed so it would be at Rick's elbow when he sat down. It used to be that she perused newspapers looking to see when auctions were going to be held or some high-profile work of art was about to change hands. She still did it, but now it was more out of curiosity than to plan a heist.

"Anything interesting?" Rick asked, as he strolled into the room.

"Nah. Dorothy's ruby slippers are going up for auction again."

He piled breakfast on his plate from the sideboard and then sat at the head of the table on her left. "And what did you do to the shower?"

"Hulk angry," she said with a grin. "I turned off the water in there, too."

"Yes, I noticed right when I tried to brush my teeth. You might have left a note."

She shrugged. "I didn't know where you went or when you'd be back. You used bottled water, I assume."

"I borrowed the bathroom next door to ours. By the way, Reg was determined to dive into the west wing this morning, and I went and told him to wait for us. Nobody goes in there alone. It was dangerous enough when we were kids sneaking about in there." He glanced toward the door. "And between you and me," he continued in a lower voice, "I don't want him picking the place clean of Richard Addison souvenirs he can auction off on eBay."

Wow. "That's kind of harsh, isn't it?" she whispered back at him.

"Perhaps. A few photos of Patricia and me showed up on news shows after the story about our break-up broke. They didn't come from me."

Like there weren't a hundred other people out there willing to sell pictures of Rick Addison if the price was right. But she knew how private he was, and how few unofficial photos of him were out there. "At the risk of repeating myself, then, why are they here if you don't trust them?"

"They're family. And...I'm not one hundred percent certain.

So, I'm willing to give Reg the benefit of the doubt." He reached out and gripped her fingers. "Which doesn't mean I'm not going to be watching."

Samantha snorted. "You know, this makes me feel a little better. Because I thought my screwed-up family relationships were an exception to the rule. If yours are messed up, too, then *you're* messed up, too. Just like me."

A soft chuckle erupted from his chest. "You make a good point."

"I do, don't I?"

Rick took her elbow and pulled her toward him across the corner of the table. "Smart ass," he murmured, and kissed her.

"Shocking," Reggie commented, strolling into the breakfast room, the Viking on his arm. "Mum and Dad won't approve." He glanced at Yule. "A pair of eggs, over easy. Eerika?"

"The same."

"You think they wouldn't?" Rick returned smoothly. "Then it's a good thing I'm not eighteen and living under their roof, I suppose." Only the grip of his fingers on her elbow told her that he didn't find the conversation amusing.

"Don't preach to me," his cousin returned, grinning loosely. "I spent the night with a woman not my wife."

Norway hit him on the arm. "You're very bad, Reginald."

The conversation didn't look like it was going anywhere good, so Samantha patted the seat beside her. "I hear you want to investigate the west wing. I'm leading an expedition there this morning if you want to join me, Reggie."

Rick's cousin sat down next to her, the Viking on his other side. "Gladly, Dr. Livingston. Shall I pack a tent?"

"Surely you aren't going in there, Samantha," Eerika countered. "It's dangerous, I hear. And dirty."

Somewhere in the past day, this had gone from her being nervous to meet Rick's family, to doing everything she could to keep herself between them and Rick's temper. The explanation he gave about not wanting to lose souvenirs kind of worked, but she couldn't help feeling that there was something else going on here. Samantha put a grin on her face. "I think I'll manage."

"And will you be joining us, Ricky?"

"I'm the one who owns the gloves and hardhats. So, yes."

Lord Rowland and Lady Mercia appeared, both chipper and so, so proper. Maybe Reggie was right, and they were totally annoyed by the way she and Rick were kissing and touching and sleeping together pre-maritally, and they were just too polite to say anything – though Reggie got away with it. If that was because Eerika had a British accent, well, fuck that. Even so, part of her wanted to apologize, to make sure they liked her, but the other half picked up on Rick's ambivalence about their presence. For the moment she'd go with the latter.

"If you're going, then I'm going, Reginald," the Viking pressed.

"I thought it was dangerous and dirty," Samantha commented under her breath, earning her a side-eye from Rick.

"It'll be an adventure," Reggie countered. "Do you have enough hardhats, Ricky?"

"Only if you stop calling me Ricky. But this place has stood for seven hundred years. I thought we might go into the village this afternoon," Rick put in. "Take Samantha and Miss Nyland for a late luncheon at The Bonny Lass pub."

"You young people do as you will," Lord Rowland put in. "If the weather holds, Mercia and I will take a stroll in the garden."

If Lady Mercia had been wearing a bonnet to go with her conservative, flowered dress, she could have been mistaken for Mrs. Bennet from *Pride and Prejudice*. Lord Rowland was suited and tied, even with this being a holiday. All he needed was to substitute a white, ruffled cravat for his thin, blue tie, and he'd be Mr. Bennet. Now they wanted to go for a stroll in the garden. These two couldn't possibly be as bland as they seemed. That made them a puzzle. She loved a damn puzzle.

Once they'd all finished breakfast and separated to gear up for the expedition, she snagged a diet coke from the huge, walk-in refrigerator in the kitchen. That was all she needed; as far as exploration, this was all the way over on the tame meter for her. Samantha trudged upstairs to the wide doors leading to the west wing of the house. No wi-fi, iffy antenna TV, and barely any electricity, but they stocked diet Coke at Canniebrae. She didn't bother with thinking it could be a coincidence; of course Rick had seen to it. For her.

"Are you certain you wouldn't rather keep exploring the attic?" he asked, topping the stairs and tossing her a blue construction helmet.

"Not today." Sam plopped the hardhat over her hair and faced the heavy, oversized doors. They even had a chain around the handles. And a big-ass lock. "Please tell me you have velociraptors in there."

"Why do you keep insisting that I secretly own a real Jurassic zoo?" Rick retorted, pulling a large key from his pocket and working it into the lock.

"Because it would be awesome." The locking mechanism squeaked and clicked. Chains rattled as they hit the floor. She shivered a little when the huge double doors moaned open, the sound echoing down a long, dark hallway beyond. "*This* is awesome," she revised in a whisper, grinning.

"Yes, all you require is some darkness, dust, and cobwebs."

"Ah, you say the sweetest things. Let's go, Shaggy."

He lifted an eyebrow curved above Caribbean blue eyes. "Which makes you Scooby, you know."

"I'm just impressed that you know who the Magical Mystery Machine gang is."

Rick leaned against the doorframe. "Of course I—"

"The Magical what?" Reggie said, as he topped the stairs behind her. Norway walked behind him. She'd donned some sort of high-fashion version of a safari outfit, with boots, scarf, khaki-colored pants, and all. Did the Viking always travel with that get-up, or had she known they were going exploring?

"It's a cartoon," Samantha returned, relieving Reggie of two of the flashlights he carried and handing one to Rick. She looked on as Reggie donned his hardhat and the Viking carefully settled hers over her styled Scandinavian locks. "I'll go first," she decided. The west wing was likely the least safe place Reggie and the Viking had ever been. In addition, this was literally right up her alley, as it were. However athletic Rick was and Reggie and Eerika might be, they didn't spend time navigating dark, treacherous corridors and rooms in search of treasure.

"Oh, I don't think so, my dear," Reggie countered. "I'm all for equal pay and all that, but I'm fairly certain my head is harder than yours."

"I wouldn't wager on that," Rick murmured as he passed by her, his fingers brushing hers. "*I'll* lead. It's my house."

Men. Samantha sighed. "Then for crap's sake stay close to one wall when you go down the hallway. The center will be weakest."

"'For crap's sake,'" Reggie repeated, humor in his voice. "Delightful." The Viking giggled.

Great. Now the Brits would think her gauche or crass and lift their eyebrows at her. "That was my serious voice," she decided.

"Ah. Good to know."

Whether they'd decided she was a stupid American or not, they at least stayed close against the left wall as they headed down the dark hallway. Most of the doors on either side were shut, and the iffy electricity in the rest of the castle hadn't made it this far – likely because of water damage to the wiring. Rick and Reggie had evidently played in this area twenty or so years ago, so she assumed it had been fairly sound that recently.

"What did this?" she asked, panning her flashlight along the top of the wall while her feet squelched over long-ruined carpet of an uncertain dark color. The rest of Rick's life – with the notable exception of her – was so orderly, that this...mess really didn't make any sense. She glanced at his shoulders as he walked a few steps in front of her.

"Time and weather, mostly," he returned, stopping at the first door on the right-hand side and lowering the latch to shove it open. "No one's lived in this wing for at least fifty years."

The room held a heavy wooden bedframe and a pair of stacked wooden chairs against the wall, with a handful of ruined books by the window and a badly sagging curtain rod with disintegrating green floor-length curtains. "Is the stuff from these rooms what ended up in the attic?" she asked, noting a lighter patch of wall in the shape of a rectangle over the mantelpiece.

"Yes. The staff had plenty of time to clear out most of the rooms."

"Only of the things they knew were valuable," Reggie commented, heading down the hallway past them. "There were odds and ends of treasure back when we dug through here. Surely some of that remains."

"I have no idea, Reg. I didn't get a chart. Generally scavenging doesn't come with signposts."

That was testy. "You know, the three of us can continue the tour if you need to make that call to Donner," she injected. Generally she was the one causing the tension; this was…weird.

"Tom can wait," Rick said in a cooler tone, and gestured for her to precede him. "I don't mind being here; I just don't see the point of it. What are you looking for, Reg?"

"I want to see our old haunts. Plenty of pleasant memories of grand expeditions. I told you that. No need to raise your hackles."

Very few people called Rick on his temper, his decisions, or, well, anything. Being a relative evidently gave Reggie more freedom than being on Addisco's board of directors. As that occurred to her, Samantha realized that she didn't like the idea that other people could – dared – talk to him the way she did. "This is all for some lead soldiers?" she asked.

"It's about memories, I suppose. Ricky – Rick – isn't the only one who's been away from this place for nearly two decades."

She heard Rick pull in a breath through his nose. "I hadn't realized you were so fond of Canniebrae, Reg."

"Well, you didn't bother to ask, did you?"

This was not good. Tension between family members meant people going away and not coming back. Or people sending other people away with the expectation that they would never cross paths again. She knew that much about families. Stepping forward, she wrapped her arm around Reggie's. "What do you remember about being here?"

"I always looked forward to the summer. We would dig for buried treasure and hunt through the old, closed-up rooms for spirits. I do remember we once found an old dagger. I stuck it in my belt, but Ricky insisted that we have it authenticated and dated. It ended up locked away in a display case."

"It did not," Rick returned. "I only told you that, when Uncle Rowland said he didn't want you walking around with a knife."

"You didn't have to say anything to my father. It was a bloody knife. Not the stone of Scone."

Hmm. She'd carried a knife at age twelve. But then she'd learned how to use it, first – and not to shave twigs into a point or carve her initials in wood. No, knives were for unlocking window and cutting wires. According to her father, if you needed it for self-defense during a burglary, then you were an amateur. And she wasn't an amateur.

She sent Reggie a sideways glance. "Not to stomp on your you-took-a-knife-twenty-years-ago rant, but that's all you remember?"

"I'm not surprised you'd take his side." Reggie rolled his shoulders. "No. That isn't all I remember."

"Good. Tell me about the treasure hunting, then."

"We were children, Reg," Rick cut in. "And it's the Highlands. They may not have leprechauns here, but I doubt there's an old house for three hundred miles that doesn't have a tale about buried treasure, banshees, and ghosts to go along with it."

"We did find the knife. And that old map." Reginald turned around to pin his cousin with a look. "What happened to that map, anyway?"

"I have no idea." Rick lifted an eyebrow. "Don't tell me that's your master plan. Find buried treasure? Because if I recall, firstly the map only *looked* old, and secondly we already searched for the treasure. It was nonsense."

"I'm not so certain of that. I say we look." He jabbed his thumb through a tear in the Victorian-era wallpaper lining the upper half of the wall. "No worrying over damaging an antique."

Well, that explained why Reggie had overruled Rick's suggestion that they avoid the west wing altogether. The good stuff had been removed or was already ruined – unless it lay beneath a floorboard somewhere. So they were tracking lead soldiers, and maybe a treasure map.

"I have this prickly feeling at the back of my neck," Reggie drawled, putting a hand on the handle of a closed door, "that some dread woman in gray will be floating in the middle of the old sitting room." Flashing a grin, he pushed down on the brass handle. "Let's see, shall we?"

No floating ghost filled the room, but the rush of cold, damp air made Samantha shiver anyway. "Was it this bad when you were kids?" she asked, glancing over her shoulder as Rick followed them into the tumbled room.

"Not quite, but close," he conceded, squatting to pick up a broom handle. "I blame this on my lack of interest in returning here." Jabbing at the floor in front of him with the stick, he made his way over to the pair of windows. The nearer one had broken out, with a scattering of glass glittering on the hardwood floor and nearly covered by a fine sheet of water.

Samantha knew the lack of interest in returning to Canniebrae had something to do with the death of Rick's mom, but he'd never much wanted to talk about it. If he did now, she doubted it would be in front of his cousin and Norway. Ignoring Reggie digging through the mildewed trash surrounding the hearth while Eerika pointed out promising shapes, she stepped across the floor in Rick's tracks and joined him at the window. Beneath her feet the floor gave with every step; it wouldn't be long before the entire wing pancaked onto itself and left nothing but a pile of stone and wood.

"Are you planning to repair this, or tear it down?" she asked, staying back far enough that she wouldn't grind the glass into the floor with her shoes. Thieves didn't make noise unnecessarily. Even retired thieves.

"I haven't decided yet. I'm inclined to think it's a total loss, historical-value wise. If that's so, then tearing it down and beginning again makes more sense."

"Christ, Ricky, you just said it's seven hundred years old." His cousin continued sorting through broken furniture and what looked like old newspapers. "Tearing it down would give you a stroke."

"It might," Rick agreed. "As I said, I haven't decided yet."

"If you don't decide soon, Canniebrae will make the decision for you." Reggie straightened. Wiping his palms on his trousers, he headed for the door. "And I think I'll pay a visit to the old library before it all falls down around my ears. I'll show you, Eerika. Used to have a lovely view of the garden."

Rick's fingers caught hers. And then he squeezed. Three times. Then three more times, more slowly. Then three quick again.

She'd never served in the Navy, but she did know a smattering of Morse code; a few discreet taps or blinks of a flashlight were far less likely to be noticed than whispering or radio traffic. Rick had just signaled her with an S-O-S. Samantha didn't know why his ship suddenly needed saving, but hell, she could swim.

Whatever it was had something to do with the old library, she surmised. Squeezing back, she pulled free and gingerly made her way back toward the hallway. With one foot on a firmer section of the floor, she stomped hard with the other. As she expected, the floor disintegrated beneath her shoe. Shifting her weight, she dug her toes into the opening and went down onto her hands and knees, throwing in a surprised shriek for good measure. "Ow!"

Reggie was closer, but Rick reached her first. "Are you hurt?" he asked, grasping her calf and lifting her foot free of the hole.

"I said 'ouch', didn't I?" she snapped back, turning to sit on her backside. She wanted to throw him a wink or something, but with Reggie that close she couldn't risk it. Hopefully Rick realized she was faking – after all, he'd given her the Bat signal in the first place. "Help me up," she continued, holding a hand out to each of them. Behind the Addison men, Eerika looked annoyed that someone else had their attention. Well, pffffth.

Together they pulled her to her feet, and she made a show of wincing as her left foot touched the floor. "Damn it. I need some ice and a beer."

With a snort, Reggie slid an arm around her waist and guided hers around his shoulder. "That's very specific."

"I've got her."

"Let Richard have her, my dear," the Viking supplied.

For a minute Samantha felt like a dog toy while Rick wrangled her away from his cousin. Evidently whatever help he wanted didn't go far enough that he meant to allow any other man putting a hand on her – even to help her walk.

"Fine. You take her; I have more exploring to do."

Stifling a sigh, Samantha twisted to look at Reggie. "Are you kidding? I just put my foot through the floor, and you think you and Eerika are going anywhere alone here? Lift my feet."

"Really?"

She elevated her left foot toward his hand. "Yes, really. You, big fella. You take the upper parts. Get me out of here."

Rick slid his arms around her ribs and took her weight as Reggie put a foot on either side of his hips and headed back toward the main part of the house. "I like the upper parts," Rick whispered into her hair. "Thank you."

"Yeah? You have some 'splaining to do, Ricky."

"Fine. As long as you never – ever – refer to me as Ricky Ricardo again."

"Deal."

7

"Not that I'm complaining about the coddling," Samantha commented, folding her arms behind her head, "but you know an ice pack isn't necessary, right? Plus my feet have frostbite already."

"Aside from the fact that you *could* have been hurt, I'm keeping up appearances. But yes, your feet are a menace on a good day." Setting aside the ice, Richard decided as long as her foot wasn't actually injured, he might as well have fun with it. Pressing his thumb along the arch of her left foot, Richard began rubbing in slow circles. After a moment she sighed, and the added benefit of seeing goose bumps travel up her bare arms at his touch wasn't anything to sneeze at, either.

"So, what didn't you want Reggie to see?"

Of course she'd realized that he'd had more in mind than safety. God knew he would much rather have her asking questions than Reginald. "It occurred to me that I didn't like the idea of my cousin digging for treasure in the ruins of my life."

She raised one eyebrow above pretty green eyes. "Really."

"Is that so surprising? You know how I like my antiques." He leaned in, kissing her soft mouth. "And you."

Her lips curved. "At least I'm in the top two."

Not for a moment did he think she'd forgotten her question, or that he'd answered it to her satisfaction. The fact that she didn't continue pressing, in fact, actually troubled him. Telling her to let it go, though, would only make it worse. How the hell had he forgotten about that damned map? And why had Reg remembered it? "I would prefer if you stayed out of that wing," he finally muttered, knowing that wasn't sufficient. He tightened his grip on her ankle. "The next time this could be real."

"Dude, I used to climb the outside of buildings for a living," she drawled. "The attic's still allowed, right?"

"Right." If this was Sam conceding to his wishes, he wasn't about to make a big deal out of it and spoil the moment, even if he did mean to pin her to the bed for the next twenty minutes as a way of showing his gratitude. Slowly he slid his hands up her leg until he pressed his fingers into the crotch of her jeans.

She drew in a quick breath. "That isn't my ankle, Brit."

"No, it isn't. What of it?"

"Did you lock the door? I don't want your aunt and uncle barging in with tea while we're doin' it."

Richard snorted. "That is quite possibly the least romantic thing you've ever said. You do, however, make a valid point." With a last kiss he stood, shirking his boots as he walked to the door.

Halfway there, someone started knocking. "M'laird?"

Damnation. Perhaps they should all have stayed at a hotel, after all. There were several nice ones just down the road. He yanked open the door. "What is it?"

The butler took a surprised step backward. "I apologize for intruding," Yule said, wisely not trying to look over Richard's shoulder at Samantha relaxing on the bed. "I thought ye might wish to know that Mr. Reginald and Miss Nyland are back in the west wing. I offered to send Malcolm with them, but yer cousin refused."

He definitely should have opted for a hotel. Next time he wouldn't be so idiotic. Or naïve. "Thank you," he said. "I'll go drag him out in a minute."

When he closed the door and turned around, Samantha had already rolled off the bed and was tying on her shoes. "I'll go distract them," she said. "With the attic, maybe. If that's acceptable, since it's your stuff in there, too."

"Firstly, you can't go distract them, because you just feigned a foot injury. Secondly, no. I'll get them. Thirdly, I don't particularly want them in my attic, either."

Samantha tilted her head. "You know, I could probably be more helpful if you'd stop being such a hard ass and tell me what's bothering you."

Having spent a good number of years working closely with men and women who followed orders and yet had their own best interests in mind, Richard knew he should have had a better idea how to manage Samantha. However she'd begun, she put him first now in her life. That fact alone both charmed and worried the hell out of him. Because the one thing she didn't do – ever – was follow orders. The other thing she didn't do – ever – was turn her back on a mystery.

"I thought you enjoyed my hard arse," he said aloud. "I'll have someone find you a crutch, and then feel free to limp about the house. Just don't go into the west wing after you went to the trouble of establishing that it was dangerous."

"I told you I wouldn't." She wrinkled her nose at him. "If the floor had been sound I wouldn't have been able to punch a hole through it, so be careful. It *is* dangerous, and you like to stomp."

"I'm too subtle for stomping," Richard retorted, and closed the door on whatever retort she was likely making.

The butler and two footmen stood at the half-open double doors that closed off the west wing. None of them looked happy, which didn't surprise him. "M'laird," Yule said, "I reminded Mr. Reginald that it's dangerous in there, but he said he reckoned he could look after himself and the lass."

Richard sighed. "Find some lumber and nails. I'll drag him out, and we'll nail the damned door shut." He caught sight of Yule's lifted eyebrows. "I know what century the door is. I can't think of another way to keep him out of here short of throwing him out a window."

"As ye say, m'laird. I'll send Malcolm in with ye."

With a nod, Richard settled a hardhat onto his head. That was the other difference between Samantha and himself; she liked – what did she call it? – lone wolf situations. Liked to handle things on her own because she knew what she was doing. He did, as well, but he employed a great many people, owned a great many businesses, and didn't mean to muck things up by being stupid. "Stay close to the walls, Malcolm. I don't want anyone else getting hurt."

"Same to ye, m'laird," the young man returned, settling another hardhat over a shock of red hair worthy of Jamie Fraser himself. Dammit, he was going to stop watching "Outlander" with Sam if he couldn't keep himself from thinking things like that.

He had a good idea where Reg would be, and Richard headed directly to what had once been the house's main library. The floor creaked beneath his feet, and he made himself be cautious. If Samantha at fifty-four kilos could stomp a hole through it, his eighty-one kilos could send him down to the cellar the hard way.

"Reg," he said, stepping into the old room and stopping just inside the doorway.

Miss Nyland, looking through the papers by the window, gasped. His cousin scrambled to his feet, a floorboard in his hands. For a minute he looked like a guilty schoolboy caught with a Playboy, which wasn't all that endearing. "You know me, Ricky. Rick. I can't resist a puzzle."

"You can't resist a treasure, you mean," Richard amended. "That's what you're here about, isn't it? That ridiculous highwayman treasure? Because the room where you hid the lead soldiers would be across the hallway from here."

"You didn't think the treasure was ridiculous when we looked for it the last time."

Richard blew out his breath. This was one of those rare times he wouldn't have minded being wrong. Wrong would have been much less disappointing. "Do I really need to point out that we were fourteen and fifteen? And do I really need to ask you to stop ripping up my floors?"

"This is the perfect time *to* rip them up, Ricky. The entire castle's a disaster, and you as much as said you're pulling this wing down, anyway." He started to wipe his hands off on his expensive-looking jeans, then changed his mind and clapped them together.

"Yes, it's falling apart. Which means it's dangerous. Which means you're risking injury for what – some old marbles? A torn edition of *Ulysses*?"

Reggie wagged a finger at him. "Why say 'most likely'? You dug through here, too, so you're just as likely as I am to know what's under the floorboards."

In the hunt for political correctness, punching had some-where become a bad thing, a barbaric response where words were supposed to be sufficient. Sometimes, though, people deserved a punch square in the face. Richard clenched his fists. "I say 'most likely', because it was eighteen years, one marriage, eight properties, a thousand antiquities, and a million miles ago, Reggie. I don't remember what I hid under the damned floor. Nor do I recall who or what inhabited the room for the previous seven hundred years. But I am fairly certain that you aren't going to find whatever the fuck it is you're after by tearing up a random room in a place you haven't been for nearly two decades."

"Ooh, profanity. That American bit's rubbing off on you." Reggie looked toward the doorway. "You. Get out."

"I... Sir?" Malcolm stammered.

"Go back, Malcolm," Richard said. "Be careful." He glanced over at the slender blonde woman. "Take Miss Nyland with you."

She sniffed. "Reginald."

"Go, Eerika. I need a word with my cousin."

Reg folded his arms over his chest as the other two left the room. "I like the clever way you brought up the amount of property you own and the large amount of money you have to sling around, you poor thing, you, all in the guise of pretending you don't remember precisely what we both know you *do* remember."

"What is it I remember, then, you ponce?"

"That map. I know you had it once, and I think you know where it is now."

So he'd been right again, damn it all. "Will Dawkin's treasure map? That's what this is about?"

"Of course it is."

Pacing carefully to the window and back, Richard took a moment to look out at the view that had decorated so many of his young summers. Back then the world had been much larger and much friendlier, and conversely much fuller of mystery and magic. Back then he'd had a partner in crime, willing to believe whatever he did. Now he had a very different partner in crime, willing to jump in with both feet just for the fun of it.

He turned around again. "The map was a hoax, Reg. Even if it had been real, any highwayman's treasure was either found two hundred years ago, or it's buried beneath so much rock and dirt and overgrowth it will never be found. I think the lads in the pub thought it would be hilarious to put one over on the laird's kid and his cousin, so they tossed a few coins into an old bear's den. We found all the treasure there was."

With a contemptuous look, Reg kicked one of the loose floorboards aside. "So the rich stay rich, and the rest of us sell cars."

They'd had *this* conversation before. "Yes, Reg. You guessed it. I'm keeping a secret highwayman's map from you because eventually I want the money for myself and, more importantly, I don't want you to get it." Shaking his head, he turned his back and walked for the door. "I'm not having this conversation. I came to get you because someone's already fallen through the floor, there's nothing here for you, and it's dangerous. Go through the floor. Maybe you'll find an old pic of mum and me that fell through a crack, and you can sell it to TMZ for enough to impress Miss Nyland."

"Bastard."

"Go to hell."

SAMANTHA SHIFTED BACK from the edge of the roof, then carefully climbed to her feet and picked her way back to the rooftop attic entrance, dropping down inside the house. "Really?" she muttered. "Treasure maps?"

Yes, eavesdropping was bad manners, but hell, at least she got points for doing it literally. Pulling off the heavy wool cap she'd put on, she shook out her hair. Her dirty and damp black clothes went into a pillow case, and after she cleaned off most of the dirt and wet leaves she donned the much more social outfit she'd been wearing earlier, slipped into the main part of the house, then to her shared room.

She could understand why Rick didn't want Reggie pawing through his old stuff, especially if his suspicions about those break-up photos were right, but he hadn't told *her* anything about treasure maps and hidden highwayman gold. That just sucked. And it was mean. And it had to be intentional, which sucked even more.

So, she was allowed to look through his sanctioned, previously-displayed past in the attic, but something about the map business was more touchy. Scowling, she tossed the pillowcase into the old, unused dressing room and moved across the hallway, through two connected rooms, and collected the cane she'd found.

Resuming her limp for anybody who might be wandering by, she made for the large second floor morning room. Rick could come stomping by any minute, and she was not going to be caught sneaking. Not even if he was being sneaky, the jerk.

"Jerk," she muttered aloud, pushing the door open with the butt of the cane.

"Beg pardon, my dear?" Lady Mercia said, looking up from a book she held in both hands.

Crap. "Oh, just my foot," she improvised, limping in to sit in the chair across the hearth from Rick's aunt. For a weird flash she'd expected the woman to be crocheting or embroidering, an old-timey matron's cap over her slightly-too-golden hair. "I told Rick I'm fine, but I'm exiled from the west wing."

"You need to be careful," Mercia returned. "I know you find stolen artwork and all sorts of dangerous things, but this house is dreadfully unsound in places."

Samantha grinned. "I'm discovering that." Since Rick hadn't tromped into earshot yet, she leaned forward a little. "Do you have any idea why?"

"Why Canniebrae is in disrepair?" Mercia gave a small frown. "The west wing has been closed since I can remember. As to why Richard never saw to it, I don't know."

Hmm. More secrets. This one, though, she figured she could sort out without too much trouble. "Rick hasn't been back here since his mom died, has he? Not till now."

His aunt sighed. "You've guessed it, then. This property actually came from her side of the family rather than from the Addison line. She was half-Scottish, you know. It always felt like faerie tales here, as silly as it sounds to say it aloud, and that went away after Rachel passed."

Rachel. Samantha had read the name before, in various articles about Rick in *Forbes* and *Business Week*, but she'd never heard it spoken. Not even by him. Of course she'd never said *her* mother's name in front of him either, but he knew why. He knew that her mom had kicked her dad out of the house and hadn't objected when Martin had taken their daughter along with his shirts and B and E tools.

This was different. It meant that even after a year together, there was stuff she didn't know about Rick. Significant stuff. Assumptions she'd made when she shouldn't have, because she'd based them on her own life. The two of them couldn't have grown up more differently if she'd hailed from Tatooine and him from Vulcan.

Now that she thought about it, Canniebrae looked like a place the magic had gone out of. After eighteen years away, though, why had he wanted to come back now? Did he expect her to wave a wand and make the colors here brighter? Or was she the ultimate symbol that the fairy tale was over? That idea kind of made her want to cry. The question, then, became what she was supposed to do about it. "Do you know of anywhere I could find out more about the folklore around here?" she asked. "Old highwayman tales and such?"

"I know they used to have storytelling nights at The Bonny Lass pub in the village. I'm afraid I never attended, though."

Oh, heavens no. There might have been cursing or drinking. Samantha shook herself. No, she hadn't grown up genteel. She damned well knew how to act like one of the upper crust, and on top of that, she had no reason to dislike Rick's aunt and uncle. They were his only family. "Thank you," she said aloud. "I may go have a chat with the owner."

Right on cue, Rick thudded into the room. "There you are," he said, then sent a nod in his aunt's direction. "Aunt Mercia."

"Richard. You look like thunderclouds."

"Yes, well, your son won't leave the west wing alone, and I'd prefer that he not kill himself falling through the floor."

"Oh, heavens. Surely it's not that dangerous?"

"It is precisely that dangerous." He turned back to Samantha.

"Care to go down to the village for lunch? I have a fond memory of mutton sandwiches at The Bonny Lass."

Aunt Mercia opened her mouth, no doubt to comment about what a coincidence that was, since Sam had just been asking about local folklore. "Sounds good," Samantha said quickly, standing and then pretending to fumble with her cane so she could stagger sideways.

"Oh, my dear!" Mercia exclaimed. "Do be careful!"

"I keep forgetting," she returned, smacking Rick in the shin with the cane as she turned around. There. That was for keeping secrets about treasures.

He grabbed her elbow, then swung her up into his arms so quickly it took her breath away. "I've got you," he intoned. "We'll be back by sunset, Aunt Mercia."

As Rick carried her into the hallway, the lights flickered and went out. "Power's oot!" echoed through the house.

"Dammit."

"What do you care?" Samantha asked, trying to decide if she wanted to comment about his bad mood or not. "We're going out."

"It's just another damned thing to take care of. There's a five-star hotel on the far side of Balmoral. What say I reserve a block of rooms there?"

"Nope."

He looked her in the eye. "Why not? Mice, rot, and no power. Why should we stay?"

"Why did you want to come here in the first place?" she countered, hoping he wasn't about to drop her on her butt.

"That is a very good question. I'll answer it later."

They descended the main staircase, her still in his arms. Ticked off as she was, she couldn't miss the fact that he was likely even angrier. She might not know much about how to be in a relationship, but she knew she didn't like it when Rick wasn't happy. "Cool," she noted aloud, flinging an arm out grandly. "This is like reverse *Gone with the Wind*."

Rick snorted. "Such a romantic, you are."

"*Gone with the Wind* is not a romance."

"Really."

"Really. If the man and woman don't end up together at the end, it's not a romance."

He slowed, his arms around her shoulders and knees tightening a little. "Are we a romance, then?"

Could he really be worried about that? Samantha put her hands on his cheeks and kissed him. "We're the best kind of romance," she returned.

"What's the best kind of romance?"

"The kind where you don't know what the hell's going to happen next, but you know the hero and the heroine will be together. Even if asteroids or giant monsters attack the planet."

Rick nodded, planting a kiss on her temple. "Figures you'd work Godzilla in there somewhere."

"You know it."

8

Thursday, 1:15 p.m.

The jeep in what had obviously once been the old stable looked like it was held together with duct tape and paperclips, so Samantha decided its name should be MacGyver. Scotland and duct tape – what else could it be? She settled into the wrong-sided passenger seat as Rick shoved it into gear and sent them toward the village.

"I thought for a minute you were going to carry me all the way to the pub."

He glanced at her. "I'm not running away."

"Never said you were." She thrummed her fingers against the plastic window. "Did you and Reggie drift apart, or was it the photo thing that made you start avoiding him?"

"Both." He slammed the palm of his hand against the steering wheel.

"Is he in financial trouble?"

"He has a flat off Cadogan Place, about a mile from mine. He drives a new Mercedes and wears Anderson & Sheppard."

"Doesn't answer my question."

Rick slammed on the brakes and the jeep veered right, nearly running them into a pine tree. "How the bloody hell am I supposed to know how much money he has?"

Great. Yelling now. Even if he wasn't mad at her, he was mad. Earlier-Sam would have made herself scarce until he finished snarling. Now-Sam was engaged, and according to magazines and talk shows, engaged and married people supported each other. "Beats the crap out of me," she said, giving an exaggerated shrug. "I figured if he's after things to sell, it must be for some reason or other. If you're not willing to give him anything, *that* must be for some reason or other. Whatever it is, I'm on your side. Fuck him."

"I didn't write the British laws of inheritance. I certainly couldn't control the order in which my father and his brother were born. Yes, my father started me out with millions. I've turned it into billions. That was me. I don't owe Reginald a damned dime." He turned halfway in his seat to face her. "I buy cars through him. Does the ponce think I *need* to do that? What more does he want?"

This really sounded like something she needed to stay clear of. "I'm just guessing," she said, anyway, "but it seems like maybe he wants to be known as Reginald Addison, and not the 'cousin of Rick Addison.'" She made the air quotes to emphasize her point. "And I don't think you can do anything about that, really."

Rick looked at her for a couple of heartbeats. Facing forward again, he backed the jeep onto the road and continued forward again. "He wants to grab hold of an old mystery," he went on, his voice still edged with annoyance. "I'm not going to help him do it. If he wants to bury himself in that muck, he's on his own."

"A mystery?" she repeated.

"No, you don't. Some things only work because they *are* mysteries. Leave this one be."

It seemed like a bad time to remind him that he wasn't the boss of her, but she said it to herself, anyway. Since she already knew this had something to do with a map and a highwayman's treasure, a little more subtle digging wouldn't cause any harm. Especially if he didn't know she was doing it. "You're mad at Reggie," she said aloud. "I'm not helping him."

"Good." He turned off the main road and into the village. "And thank you."

"Don't mention it."

He pulled into a small parking lot where a goose and a bicycle took up half the remaining spots. As he pulled free the key, Samantha opened her door and hopped to the ground. No one here knew she'd claimed a bum ankle. If she decided to come down here later on her own, she wanted the option of moving unremembered and unseen – if that was even possible in a village of four hundred or so people.

"*Are* you on my side?"

She looked over the hood of the jeep at him. "Of course I am."

"We've been on opposite sides before."

Great. Another surprise conversation – just when she'd thought she was getting the hang of being part of a duo. "I don't get why you're asking me that. Do you think I have secret plans to tell Reggie you keep a stash of Peanut Butter M&M's in your desk or something?"

"I know you heard the words 'treasure map' this morning, and there you stand, not asking me a word about it. I may be the suspicious sort, and I may even be paranoid on occasion, but even taking that into consideration—"

"You're a jerk." Turning on her heel, stifling the thought that he made a really good point, Samantha marched up to the paned-glass door of The Bonny Lass. The chalk sign hung in the window said it was open, so she pulled open the door and stepped inside.

The half dozen men inside the long, low-ceilinged room all looked up at her. For a second, she thought she'd walked into a Tarantino movie. Nobody pulled out a machete or one of those big *Braveheart* claymore swords or anything, and so she nodded at the giant behind the bar. "Do you care if I sit by the window?"

"Nae. Plant yerself wherever ye like, lass."

She smiled. "Thanks. How's your mulled cider?"

"Nae as good as my straight whisky, but I reckon it willnae kill ye." The barkeep looked past her, straightening to his full height as he did so. "Bless my eyes. Lads, MacKenzie down at the post office had the right of it; the laird's returned to Canniebrae."

"I'll have a glass of that straight whisky you just recommended," Rick said, his voice as smooth as if he hadn't been accusing her of being a traitor thirty seconds ago. She ignored him as she claimed the seat looking out the window.

The chair opposite her pulled out. "So I'm a jerk because I pointed out that it's curious you're not more curious?"

"That's not what you said." She kept her gaze out the window, following the path of the wandering goose as it grazed along the base of the shop wall opposite, pausing to shake rain off its gray back.

"If you're going to be petulant, then let's head back to the house," he murmured, pulling out his wallet to pay for the drinks they hadn't even received yet.

"'Petulant,'" she repeated, snapping her gaze back to him, to that lean face and those Caribbean-blue eyes presently glaring at her. "You asked if I was on your side. What the fuck have I ever done, since day damn one, to make you ask that question?"

That had done it. The more she thought about it, the madder she got. Yeah, she'd done some stuff behind his back, mostly to protect him. But she'd never – ever – done a single damned thing to harm him. Not from the moment they met. And taking his side had ended her career (illegal or not), most of her so-called friendships, and the entire path that she'd set for her life.

His eyes narrowed. People didn't call him out on stuff, and most of them didn't argue with him. Well, she wasn't most people, and if he thought he could insult her just because he was mad about other crap and she was convenient, he either needed to be set straight or she needed to pack her bags. She glared right back at him.

A pair of glasses hit the table in between them. A glass and a pewter mug, but it was enough to make her blink and look up as the giant folded his arms across his chest. "Ye're the mysterious American lass the laird's set to marry, aye?" he asked.

Rick's jaw jumped. He wanted to answer for her, she knew, make sure she didn't say something that would raise questions. Something like "maybe", or "we'll see about that". She smiled. "That's the rumor."

Chuckling, he cocked his head. "Canniebrae's been empty for near twenty years now. The pair of ye thinking to settle in the Highlands?"

"I—"

"Mostly attempting to escape the press," Rick interrupted.

Samantha couldn't help staring at him. He'd actually just spilled the plan. Out loud. To a stranger. Either the thing with his cousin had sent him off the deep end, or... Well, it had to be that, because otherwise, cripes.

The big Scotsman nodded. "We're a fine place to hide out for a time, then. The tourists come in summer, and a few to see the snow in the winter. Ye willnae be staying through the winter though, aye? They say it gets a might cold up in the castle these days."

"Just a few weeks," Rick returned. "And I'd appreciate if no one here spreads the word about our presence."

"Dunnae ye fret about that, m'laird. We ken how to keep a secret. I reckon ye've got a few ye keep, as well, aye?"

"Clearly I couldn't say."

With a snort the giant wandered off to repeat the exchange to the men who'd gathered along the bar. Rather than go back to a glaring contest, Samantha picked up the mug of mulled cider and breathed it in. Warm and cinnamon and that faint antiseptic smell of liquor that made her dislike most of it. Settling with her back against the window, she took a swallow. Not bad, actually. "That was weird."

Rick shrugged. "They're the 'second quaintest village in the Highlands,' remember? I doubt they want our paparazzi circus coming around."

It made sense, but he practically had a doctorate in keeping his business to himself. To blurt it out like that--

"Why haven't you asked about the treasure map?" Rick asked, interrupting her train of thought with a much more annoying one.

She took another swallow of her cider. "I'm not answering you until you apologize to me. That really pissed me off."

His glass left the table. A second later it returned, empty. "I'm sorry. You're right. I know you're on my side. I should have asked whether you mean to go after the so-called treasure on your own."

"That's the stupidest apology ever. So you keep your treasure map and arguments with your cousin to yourself, and I'll keep cataloguing the castaways in your attic. If you want me involved, you ask me. Otherwise assume that family spats make me queasy, and I don't want to go anywhere near them. Especially the ones about money."

And if she meant to find out more about the treasure map, that was *her* business. It was practically self-preservation. As for any treasure that might fall out of a wall somewhere, Rick could have it. She loved the chase; the idea of treasure, especially if it was old, fascinated her, but even when he was being a stubborn jerk she chose Rick Addison.

He was still mad at whatever, so after half an hour she got up and left the pub. The rain had dwindled to a scattered mist, and she ignored it as she walked up the street. Big bowls of flowers hung from the eaves, making the shops and tiny market look even more quaint than they already were. It was nearly five o'clock, and the hardware store, bakery, and grocery were already closed for the day. The sidewalks probably rolled up at sunset – which hit pretty early this far north.

Small houses one street back more than likely belonged to the shop owners. Some of them looked at least Shakespeare old, but she didn't feel like going sneaking around the neighborhood just to look at exposed wooden beams.

"It's livelier during the summer," Rick's voice came from a few feet behind her. "At least it used to be. Orrisey gets a fair business from tourists looking for Balmoral."

For a couple of seconds, she debated whether to ignore him. She didn't do fights well, because the ones she had tended to be more about survival and staying out of prison than pride or whatever it was that was bugging him. Plus, he argued and negotiated for a living. "My ankle's going to be better tomorrow," she said instead, turning to face him. "I'm not going to keep limping around for no good reason. If you want to keep Reggie away from the west wing, you're going to have to come up with something better than rotting floors. Tell him whatever you want; I'll back you up because *I'm on your side.* But don't expect me to buy what you're selling."

He cocked his head. "I need to remember that just because I want to fight doesn't mean I should settle on you. Aside from the fact that you're fiercer and more stubborn than a bulldog, you're the one person more precious to me than whatever the surrounding stakes might be."

"That's better," she conceded.

"I don't apologize well or easily."

"Yeah, I know that. I don't, either. But seriously, if you want to fight, put on some gloves and tell me. I don't mind a black eye in a fair fight. This crap, though?" She gestured between them. "No es bueno."

As quick as Samantha was, he didn't think he'd ever manage a punch even in a fair fight – not that he'd ever strike her. Interesting that she preferred that to word-battling, though. "I'll get a punching bag," he said aloud. "I'm not hitting you."

"It felt like you did."

Samantha turned around again, wandering up the nearly-deserted street. He'd seen her cry once or twice, though she'd never admitted to it. But he heard it in her voice just then, and he stood rooted where he was. She'd said she was angry, and he'd been angry, as well. Not at her, initially, but that didn't really signify. What did signify was that he'd hurt her.

He'd divorced Patricia four years ago now, because she'd slept with one of his closest friends. Now, though, he wondered how much he'd had to do with her going elsewhere for sex or comfort or whatever it was she'd been after. They'd argued, of course, but it had always seemed insignificant. Afterward, she'd always apologized.

Samantha didn't apologize. Not unless she'd been in the wrong. And she never backed down from a fight – especially one that he flung at her for no good reason other than that he was annoyed at Reg and old secrets he'd nearly forgotten. Until two months ago she'd also had a go-bag, as she called it, filled with necessaries and stashed under the bed or in the closet in case she needed to grab it and disappear into the night. He'd destroyed it, and she'd never made a new one. Not that he knew of. The idea that he could push her hard enough to make her regret that decision, or even act on it, made him feel ill.

"Sam?"

She turned around, still backing nonchalantly away from him. "What?"

"I don't have anything clever to say. I was wrong, and I'm sorry. I know you're on my side. I should never have said otherwise."

Stopping her retreat, she strolled back up to him again. "Okay." Samantha continued past him, back in the direction of the jeep.

"That's it?"

"What? You were a jerk, I was offended, you apologized, I accepted. Am I supposed to demand jewelry or something? I haven't read that book. Come on; Reggie's probably in the west wing again, and *I'm* not stopping him. That's on you."

He'd known her for a year. Yes, they'd begun as adversaries of a sort, but she'd chosen sides quickly and decisively, and never looked back. And she still surprised him at least once a day. Today, evidently, he'd surprised her. Richard clenched his jaw. She hadn't found him because she was looking for a boost in Society, because she wanted to be a marchioness and attend tea with the Queen. She didn't need his money, because she had her own. Illegally-acquired and likely tainted with all sorts of legal problems, but she'd lived on it before they'd met. She didn't want his high profile, because she felt much more comfortable in the shadows, blending in. In short, she had several reasons for not wanting to be anywhere near him, and one – that he knew of – for staying. And that would be his warm and giving personality. Lesson learned. He declined to repeat his mistakes, and he bloody well had a very good reason not to do so this time.

Pulling the keys from his pocket, he handed them to her as he caught up. "You drive."

"You're so cool." Yes, she also liked his cars.

He might have remained unsettled longer, but Samantha's driving on the muddy, winding road left little room for anything but stark terror. It was actually a relief; if she'd been careful, he would have been worried. By the time they skidded up to the old stable, he felt a certain joy at just being alive.

"That was fun," she said, tossing the keys to Rob, Canniebrae's mechanic and driver.

"After I go vomit I'm certain I'll agree with you," Richard returned, handing her the walking cane.

She made a face. "I'm healed tomorrow," she pointed out again, and assumed her limp as he kept pace with her across the yard and up to the kitchen door.

Rolling his shoulders, he held the door for her. As a man who prided himself on knowing how people were likely to react, he'd stepped into a very large pile of horseshit here. He'd never been able to control Samantha, and eventually he'd learn to stop trying to do so. But Reg? Richard had always been the leader in that duo. This digging through the ruins thing needed to stop, both because it was dangerous and because he didn't want it happening.

Time to stop tiptoeing, then. Having a reputation for ruthlessness didn't mean anything if he couldn't lean on it once in a while. "Yule, where's my cousin?" he asked, as the butler met them in the kitchen.

"In the library, m'laird. Making a mess, if I may say so. He always was a willful lad, but some of those books are bloody first editions."

"I'll see to it." Richard put a hand on Samantha's shoulder.

"I'm snagging a diet Coke and some crisps and going to limp around upstairs," she said, elbowing him lightly in the ribs as she limped by him, still managing to look graceful. "Good luck."

One whisky even on an empty stomach hadn't done much to him, but he nevertheless tried to measure what he meant to say to his cousin before he reached the library. Family was sticky. You couldn't fire them, for one thing, and they always knew more about you than felt exactly comfortable. There he was, rich and semi-famous (to quote Samantha), and engaged to a woman who detested publicity. Reg had made money off him before – of that he remained reasonably certain – and he had more to lose than privacy or pride now.

"Reg," he said, pushing open the library door.

His cousin – or his cousin's arse, to be more precise – glowed moonlike as it thumped up and down over the splayed figure of Eerika Nyland. *Fuck*. Literally.

"Christ, Rick, get out!" Reg bellowed, twisting his head around as Miss Nyland gave a garbled shriek.

"Lock the damned door next time," Richard returned, refusing to be anything but affronted that this was going on in his bloody library. "And don't damage the first editions." He pulled the door closed.

As he climbed the stairs to the first floor he reflected that a few years ago what he'd just seen would have deeply annoyed him, mainly because this was his house, his territory, his damned library, and he didn't particularly want them here in the first place. Now, though, he felt a bit more…circumspect. In addition, he knew someone who would find it all hilarious.

He found her in the music room, which now consisted of a grand piano that had seen much better days and a selection of antique musical instruments decorating the walls. She sat in one of the chairs ranged around the room and munched on a potato chip as she studied an old violin just above her eye level. "It's not a Stradivarius," he commented, shutting the door and leaning back against it.

"I just like the color – the patina – of the old varnish on the wood," she said absently. "It looks deep, like you could stick your finger into it." She faced him. "That was a quick conversation with Reggie. Was anyone killed?"

He dragged a chair around beside her. "So, I shoved open the library door, ready to remind Reg that the books he was flinging about were mine, and that if he wanted to remain here he would respect my property. In—"

"Diplomacy, thy name is Rick Addison," she put in, grinning.

"Hush. I'm not finished yet. So, I shoved open the door, ready to demand respect, and what should I see but Reggie's arse in the air, naked as anything, on my Persian rug with Miss Nyland beneath him."

"*You didn't,*" she said, sotto voce, her green eyes widening with what could only be glee.

"I did."

"What did you say?"

"They yelled at me to get out, I told them to lock the door next time and not to damage the books, and I came up here to tell you."

Laughter burst from her chest, bubbly and genuine and infectious. "You mentioned the books anyway!"

"Of course I did." Chuckling, he snagged one of the crisps from her bag.

"You are *so* awesome."

"Yes, I know."

Samantha leaned her head against his shoulder. "Just keep in mind that now he's embarrassed, so he'll probably try to catch you doing the same thing."

"That would be unwise." Especially if Reggie brought along a camera. God, what a disaster that would be. His amusement cooled considerably. "We're double-checking the locks from now on."

With a distant thud the lights flashed out, leaving them in the early evening gloom. "Power's oot!" began echoing through the house.

One low note sounded from the piano, echoing into the silence. Beside him Samantha didn't move, but he could feel her coming alert. "You heard that, right?" she whispered.

"Probably a mouse in the works," he returned, sending the dark corners of the room a glance, anyway.

"Mm hm. Any objection if I call Stoney and have him send me some gear? Infrared camera, temperature monitor, stuff like that?"

He looked down at the top of her head. "Ghost hunting?"

"I'm asking because if anybody's here, they're probably related to you. It'll be fun."

Back in Florida he might have scoffed at the notion, but this wasn't a luxury mansion built in the 30's, full of sun and sounds of surf. This was Britain, a few hundred miles from where the two of them had uncovered a family heirloom that had produced so many coincidences he could barely call them that, and with a few hundred – or thousands, rather – years of history literally beneath their feet.

"I have no objection," he said aloud, standing and pulling her to her feet. If she preferred to look for invisible things rather than hidden things here at Canniebrae, he had no objection whatsoever. Maybe she could even pull Reg and his Viking into the hunt. If anyone could distract the undistractable, it would be Samantha.

9

Friday, 9:20 a.m.

"Yeah, I can swing by and pull the infrared goggles out of storage," Stoney said, his voice cracking and distant on Rick's office phone. "What the hell's an EMF detector?"

"It detects electromagnetics," Samantha returned, resting her elbows on whatever business deal Rick had left on top of his desk. "Power lines, ghosts, stuff like that."

"Uh, huh. So now you're a ghostbuster."

"Yep."

"I was being sarcastic. What's up? Really?"

She smiled at the phone. "A bit of a mystery. Maybe even a ghost. You have the whole list? Four stationary night-vision cameras with infrared, four portable ones, a monitor and cables, four digital recorders, my infrared goggles, and say six walkie-talkies with at least a two-mile range." If they couldn't use cell phones, maybe walkies would solve the big house problem.

"And a partridge in a pear tree," he finished. "I've got it. Not my first rodeo, kiddo."

"It is your first ghost hunt." Samantha leaned out into the hall-way, then ducked back into the deepest corner of the office. "I have no internet or cell service here," she continued, lowering her voice. "Look up anything on Scottish highwaymen or known serial robbers in the area around Balmoral and before the 1900's, will you?"

Silence crackled back at her. "You catch a whiff of something?" Stoney finally asked.

"I don't know. I'm just looking for some info. Not a score."

"Yeah, you keep telling yourself that. In the meantime, I'll express ship your 'ghost hunting' equipment." The way he said the words, she could practically hear the air quotes.

"There could be treasure *and* ghosts," she retorted, keeping her voice as quiet as she could manage and still be heard over the bad connection. "But I'm mostly curious about the treasure. The equipment might help me look for it. Info to me only, dude. Okay?"

"Yep. Oh, and Aubrey wants to know if you like the name Max Zellicon, or if it's too on the nose."

"Too on the nose for what?"

"For you. I think he's writing a book about you."

She held the phone away from her ear to scowl at it. "One, I am not a Max or a Maxine. Two, no effing way is he writing a book about me. If he does, he's fired. You tell him I said that."

"He said I could be Wallace Granite. But okay, I'll tell him."

"If that was your name, I'd be calling you Granny instead of Stoney. Think about that."

"You're an evil woman," Walter Barstone returned. "I'll let you know your stuff's ETA as soon as I get it shipped. Up to you to figure out what to tell his lordiness."

"Thanks, Granny."

She heard him snort as the call cut off, and leaned against the wall once she'd set the phone's receiver back into its cradle.

Aubrey couldn't have been serious about writing a book based on her. Aside from the fact that he knew almost nothing about her before the past year or so, *The Adventures of Max Zellicon* would send a lot more suspicious glances in her direction. She couldn't afford that either for herself or for Rick.

If Stoney couldn't give her some assurance that Aubrey had stopped his semi-biography or whatever the hell he thought he was writing, she would have to give the former professional lady's escort a serious talking to. Just the idea of a story about a thief and a rich guy, however much he altered the details, gave her the shakes.

Two sets of footsteps left the stairs to turn in the direction of Rick's office. Her first instinct was to sink beneath the desk, but for crying out loud, she hadn't done anything wrong. Not even slightly shady, really. She was legit here.

The footsteps stopped before the half open door. "Rick?" Reggie asked, rapping his knuckles against the doorframe. He leaned in. "Samantha. I don't suppose you have any idea where Ricky is, do you?"

"Last time I saw him he was out on the drive with two utility guys. They want to drill holes for the internet router and the satellite, and he doesn't like that idea very much."

Eerika stepped in around Reggie. "Thank goodness you're here, Samantha."

"Was I missing?" she asked, before she could rein in the sarcasm. Oh, well. She was supposed to be a touch upper-crusty, after all.

"What? Oh, ha ha. No. I've heard the village is very quaint, and I want go. But Reginald won't take me. We must go find a bakery and a kilt shop, and of course some shoes. Say you'll come."

A bakery, a kilt shop, and shoes. What came next in the way of quaint Scottish village shops – a bagpipe boutique? But this was what girlfriends of guys with money and good bloodlines did, right? Go to out-of-the-way places and buy expensive shit? She could use the practice, she supposed. Plus, Eerika knew more about Reggie than she did, and that could be useful. "Sure. I'll grab my jacket and meet you downstairs."

The Viking flashed her a pearly white smile. "Splendid." She put her well-manicured hand on Reggie's shoulder and gave him a peck on the cheek. "You boys go have your fun. Samantha and I will be back after lunch."

Huh. Now a peek in the windows of three shops had turned into a four-hour excursion. Well, she'd gotten more accustomed to Rick's lifestyle over the past year. It couldn't hurt to learn a few things about how to be a girl blueblood from a girl blueblood.

While Eerika went to find her clutch and shopping shoes, whatever the hell they were, Samantha snagged her light jacket off the bed post in the master bedchamber and trotted downstairs. In the foyer Yule was actually using a ruler to center a vase of thistles on the side table, and she paused on the bottom step to watch that for a second. Thank crap her dad hadn't been a vase measurer, because she wouldn't have been able to follow his footsteps and still keep her sanity. She did get the whole thing about running a small army of household staff and taking pride in good work, but that world was way too small for her.

"Miss Nyland and I are going into the village, Yule," she said, resisting the urge to hop down the last step into the foyer because she supposedly had a bum ankle. "I think we're having lunch there."

The butler nodded as he folded up his ruler and stuck it into an inside pocket of his black dress jacket. "The forecast is for sun, so ye've chosen a fine day for an outing."

"Thanks. Let her know I'm getting the car, if you don't mind."

"I dunnae mind at all, Miss Sam."

Rick was still on the front drive, now looking at some skinny brown PVC pipes that she figured the cables would be run through. "Eerika and I are going into the village," she told him, interrupting a pretty impressive scowl.

"There has to be a way to run cable without either drilling a hole through the stone or having pipes crawling up the outsides of the walls," he grumbled. "We managed it at Rawley Park."

"Rawley Park's walls aren't solid stone," Samantha noted.

"Not helpful."

"Well, do you have a dungeon here?" she asked, only half joking.

"I have a wine cellar which may or may not have been a dungeon at one time."

"Ooh, that means it totally was. Why haven't I seen it, then? Anyway, if you want to bother digging trenches through heavy dirt and permafrost, you—"

He planted a kiss on her mouth. "I'm there. Be patient with Miss Nyland." Brushing his fingers against hers, he faced the two utility guys. "Make some calls, lads. We're going in through the cellar."

The keys for the four cars – well, one car, MacGyver the jeep, an old SUV that they used for bringing up supplies, and a three-wheeled...thing – hung on nails on an inside post in the stable. She snagged Mac's keys and hopped into the red jeep.

With the sun out, she was tempted to unsnap the plastic roof, but Norway had probably spent five hundred bucks on her hair, and Rick had just reminded her not to rile the near in-laws, so she left the top on the jeep. Instead she turned the key and fed the beast some gas, grinning as it roared to life.

Eerika came out the front door as Samantha pulled up. Apparently shopping shoes had two-inch heels and were bright blue, and were worn with a matching over-the-shoulder handbag and a pretty, patterned cardigan. The whole outfit screamed, "look at me, I'm rich and sophisticated," even with slim-fit jeans and a pink heart T-shirt. To Samantha's eyes the ensemble also said "steal my purse because I'm rich and I'll never be able to catch you in these shoes," but this wasn't New York or Paris, or even London.

"Ready?" she asked, leaning left to shove open the passenger door.

"Oh, brilliant," the Viking said with a bright smile, and clambered into the seat. "It's so rugged here!"

"It does have that backwoodsy feel," Samantha agreed, putting MacGyver into gear and resisting the urge to stomp on the accelerator. Not everyone was an adrenaline junkie, and Eerika seemed to be trying very hard to look...perfect.

"I half expect to see William Wallace emerging from the trees. But there haven't been as many kilts as I expected."

"Well, it's autumn. Nippy and way fewer tourists."

"Oh, yes. London's crushed with tourists in the summer, all of them asking where the nearest MacDonald's is." She put a hand to her mouth. "I don't mean you, of course. You're not one of those."

One of those what? Normal Americans? No, she wasn't. Until six months ago she hadn't even had a real driver's license. As for her passport... Well, that beauty was worth every one of the ten thousand bucks it had cost her. Getting a legit one of those after she married Rick was going to be tricky. "Thanks," she said aloud, because it seemed like she should say something. "Do you come to Scotland often?"

"This is my first time. It's so odd, isn't it? I've lived in London for my entire life, I've been to Paris and Milan and New York, and I've never been to a place just north of me, on the same island."

Samantha hoped they weren't going to start listing all the places they'd ever visited. MacGyver skidded a little on the muddy track, and she downshifted to take the next curve. "There are a couple of states I've never been to," she returned, though Idaho and Alabama *were* on her to-do list. "There are only so many hours in a day."

"And only so many days in a year," Eerika added. "Precisely. One must hit the highlights first."

So, Scotland wasn't a highlight for Miss Nyland and her shopping shoes. Samantha liked figuring people out, but this was already exhausting. Maybe she needed to try edging a little closer to upper class. "Rick said Reggie has a flat just off Cadogan Place. That must be lovely. Do you share it with him, if you don't mind my asking?"

Eerika chuckled. "You Americans are so direct. I'll just say I have a toothbrush there."

"Fair enough."

"But what about you? How in the world did you manage to catch Richard Addison's eye – much less get him to ask you to marry him? I think half the single women in the world wept that day."

That was a total exaggeration, though she did get vilified a lot on the *Rick's Chicks* Facebook page. She knew that because she liked to check in on them. They liked to appear outside the Solano Dorado gates on odd days, trying for a glimpse of Rick. She liked having a heads-up for things like stalkers. "He hired me to find some stolen artwork, and we just hit it off. It helps that we're both into art and antiques." She'd told that version so many times she could almost believe it herself, if not for the bomb shrapnel scar on the back of one thigh.

"I know what you mean. I learned *so* much about cars when I met Reginald. Men love women who share their interests." She abruptly went digging into her purse and produced a pen and paper. "I'm writing that down. My producer will love it."

"Your producer?"

"Oh, yes. We're working on a show for me. Something that follows me through my day, while I dispense advice and have fabulous adventures."

Wow. Somebody liked herself a whole lot. "Oh," she said aloud. "Cool."

Aside from the self-absorption, the way Eerika viewed Reggie's interests sounded a lot like the way Samantha viewed a mark she meant to rob. If she needed to get close, she found out what he or she liked and did some research. From the beginning she and Rick had shared an interest in the art world – and while her plan to steal something he owned had brought them together, she'd never faked a damned thing where he was concerned.

She hadn't realized how long the silence had stretched out until Eerika put a fake-sounding laugh into the middle of it. "I just realized how very mercenary I must sound. Everyone wants to do their own show, after all. But I already have contacts, and an absolutely unique hook. I can't tell you, of course, but it will be fabulous. A guaranteed smash hit."

"Is Reggie going to be involved?" Samantha asked, smothering a shudder. Norway might be excited by the idea of being on camera, but that kind of thing gave her former thief self the shivers.

"Reginald's all for it. He says he keeps me grounded, but I give him wings. And those Addison boys are very driven, aren't they?"

Firstly, at least one Addison wasn't a *boy*. Considering where *she* came from, Samantha wasn't about to start an argument over who was good for whom, though. Instead she pasted on a grin. "You're preaching to the choir, sister."

Eerika's chuckle sounded a little more real this time. "Of course I am. And we are sisters, of a sort, aren't we?"

Sure, they were. "The very definition of," she said aloud, as she turned MacGyver onto the cobblestone main street of the village. "Bakery, or search for the kilt shop? Or shoes?"

"Kilt shop. Oh, and perhaps we could find where they make the bagpipes."

Huh. So this was the hell she was signing up for. Still, learning the layout of the entire village couldn't be a bad thing. If they had a museum or a historical society, she would slip back into Orrisey with a few questions – and without her brand new, man-eating, fame-hunting sister.

BY THE TIME the local utility workers had made arrangements for a bulldozer and a trencher to come up in the next couple of days, Richard felt ready for a jaunt into the village, himself. Simply because it was a small matter to drill a hole beneath the eave of most houses didn't make it acceptable to do so with a castle that predated America by over five hundred years.

As for handing Canniebrae to the National Trust, over his dead body. He had a plentitude of respect for the Trust, but this was his place, his property. His headache. Stomping mud off his hiking boots as he went, he headed for the front door.

Yule opened it before he could reach for the handle. "M'laird, Master Reginald says his father would like a word with ye," he intoned. "Ye'll find Laird Rowland and Lady Mercia in the garden."

So much for catching up to Sam. "Thank you, Yule."

"It's good to have the family back at Canniebrae, m'laird, if I may say so."

Richard slowed his exit down the hallway. "I stayed away for too long."

"I can see from the improvements ye're chasing that ye mean to be here more often, now. Would that be accurate?"

"Depending on our success with internet and electricity, yes. I think so. I hope so."

"Fingers crossed then, m'laird," the butler answered.

Halfway down the long portrait-lined gallery that bisected the central part of the house, the lights went out again. The hallway had been dim and windowless before, designed that way to protect the artwork, but now pitch blackness settled around him. Richard stopped; too many antique chairs and side tables lurked against the walls for him to risk maneuvering. Instead he dug into his pocket for his phone.

Something distinctly thumped a few feet behind him. Sliding

the phone's control panel up with his thumb, he tapped the torch-light icon and whipped around. Nothing. He panned left to right, half-expecting Samantha to leap out of the shadows at him. She'd done it before. Still, oil-painted faces, edges of chairs, dimming to black beyond the reach of the tiny light, loomed around him.

Satisfied he wasn't about to be assaulted and ignoring the pricking of the hairs at the back of his neck, he resumed his trek toward the rear of the house by weak phone light. He was thirty-four years old, and he was not going to succumb to Samantha's fantastical imaginings of ghouls and ghost hounds, and he was not going to hurry his steps.

The far door came into view, and he reached for the handle. As he touched it, another thump sounded, just as close behind him as the previous one. Richard snapped around, his free hand clenched into a fist. Again, nothing. "For fuck's sake," he muttered, and reached behind him to push open the door. Keeping his front to the black hall and feeling like an idiot the entire time, he backed out into the adjoining hallway.

Samantha was not going to hear that he'd been spooked. Not ever.

From the hallway he headed through the sun-filled conservatory and outside down the wide, shallow granite steps that opened into the immense garden. His aunt and uncle sat on the edge of the central fountain, the two of them dwarfed by a godawful Poseidon with water spewing from the conch shell in his hands. Richard had decided long ago that an in-law had gifted the fountain to his Victorian-era relations, because he preferred to think that his own bloodline on both sides had a better eye for true artistry – and certainly a better grasp of good taste.

"You wanted to see me?" he asked.

"We'd like you to tell us a bit more about Miss Jellicoe," his aunt said. "We're to welcome her into the family, but all we know of her is what we've seen in the tabloids or on the telly. Of course no one can believe those things. Or wants to be seen reading or watching them."

Strictly speaking, Samantha was none of their business. He was the head of the family, he controlled the title, he owned by far the greatest portion of the wealth. Yet he had asked them here specifically to meet her. He was also keenly aware that aside from Walter Barstone – and perhaps Aubrey Pendleton, who was only a recent addition – she had only him in her life to care about her. They were quite literally her only family, and neither of them were blood relations. She needed more family in her life. Even his, he supposed.

Blowing out his breath, he took a seat on the bench opposite the two of them. "Her family tree is a bit shady," he said, measuring his words very carefully despite the fact that he'd gone over this conversation in his head at least a dozen times. Whatever else happened, Samantha was to be protected. "Her father, especially, flirted with the dark side, as she says. She's a wonder at what she does, and knows more about some of the pieces of my collection than I do."

"You're certain she's not out to hook a rich husband?" his uncle asked, sitting forward with his elbows on his knees. "We adored Patricia after all, and she—"

"I recall what Patricia did," Richard interrupted, unwilling to rehash a marriage that had been a disaster from its beginning to its end three years later. "Samantha has her own money, and she would much rather I wasn't the Marquis of Rawley. She dislikes the spotlight." Dislike would suffice, though he'd put it closer to the fascinated horror a vampire had for the sun.

"She seems charming," Aunt Mercia put in a little hurriedly. "And genuinely interested in Canniebrae. I didn't recall much of the highwayman legends, but I did direct her to The Bonny Lass. I know they tell stories of it there from time to time, or at least they used to."

Richard sat so still for a second, he wasn't certain he was

breathing. She'd found the mystery, damn it all, and she hadn't mentioned a thing about it to him. And unlike Reg, she had a good chance of figuring it all out.

"Should I not have sent her into Orrisey, Richard?" his aunt asked, her smile tight.

"No, that's fine," he returned, forcing his teeth to unclench. "She's fascinated by history, which is why I decided to introduce her to Canniebrae in the first place."

"I'll just come straight out and say it, shall I?" his uncle Rowland fisted his hands, straightening. "I had a solicitor friend do some checking. Miss Jellicoe's father was a thief, Richard. A fairly notorious one who died in prison. He specialized in art and jewelry, and there was some question about whether he had an accomplice."

"I'm aware," Richard returned, digging in to hold onto his temper. It made sense they would look into Samantha's past; unless he produced an heir, the Rawley title and all the wealth tied into it would go to Uncle Rowland and his offspring – meaning Reg. So would the remainder of his empire not already allocated to Samantha and to various charities and foundations.

"Richard, your fiancé's father was a convicted felon," Rowland repeated. "They think he had a partner."

"I'm aware," he repeated. He was also aware that the deceased Martin Jellicoe was anything but, and that the father had many fewer scruples than did the daughter.

"And you still think she isn't gold-digging? Don't be naïve, lad. Patricia turned out badly enough. This could be so much worse."

The Richard of a year ago would have taken that moment to tell his nearest relations to mind their own fucking business and get out of his house. They knew that, too; he could see it in his uncle's tight shoulders and his aunt's desperately sympathetic expression. Luckily for them the Richard of today had seen what a truly dysfunctional family looked like in the Jellicoes, and he had a much better grasp of what true disaster and peril were, in contrast to a bit of awkwardness and discomfort.

"If you can't see how much I adore her and how happy she makes me," he said aloud, "then I can only pity you. She's mine, and I'm hers. I cannot explain it better than that. So, you can either embrace her, or stay clear of us. You have the next two weeks to decide which it will be."

"You have a very long line of titled ancestors on both sides who would not approve."

Standing, Richard nodded at his uncle. "Yes, but they're dead. I'm not. And I love Samantha."

At this moment he also wanted to lock her in a closet to keep her from digging into the legend of Will Dawkin and his treasure, and keep her in there until she told him how the hell she'd gotten hold of the tale. *He* hadn't told her whose map Reg was after, and he didn't think Reg would do so, mainly because his cousin wouldn't want to have to share the treasure if the tales turned out to be true.

By the time he made his way back through the conservatory, the power had been restored. Even so, he decided to head up to the second floor via the plain rear stairs instead of trudging through the more direct route of the portrait gallery. If the dead relations disapproved of Samantha and were attempting to let him know that, he wasn't going to make it any easier for them.

She'd caught a whiff of a story about highwayman treasure, then, and had neglected to mention that to him. Well, he wasn't going to make digging into it any easier for her, either. He made for the library. Amid the old Shakespeare folios and early editions of Robert Louis Stevenson, Robert Browning, and Arthur Conan Doyle he knew there were scattered books on local specters, high-waymen, and Jacobites. One by one he removed seven books that delved into the life of Will Dawkin.

Under normal circumstances he would have hidden them in the attic, but that space had become Samantha's base of operations. The cellar was out, because workmen would be crawling all over it in the next couple of days. With the books in his arms he made his way up the hallway and tried to decide which spot in the old, rambling house would be most boring to a woman who lived to dig into trouble.

Ultimately, he decided on the old dressing room directly connected to the bedchamber they shared, in the bottom box of a stack of well-worn hat boxes. Hats didn't preserve well, and didn't carry much value as antiques, and these boxes looked…damp and distinctly uninviting – but not in an obvious way. They'd dumped their suitcases in here already, so hopefully she'd already declared the room boring. There. They'd come to Canniebrae to escape, and for her to meet his relations. Not for Samantha Elizabeth Jellicoe to go digging after some mythological treasure trove. Or for Reg to do it, either.

Richard paused as he left the dressing room. Where was Reg? He hadn't gone with Sam and Eerika, he hadn't been in the library, and he wasn't in the conservatory or the garden with his parents. If he was back in the damned west wing, the gloves were coming off.

Striding to the front of the house, Richard leaned over the balcony railing. "Yule! Where's my cousin?"

"I dunnae ken, m'laird," came the answer. "Sorry to say I've been going over the shopping list with Mrs. Yule. I'll get him tracked down for ye."

"I'll be in the west wing," Richard snapped back.

They'd chained the door to the wing again for the sake of safety. Samantha could get in if she chose, but then she knew what she was doing. Before he reached the end of the hallway he could make out the chain hanging from one door handle, the lock open. Apparently Reg had some skills of which Richard hadn't been previously aware.

Even as he shoved open the door, he couldn't believe his cousin would resort to thievery to fund his lifestyle. Embezzlement, perhaps, but high-end cat burglary took planning, effort, finesse, and discipline. Reg lacked at least two of those. Since the key remained in his pocket and the lock wasn't cut, though, someone had picked it.

"Reg!" he yelled, remembering to keep to one side of the damp hallway as he stomped deeper into the west wing. "If you've fallen through the floor I'm bloody well leaving you there!"

The sound of his voice echoed and flattened, unanswered. The owner of a multi-billion dollar empire, contracts on his desk awaiting his signature, house renovations he hadn't intended already beginning, and there he was tramping over rotting floors because his idiot cousin wouldn't give up a childhood dream of finding treasure.

"Reg!" he bellowed again. "Do not fucking make me track you down!"

A shadow crossed a doorway toward the end of the hallway, and he moved toward it. Bits of damp plaster thunked onto the ruined carpet around him as the ceiling gave up its life piecemeal, but he mostly ignored the mess as he drew closer.

After the oddness in the portrait gallery he half-expected the old bedchamber to be empty. Even so, when he turned into the doorway to see nothing but some wooden bed slats and a pile of ruined wallpaper, he stopped short. It hadn't been a ghost, because there was no such thing. Cursing, he stepped into the room.

Directly to his left in the far corner, a figure hunched against the floor, digging at the baseboard. For a quarter of a second, he thought perhaps Gollum had moved into the ruins, looking for his Precious. Richard blew out his breath, relieved and pissed off all at the same time. "So you couldn't even muster a 'bugger off' to let me know you weren't dead?"

Reg kept prying at the old wood with what looked like a screwdriver. "Bugger off," he grunted.

"Too late for that now. You made me come after you. Get off the floor before you fall through it."

"I know it's here, Ricky. This house might be yours now, but it wasn't when we found the map. It's half mine, and I want my share."

"Oh, for God's sake. I told you, that map was a joke those blokes at the tavern played on the rich lads from the castle, and it's long gone. Why are you so desperate for this nonsense?"

"It's not nonsense, it wasn't a joke, and you didn't toss it away. I will find it. If you aren't interested, I'll happily claim the entire thing."

Richard shut his eyes for a half-dozen heartbeats. "I threw the map in the fireplace the afternoon my mother told me about her cancer," he stated, keeping his voice as flat as he could manage. "It seemed completely stupid and frivolous in comparison. So even if it had been real, which it wasn't, it no longer exists. If you want me to apologize for thwarting some plan of yours to recover a few glass beads and call yourself a treasure hunter, then I suppose I'm sorry."

His shoulders hunched, then Reg straightened and turned around. "I can't figure it out," he said, the screwdriver held low in one hand. "Did you find the gold and just add it to your bank account, or do you like knowing it's nearby with no one else able to touch it?"

"Did you hear what I just said? The map has been ashes for nearly twenty years. Whether what it led to was highwayman's gold or a pile of sticks, there is no way to find it. When the hell did you become so bloody obsessed with it?"

"When you invited us back here and I realized I have as much claim to it as you do. *We* found the map. *We* tracked down the stories. It's half mine. That's what annoys you, isn't it? That you'd have to share. Because that isn't how you operate these days."

Richard looked at his cousin. As children they'd been close, with him less than a year older than Reg. They had adventured together during the summers. Even before the heart attack that had killed his father and left him a millionaire at nineteen, though, they'd drifted well apart. Reg had dipped his toes into racing, only to discover that sponsors were both necessary and required a certain level of decorum and acceptable behavior from those representing their brand. The younger Addison cousin had never liked being told what to do.

Car sales had come next, and he wasn't shabby at it or anything, but until this second Richard had never wondered whether Reg was happy doing it. Before he'd met Samantha, words like "happiness" and "satisfaction" where business matters or other people's personal lives were concerned, had never really occurred to him.

"Do you want money, Reg?" he asked, setting one hip against the doorjamb. "Are you in over your head or something? Do you want me to write you a check?"

"Yes, because more than anything else I want to be indebted to you. I want to wake up every morning and have my first thought be 'thank God for cousin Ricky'. Without cousin Ricky who knows where we'd be?"

"Then what the fuck do you want?" Richard snapped back. "Because there's nothing like offering a hand and watching it get bitten off."

Reg's tanning salon hue paled a little. "I want to be Reginald Addison. Not Rick Addison's cousin, or a member of Rick Addison's extended family. Highwayman treasure uncovered in the middle of the Scottish Highlands by entrepreneur Reginald Clarke Addison had a damned fine ring to it." He jabbed the screwdriver hilt-deep into the wall and stomped past Richard, just missing a shoulder shove that he likely didn't have the guts to risk. "And I don't believe for a bloody second that you burned that map. You've never destroyed anything old or remotely useful. Go on with your tale, but peddle it to someone more gullible than I am."

Richard stayed where he was in the doorway of his old bedchamber as Reg cautiously stormed down the rickety hallway.

Bloody wonderful. Reg refused to give way despite all evidence to the contrary, and now Samantha had her fingers into a nice slice of mystery. Chaos, where he'd wanted a few weeks of peace.

One thing was damned certain; he was going to have to find a better hiding place for the map.

10

Friday, 3:10 p.m.

"I suppose it's charming enough," Eerika said, as Samantha parked MacGyver in front of the stable, "but the second quaintest in the Highlands? That shoe store, for example, doesn't carry nearly enough variety. Not a Ferragamo or Louboutin in sight. I can't believe no one here wears at least Vuitton. I refuse to leave my flat without at least one pair. If anyone ever—"

She kept talking, but Samantha missed part of it as she hopped out of Mac and tossed the keys to Rob. She'd put a layer of mud over the red paint, and that would never do while the laird was in residence. After she retrieved her shopping bag and purse, she glanced back at him. "The three bags in the back are Miss Nyland's." Clearly Norway didn't carry her own bags into a house, and well, *she* wasn't going to be a Sherpa today.

"No worries, Miss Sam. I'll see 'em upstairs."

"Thanks, Rob."

"—really dress up for dinner, don't you think?" the tall blonde went on, as they met at the back of the jeep and walked up to the house. "The boys will be so impressed. We'll have to include Lady

Mercia, as well. She'll never forgive us if she comes downstairs in a house dress and we're dripping in pearls."

Samantha had brought a few show-stopper gowns because Rick liked to try to surprise her with outings. Dressing up to go downstairs was totally an English aristocrat thing, and since he was an aristocrat she was willing to do it. Going Evita Peron was okay, too, but not without informing him first. The other guys were on their own. "Sure," she said, since Eerika seemed to be waiting for a response so she could start talking again.

"Oh, I knew you'd be a sport about it," the Viking gushed. "It'll be our secret. They'll be so surprised. I can picture it now."

Before Eerika could suggest a sisterly bonding ritual involving shoes and crumpets or something, Samantha backed into the morning room, then turned and dashed through the connecting door into the downstairs sun room, and from there up the side of the house to the servants' stairs. Somewhere behind her she could swear the woman was still talking.

Just for the hell of it she clambered onto the railing to ascend the last few feet to the second floor, then did a front flip to land in a crouch at the edge of the hallway. It couldn't hurt to keep her skills sharp, plus Norway had her wound up like a crocodile at dinner time. A little adrenaline release kept her from having to bang her head against the wall.

She straightened to see Rick standing outside his office door, gazing at her. That wasn't good. It wasn't that she was trying to hide a flip or two from him; what bugged her was that she hadn't realized he was there. Damn, she really was slipping. Time to put in some practice runs.

"That's a little hard on the furniture, don't you think?" he commented, folding his arms over his chest.

Hmm. "The classic 1950's revival oak servants' stair railing?" she returned, strolling toward him. "I don't think so. What's up?"

He continued to watch her levelly as she approached. "How was shopping?"

"Loud. I mean, I can carry on a conversation with just about anybody, but I think the Viking might be a cyborg. I could barely get a word in. I finally stopped trying. The weird thing is, I still don't know anything about her except that she wants to be on TV." The hairs on her arms lifted as she spoke, and she stopped just out of his reach. Rick was stewing about something. She could see it in his direct gaze, in his still expression.

"Nothing else at all?" he countered, in the same flat tone he'd been using since she appeared Olympics style.

"Well, I know she went after Reggie specifically, and that she was kind of mercenary about it, and I know she likes not just nice things, but *really* nice things. She knows way more about purses than I ever want to learn, which makes sense since she's a professional shopper. But nothing about her family, and nothing more specific about her past than that she's always lived in the good part of London." Samantha tilted her head. "And what have you been up to?"

"Just the usual. Defending your character to my aunt and uncle, popping in on Reg prying off baseboards in the west wing, offering him money to stop destroying my house and having him fling it back at me while he called me selfish."

That stopped her. "You offered your cousin money to leave your stuff alone?"

"I tried to talk to him, but he wasn't interested. The offer came next, because the fact is I won't have him digging through my things. He and everyone else here will leave them be. Is that clear?"

Ah, so that's where they were. "Aunt Mercia blabbed about the highwayman lore chat we had, eh? So is the attic still okay, or is that hands off, too?"

He lowered his chin a little. "Attic's fine."

"Then I'm going to drop off my shopping bag and then go look for a John Singer Sargent. Or maybe a Monet. Back later. Bye." She walked off toward the master bedchamber. "Hey, just FYI, I think someone shoved a stick up your ass. You might want to get that looked at."

A half dozen second later his office door slammed with a thud that reverberated up and down the entire floor. Well, crap. He knew she wasn't good at the arguing thing, but issuing imperial decrees wasn't going to make her bow. He could have asked her directly what she knew about Will Dawkin, and she probably – *probably* – would have answered him directly.

Instead he'd gotten all "you shall not pass," when he could have just explained what he was being so touchy about. Now she'd forgotten to tell him that Eerika wanted to play high-style dress up for dinner. Then again, if he preferred to deliver commands instead of ask questions, that was the result.

She popped by their shared room to drop off her new hand-bag, then snagged a flashlight and went up into the attic again. It ran the whole length of the middle and east wing of the house, dipping low in some places, narrowing and dead-ending in others, with walls and doors separating one section from another. She'd begun at the front middle because it was nearest the stairs and the Gainsborough had almost immediately caught her eye, but there was plenty more to look through.

Rick knew she'd asked about the highwayman, but he was okay with her scouring the attic. That meant either the map Reggie was after wasn't in the attic, or it was hidden well enough that Rick figured she would never find it. *That* possibility made this kind of an irresistible challenge.

Even better, she wasn't going behind his back to find it – as long as she confined her search to the attic.

Now he knew where she'd been sorting through things up here, so it made sense to relocate as far from that point as she could manage. First, though, both to satisfy her own curiosity and because even the attic over the abandoned west wing was still technically in-bounds, she shoved a Louis XIV bureau out of the way and tried the door separating that part of the attic from where she'd been working.

It was locked, of course, so she crouched down, held the flashlight cradled between her shoulder and her neck, and pulled the lockpick from her pocket. The lock was the big brass pirate jail kind, and with one twist and two bumps she had the thing open.

"Ta da," she muttered, straightening to drop the flashlight back into her left hand.

The door was swollen and wedged into the frame, and so she put her shoulder and hip to it and shoved. The screech it made as it scraped open raised the hairs on the back of her neck. In the old days that kind of noise would have cut her career short and sent her straight to the slam without passing go.

A second later she was glad she'd hung on so tightly to the door, because the floor just beyond it wasn't there. "Jesus." She crouched in the doorway, looking down to see a waterlogged drawing or sitting room directly beneath her. The closed west wing had a second, unchained entrance then – though she wouldn't recommend anybody take that first step. It was a long way down.

The attic continued after that seven-foot-wide opening in the floor. None of it looked awesomely safe over there, and if not for the old trunk and crate she could see in the far corner, she would have shut and locked the barrier door again. But at the moment the trunk and the crate were treasures, an unknown separated from her by a hole in the floor and thirty more feet of uncertain footing beyond that.

Widely-spaced rafter beams continued above her head and on down to the end of the attic. They looked fairly sturdy, but with all the leaks below she could bet that some of them were rotted. The slightest touch would turn them into goopy sawdust.

Huh. If this had been an actual paying gig she probably would have rope with her, along with gloves and maybe even a saw so she could remove a timber upright or two and make herself a bridge over the opening. This entire house, though, or at least the majority of it that wasn't already ruined, was a historical treasure. Dismantling the good bits made her feel icky.

And when she thought about it, the rest of the attic over the ruined wing had been emptied out. Something about those two containers had made them unworthy of rescue. For all she knew, they were both empty.

Or they'd been left until last because they were heavy, and the floor of the attic had fallen out before they could be moved. Both of those scenarios made sense, damn it all. Frowning, Samantha dug her fingers into the wrecked edge of the floor in front of her. With the exposure to cold and wet for who knew how long it flaked away like stale crackers. Chances were, if she jumped across she'd go right through the floor on the other side.

Dusting her hands off, she straightened. Old, pre-Rick Sam might have risked it, and this Sam was tempted, but neither Sam was stupid. She knew Canniebrae's staff had moved all the shit the family wanted to keep and put it in the sound part of the attic. Those boxes, then, weren't anything anybody particularly cared about. "Ergo, Sam won't be playing the part of crash test dummy today," she murmured, taking a step backward to clear the doorway.

She was being totally sensible, but of course she was the only one who knew that. Just like if Rick would tell her why he wanted everybody to stay away from the Will Dawkin business, she would probably drop it. But whatever it was, he'd lumped her in with his cousin and decided they weren't worthy of his secrets. And he definitely had a secret.

Leaning out over the hole in the floor, she reached for the door handle. At the same time she heard the top stair creak behind her. Samantha took a breath, lifted her back leg for counterbalance, and grabbed onto the door. At least whoever it was wouldn't be able to throw her through the hole, that way.

"Don't you dare," Rick snapped.

She shifted her grip on the handle and continued dragging the ill-fitting door back into place. It took a lot of hauling and that high-pitched squeaking, but with a last heave she got it shut again. That done, she locked it and shoved the chest of drawers back in front of the door.

Only then did she turn around. "Don't I dare what?" she asked, shaking damp dust and cobwebs off the front of her shirt.

"Don't you dare go into that part of the attic," he returned, his tone lowering. "It's dangerous."

"Hence me standing on this side of the door, dude. Anything else you want to forbid me from doing, my lord? Jumping off the roof? Running myself over with the jeep? Oh, I know – you should dare me not to stab myself in the face."

"That's enough, Samantha." His face was shadowed, but she could hear the sharp, hard annoyance in his voice. "You were at least thinking of making that jump, unless you already did it."

"Of course I thought about it. Then I decided, all on my own, that it would be a stupid risk. There's nothing you wanted to keep over there, because if it was something you valued, it wouldn't still be over there." She folded her arms, ticked off enough at his trying to order her around that she didn't feel like changing the subject. "So, anything else you want to accuse me of? I know something's got you all clenched up, sport."

"I am not all clenched up. Is it too much to ask that you stop rattling doors you have no business walking through?"

"And which doors are those? The one with the non-existent highwayman treasure that's so made up you have a stroke any time somebody mentions it? *My* question, Mr. Uppity, is why it's any of *your* business."

"You have—"

"Nope. You give me a straight answer or you back the fuck off, Rick. I love you. But you do not employ me, and you do not own me."

"A simple 'leave it be' won't do, then?" he retorted. "Not even if I add a 'for my sake'?"

"Maybe if you'd led with that. I guess now you just have to hope I don't find anything, and that if I do, I decide to keep it to myself instead of going to your cousin."

That last part was probably mean and unnecessary, because the odds of her turning info over to Reggie instead of Rick, if she shared at all, were pretty tiny. Infinitesimal. But crap. If he wanted her to take things on faith, he was going to have to give her some credit for not being an idiot. Today he didn't seem to be inclined to do that.

His shoulders rose and fell. "Do your bloody worst, then. Chase your tail, cat burglar. You won't find anything."

Wow. *That*, she hadn't expected. An actual challenge for her to find something – which made her wonder if maybe there was nothing to find, after all. Except that even the way Rick dismissed the whole thing made her think otherwise. Anyway, now it was game on.

Rick stomped back down the attic stairs. "Hey," she called, before he could clomp out of earshot, "The Viking wants the girls to dress up for dinner. Really dress up. It's a stupid surprise for the guys, I think, but I know since Patricia you don't like shenanigans pulled on you in public."

The footsteps paused, then resumed. "I love you too, by the way," drifted up to her.

Cool. She hadn't wrecked that, anyway. The whole fighting and still staying together thing still felt weird, and she had no idea if she was doing it right. But yay, one point for her, she guessed.

Ö

RICHARD CHECKED his Rolex as he shrugged into a dark-gray formal tuxedo jacket. He dressed for business dinners all the time, and for charity events and the occasional high-end auction. He hadn't formally dressed for the express purpose of sitting at his own table with his own family, though, for years. The rare Christmas in London, though he made an effort to be elsewhere when that time came around.

Tonight he would likely have dressed in jeans, a jacket, and an open-collar dress shirt, and that was only for the sake of his old-fashioned aunt and uncle. The heads-up from Samantha had altered that. Because while he didn't give a damn if Eerika Nyland wanted to pretend this was a royal dinner, he wasn't going to dress shabbily when Sam meant to do otherwise.

Looking down, he straightened a few things and made another attempt to tie the long laces of his shoes. Perhaps he should have opted for his standard tuxedo, but this wasn't New York or London. This was the Scottish Highlands.

It all might have had to do with the fact that he was still annoyed as hell with Samantha, because as he reviewed their conversation it almost felt like she'd maneuvered their argument in order to give her a way to delve into Will Dawkin's supposed treasure, when he'd been trying to prevent that very thing. Now, though, the gloves were off. He couldn't risk moving the map now because she would be watching for any clue. What he *could* do, though, was distract her.

Once he got rid of his relations, he could sweep her off to Rawley Park and hopefully find some new acquisition that required her expertise. They were more likely to be discovered by the paparazzi there, but Rawley did have some high, sturdy stone walls, and top-of-the-line security. More importantly, it wasn't Canniebrae.

Of all the reasons he hadn't wanted to return here, it figured that a decades-old rumor of treasure he'd nearly forgotten about would be what tripped him up. He should have known better.

Finally satisfied that everything was where it was supposed to be, he went down the hall to his office. A couple of cable coils were stacked in one corner, which seemed rather optimistic given that the bulldozer hadn't yet arrived from Inverness. Regardless, he meant to drag Canniebrae into the twenty-first century by the end of the month.

He'd dressed early to avoid crossing Samantha's path, and he spent the next hour in his office finalizing his revisions and signing off on two other deals that he would mail off tomorrow. In the morning he was going to have to visit The Bonny Lass for their internet so he could email his contract changes to Tom. Finally, he sat back. This afternoon Samantha had made him angry enough to spit nails. There she'd stood, in the actual doorway of the place he'd asked – well, ordered – everyone to avoid, and the argument had ended with the two of them agreeing that she could do whatever the hell she wanted.

For Christ's sake, he made deals for a living, and she'd danced around him like a cheetah with a sloth. He could curse her stubbornness and her cleverness and her damned curiosity, but they were the very things that had drawn him to her in the first place.

Reg he could turn aside, or buy off if need be, but Samantha required a much more cautious approach. He wanted her in his life. He needed her there. She'd opened what he'd already considered a very large world into a completely new dimension where the sun shined brighter and the shadows looked darker than he had ever realized. Samantha stood at the center of the whirlwind, where all he could do was hold on for dear life and hope he didn't burn up on re-entry.

The dinner gong sounded from the depths of the house, the signal for the diners to gather in the parlor that adjoined the formal dining room. Ignoring the evening chill traveling up his legs, he headed down the stairs and up the main hallway.

As he stepped into the parlor the opposite door opened. Samantha glided into the room, and his brain stopped working.

He had no idea where in hell she'd gotten the dress she wore, but damn. Emerald green silk topped with spaghetti straps and flowing from a gathered waist into a flowing, calf-length skirt with a slit up the left thigh. Green beads flowed diagonally across the material like a glitter of shooting stars, and she wore matching green three-inch heels. With her auburn hair swept up by silver combs and one of the delicate silver chains he'd given her glinting at the base of her throat, she would have drawn attention among empresses and kings. The sight made his mouth dry and his cock sit up and take notice – which could be tricky considering what he was wearing.

She canted her body a little bit sideways to him as he crossed the room to her, which reminded him that they were arguing, and she of course would already have picked out three escape routes if need be. "Wow," he said aloud, taking her in all over again.

"Does that mean you're being nice now?" she asked, her own gaze sweeping down to his feet and up to his face.

"It means I thought we'd resolved that you would attempt to find the unfindable, and I would attempt to thwart you at every turn."

She lifted an eyebrow. "You're my nemesis now?"

"That depends on whether nemeses are permitted to have sex and hold hands on occasion."

"Like I'm going to disagree with that while you're wearing a kilt," she returned, amusement in her voice. "Because you, despite being stubborn as frack, are the most awesome boyfriend ever." She leaned in. "Are you wearing underwear?"

"What's the saying? If I were wearing anything under it, it would be a skirt? It's not a skirt."

Samantha grinned, reached out to flick his boar's hair sporran. "This outfit's gonna have to travel with us from now on."

"Just don't call me Jamie Fraser. Or Braveheart."

"I'm not making any promises." With her heels on, the top of her head came to just above his nose, so it didn't take much effort for him to lower his head and reach her upturned mouth. Yes, they remained at odds, but she did have quite a reasonable streak right alongside the stubborn one. It was entirely possible that she

143

would wake in the morning and decide to drop the entire treasure chase. He would definitely do his damnedest to convince her of other ways to keep the two of them occupied.

The door behind him opened again, and his aunt and uncle walked in, both of them dressed to the nines. Richard stifled a frown. From what Samantha had said only the females were to know about the dinner garb. He looked at her again to find her attention on his relations as well.

"Huh," she muttered.

Before he could respond to that, Reg and Miss Nyland joined them, his cousin in a damned tuxedo. The Viking, as Samantha referred to her, had somehow wriggled into a skin-tight red dress with one shoulder strap, and a hole from just below her breasts to just above her navel. Like Sam she wore ridiculously high heels, hers a red sandal with bindings all the way up her calf.

Perhaps he was prejudiced, but the tight fit had the effect of making her look desperate for attention, completely at odds with Samantha's elegant sexiness. Even that, though, wasn't his first thought. "Was I the only one not supposed to know we were dressing up?" he murmured, catching Sam's hand in his.

"It kind of looks like it," she returned in the same tone. "I don't get why, though. The only thing I haven't told you about tonight is that I'm not wearing any underwear, either."

"The... Well, now I can't recall what I was going to say," he murmured back. Abruptly he felt better about all this. And yes, he would have been mildly annoyed to see everyone but himself dress for dinner. At the same time, it was small, petty, contrived, and very like a reality show stunt. Compared with some of the turmoil he and Samantha had survived, supremely insignificant. It did give him a very good indication of just how shallow and desperate for attention Reg's significant other was. The Viking did have her phone with her, swiftly handed over to Reg. Was that it, then? Had she meant to record his anticipated annoyance? A reality-television style stunt, indeed. And it would not be allowed. Not here, and not with him and Samantha involved.

"We all clean up well, don't we?" Reg straightened his bowtie. "I see you went native, Rick."

"Chicks dig kilts," Samantha put in, before Richard could comment on Reg's resemblance to any number of head waiters. She wrapped both hands around his arm. "How do they say it? 'Ye're a braw lad, Rick'."

Again her Highlands accent was, of course, spot on. Then, even though he knew that she was aware that his aunt and uncle had some rather serious reservations about her joining the family, she released him and glided up to them with a broad smile.

"You look fabulous, Lady Mercia," she said, reaching out to squeeze one of his aunt's hands. "That necklace brings out the green in your eyes. It's North Carolina emerald, isn't it? The color's so deep you could almost sink into it."

Of course Samantha would know a stone's origins simply from its color. His aunt looked flattered, but a little cautious. Considering that they knew at least some of Martin Jellicoe's history as a jewel thief, he wasn't entirely certain that Samantha had taken the correct tack. And that was extremely unusual for her.

Aunt Mercia put her free hand over the silver-bound stone. "It is, I believe. Rowland gave it to me for our last wedding anniversary."

Samantha's smile deepened, even as Rick moved into rescue position. "My dad was kind of a notorious guy, but he would never touch emeralds. He always said a vain woman insists on diamonds because they sparkle, a greedy woman wants rubies to make her look desirable, but only a husband who's memorized the color of his wife's eyes gives her emeralds. They were kind of sacred to him, I think."

And just like that she'd won them over, at least for tonight. Uncle Rowland put an arm around his wife's shoulders, both of them melting into smiles. As Sam released Aunt Mercia's hand and strolled back to Richard's side, she flashed him a swift grin.

At that moment he realized two things: She'd completely made up her father's quaint saying; and Eerika Nyland was wearing rubies. "You haven't made a friend tonight," he whispered, offering her an arm as Yule appeared to throw open the formal dining room's double doors and announce dinner.

"She meant to embarrass you. I don't want to be her friend."

He took a slow breath. She was an F-5 tornado, and for some reason she'd chosen to stop spinning long enough for him to catch her. "I thought you and I were still at odds."

"We're at odds because you're a jackass. That doesn't mean I wouldn't fight a dragon for you."

"Is she a dragon, then?"

"Nope. A snake, maybe. I'll figure it out."

As they took their seats, him at the head of the table and Samantha on his right, he sent a swift glance in Norway's direction. Reg tended to go after glamour and looks and money, and she at least gave the appearance of having all three. At the same time, Reg had told him that she hadn't bought the car that had been the ruse to bring them together.

Perhaps she did need some figuring out. Not because she might be digging after Reg's money, however. Because of the look she sent at Samantha when no one else was looking. Sam might be willing to slay a dragon on his behalf, but that was nothing compared to what he was prepared to do for her.

11
_____

Saturday, 3:07 a.m.

Samantha opened one eye. Beside her, one arm draped across her hips and the other beneath her head, Rick breathed softly against her forehead. He still wore his kilt, and if she had any say in his wardrobe choices he wouldn't ever be wearing anything else. *Hoo, baby.* With the heavy blue curtains shut it could have been broad daylight outside, but the still air and the quiet house, even the tap of a breeze-blown branch against the window, felt like night.

Night had always felt like it belonged to her. Most people would be sound asleep, but she wasn't most people. Taking a breath, she lifted his arm and rolled out from beneath it. That done, she picked up her phone and scooted silently to the floor. Just after three o'clock. Heavy shadows, sinking moon, and deepest sleep – mortals beware. The cat burglar stirred.

The ex-cat burglar, that was. With a sigh she slipped into the bathroom, because even burglars had to pee once in a while. Back in the room she stood by the door, listening to Rick's steady breathing. After awesome kilt sex he wasn't likely to wake up because of her minimal pitter patter, but she waited anyway. This was solo time, and she didn't feel like either explaining or arguing.

Silently she pulled on the dark sweatshirt and black jogging sweats she'd tossed into the old dressing room, donned her sneakers, and tied her hair back in a loose pony tail before she slipped into the cold hallway. A dim light had been left on at either end of the corridor, but that left a lot of room for shadows in between.

Going down the stairs she kept close to the wall and avoided the typical old house step-squeaking. All of Rick's other properties were pretty high tech, and she'd even made him upgrade the system in Florida in order to keep out nefarious types other than herself. She'd learned how to beat all of them, which made no-tech Canniebrae no kind of challenge at all.

But it was still night, and she still didn't want anyone else spotting her, so that was sort of fun. She grinned as she darted across the hallway and into the library, putting her weight against the handle as she pushed the door shut so it wouldn't creak. The library hearth was dark, so she turned on her phone's flashlight. It was too much light, and she lowered the brightness level and made sure the curtains were shut. Unless somebody walked in on her, she was invisible. Even if someone did, she had a good chance of going unseen.

She'd already found the local ghost lore book, and if she recalled correctly – which she did, with her near photographic recall – the local legends book was on the same shelf. Except that it wasn't. Samantha squatted in front of the row of books. Ghosts, churches, plants, villages...and six inches of space where books weren't.

"Dammit, Rick," she muttered. Whatever the hell it was about Will Dawkin or his legend or his rumored treasure, Rick really didn't want her digging into it. He didn't want Reggie doing anything about it, either. Reggie already knew things that she didn't know, but she was *not* going to go to Rick-light for information. She couldn't – not while Rick was pissed off at him. Aside from that, if anyone at all was going to find this whatever it was, it was going to be her.

Okay. No book on local Highlands myths and legends, but there were always tourist books. Villages always had some hook, some fanciful story, with which to attract tourist dollars. She pulled out the Balmoral-printed *Villages in the Shadow of the Cairngorms* and sat cross-legged with her back to the shelf.

Because she needed a starting point, she began with the area directly around Canniebrae. Some sort of map had been here, and that made here important. Orrisey was just a mile down the lane, and on Canniebrae land. According to the book, it boasted a picturesque church, once known to shelter first Catholic priests and then Jacobites. It averaged blah blah blah of rain per year, had gotten electricity fairly early for a place this remote, and its oldest building was The Bonny Lass tavern, which had begun as a coaching inn some six hundred years ago, and was now a locally-renowned pub.

Blah blah local whisky, and for ten years beginning in 1738 the infamous highwayman Will Dawkin had been known to share a drink with travelers and then follow them down the road, where he would don a mask and caped greatcoat and rob them of everything but the clothes on their backs. "Ha," she breathed, turning the page to view a facsimile of a wanted poster showing a hulking guy in a Dracula cape, a black hat low over his brow, and a black cloth covering his face from above his nose to below his chin. With crazy arched brows, wide-set, narrowed eyes, the old-timey cops might as well have been looking for Bela Lugosi.

The next paragraph actually said that on one particularly dark and stormy night Will Dawkin vanished, never to be heard from again. Ooh. *And* his hoard of riches was rumored to be somewhere in the hills above Orrisey, though no one as of yet had recovered any of the loot.

"Bingo."

Usually her next step would be a combo of library and internet. Rick apparently had the books she would need – which explained why he'd told her to go ahead and do her worst – and they wouldn't have internet until next Tuesday at the earliest. Okay, maps, then. An old map, preferably. Climbing to her feet, she went back to searching the shelves. A couple of street atlases and a topography of the world book, but nothing that gave her an old overview of the countryside. A couple more empty spaces on the shelves though, of course.

Grimacing, she turned around. The tourist collectibles shop down past the tavern had had some long tubes in a basket, but the Viking hadn't wanted to set foot inside. That meant tomorrow, and business hours, and other people. Sure, she could trot down there and risk it tonight, but that would mess up her karma in some horrible ways. Sam Jellicoe never had and never would steal from mom and pop shops.

So yay for her rules, but they still left her mapless. Standing, she replaced the atlas. She'd bet her underwear that the books Rick had pulled out of his library could give her a few more clues, but going after something he'd hidden from her on purpose crossed a couple of other lines.

"Well, this sucks," she murmured. That treasure map Reggie seemed obsessed over could always be up in the attic, but it just as likely wasn't. In this house and without any clues, finding it could take her a week or more, if it actually existed.

She could do an aerial survey with a drone if she had one, which she didn't. Balmoral might well shoot it or a circling helicopter down anyway, just on principle. The Cairngorms loomed up behind them, but climbing a mountain seemed kind of desperate at this point. GPS was out because no cell service. The gods of nefarious deeds didn't seem to be willing to offer her any breaks on this one.

Samantha glided to the window and looked outside. A quarter sliver of moon hung at about its midway point, turning the trees a silver blue that deepened to murky black shadow below. A clear night in the autumn Highlands. That couldn't be too common. Hmm.

The widow's walk. With a loose grin she snagged the atlas again, found a couple blank sheets of paper and some pencils, then went up into the attic. She unlocked the hatch that opened onto the roof, and a few seconds later she was outside. An iron rail ran around the top section of roof, but she wasn't about to count on something that practically screamed "come, let me lead you to your doom". The iron lattice walkway looked even less promising than the floor in the west wing.

Ignoring them, she climbed up beside a chimney, shoved at it a few times to make sure it wouldn't come down tonight and take her with it, then sat back against the upslope side. The view would of course have been much clearer in daylight, but then the whole other people peskiness came into play.

Using the atlas as a lap desk and drawing a rough outline of Canniebrae in the center of the page with the village in the lower right, she sketched in the river Dee, the hills, the loch, and the valleys immediately around them. She had to leave some blank spaces where trees obscured her view, and a chunk of the twists and turns of roads and trails were pretty iffy, but she had an idea how to fill them in. Rick liked horseback riding, and he would jump at the chance to pull her away from her investigation.

An hour later she'd filled four sheets of paper with Canniebrae's surroundings, her face and hands were numb with cold, and she figured she'd pushed her luck far enough. She left the sketches in the attic, replaced the atlas, and headed back into the master bedchamber.

Rick still lay there, thankfully, and she stripped out of her dark clothes to hike herself onto the bed and crawl beneath the covers beside him. The chill felt like it had sunk all the way to her bones, and he practically radiated heat, so she surreptitiously snuggled her back up against his chest.

"Christ," he mumbled. "Where did you go, the North Pole?"

Dammit. "Scotland is cold," she chattered, and turned around, shoving her hands into his chest and her face against his neck.

He actually flinched. Instead of shoving her back out of bed, though, he growled and wrapped his arms around her, pulling her tighter against him. "Next time you go sneaking about, put on a bloody hat and gloves."

Now might be a good time to point out that if he hadn't hidden those books she wouldn't have had to go sit on the roof, but on the other hand she'd kind of maybe pushed him into pulling out the books in the first place. He would totally point that out, too. "Maybe I'll just wear *you,*" she said instead. "You're nice and warm."

"Thanks, but we can mess around after you warm up. You're cold enough I'm genuinely terrified that if I go in, my cock might break off."

She snorted, kissing his throat with her cold lips. "Neither of us wants that. Just some nice, close cuddling." Samantha wrapped her feet around his.

"Good God, you're killing me. I've changed my mind. I want to be a bachelor."

"It's too late. You're all mine now. Every toasty inch of you. Snuggle up, buttercup."

Sex probably would have warmed her up nicely, but she wasn't sure he would have liked her cold appendages groping on him. Little as she generally liked being trapped, this didn't quite feel that way. Instead it was...nice. Warm and safe and comfortable and kind of heart-lifting. *Great.* Now she was getting sappy.

"Sam?" he murmured.

"Hmm?"

"Wherever you went, were you safe?"

"Yes. Just not well-enough insulated."

And still tempted to tell him just what she'd been up to. But he wouldn't tell her what had him so wound up about the supposedly non-existent highwayman treasure, even if it would stop her from prying into it – which it would. So stale, meet mate.

"Okay, then. Good."

"RIDING," Richard repeated, an eyebrow lifting before he could gain control of his own skepticism.

Seated on one of the chairs facing the master bedchamber's fireplace, Samantha stomped into her second hiking boot. "With you. Not to go bronco busting or anything. Just, you know, a walking tour of your realm, my liege."

Samantha liked going on runs, driving fast cars, flying helicopters when she could get away with it, and riding in airplanes. Her feet and the machines did what she wanted them to, when she wanted them to do it. A horse, though, had a mind of its own. One that might not agree with what its rider wanted. That wasn't *his* opinion; she'd stated that very thing the last time he'd tried to take her riding.

"I'll have two horses saddled after breakfast, then. You can have me until noon. I want to be here if and when the bulldozer arrives so I can mourn the destruction of my front drive."

"Me, too. There could be Roman artifacts here, even though it's kind of too far north for that. Celtic would be awesome, though. Or Norse."

"Or feet of accumulated oyster shells and some glacial rocks," Richard returned with a grin. "But I don't want to crush your dreams of legitimate archaeology, so we'll be back in plenty of time."

"Cool." Snapping to her feet, she slid her arms up around his shoulders, leaned up along his chest, and kissed him.

Richard kissed her back. It would have physically hurt him not to do so, even if this morning did feel just a little too perfect. Some voracious morning sex that had begun before dawn, no arguing, and Sam willing to go riding with him. The Highlands was the most dramatically beautiful place they'd been together, so it could simply be the scenery. Or she was leading him somewhere, and he was trotting along happily behind her as long as he could ogle her arse.

In his defense, she did have a nice arse. And over the past year he'd learned that going along with her netted him more cooperation than trying to shut her down – in which case she went ahead with whatever she thought was necessary anyway, and just did it behind his back.

He wasn't her damned parent, telling her what she could or couldn't do. But keeping her safe, by which he meant both alive and out of prison, had just about a year ago become his first priority in everything. He ranked it right alongside keeping her with him. That was why he'd had Tom Donner make up a list of which countries didn't extradite to the United States, and he'd memorized it. That wouldn't help if Interpol caught up with her for a crime in Europe, but they spent most of their time in America, and so it was from there that any threat was most likely to come.

"What's up?" she asked, eyeing him.

"I'm just wondering whether I should hire a film crew to document your first ride." With another kiss he lowered his hands from her hips. "But first I need some breakfast. It takes a great deal of energy to be as heroically warm and sexy as I was last night."

"Mm hm. You did earn a pretty damn hearty meal. Let's go, then. I want to know if Norway's still in a huff."

"You're not planning on making more trouble, are you?"

"She started it. I prefer to make my own trouble."

"It could have been an honest mistake. You told me. My aunt told my uncle, and Norway, as you call her, told Reg."

"I checked with your aunt. Norway told her and your uncle we were all dressing up."

Richard pulled open the door and stood aside to let her precede him. "It still could have been an oversight."

"Fine. You be all naïve, and I'll watch our backs," she said over her shoulder, as she passed by him. "By the way, your aunt's taken up painting, and she's not half bad. She brought photos to show. You should ask her about them."

For a woman without a family, Samantha had a keen sense of where repairs between relations needed to be made. Even the ones he'd caused by his own stubbornness. True, a just-orphaned nineteen-year-old didn't want to be told what to do by a probably well-meaning aunt and uncle, but he wasn't nineteen any longer. "I will."

"Good. And I want a calm horse. A really calm one. Half dead, even."

The scent of warm bread and bacon met them halfway down the stairs. Inside the breakfast room a hot pot of coffee awaited him, while a glass of ice and a can of diet Coke had already been placed at the spot where Samantha generally sat. Perhaps things felt too perfect because they were just perfect enough.

Or not. As he piled bacon and over-easy eggs on his plate, Reg and Miss Nyland made their appearance. He wasn't about to greet them first, on the very good chance that neither of them would respond. Because whatever he'd told Samantha about innocent mistakes, he didn't think last night had been one of them. Power, negotiation – they were like part of his own nervous system. Reg wanted something, and he had no intention of aiding his cousin in any way. He, therefore, had the position of power. He wasn't about to give it up in exchange for an unanswered hello.

"Good morning," Samantha said, smiling as she and her plate took their seats. "Rick and I are going horseback riding this morning, if you want to join us."

Richard sent her a quick frown. Samantha inviting other people to witness her attempting something at which she had no skill didn't make any sense. "Really?" he whispered, as he moved around behind her.

"Oh, riding sounds delightful," Eerika gushed. "I haven't ridden in ages. Might we, Reginald?"

"There's nothing else to do here but play cards with my parents," Reg answered stiffly. "We may as well."

The pair went over to the sideboard, and Samantha leaned over toward him at the head of the table. "Reggie can't be pulling down walls if he's with us," she whispered back.

It was for him, then. She was willing to risk being embarrassed in exchange for keeping his cousin from digging through the west wing for a few hours. The cynical half of him also had to note that going riding would keep Reg from finding any treasure before she could do so herself, but one thing at a time. "The heavy equipment is supposed to be here by noon," he said aloud. "I've also sent for my architect and a structural engineer. It's fairly obvious that I won't be able to repair the west wing, so I'll be replacing it."

That got Reg's attention. "You'd just tear it all down, then? What if I were to send for a historian? Someone who might object to you ripping things apart without assessing what the country could be losing?"

Richard finished chewing his mouthful. "Be my guest. Who knows? After I restore the place I may decide to hand it, and a large endowment, over to the National Trust after all. Or I may change my mind again. At any rate, I'm opening a museum that should bring a large amount of tourist money to Devon and won't cost the county a penny. Don't be an idiot and think you can convince them to sue me over some rotted wood and ruined carpet."

Something rammed into his shin beneath the table. Hard. His only suspect was in the middle of wolfing down an omelet, her gaze on her plate. If she expected him to cow or to sit quietly while his own cousin threatened him, she didn't know him very well. But then, she *did* know him very well. He took a slow breath.

He'd just shortened Reg's timeline to find the treasure, and then he'd taken the bait when Reg had threatened him, giving his cousin the excuse to avoid going for a ride so that he could go digging instead. After Samantha had gone to the trouble of arranging for Reg to be away from the house in the first place.

"But beneath all the stomping and blowing," he went on, "we're still family, Reg. We've drifted farther apart than we should have, and I'd like to amend that. If you're still set on going on a treasure hunt, I'll give you a day or two to dig through the rubble – as long as you stay safe while you're doing it."

Reg remained on his feet, chest out and shoulders squared. Eerika, though, sank down gracefully onto a chair. "You know you're always grumpy before you've had your breakfast, Reginald. Let's eat, go riding, and then decide if you're still indignant or not."

"Sure, if Ricky apologizes for calling me an idiot."

So now they were back in public school again. "Certainly, if you stop acting—"

Crack. Samantha's boot found his shin again.

"—like I'm personally trying to ruin your life," Richard amended, making a mental note to purchase shin guards before his next argument with Samantha. "Which I am not."

With a pause for dramatic effect Reg deflated enough to take a seat. "Not quite an apology, but I'll take it. I suppose I have to, if I want to be invited to the wedding."

"I'd invite you anyway, Reggie," Samantha finally put in. "You're Rick's family. No fisticuffs is good, though. I've never ridden before, and I really don't want you guys bellowing at each other while I'm trying not to be killed."

Miss Nyland chuckled, clapping her hands together. "You've never ridden? Oh, if you're going to be an English lord's wife you must learn."

"Because we're time traveling back to Jane Austen days?" Samantha suggested.

"If only we could! But there are charity rides, the polo matches where Rick already shows so well, pony judging... So many things! I'm happy we can assist you!"

"Oh, good," Samantha said, gulping down her soda. "You can never have too much help."

A little too much help would serve her right for kicking him. "You're a horsewoman then, Miss Nyland?" he asked.

"I've won several ribbons, if I say so myself. And please do call me Eerika. You've given your leave for me to call you Rick, after all."

He didn't remember doing any such thing, but it didn't matter. "Eerika, then. I'm certain Samantha would appreciate any pointers you're willing to offer."

The tall blonde picked at her plate of fruit. "With pleasure. Will you be riding in the proper style then, Sam?"

"If you're talking about riding sidesaddle, no way. I'm going to be holding on with everything I've got."

"We can't have that. Not with you being an American. Once you become a marchioness, you'll have duties."

Samantha turned her head, pinning Richard with a look that might just keep him awake at night. "Duties?"

"We'll talk about it later," he said, reaching over to take her hand. He was accustomed to battling on several fronts, and the two of them were already at odds over the highwaymen nonsense, but this... This one could do some damage if he couldn't head it off. "It's nothing you can't handle."

"Says you." She set aside her fork and stood. "I'll be out at the stable trying some bribery." On her way out she liberated a pair of apples, dumping them into her jacket pockets.

He wanted to go after her. She had a history of fleeing when she felt trapped, and he wasn't about to let her get a head start. On the other hand, she hadn't made a run for it in weeks, even when he'd asked her to marry him. She loved him. He knew that. He was going to have to trust in it sooner or later.

Deliberately he took another bite of his eggs. "I want your word, Reg, that you won't go into the west wing alone, and that you'll wear a hard hat. I'd ask that you not blame me when you don't find anything, but that would make me delusional."

"Why don't you tell me where the map is? Then you won't have to worry about me blaming you for anything."

"I told you what happened to the map." Finishing off his coffee, he climbed to his feet. "And for God's sake keep in mind that I invited you here to meet my fiancé. Make an attempt to do that, will you? If it doesn't interfere too much with the reason you actually came here, that is."

Even without Samantha there to kick him he knew he was pushing things again, so instead of elaborating on what he thought of his cousin's new obsession he inclined his head and gestured them toward the hallway door.

"Don't I even get to finish eating?" Reg asked.

"No. Samantha's out there getting nervous because you two had to talk about duties and obligations, so we will go out now and reassure her. We will compliment her efforts, and we will be extremely supportive and informative. Is that clear?"

"Of course we'll be helpful," Eerika said, pulling on a jacket. "I certainly never intended to be anything *but* helpful. Sam and I are practically sisters."

Reg drew even with him as they left the house for the front drive. "Miss Jellicoe doesn't strike me as being particularly shy or fearful."

"She isn't, generally. But she is private. She would have to engage with the aristocracy as much as I do, which is almost never."

"I'm not the one who mentioned charity rides and pony judging. That was Eerika. She'd give her left arm to have those obligations. Showing off in front of rich, snobby women gets her off."

"Then why is she with you?" Samantha had mentioned that

Miss Nyland's pursuit had evidently been very focused on Reg, as well, but he wasn't about to have that discussion.

"Ha ha. Very amusing. Just because you absent yourself from the obligations of your station doesn't mean the rest of us do. Dad, Mum, and I always attend the Derby opening, Wimbledon, Parliament, and all the other things you so studiously avoid. Hell, I'm practically your official stand-in. Didn't you know that?"

"Honestly, it's never really crossed my mind. But don't expect me to believe for a second that you get nothing out of it."

"Oh, I get tail like you wouldn't believe. There's a whole cult of aristocracy groupies. After William and Kate's wedding I didn't even surface for a week."

Richard glanced ahead of them as Eerika slipped into the stable. "Is that where you caught Eerika's attention? Before she pretended to buy a car from you?"

"Yes."

"Then we'll call it even."

Perhaps he needed to pay more attention to his inherited obligations. He'd always put them second to his business ones, and since he'd met Samantha they'd fallen even further down the list. No, she wouldn't wish to participate in some of it, but his thief had a soft spot for charities and causes. He could certainly afford them, and he could use some more good karma. Anything to insulate Samantha a little better from her past misdeeds.

Inside the stable, closed off from the part they now used as a garage, waited half a dozen horses and a trio of grooms. He'd had them brought up from Rawley a few weeks ago, when he'd first decided Samantha needed to meet his family. Samantha leaned up against one of the stall doors while a foot or so in front of her a large chestnut mare sloppily chewed up an apple.

"You've met Lily, I see," he said, walking over to join her.

"She wasn't at Rawley Park. Where's Molly?"

"Molly's still at Rawley. I thought you might like Lily. She's nearly in a coma, she's so calm." He tilted his head. "You remembered Molly?"

Samantha pointed at her head. "Really? Have you met me?"

"Point taken."

"Briggs said you've acquired a new gelding. Major Pumpernickel or something."

"So you remember a horse you barely set eyes on, but you can't remember my new bay after you were clearly just introduced?" Richard put a hand to his ear. "Say his name, Sam, if you expect his support and assistance."

"Fine." She took a deep breath. "Major General Llewelyn Alberic Emilius Price-Davies. Named for the English recipient of the Victoria Cross who died in 1965 at the age of ninety-five."

"Going for extra credit points, are you?" He put an arm across her shoulders and pulled her against his side. "I know you don't like displaying any sub-par skills in front of other people. I appreciate this, my lass."

She smiled. "My lass. I like that. Just remember that you owe me one."

"Thankfully you won't let me forget."

He *did* appreciate it. Yes, he'd now more or less given his permission for both Reg and Samantha to go digging through the ruins, but neither of them would be doing it this morning. Neither of them would be finding the damned map there, either, and Sam had no access to details of anything. Reg already knew the tales, but if he hadn't figured anything out by now, he never would.

The part of him that liked taking risks, the part of him that dove straight into the deep end after Samantha, looked forward to watching her try and fail because he'd already taken steps to see that she would do so. He'd caught her once, but that had been in the process of working with her to solve a crime. This time they would seem to be at cross-purposes. Nemeses, as she'd said. And he really wanted to win, as much as he wanted to see how she would handle losing.

"Briggs, let's put Lily in the pen, shall we?" he said aloud. "She won't take off on you, Samantha, but this way you won't have to worry about it."

"I'll see to it, my lord. Let's get the rest of you mounted first, though." The English groom sounded out of place here, but he knew what he was about. He nodded at Samantha. "Lily's a sweetheart, but any animal's easier to control while they're moving than while they're trying to stand still."

"Okay. I'm not about to argue."

They put Reg up on a black gelding named Pitch, while Eerika chose Lady, a gray mare trained for sidesaddle. He could see Samantha eyeing the rig as they all went outside and Reg lifted Norway onto the saddle. "Lily's not trained for a lady's saddle," he murmured. "I reckoned you'd be more comfortable with cowboy-style riding."

"Damn straight," she returned, climbing up the bottom of rail of the pen to watch Briggs saddle the chestnut mare.

"I thought you wanted to learn how to ride properly," Eerika said, walking by on Lady and circling back again, and not sounding the least bit supportive or helpful despite her promise to be both. "You're already at a disadvantage because you're, you know, American."

"Oh, get me the fuck up there," Samantha muttered, and stepped up to hop gracefully over the railing.

Richard wanted to hand her into the saddle himself, but Briggs had been right about moving being easier than standing still. He swung up on Major, sending the bay over beside the gate. Was Samantha going to play the part of the neophyte equestrian, or would she be herself? It was difficult to tell the difference sometimes.

With Briggs holding Lily's bridle and issuing softly-spoken instructions, Samantha took hold of the saddle horn, put her left foot in the stirrup, and swung herself up into the saddle with all of her usual easy athleticism. The groom specialized in first-time riders, and after having him on the payroll for six months Richard was supremely gratified to see just how good he was at his job.

She took hold of the reins as Ross guided Lily in a wide circle and gave instructions on steering and braking. Once she'd attempted the various controls Ross stepped back and sent her around again. The moment Samantha smiled, Richard leaned down and unfastened the gate, then pulled it wide.

12

Saturday, 12:07 p.m.

After three hours of torture, and however independent and self-sufficient she considered herself, Samantha was extremely grateful to see Rick hop down from Major and then walk over to half-lift her out of her saddle. When her feet touched the ground, her legs wobbled. "This, I don't like," she grumbled, grabbing onto his shoulder. Three hours in the saddle, her brain making a geographical survey while her ass chafed – it had better have been worth it.

"Give it a second. Did you like the rest of it?"

Even without her map survey making the excursion necessary, the weather had been brisk, the trees except for the pines starting to turn red and yellow along the outermost limbs, and a trio of deer and a fox had trotted across their path. "Of course I did. It's stunning here. The company ain't bad, either."

Rick grinned. "Good. I like it here, too. More than I realized. Once the west wing and the power and internet are all useable, I think we should spend more time here."

"Because it keeps me away from civilization?"

"Because it's peaceful and a little slower, and because I do want to catalog what's in the attic and move some of the pieces to the Rawley Park museum." He leaned sideways and kissed her. "Agreed?"

"Agreed."

It would be weird, but she couldn't deny that a quieter and slower pace once in a while would probably be good for her. She knew it had to be good for him to relax a little more, as much as he liked making deals, scouting businesses, and being an all-around high-powered bad ass.

Feeling began returning to her legs, and she straightened. "Are you off to go digging through the ruins for missing treasure maps, as well?" Rick asked, shifting his grip to her hand. "I notice Reg didn't waste any time heading that way."

"Nah. I think I'll head back to the attic."

He lifted an eyebrow. "Are you giving up, then?"

Samantha shrugged. "Reggie can do it his way. I've got a couple of other ideas." For some reason Reggie had fixated on the map as being the only way to track down Will Dawkin's treasure, probably because in the long run he thought it would be easier to follow someone else's path than make his own. She happened to disagree with the single-minded approach, but she wasn't about to distract Rick's cousin from his search.

Yule met them at the front door. "Miss Sam, a set of boxes arrived for ye by special delivery. I put 'em in the morning room. "M'laird, ye've something waiting for ye in the morning room, as well."

"Ooh, my ghost hunting gear." Her need for it had shifted a little, but an infrared camera could come in really handy if she went looking for likely hollows or caves in any of those ravines she'd spotted.

"Are we going ghost hunting?" Norway asked from the landing above them. "How exciting!"

Oh, yay. Any distraction in a storm, though, Samantha

supposed. "Well, I figured if there are ghosts anywhere, it would be in a half-collapsed seven-hundred-year-old house. Let me look through the stuff, and maybe we can set something up for tonight. We'll do a group hunt."

Rick sent her a glance that might have been gratitude, then walked into the morning room. Resisting the urge to rub her bottom or do the John Wayne sidle, Samantha followed him to collect her gear.

As she reached the doorway, Rick reappeared. "I had nothing to do with this," he stated, putting his hands on her shoulders and walking her backward. "I swear it. I had no idea."

"What the frack?" she returned, dodging around him. "You're starting to scare me, du—"

She clamped her mouth shut over the rest of the sentence. Halfway back in the room, wearing cowboy boots and a ten-gallon hat, stood a six-foot tall dad bod of a Texan. He frowned as he caught sight of her. "You haven't run off to the big city yet?" he drawled.

"Tom fuckin' Donner," she retorted. "Your lips get chapped from not kissing Rick's butt every day?"

"Children," Rick broke in, moving past her. "What are you doing here, Tom?"

Donner jabbed his finger toward a briefcase on the couch. "Kigomo won't give up his majority shares in Himori Gaming."

Rick frowned. "That was the entire reason I agreed to his price."

"Yep. So no phone, no internet, and forty-eight hours until the deal goes through unless we challenge it. Hence, me here in the Highlands of Scotland."

"Bloody... Okay. Let's go up to my office." Leaning sideways, Rick kissed Samantha on the temple. "I'm sorry. This can't wait."

Okay, she got that. Millions of dollars and Rick's control of a very cutting-edge gaming company at stake, plus a looming dead-line. That didn't mean she had to like having the Boy Scout lawyer around. Blowing a raspberry, she hefted the first of three boxes sitting in the corner and hauled it upstairs. Two footmen arrived at her bedchamber a minute later with the other two.

From the weight and quantity of boxes, Stoney had included an entire ghostbuster, some assembly required. She hoped it was Venkman. Slicing open the first one, she wasn't surprised to see he'd even sent batteries and plug adaptors to go with the cameras, tripods, and digital recorders.

She'd always half believed in luck and good and bad fortune, and after she'd found that bad luck diamond in Rick's stable she considered at least part of the whole paranormal thing proven. The power going out, things falling over for no good reason, the odd sounds and cold spots – it could be age and mice and damp, or it could be something more. Like she'd said, the house was seven hundred years old and settled in the middle of the turbulent Scottish Highlands.

Plus, the hunt might keep people occupied while she did a little more digging. All she needed was somebody to help coordinate the fun so she'd have a little wiggle room for sneaking.

Maybe Donner being here had a bright side, after all. It meant Rick had broken the no sidekicks rule. Samantha sat back. Hopefully Stoney still had a warm coat.

"How the hell did this happen?" Richard slammed the thin stack of papers onto his desk.

"You may think you slipped away from Palm Beach unnoticed," Tom returned, holding his phone over his head and pacing every corner of the room, "but even though the tabloids don't know where you are, they haven't stopped talking about you. 'It's been five days since billionaire Rick Addison and his fiancée vanished. Did they elope?' Goes on every night."

"And?" Richard prompted. For God's sake, there had to be more important things going on in the world.

"I think Kigomo saw all the coverage and figured he'd slip in a clause or two just before the sale deadline. You could cancel your purchase, but only if you file in the next…" He checked the time on his phone, "forty-three hours. Or it goes through as is."

"There's internet down in the village. Let's see what we can get done here, and then drive down to the pub to send some emails and make some damned calls."

"Doing big business in the pub. Not even the good old days were like this."

Richard drew a breath. This was all supremely aggravating, but it could have been much worse. "These are the good old days. Neither of us is old enough to spend our time looking backward yet."

"Yeah, well, you don't have a kid in college. I'm nearly forty, for crying out loud." Finally, Tom gave up on finding a square foot of cellular service and dropped into a chair. "What was in Jellicoe's boxes? Her wilderness survival supplies?"

"Ghost hunting gear."

Tom snorted. "What? Oh, this is better than I even imagined."

"No, it's worse. It's a distraction. She and my cousin are both after a treasure I told them doesn't exist, and she's trying to slow Reg down. Her with spy equipment gives me the shakes on a good day, whatever she claims it's for."

"Well, I need more information now."

"Nope. If I'm not saying anything to Samantha, you can be damned certain I'm not talking to you about it." With a growl he flipped open the folder in front of him and pulled his seat forward. "Let's take care of this, shall we?"

Wincing, Samantha shed her jeans to rub some aloe lotion on the insides of her thighs. She did enough lifts and squats that her leg muscles were only a little tired, but man did that sitting in the saddle thing chafe. Maybe that was why Norway preferred to ride side saddle. Samantha might have listened to an explanation about that, for crying out loud.

Giant band-aids were out of the question, so she settled for a loose pair of sweats. Across the room someone thudded into the closed door, then knocked. "Samantha?"

"Just a sec." Flapping the insides of the legs to encourage the lotion to dry, she waddled over and unlocked the door.

Rick looked her up and down. "Did I miss the good part?"

"Now I know why John Wayne walked the way he did."

He brushed a finger down her cheek. "I've heard that wearing Spanx beneath your jeans helps with chafing."

"I could have used that bit of information a few hours ago, bucko."

"Sorry. Tom and I are going down to The Bonny Lass to borrow their wi-fi. I *will* send him back to Florida as soon as I can."

"I know." She smiled, going up on her tiptoes to kiss him. "I get it. I was there for the two months you guys worked on the Himori deal."

"Thank you for understanding."

Yeah, he might want to hold off on thanking her. "I'll give you a million dollars if you bring me back some Spanx from that dress shop in the village. If they carry Vera Wang, I'm pretty damn sure they have shit to hold in your flab."

"Done." He kissed her back. "We'll be away a few hours. You and your chafed thighs stay out of trouble." He started away, then turned around again. "I put my uncle in charge of the front drive excavation, so he's dealt with. My aunt's in the library, and you know where Reg and Norway are."

She liked that he'd taken up her nickname for the gloriously

Scandinavian Eerika Nyland. "Roger that. I'm going through my spook gear before I do more rummaging in the attic."

Once he headed back downstairs she shut the door again. A couple of hours could be really useful. Damn her chafed thighs. Scowling, she hefted the infrared camera. That gorge she'd spied was a good mile away. She could run it, but the ouch factor made her hesitate.

She was accustomed to weighing the whole risk versus reward thing. Here she knew the risk, but the reward was iffy at best. Rick claimed it didn't exist. She wouldn't even have known about it if Reggie hadn't started bitching.

The Spanx thing did give her an idea, at least. Shedding the sweats, she pulled out the skin-hugging pair of jogging shorts she'd brought along. It took a couple of curse words to get them on, and once she'd managed it she tried a few steps. They rubbed a little, but not nearly as much as the sweats had. She pulled the baggy black sweats on over the shorts because Scotland, then grabbed the infrared camera and went up into the attic.

Before she snagged her handmade maps she carefully opened the door that overlooked a big part of the west wing. Reggie should have realized that Rick wouldn't permit him to search there if that was where the map was, but hey, not everyone could be a criminal mastermind.

She could hear Reggie below, arguing with Norway about something, though their voices were low enough that she couldn't quite make out what they were saying. But they weren't happy, so they definitely hadn't found anything. Good. Because while she was honestly trying to like them, or at least Reggie, the more she heard and saw the less enthusiastic she was about this part of the Rick familia. And coming from her background, she was pretty lenient.

Quietly she shut the door again. Her maps lay across an eighteenth-century gaming table, to which she'd pulled up a Regency-era spindle-backed dining chair. All she needed was a Tiffany lamp or two, and this could be her cozy little office. It had a lot more character than Rick's office space downstairs did.

Working from memory she sketched in the road and pathways she hadn't been able to see from the roof in the dark. Hillsides, a couple of streams, the steep-edged gorge Rick had avoided, thick clumps of trees, rocks, every topographical feature she could recall. Okay. It wasn't perfect, and she didn't have all the tales of Will Dawkin, or his supposed treasure map, to go by, but she did know a lot about the politics of seventeenth- and eighteenth-century Scotland. She also damned well knew how thieves thought. Even oldie moldy ones.

Working through the *Beautiful Villages* book she made a note of which places Will Dawkin had reportedly been seen, or had a drink, or held up a coach, plus who his more famous victims were – or at least the ones the book's author had found interesting enough to mention. When she plotted them out, they centered around Orrisey. He must have been a local, but he'd struck there as often as anywhere else. A local without loyalty, then.

Finally, she stretched and sat back. With some more detailed info about Will Dawkin she would definitely have been able to narrow things down a little more, but unless she could turn up the books Rick had hidden from her, she would have to make do. Going through the history of the area and a couple of limited tourist maps in the village book, she had discovered one thing, anyway: That gorge Rick had skirted, even if it had roused her interest at the time, was a red herring. Several robbers and one other highwayman had been caught there, because it was only accessible from one end. A local highwayman, and one clever enough to vanish into thin air, would not venture in there. Not even to hide something. A good thief always had at least two ways to exit any given location.

Samantha leaned forward again, looking at the half dozen spots she'd circled as being possible locations for hidden treasure.

Each one left a fairly large area to search, but once she saw them in person she'd be able to narrow things down. The—

Something metallic clanked against wood in the near corner of the attic. She picked up the flashlight she'd set beside the camp lantern and flicked it on. Nothing moved. It could have been a mouse or a rat, of course, or the house shifting thanks to the earth being bulldozed out from under it. Or…

Standing, she picked her way over to the corner. Whatever it was had hit the floor and had sounded small. In a tiny clear space, she spied it – a hammered copper bracelet. She had no idea where it had come from, but she retrieved a walking cane and hooked it, lifting it until she could get a hand on it.

It was pretty, but not particularly old, and it really needed a good cleaning. Sighing, she checked her phone for the time, the only thing the magnificent specimen of technology was good for right now. Nearly four o'clock. She put away her maps, pocketed the bracelet, and headed downstairs. The next trick would be finding the time and space to go outside and do some close-up investigating. She supposed she could just tell Rick what she was doing, but that was so against the thief code that just the thought almost made her break out in a rash. Plus, there was no way she was going to let Reggie know anything.

"There you are," Rick said, from the bottom of the attic stairs. "I don't suppose you've uncovered a Rembrandt or a da Vinci."

"Not yet. Just this. It bounced to the floor on its own." She pulled the bracelet from her pocket and held it out. "Something an ancestor wanted you to find?"

He snorted. "More likely something my ancestors were trying to vomit out of the house. It's Patricia's. Or it was."

As soon as Rick mentioned his ex-wife, Samantha grimaced. According to him, he and Patricia had been young and stupid and good in theory, and he'd figured her ease in high society would only help him in his business dealings. That didn't change the fact Rick had married someone else, had asked for someone else to share his life before he'd asked her. Then again, everything had ended badly and Patricia was a complete wreck these days, so points to Rick for having the guts to try it again. And she was *not* Patricia. For one damn thing, she would never cheat on him. Ever. Even when she wanted to knock him around until he told her what he knew about some local legend of treasure.

"What do you want to do with the bracelet?" she asked, shaking herself out of those useless cobwebs.

"I don't care."

"Cool." Taking a step backward, she opened the attic door and tossed the bracelet inside. "It's a regular found and lost up there."

"Mm hm. How's your…bottom?"

"It's not my bottom. It's my thighs and girl parts. I put on my jogging shorts, so it's a little better."

"Good. I bought you three pair of Spanx. The salesgirl nearly fainted when I walked into the shop."

"Thanks. Speaking of pains in my ass, though, where's Donner?"

"Unpacking. I'll need him for at least another day, I'm afraid."

"Which room?"

"The one with the blue wallpaper. Why?"

"Because I've determined that the blue room is the most haunted location in the entire house. We'll be starting our investigation there tonight."

He threw his arm around her shoulders and tugged her against his side. "Don't be too hard on him, please. By showing up when he did, he's likely saved me a couple million dollars and a lot of embarrassment."

She heaved an exaggerated sigh. "Okay. I won't tell him his room is haunted until tomorrow."

Plus, by this time tomorrow she might be asking Rick for a little forgiveness. She could stand to build up some good karma points before then.

13

Saturday, 9:39 p.m.

This was *not* what Richard had envisioned for his evening. On the upside, Samantha's chief crony Walter Barstone had sent some walkie-talkies along with the so-called ghost hunting equipment, so at least they could now communicate inside the house without tromping up and down the stairs. On the downside, t—

"Rick, tilt it up and just a smidge left, will you?" Samantha's voice came over the walkie-talkie, interrupting his thoughts.

Clenching his jaw, he tilted the night vision camera standing in the corner of the portrait gallery in the direction she'd requested. He hadn't said a word about the noises he'd heard there in the dark, but the fact that she'd assigned him this precise space out of all the rooms in the house did not sit well with him. At all.

"Perfect," her voice acknowledged tinnily. "Come on back to Spook Central."

He lifted the walkie-talkie. "We are not calling the formal dining room, 'Spook Central.'"

"Fine. HQ, then. Reggie, your camera's fine. Yule, can you pick up the library tripod and move the whole thing about a foot backward?"

"Aye, Miss Sam."

A pause. "Nice. Now I can see all the bookcases and the doorway. Okay, gang, head back here and turn out the lights as you leave each room."

"Why would spirits care if the lights are out?" Richard asked, sending a last look back at the long, empty hallway before he turned the old-fashioned switch and backed out of the room as it dove into darkness.

"It's not for them; it's for the cameras. Plus, if a ghost tries to form as a shadow, it's easier for them to do it in the dark."

Clearly she'd been watching a great many paranormal television series, because as far as he knew she'd never delved into this sort of thing before. Night vision goggles and walkie-talkies, yes – but not for anything as whimsical as ghost hunting. He rolled his shoulders. The most likely scenario was that this equipment was for something else, but she did have a superstitious streak. If this became her new hobby, then, he would accept it, but he didn't quite feel up to encouraging it. Especially if she meant for him to participate.

"Jellicoe, I'm still in the grand ballroom," Tom's voice came. "And only because my wife likes you. How's the view?"

"Oh, Donner. Yeah, you're good. I forgot you were there."

Richard chuckled. Yes, they each had serious reservations about the other, but lately he'd been detecting an undercurrent of at least mutual respect if not affection in their non-stop battle. With a thief on one side and a lawyer on the other, perhaps that was good enough.

Detouring down a short flight of stairs, Richard met up with Tom as the former Texan wrestled with a hundred-year-old table lamp. "Stop pawing at it like a grizzly bear," he said, and leaned down to pull the delicate chain hanging inside the shade.

"We're really going to spend the night doing this?"

"A few hours, anyway. I'm calling it familial bonding."

"Uh huh. Where are your aunt and uncle?"

"Locked in their room and refusing to come out till morning."

"Your life has gotten really odd over the past year."

With a grin, Richard clapped Tom on the shoulder. "Yes, it has, hasn't it?"

They returned to the dining room to see Samantha sitting in front of the monitor and labeling the four input lines, while Reg had a hand on the back of her chair and leaned over her shoulder, ostensibly to gaze at the four-way split screen. At the other end of the table Eerika looked through the infrared camera and passed her hand in front of the lens.

"That's the kind of familial bonding you wanted?" Tom muttered under his breath, his gaze on Reg and Samantha.

"No, it is not." He moved around to Samantha's other side, leaning down to kiss her on the cheek. "Any shadows or levitating chairs yet?"

"Goodness!" Miss Nyland exclaimed. "If that were to happen, I would perish on the spot!" She set aside the camera. "Do you think we'll actually find anything? This could be very good for my show. Oh, could I have the recordings afterward?"

The hell she could. Samantha shrugged. "We'll see. As to whether we find something, that's not really up to us. Just keep in mind that these spirits, if there are any, are Rick's ancestors. So no calling them names or trying to piss them off to make them show up. You can ask for their help and cooperation, ask them to answer questions or knock on walls or turn on flashlights. We might not hear anything tonight, but with the digital recorders on, we might pick up something anyway. Any questions?"

"How long have you been doing this?" Reg asked, shifting a little as Richard accidently crowded him away from Samantha.

"Just once in a while," she lied smoothly. "I spend a lot of time in old places. We've just accidently found a couple of 'maybes', but put together they kind of add up to 'unexplained'."

"Who's 'we'?" Norway asked, moving over to join them behind Samantha's chair. Sam couldn't possibly like having this many people standing behind her, but she didn't show it. "You and Rick?"

That was not going to be allowed to stand. A hard-charging businessman did not pursue the paranormal unless he wanted to show the world a very large chink in his armor. He did *not* want to read about his penchant for ghost hunting in the tabloid news. He opened his mouth to deny his involvement, but Samantha chose that moment to stand, elbowing him in the ribs as she did so.

"Yeah, right. Rick's only doing this because he doesn't want me wrecking the furniture. I was talking about my adopted dad, Walter. He knows a lot about cameras and photography, and we end up partnering up sometimes trying to figure out how security might have been disabled, stuff like that."

"Ghost hunting is an offshoot of antiquities recovery I would never have expected," Reg put in, "but it does make sense."

"Right, 'recovery'," Tom mouthed, and Richard scowled at him. Good God, this had begun as a quiet, low-stress holiday. Now they were treasure hunting and ghost hunting and Tom wanted to blab about Samantha's criminal past. They'd be lucky if any of them made it out of Canniebrae unscathed.

Samantha had extricated him nearly flawlessly, even if she'd been the one to drag him so close to the edge in the first place – but then he was becoming accustomed to that, these days. The other bit, the quick and masterful defense, was what stopped him for a moment. He needed to stop pushing at her, demanding that she somehow prove she'd left the dark side behind, demanding that she prove she was on his side. Because she *was* on his side. Truly. She'd already proven it, long before today.

He took her hand as the other three divided up digital recorders, EMF detectors, and night vision goggles and cameras.

"I quite adore you, Samantha Elizabeth Jellicoe," he murmured. "You know that, yes?"

She looked up at him, a slow smile curving her mouth. "You're just saying that because you can't get into my pants tonight, aren't you?"

Richard tightened his grip. "Sam." Yes, she liked to jest, and yes, emotions still tripped her up sometimes, but she had to know by now that he would give up everything, including his life, for her.

Samantha faced him, taking his free hand in hers. "I know it," she whispered. "You're my...best thing, Rick. It scares me a little how much I love you."

"What are you two whispering about, over there?" Reg asked. "If anyone means to jump out of the dark and scare me, expect to be punched in the eye."

Ignoring the interruption, Richard brushed straight auburn hair out of Samantha's face, then tilted her chin up and kissed her. Sometimes, just sometimes, the winds calmed and the storm eased, and there she was – not the cat burglar, or the adrenaline junkie, or the puzzle solver or the chaos lover, but just her. Samantha. He lived for all the moments, but especially those.

"People are staring, James Bond," she whispered, twining her fingers with his.

"Let them stare, Xena, Warrior Princess."

Her grin deepened. "You say the nicest things." Finally she sighed and backed away. "Okay, Spengler, Venkman, and Stantz. Let's divide into two groups and get going."

"Who's that?" Eerika asked, pulling the night vision goggles down and with that one question probably dooming any chance of a friendship with Samantha. To not know who the *Ghostbusters* were was to be irredeemably uncool.

Samantha sighed, very quietly. "Nobody. I'll go with you and Reggie. Sorry, Rick, that means you get Donner."

"I'll manage," he said crisply.

Considering that neither Reg nor his girlfriend were particularly pleased with Samantha right now, he had to admire her fortitude. Of course she might have decided to use the opportunity to grill Reg about the highwayman's map – which was fine with him. If they chose to go about chasing their own tails for another week or ten days, he would be able to declare the holiday over and remove Samantha to Rawley Park and the rest of them to wherever they chose to go, as long as it wasn't here.

Even if she did decide to quiz his cousin about highwayman Will Dawkin, without a map and without any idea of the lay of the land it wouldn't do her much good. Hopefully. Reg was greedy and obsessed enough that he likely wouldn't voluntarily share any information, anyway.

"Tom and I will take the ground floor," he said, picking up a torch and his walkie-talkie. Despite Tom's vocal skepticism of this adventure, the attorney was loaded down with enough devices for the two of them, so he didn't bother taking any more himself. One lunatic talking to the walls in the dark would be plenty.

"Sounds good," Samantha returned, hefting one of the infrared cameras. "If anybody falls over something or makes a loud noise, report it. Same if you hear something, so we won't end up investigating each other."

"I had no idea paranormal investigation was so technical and complicated," Eerika commented.

"Just trying to keep everybody from breaking their necks in the dark," Samantha said.

They parted company at the main staircase, while the surprisingly obliging Yule went to keep an eye on the monitor. Richard and Tom headed downstairs to the foyer, the light from their torches bobbing against the old walls and feeling creepy in a way that the semi-regular power outages hadn't managed. "What say we go get a beer?" Richard suggested. "The staff's gone home or turned in early, so we'll have the kitchen to ourselves."

"Listen, I don't even know what day it is right now, but I kinda want to look around first. I mean no offense, but this place is spooky in the dark. Kind of ghosty, really."

"I thought you'd be more put out that Samantha's enjoying it here. I think she's having a better time than I am, truth be told."

Tom shrugged. "Truth be told, the past week's been borderline dull without any of her lunatic shit for me to rant about. But don't you dare tell her that. It's attorney-client privilege."

"That generally works the other way, doesn't it? For the client and not the attorney, I mean."

"Shut up and help me hunt for some ghosts."

☼

SAMANTHA TURNED the infrared camera on Reggie and Eerika, observing as Norway made nervous sounds and kept her hand wound into the back of her boyfriend's jacket. It dawned on her that Eerika acted just like a shallow, dimwitted, bimbo blonde from some 1980's television show.

She didn't miss a beat, really, from the lack of familiarity with popular movies to the obsession with shopping to her helplessness and reliance on big, strong menfolk to protect her, to the way anything technological was clever and marvelous and far beyond her ability to decipher. If they'd had internet, Samantha was pretty confident that Eerika would be a wiz at texting and twittering and instagramming. Even without cell service she'd taken about a hundred thousand selfies in four days. The Viking wanted to be a reality show character so badly she'd turned herself into one.

From the few conversations Samantha had had with Reggie, *he* wasn't stupid. Rick-light, maybe, but in most circles that could still be pretty impressive. For him to have paired up with Eerika, especially to the point that he'd introduced her to his parents, he had to have found *something* interesting about her. Maybe she was just really good in bed, but for somebody as fame-adjacent as

Reggie was, a good fuck buddy wouldn't have been that hard to find.

What was it, then? Was Eerika's dimness really an act? If so, why? "Let's stop here," she said aloud, deciding the middle of the portrait gallery worked as well as anywhere else. Plus, it was atmospheric as hell. "Eerika, turn on the digital recorder, and we'll ask questions. Leave some space in case anybody answers." That was what they used to do on *Ghost Hunters*, anyway. She'd watched those paranormal shows a lot before she'd met Rick. A couple of times their use of new night-vision tech had come in really handy. And now their spook-hunting tips had, too.

Norway tapped on the recorder, putting her free hand over her chest. "My heavens. I don't know what to say. What if something answers? I *will* faint."

Inwardly Samantha sighed. This would have been easier if Norway had fled to lock herself in the room she shared with Reggie. Since the Viking hadn't, though, Samantha had an idea or two how to make her useful tonight. Now she just needed to prime the pump. "Like this. Can you tell me your name?" She waited a beat. "Did you live here at Canniebrae?" Pause. "Did you work here?"

"Oh, I hope we won't be speaking to chamber maids and scullery girls," Norway broke in. "Do you think we will, Reginald?"

"Servants spend more time at a big house than the owners do," Reggie commented. "If anyone's here, it's probably one of them. One of Aunt Rachel's relatives would be more interesting, though."

"It doesn't even have to be someone who lived here," Samantha added, lowering the camera to make it less obvious she had it pointed at them. "A spirit could be anyone who experienced strong emotions, negative or positive, in the area, anyone with unfinished business or an undiscovered secret, a lost love, a missing child, anything."

The temperature on Reggie's face didn't change, but behind him Eerika's warmed by several degrees. Embarrassment or excitement. Well, nothing embarrassing was going on. Fear, dread, or worry would lower face temperature as blood rushed away from the surface to protect vital organs. Yep, there she was, Sam Jellicoe, lie detector *and* ghost tracker.

"So I can ask anything?" Eerika repeated.

"Sure. Then play back that bit of recording and listen to see if anything shows up." Sam straightened. "In fact, you guys do that, and I'll check out the rest of the room with the thermal camera."

Norway's face got even warmer. Reggie's didn't, so either he didn't share his girlfriend's excitement or he hadn't caught onto it yet. Hm. Samantha figured she'd made it pretty clear that a certain highwayman might be hanging around without just coming out and saying it. If that was what Eerika was reacting to, it was interesting for two reasons: One, Eerika seemed more interested than Reggie; and two, Eerika had figured it out first. Somebody was pretending to be stupid. Probably for dramatic purposes.

She moved away from the pair, panning down the length of the room so she could bite off a short piece of duct tape and put it over the camera's red indicator light. No sense letting them know she was recording them. At the same time, she turned up the camera's microphone sensitivity; they'd probably be whispering their questions, and she could listen to them later.

She gave it about twenty minutes, making a mental note of the time stamp a couple of times when Reggie caught on to whatever had Eerika excited, when their body temperatures rose and fell. Checking the digital recorder would be more para-interesting, but as long as she had the audio on the thermal, their questions and conversation should be there for her listening and viewing pleasure.

"Anything interesting?" she asked, removing the tape covering the recording light. "I got a couple of temperature fluctuations, but old houses have drafts. Nothing I could declare paranormal. Maybe when I go through it again."

"I think I heard a few whispers," Norway whispered, "but I want to listen to it again. Maybe we can do that in the morning. If we find anything, we'll play it for you."

Yeah, like that would happen. If the two of them hadn't just spent the last twenty minutes asking a highwayman ghost where he'd hidden his treasure, she would eat Donner's ten-gallon hat. And the questions they'd asked were the reason she was never going to set ears on that tape. But with the infrared camera's audio, she didn't need their stupid digital recorder. "That would be great. It'll save me from having to watch and listen to everything on my own."

In the deflected glow of her flashlight, she saw Eerika smile. "I'm so glad we're getting on again, Sam. I do want us to be friends."

Samantha decided she was going to have to go along with that, for a while, anyway, if she ever wanted to figure out this mess. Which she did – both because Rick had challenged her, and because she loved unraveling a damn puzzle.

From the portrait gallery they went into the huge ballroom, the music room, the billiards room, and a couple of the long-empty bedchambers. With Norway hearing – or pretending she heard – scary noises in every squeak of every floor board and jumping around like a kangaroo, any self-respecting ghosts would have stayed well away. Especially if they were related to Rick and had any of his common sense and taste.

When she figured they'd been at it long enough to convince squad Reggie that the paranormal investigation was the actual focus of the night, she radioed Rick. "You guys find anything interesting?"

"Tom tripped over an ottoman and nearly broke his neck, but not much other than that."

"Nifty. Let's meet back in the dining room."

"Roger that."

"Thank God," Donner's voice exclaimed, more faintly.

She grinned at the walkie-talkie before she pocketed it again. "Ready, team?"

"Absolutely," Reggie returned. "It's past my bedtime." He picked up the EMF detector and digital recorder and gestured for Eerika to precede them. "I've noticed you and my cousin's faithful companion seem somewhat...antagonistic. Considering Tom Donner's had a stick up his arse since I've known him, please tell me you discovered some horrible secret of his. An affair? A gambling addiction? A drug addiction?"

What *was* the public explanation for her and Donner's antagonism? They'd never really come up with one, and when he'd arrived they'd just taken up where they'd left off without considering what their audience might think. That had been sloppy. And short-sighted. And careless. "Donner's a die-hard Houston Astros fan," she improvised, looking for something stupid but plausible. "I adopted the Chicago Cubs a long time ago." She grinned. "It's American baseball. Do you follow it?"

"Baseball? No."

"Yeah, it's kind of ridiculous, but since the Astros won the World Series he's been a real jerk. I lost a hundred bucks to him because I went with the Dodgers."

"You should've known better," Donner said from behind her, as he and Rick reached the hallway outside the dining room. "And you still haven't paid up."

Oh, so now he was willing to play along. That figured. "I'm not over my shock and disappointment yet," she countered.

"Mm hm."

She pushed open the dining room door to find Yule snoring in front of the monitor. Swiftly she turned around to face the troops behind her. "That was a long evening," she said, a little too loudly. "Whoever wants to do their own re-listening or watching, keep hold of your equipment. Otherwise hand 'em over and I'll go over everything. In a day or two we'll have a ghost busters meeting and share our findings."

"Whether we gathered any evidence or not, that was quite exciting," Norway exclaimed. "I expected every shadow to leap out at us!"

Once she had an armful of equipment, Samantha turned around again to face an awake and alert Yule. "It was kind of slow from our end, Yule. Did you notice anything at all? I know it's hard to watch all the feeds at the same time."

"I didnae notice anything, nae," he said, pushing to his feet. "But I cannae guarantee that nothing got by me."

"Thanks for being a first pair of eyes," she said. "I'll go over everything again whether you noticed anything weird or not, just to be sure."

Donner set his EMF detector down on the table. "Well, if y'all don't mind, I'm going to bed. I have a feeling tomorrow's going to be busy."

"Keep the walkie-talkie on, Tom," Rick said. "I think we all should, at least until we get the wi-fi put in. Let's say channel three."

The attorney hefted his radio. "Ten-four. But for God's sake give me at least an hour or two of sleep."

"I may give you as much as three hours," Rick returned. "Let's say eight o'clock. That's..." He checked his watch, "five hours. We'll meet for breakfast."

"Consider me asleep, then. Good night, all."

"Us, as well," Reggie put in. "We have a full day of recordings to review and exploring to do."

That made Rick clench his jaw, but he nodded. "Good night, then. You as well, Yule. We'll see to this mess tomorrow."

"Aye, m'laird. Good night."

Once they were all gone, Samantha sat to shut down the stationary cameras and disconnect the feeds from the monitor, then make sure all the portable equipment was turned off. When she looked up, Rick was leaning against the wall by the doorway, gazing at her. "What?"

"Yule was asleep, wasn't he? That's why you blocked the doorway and started making all that noise."

"The man gets up at like five o'clock in the morning. This is *way* past his bedtime."

"I wasn't criticizing him for dozing off. It was just a nice gesture. He would have been embarrassed if we'd caught him snoozing."

She nodded. "Thanks." Retrieving her thermal camera and some headphones, she stood again. "Ready?"

"Yes, ma'am. Not all of us are creatures of the night like you are."

"Yeah, well, I'm a lot less nocturnal than I used to be."

Rick slung an arm around her shoulders as they left the room. "And I'm very glad of that. But you're not *too* tired, I hope."

"I have chafed thighs, dude. You can have me from the waist up."

"That's where some of my favorite bits are," he returned, "but that's not what I meant."

"No?" she asked, leaning into his ribs.

"No. In the village I found graham crackers, marshmallows, and chocolate bars. They're up in our bedchamber by the fireplace."

"S'mores? You hunted down s'more fixings?" His art collection fascinated her, his money (and the way he could simply spend it without somebody coming calling to ask where he'd gotten it) made things both easier and more difficult, but the small things, the ones even she could never expect – they were why she'd fallen so hard for him. Why she fell for him every damn day.

"Well, it might have been a little more complicated than that, but yes. I thought it might be a nice way to wind down from a long evening of ghost hunting."

"You just made all my feelings happy."

He smiled as they walked together down the long hallway. "You called Walter the minute Tom showed up, didn't you?"

Okay, she was definitely going to have to come up with some new moves. "Maybe. Did you notice how swell Norway and Reggie and I were getting along?"

"Yes, I did. When does Walter arrive?"

"Sometime in the morning, I would guess."

"Will Aubrey be joining us, as well?"

She shrugged against his side. "I don't know. Stoney thinks I adopted Aubrey without checking all his papers first, so probably not. I could be wrong, though."

"Any idea what we're telling my family Walter does for a living? Other than help you with ghost hunts, of course."

"He's an antiques dealer," she responded promptly. "It's even the truth."

"Technically he's an antiques *fence*. That's not quite the same."

"Yes, it is. Money changes hands, and the buyer gets the goods. But I prefer s'mores to semantics, unless you want to spend the rest of the night lamenting and arguing over my life choices."

He didn't seem to be angry. In fact, he dragged her even closer and kissed her forehead. "Tom said it was too quiet in Palm Beach with us gone."

"He missed us?" She snorted. "He missed *me*?"

"He would eat his own tongue before he admitted that to you, so be nice about it. I figure perhaps Walter feels the same. But when Tom goes, Walter Barstone goes."

"Deal." Freeing himself, she pushed open their bedchamber door. "But first, s'more me."

"With pleasure, my lass."

14

—————

Sunday, 8:19 a.m.

"No. Read that last part to me again," Tom said, his Texas twang intensifying as his frustration increased. He banged the phone's receiver on the desk. "Mansour? Hello?... No, I didn't catch it. I need the last paragraph again."

Across from the desk, Richard sat in the deep window sill of his office and watched the sun edging into the southeastern sky. "Tell him to email it. After breakfast we'll go down to the pub."

"Man—Mansour? No. Just no. Email it. I'll get back to you in an hour or so. Yes. One hour." Grumbling in the nonsensical way he'd mastered since becoming a father – words that sounded profane but weren't – he set the receiver back into its cradle with exaggerated care. "How are you so calm? All this crap should be driving you crazy."

"I was actually thinking that you've taken to the country life about as well as you expected Samantha would." Richard straightened. "Don't mistake me, though. Kigomo annoyed me. I don't mean to allow him to get away with it."

"Now that's what I wanted to hear. Lead the way to the breakfast room, because I couldn't find it with a compass."

That explained why he'd found Tom this morning talking to himself outside the billiards room. Canniebrae had never been particularly disorienting to him, but then he'd grown up spending time there. He did recall thinking as a young boy that the place featured an endless number of doors and rooms to explore.

Samantha, of course, had figured out the layout almost immediately. Whatever arguments there were for nature versus nurture, she, the way her mind worked, was a marvel. He didn't think he would ever tire of trying to figure her out.

"Honestly," Tom said as they walked, "with the electricity and the phones and the wi-fi and the internet as they are here, I don't know how either of you have been able to stand it. The—"

"What?" Samantha said, as she emerged from the breakfast room, a can of diet Coke in one hand. "You can't hack it here, Donner? Ready to flee to London?"

"I'd just like to point out that *you're* not trying to save a two-billion-dollar deal," the attorney retorted.

"Nope. I'm ghost busting." She hefted the camera in her other hand. "I'll be in the attic if you need me." Stretching up, she gave Richard a soft peck on the lips. "Take your walkie-talkie with you when you go into the village. It should have just enough range."

"So she's hiding out in the attic like Mr. Rochester's looney wife?" Tom commented, eyeing the two of them.

Samantha laughed, the sound floating back over her shoulder as she headed away. "That's me, Bertha Mason Rochester. Points to you for knowing your Charlotte Bronte."

As she turned the corner and vanished, Tom led the way into the breakfast room. "Katie actually forced me to sit through the Michael Fassbender movie," he confessed.

"It still counts," Richard returned, trying to decide when, exactly, he'd gone from being troubled by the animosity between Tom and Samantha to being amused by it.

"And why is Jellicoe hanging out in your attic?"

"That's where all the good stuff from the collapsed wing was stored, plus at least one Gainsborough and God knows what else that's ended up there over the years. She's cataloguing." Which was fine, except that she'd more or less declared that she meant to go after the highwayman's treasure. If she'd given up, it was the first time he could recall her doing so. If she hadn't given up, though, what *was* she doing in the attic? He wanted to go take a look, but the damned clock was ticking on the Kigomo deal. Richard was generally fine with multitasking, but this was getting ridiculous.

And then it got worse. Yule hurried into the room. "M'laird, there's a man at the door. He claims to be here to see Miss Sam, but..."

"Is he a large black man?" Richard asked. "Short hair graying at the temples, and a scar through his left eyebrow?"

"Aye, m'laird."

"Walter?" Tom mouthed.

Richard nodded crisply. "Show him up to Samantha in the attic. And he'll need a room."

"Aye, m'laird." Yule started out of the room, then paused again. "I'm nae certain what to make of him, m'laird. He's dressed like an Eskimo."

If he didn't explain Walter, rumors and speculation would flood the house. "He's Walter Barstone. Samantha's adopted father." He sighed. "He's family. Family who doesn't like the cold."

"Of course, m'laird."

Oh, this was just perfect. He'd be out of the house for a good part of the day, giving Samantha plenty of time to tell Walter everything she knew about the highwayman treasure and enlist her cohort's assistance in tracking it down. Which meant that now he was going to have to decide how far he was willing to let this go, and what he was willing to do to put a stop to it. And whether he needed to bring anyone else in on his side.

As far as he knew Reg and Miss Nyland were digging through

the ruined wing again, though he supposed eventually even his cousin would have to realize that either the map didn't, in fact, exist any longer, or it wasn't where he thought it was.

"All in all," Tom asked, "are you wishing you'd stayed in Palm Beach?"

"Not so far, but that could change." Soon, actually.

○

SAMANTHA LEANED CLOSER to the camera's monitor, as if that would make the volume on the headphones go above ten. Norway might be smarter than she let on, but the woman had the investigatory skills of a moose, at least where asking questions to empty air was concerned.

"Is Will Dawkin here?" came faintly to her ears, followed immediately by, "Let's listen back and see if he answered," followed by five repeats of her slightly garbled question from her recorder.

"Patience, Sam," Samantha breathed, resisting the urge to forward the camera's recording. This bit was only twenty minutes. She just hoped it wouldn't be twenty minutes of listening to the same two questions rewinding over and over.

"Will Dawkin, if you're here, please make a sound for us." Pause. "Did you hear anything, Reginald?"

"No. Play it back."

Samantha knocked her head against the chest of drawers.

The request repeated. Twice. "I don't hear anything," Eerika commented quietly.

"Should we ask Sam if we're doing it correctly?"

"Oh, yes, and while you're at it, ask her if I'm wearing greedy colors tonight or not, why don't you?"

"Move past it, Ree. She's American; they're all rude." He paused, the warm red and yellow blob of his form leaning toward his girlfriend. "Are you recording that?"

"Oops. How do I erase something?"

That went on for at least a minute, so Samantha popped the top of her soda and took a drink of diet Coke. They thought she was rude. Hah. She'd been going more for fresh-faced and forthright, but rude was close enough where these two were concerned. If they cared to become acquainted with her any more deeply than she did with them, she'd eat a cobweb. Usually watching and learning about people kind of fascinated her, but she knew these guys already, or at least their type. They were the sort she most enjoyed robbing.

"Sam, this is—"

She jumped, yelping, as the dark figure topped the stairs behind her. In the same swift heartbeat she recognized the form, paused the playback, and slipped out of the headphones before she rolled to her feet. "You came!"

"Of course I came. I'm not happy about it, but... Is that a Bernini?" Stoney veered sideways, pulling out his phone and flipping on the flashlight as he leaned down to examine the white marble bust.

"Yep. Louis the Fourteenth. I found a Gainsborough a couple of days ago."

"I'm telling you, kid, if you ever change your mind about this guy we could buy a country with the proceeds."

"Not changing my mind." Once Stoney straightened she hugged him, then pointed him toward the chair she'd vacated. "I have a story to tell you, and then I need your help."

He eyed her as he took the seat. "What kind of help?"

"A heist. Maybe."

"Honey, don't get me all excited if you're just going to crush my hopes again."

She perched on the edge of the chest of drawers and told him about the highwayman thing, from Reggie's nastiness over a reportedly non-existent map to Rick's line in the sand and the missing books from the library, to the maps she'd made and her ploy to sneak clues off of Reggie and Norway last night.

"Show me what you've sketched out," he said when she'd finished.

Samantha dug out her map pages and handed them over. "You agree with me, then? There's something out there?"

"Addison tells you everything. If he knew for a fact nothing existed, he'd have a story about how he looked and found nothing. By my thinking he found something, and for some reason he doesn't want his cousin – or his own wife-to-be – to know what or where it is. Ergo, it's illegal and it's valuable."

Samantha had walked down the same path, but she'd stopped short of that ending. "Rick might be sketchy but outright illegal's pushing it, don't you think?"

"Look in the mirror, honey. Are you sketchy, or illegal? He's kept who you really are secret from his own family."

"He's more just fudged some of the details."

Because he was Stoney he'd kept his voice low for the entire conversation, but there were still enough greedy, prissy ears around here that she couldn't help glancing over her shoulder. She might not have a bounty on her head, but some of the pieces she'd liberated had hefty return rewards. If someone did turn her in, it would probably end up being pretty lucrative for him or her or them.

"How accurate is the topography?"

"Pretty accurate. I went horseback riding for three hours yesterday so I could take a closer look. I cross-shaded the sections I haven't been able to verify."

"You've got what, six possible locations for burying something?"

"That's as far as I could narrow it down from the one look – presuming he didn't just shove the goods under a fallen tree some-where and they've washed down into the loch." That was possible,

193

she supposed, but it didn't fit with Rick's current secrecy and annoyance. Aside from that, Will Dawkin seemed to have been a competent thief, so fallen-logging didn't make sense. "I'm listening to a recording right now, but all I've gotten so far is the urge to barf."

Stoney lowered the pages to his lap. "Are you really going after it, then? And what if you find it?"

Samantha grimaced. "I don't have to have an answer for that yet, do I?"

"You're really asking me that?" he retorted. "You never go in without a plan to get out."

"This isn't Fort Knox," she retorted. "And I'm thirty percent sure the treasure isn't even a real thing. So give me a frickin' break."

"Uh huh. Then I flew overnight from Florida, took a tiny plane to some no name airport, and then hitched a ride into the middle of nowhere with a guy carrying sheep in the back of his truck, just so I could help you dig into something you might not want to dig into even if we track it down? Or am I your token underworld character because your boyfriend brought Donner in after he said he wouldn't?"

"Isn't it enough that I'm a little...confused morally, so I called you for back-up?"

He eyed her. "Excuse me, but in this new chapter of your life, the one where Rick Addison is your white knight, doesn't that make me the Dark Side? The Darth Vader of your little tribe?"

"Oh, please. You've always been my Yoda."

"I'm not here to talk you into doing evil, then?"

That made her frown, mostly because in a way it was kind of true. "Nope," she said anyway. "It's just a tangle, and I need you to machete me into the open. Plus I have a lot of ghost hunting audio and video to go through, and you like that stuff." She tagged him lightly on one muscled shoulder. "Plus I'm outnumbered by posh, and I missed you."

With a loud sigh he set her maps aside. "Fine. Do you have any idea where the billionaire stashed those books? Having them to look through would narrow down your potential treasure spots by a lot, I would imagine."

"He put 'em somewhere he figured I would never think to look. But it's a big house with a shit ton of obvious but not obvious places to put a couple of old books. Do you want to look for those or finish going through the highwayman séance tapes?"

"Séance. I'll do the rest of the recordings, too, and whatever else you brought up here, so it looks like you were actually doing an investigation, and not tricking people into talking about a treasure so you could record them."

"Thanks, Yoda." She kissed him on the cheek, moved her diet Coke closer by his elbow, and gave him her walkie-talkie. She would have to snag Donner's, but he and Rick were practically joined at the hip, anyway.

Rick and Donner were still in the breakfast room when she found them. For a second, she thought about just picking the attorney's pocket and going on her way. He already thought she was a one-woman crime syndicate, though, and she hated giving his theories more fuel. "You guys still going into Orrisey?"

"We are," Rick returned, reaching for her hand as she stopped beside him. "Walter found you?"

"Yep. He's helping go through the ghost tapes. I need the monitor for the cameras, though. May I borrow your walkie-talkie, Donner? Pretty please?" He'd probably make her say that last part anyway, so she headed him off.

He pulled it out of his coat pocket and handed it over. "You scare me when you're polite like that."

She flashed Rick a grin as she turned back for the stairs. "You're just saying that to try to get me to be nice to you. It won't work." As she ascended she switched the radio two frequencies up to avoid including Reggie and Norway, and Rick, in her conversation with Stoney. "I'm on air," she said, lifting it. "The others are two below this, if we want to go public."

"Roger," Stoney's voice came back to her. "Good hunting."

"You, too. Lemme know if you catch anything interesting."

"Bring me some scones or something next time you head up here. Last meal I had was airplane pretzels and some gum from the sheep guy."

"Ten-four."

Lady Mercia – Samantha still wasn't ready to call her "aunt" yet, even if it had been offered – hadn't made it into the library yet this morning, so Sam made another circuit of the bookshelves in case Rick had just moved the highwayman books he considered pertinent to her search. This didn't seem like a place she wouldn't check, though, and she wasn't surprised not to find them.

She would have been out shopping with Norway when he moved them, so they could literally be anywhere. At least if she'd been in the attic she would have had one place she could eliminate. But no, she could have been sitting on them up there, for all she knew --- except that he knew she was digging through all that stuff. Rick liked taking chances, but they had to have a logic to them. Given all the more likely hiding places, she didn't think he would have risked dumping them up there.

Where the hell, then, would he think she was unlikely to look for a pile of books she really wanted to find? It wasn't like there was a room filled with glass-eyed antique dolls in the house...she hoped. Shuddering, Samantha went one door past the library, peeked in at extra chair storage, and backed out again. Too easy.

What, did Rick think she just wouldn't notice? Or was she overthinking how sneaky he would be about it? Maybe they were just under a couple of unused chair cushions.

She could do without the additional info the books would provide, but that would mean additional time spent on outdoor treasure hunting. Rick would know what she was up to – and Reggie might figure it out, too. The more she could narrow it down on paper first, the better.

Okay. Rick logic. Tricky, but with sound reasoning behind it.

According to him, the last place she would look would be Donner's room, but the lawyer hadn't yet arrived when the books vanished. Reggie and Norway's room? Nah, he wouldn't put more information in his cousin's reach even if Reggie thought all he needed was the map. His aunt and uncle's room? Rick was a proper Brit. Proper Brits didn't sneak stuff into the rooms of their elders.

Their room? That would be kind of...clever, really. Huh. The odds were against it, but it would be totally easy to search – especially now, with Rick headed down to the village.

Feeling kind of stupid, Samantha headed up the hallway, climbed the stairs, and slipped inside the room she shared with him. She closed and locked the door, because no way did she want to get caught tossing her own room.

"Okay, Sam," she muttered, rubbing her hands together and blowing out her breath. "Let's make this quick, and never speak of it again."

Sinking onto her hands and knees and then lowering to her stomach, she flipped up the bed skirt to look beneath the nose-bleed-high piece of furniture. Without her phone light she wouldn't have been able to see all the way back, but other than a sack and some dust bunnies that probably dated back to the Highland Clearances, it was just a lot of space.

They'd both unpacked into the old wardrobe and chests of drawers, with the suitcases relegated to what used to be the formal dressing room with its old hat boxes and dressing table and chair and more old shoe boxes. She went through her drawer, then Rick's, then went into the dusty dressing room and opened their suitcases. Nada.

The one bookcase in the bedchamber had more knickknacks than books on it, but she checked there, too, just in case. "Dammit." Grumbling, she stomped back into the dressing room to shove the suitcases back into their corner, then sat in the single dressing chair.

This was getting embarrassing. If she couldn't outfigure Rick in the "hiding goods" department, maybe it was a good thing she was mostly retired. Or had being mostly retired for the past year dulled all her instincts? Either way, this sucked.

"Stupid, stupid, stupid." Next, she'd be on her hands and knees digging through the boxes of mildewed ostrich feather hats and shit and yowling at the moon.

Wait a minute. Narrowing one eye, she looked at the uneven stacks of round hatboxes. She liked antiques, but moldy old hats didn't much interest her at all. Unless they'd been carefully stored and preserved, hats in cold damp just turned into lumps of blech. Pursing her lips, she toed the top box in a stack of three.

It wobbled, then tipped over. A damp-looking straw hat with fake flowers that had probably once been silk daisies plopped onto the floor. Great. Now she was going to have to clean that up. Even so, she'd committed now. Using her foot again, she pushed the next one down. At the least knocking over stacked things helped her push back against her frustration. If Rick got the idea that he could outmaneuver her, well, that would be setting a very bad precedent.

The bottom box wouldn't tip, so she shoved off the lid with her toe. Then she stared at the contents for a good, long minute. *Bingo.* Pushing a fist straight up into the air, she slid down the front of the chair to sit her bottom on the floor. Five books. *Legends of the Scottish Highwayman, A Dangerous Occupation, In the Shadow of Balmoral, The History of Highway Robbery,* and *Stand and Deliver: A Guide to History's Lawbreakers.*

Swiftly she set them aside, then closed the empty box so she could stack the other boxes back on top of it. Even the yucky straw thing only made her wipe her fingers off on her jeans. The books she bundled into her spare jacket before she retreated with them back to the attic.

"Found 'em," she said, setting her bundle down on a side table.

"That's good, because most of the audio on your thermal

recording is pretty spooky messed up," Stoney returned, straightening to flex his arms. "I think you found a ghost. Where's my scone?"

Her heart beating a little faster, Samantha picked her way through the mess of antiques to where Stoney sat. "I'll get you a sandwich in a minute. Ghost first."

"Yeah, well, I'm not ready to swear in court what it is," he said, "not that you'd ever find either of us in a court, but it's... Well, take a listen for yourself."

He backed the thermal recording up to seven or eight minutes after she'd stopped her own review, then handed her the headphones. Once she'd adjusted the small playback screen so she could see it, he reached over and hit play.

On one side of the screen Reggie and Norway sat side by side, her right hand up as she held out the digital recorder. "Is it true, Will Dawkin, that no one has ever found your treasure?" Norway asked, then paused. "Yes or no, is it hidden in a cave?" Another pause. "In a tree stump? Under a r—"

The low rumble at the edge of Samantha's hearing unsettled her. "Jesus."

"I nearly fell out of my chair," Stoney said. "Did you make out any words?"

"I definitely heard something." Rewinding it, she turned up the volume, putting both hands over the earphones.

"Leave me alone," she heard, low and soft. "Not for you." Then the audio went out completely for a couple of seconds before it popped back in.

"Wow," she murmured.

"What did *you* hear?"

She looked over at Stoney. "I got 'leave me alone' and 'not for you'."

"Huh," he returned. "I heard 'leave me my gold' and 'Nosferatu'."

Samantha squinted one eye. "Well, they're similar, but I don't see why an old spirit would say the name of a 1922 horror film."

"Maybe he's a fan," Stoney said dryly. "Or it's audio matrixing, and we really just heard nothing but your stomach growling."

"Yeah, so loud I blew out the audio." She snorted. "Norway's going to flip out when she hears this." And somehow that had become the best part of all this – the idea of scaring Eerika so badly she would go fleeing down the front drive in her expensive shoes. Samantha had set up this whole ghost tracking thing so she could spy on Reggie and Norway. The fact that she'd actually found evidence of something was pretty damn awesome.

"Norway?"

"Rick's cousin's girlfriend. Eerika Nyland. You'll get it when you see her as something other than heat blobs. Very Scandinavian." She tapped the camera. "Did you find anything else?"

"Not yet. I had to listen to that one thing about forty times. You check the books, and I'll keep going with this. I'm past your spy cam work, and I have a couple of notes for you, but I want to know if anything else stopped by to chat."

"Deal. I'll get another pair of headphones so I can at least listen to Rick's digital recorder while I read. Plus, I owe you a sandwich."

"If we find a highwayman's loot, you're going to owe me more than that. And if that spook comes after me, I'm going to make it my business to haunt you for getting me killed in the world's coldest place."

She could totally argue that Scotland in September was not the coldest place on Earth, but Stoney was cranky enough already. "Got it. Sandwich, hold the spooks."

Wow. Now she had a maybe warning that was probably aimed at Reggie and the Viking and that could easily be interpreted to be about the treasure, and she had enough information on hand that she would hopefully be able to at least halve her search area. Time to do some reading.

15

Sunday, 12:12 p.m.

"I'm getting all dirty, Reginald," Eerika said, dropping the crow bar she held and putting her left hand around her broken right pinkie nail as if that would mend it again. "And I didn't see a nail salon in Orrisey. This is stupid."

"It's not stupid. Your nails are rather ridiculous anyway, don't you think? How do you even use your phone?"

"That's what the stylus is for." She sniffed. "And don't be angry at me because *you* can't find anything. We've torn up every floor board in this entire room. The map's not here."

"Oh, it's here." Reginald tossed his hammer aside. "It's just not *here*. He moved it."

Using the back of one filthy hand to swipe blond hair out of her eyes, she frowned at his backside. "Then why are we still ripping up floorboards, for heaven's sake?"

"To make certain it's not here."

"Now you're being ridiculous, Reginald. You told me—"

"I told you there was money and fame here that Ricky could

only claim if he got to it first. He hasn't done so. Which means I will."

"How do you know he hasn't?"

Reginald straightened, his slightly bland features forming into a pleasant smile that made him look more like his cousin. "Two reasons. First, Ricky can't keep his purchases and discoveries to himself, especially if they're rare and valuable. He'll do an interview with some magazine or newspaper or something to explain what perfect taste he has, and why he's saved some old stick figure from historical obscurity. But there's never been a whisper about Will Dawkin's treasure. Second, he's extremely worried that we're looking about in here. He nearly threw a tantrum when he found me in here the other day, and then he actually offered me money to stop searching. The—"

"He offered you money?" Eerika interrupted, trying to keep the annoyance from her voice. "How much money?"

His smile sagged a little. "He didn't name a figure. What do y—"

"Reginald," she cut in again, bending down to pick up her crowbar and gratified to see his attention on her chest as she straightened once more. "I could do an entire series around an unexpected windfall. Money doesn't have the same ring as highwayman's gold, but it might work. We'd have to change the name of the show, of course, but I'm not married to *Booty Queen*, anyway."

He took the crowbar out of her fingers, then straightened to give her a soft kiss. "I like *Booty Queen*. But Rick's charity money wouldn't be enough. I negotiate price against product for a living. Trust me. Finding the treasure wouldn't be charity. It would be mine. Ours. As would all the publicity we get from digging up Will Dawkin's treasure."

Stifling her sigh at the fragile egos of men, she furrowed her brow in the pout she'd been told was her second most attractive expression. "Darling, *Booty Queen* only happens if we find the map." She sniffed. "I am getting impatient, Reginald. I don't know how many more times I'll be able to tolerate going shopping with that woman."

"Eerika, I will find it for you. The map and the treasure." He kissed her again, this time on the forehead. "I promised you a treasure, and I promised you that this would be the thing that moved me so far beyond being just 'the other Addison, you know, not Richard', that *he'll* have to make an appointment to see *me*. And that producer friend of yours will have to make an appointment to see you, because you'll be busy being a star."

Well, he sounded very certain of that. At the best she could be married to the famous Reginald Addison and he could be married to the even more famous Eerika Nyland. At the least it would be nice not to have to go to the bother of pretending he was Richard Addison when he climbed on top of her. Folding her frown into a smile and stepping closer to rub her chest against his, she took his free hand. "You make me wet when you talk like that. It's just that you've been promising me that highwayman's treasure for weeks. I want it. I want it now. I want to see you tell your cousin you found it. I want that tiny rude woman to know she settled for the wrong Addison cousin. And I want all the fame that comes with it."

"You make me hard when you talk like *that*," he said thickly. "What say we go take a shower and wash all this dirt off each other, and then figure out why Ricky's American has been spending so much time in the attic? Especially when Ricky claims she finds lost things that are worth large piles of money?"

Thank Christ. She'd been nudging him toward the idea of using the American's claimed expertise for the past two days. It had become clear to her almost immediately that all Reginald had was a theory and a vague idea. She'd sharpened it as best she could, but they had a limited amount of time here, and with the months she'd invested in Reginald she required a payoff. A very lucrative one. That was what she'd been promised, after all. If Sam

Jellicoe was capable of providing it, then she must be convinced to do so. There didn't appear to be any other option.

Her mother had always said that a man with possibilities and no ideas needed a woman with intelligence and ambition. Reginald was that man, because the little American already had her claws into the good Addison. And by God, Eerika Eunice Nyland was that woman.

Ö

LIGHTNING SLASHED across the windows along the front wall of The Bonny Lass. The sky had been lowering all morning, and according to Jamie MaCafferty, the pub's owner, they were in for a bit of a blow. By Highlands standards that could well mean something apocalyptic.

The lights flickered overhead. It could also mean the end of their internet and wi-fi. Tom glanced over the screen of his laptop, then went back to typing. Generally the two of them would be pacing, contract revisions in hand, while someone else typed up changes for immediate review by the other party involved. These were not normal circumstances, and as thunder rumbled again Richard had the distinct impression they were running out of time.

"Do you have it?" he asked. "I'll still step in to purchase Himori Gaming, but if that bastard Kigomo stays on, my offer shrinks to four hundred million because of the impediment his presence will cost my business and my reputation. Let's see how their board likes that."

"You're sure they won't just back out of the whole deal? A hundred seventy million is a lot to lose in exchange for keeping one bastard on the payroll."

"They can't afford to back out. That's the problem when a company puts all its resources behind a billion-dollar enterprise that gets a unanimous 'worst game of the year' vote."

"Yeah, Rick Addison swoops in and suddenly your company will be working on a Godzilla VR game for his girlfriend."

Richard grinned. "I am not making anyone work on anything. I am going to run the next big game idea by your children before I sign off on it, though. There will be no *Slip and Slime 2.*"

"And thank God for that. I've never heard so much whining about how many hockey goals my kids had to make before they earned enough points for ladder steps to climb a slide or some such crap."

"Less complaining. More typing."

"Don't worry. Mrs. Prendergast didn't give me an A for being the slowest typist in typing class."

Richard pushed to his feet. "There'll be a mug of mulled cider and cinnamon whisky waiting for you to hit Send."

"I'm getting there. Go away."

He'd been planning on that, anyway. The pub was nearly empty at the moment, with just Jamie and a couple of old timers in the far corner playing darts. Richard strolled up to the long bar.

"What can I get ye, m'laird?" Jamie asked.

"Two mulled ciders with cinnamon Benedictine, if you please."

"It's a good day for it, I reckon."

Richard leaned an elbow on the bar. "My cousin's been a little curious about some of the old legends since he came to visit," he said quietly. "I've been putting him off, but he may decide to go digging. Is there anything new I need to make him avoid?"

The pub's owner squinted one eye. "If ye've come here to allow trouble, all these villagers will wish ye'd left us abandoned."

"I think you know I have Orissey's best interests in mind. Be patient and I'll attempt to do the same."

"I keep to that very same philosophy, m'laird. But I'm one lad. There are those a wee bit more worried than I am. You giving yer word and all."

Clenching his jaw, Richard nodded crisply. "I will do my part. If things move beyond my control, I will let you know." At least at this moment Reg was clomping around so loudly that no one but Richard and Stoney had any idea Samantha was the real threat. But he still needed to stop both of them.

Jamie inclined his head. "I appreciate that. Here lately or nae, ye've done well by us, m'laird. At least most of us think so." He set the mugs on the bar top.

"Then most of you are welcome." Picking up the mugs, Richard returned to the table. "Sent?"

"Just. I added another forty-eight hours for final signatures, because Scotland."

Which also meant Tom would be staying for at least another forty-eight hours – which meant Walter Barstone would be about for at least that long, as well. Businesswise it made sense. It was all playing hell with his blood pressure, though.

Tom sipped from his mug. "You could just let this go."

"No. People don't get to alter the rules midway through a game in the hopes that I'll leave my marbles and go home. It sets a bad precedent."

"I get it. I'm just saying you c—"

The lights flared and went out.

"Well, that's that," one of the old-timers drawled. "Wife willnae like sitting alone in the dark." The three men got up, put on heavy slickers, and left the tavern.

"We may as well go, too, before the road washes out." Richard handed over the waterproof case as the attorney shut down his computer.

"Do ye want me to send word up when the internet's back?" Jamie asked, walking over to collect the used plates and glasses.

"Please do. I imagine we'll have at least one more day of this."

"Ye help us honor our way of life, and I'll keep welcoming ye back, m'laird."

No, that didn't sound odd at all. "I'll hold you to that," Richard said for good measure.

Outside they hurried through the driving rain to the jeep and jumped in. "I think Scotland might hate us," Tom noted.

"Scotland doesn't care," Richard replied, putting the wipers on what Samantha termed "ludicrous speed". Living most of the year in Florida meant being accustomed to heavy rain and the occasional hurricane. Here, however it also meant steep terrain, muddy roads, and overrun streams cascading down mountainsides.

If he hadn't been keenly aware that he'd left Samantha at Canniebrae with his relations and her literal partner in crime, he would have been tempted to put himself and Tom up at one of the bed and breakfasts that had sprung up in the village since *Braveheart* and the *Outlander* had made the Highlands so popular with tourists.

"How are you helping them honor their way of life?" Tom asked. "By buying drinks?"

"Technically I own the village," Richard said, wondering how many twisted tales he could hold onto before it gave him a stroke. "Or the land it's on, anyway. I keep the rent low, and Orissey becomes the second quaintest village in the Highlands." That sounded fairly straightforward, at least.

"Gotcha. When I leave," Tom said, doing a valiant job of trying not to look terrified as they skidded up the road, "how are you going to work it with Barstone?"

"I won't work it with Barstone. I'll work it with Samantha. She knows you came up here because you had to. You leave, he leaves. That's the deal."

"And if she doesn't agr—"

"That's the deal," Richard cut in. "I have every confidence that she concurs."

"Yeah, well, I'm glad you're confident, but I'd be even happier if you slowed down a little."

Richard took a breath. Yes, every moment that went by with Samantha digging into highwayman legends, especially with

Walter there to help her, did make him a little keener to get back to Canniebrae. At the same time, the man sitting beside him was a husband and a father. He eased his foot off the accelerator.

"Thanks."

"As convinced as you are that Samantha will be the death of me," Richard pressed, "she's a huge incentive for me to remain alive and healthy. That's the only way I'll be able to keep up with her."

"I ain't gonna argue with you while you're driving," Tom drawled.

Just as well; the attorney would never win that fight. But it did remind Richard of that other problem waiting back at the house for him. "If I wanted to write someone a substantial check, say," he began, picking through his words, "how much do I have to hand?"

Whatever bee had gotten into Reg's bonnet, his cousin hadn't shown any inclination to give up digging for buried treasure. Reasonably, the only way to counter a treasure hunt was with money. Enough money to convince Reg that it was no longer worth his time to continue digging, whether an actual treasure existed or not.

Tom sat up straighter. "Wait a minute. Just who are you buying off? Because if it's Jellicoe I might be willing to chip in a little of my own money."

"It's not Samantha, for God's sake."

"Okay, okay. A man can dream, can't he?"

"How much?"

"You've got some cash flow tied up with this Himori deal because the numbers keep changing," the attorney mused. "And I'm not your accountant. But off the top of my head I'd say you've got about two million to play with if you don't want to bother with shifting funds or cashing out assets."

Two million. When he brokered deals for high-end cars Reg likely made seven or eight thousand dollars. An offer of a million or two in exchange for not digging up floorboards and chasing a two-hundred-year-old rumor seemed more than fair. The question was if offering anything substantial would convince Reg that the treasure was real and that it was worth more than the bribe.

"Do you need me to write up an agreement or something?" Tom asked.

"Not yet. This is a little tricky. Another reason Rawley Park might have been a better location for this holiday."

"Just don't blame me. I only suggested the two of you go somewhere remote and maybe out of Jellicoe's comfort zone."

"If I'd known Reg was still obsessed over something none of us have even mentioned over the past eighteen years, I would have decided differently." As for Samantha's comfort zone, he hadn't yet found the edges of that, either.

"You know, I'm a pretty good lawyer. If you tell me what you need, I might actually be able to help you."

"I appreciate that. It's not my tale to tell. I gave my word."

"It's been eighteen years? You would have been what, fifteen? Whatever you did or said or agreed to isn't legally binding. Not when a minor is involved."

"Spoken like a true attorney." Richard tapped the brakes as a trio of deer bolted across the road. "It's morally binding. I'll deal with it. It just might take a good portion of that two million."

"Okay. My feelings are a little hurt, but okay."

"*Your* feelings? Just imagine Reg and Samantha's."

"Jellicoe's part of this, too?"

"She's dabbling. I don't know how serious she is about it. Not very, hopefully. Because if she went in full bore she would run circles around Reg, and I wouldn't be able to buy her off." Given the limited visitor population at this time of year, the blame for any treasure discovery would land on his doorstep. Whatever happened would be his responsibility – and with two stubborn, independent people refusing to listen to him and making him scramble to keep some semblance of control, this was maddening.

"You think Jellicoe's here to pull a job?"

"No. Of course not." He grimaced. "Probably not." Not until he'd half pushed her in that direction, anyway.

In fact, now that he considered it, he couldn't conceive a reason why Samantha would have given up on this chase. He'd mostly denied it existed, had refused to give her any information about it, and had then more or less challenged her to do her worst. Yes, he'd seen to it that she had no access to more facts and no real chance, but that didn't mean she'd given up. If she was still hunting, though, she'd certainly been very low key about it.

A shiver ran down his spine. She saw a puzzle and a challenge. She knew nothing about the stakes or the consequences. How much could he even tell her that wouldn't cause him to break his word – or worse, convince her that this was something she couldn't resist?

"We're um, going very fast again."

At Tom's high-pitched protest, Richard slowed down once more. Fifteen minutes wouldn't solve anything one way or the other, unless he ended up dead. And he had other plans.

Just as they stopped at the head of the drive, the sky opened up. Christ. He'd thought it had been raining hard before. Another half dozen degrees colder and it would have been sleet. As it was, every drop stung like ice, and it came down thick as a waterfall. Swearing, he shoved Tom into the foyer ahead of him, and then stumbled in behind.

"Ye've seen some Highlands weather now, I reckon," Yule said, trading Richard's light jacket for a rough towel. "We'll have snow by sunrise. A month early, this year."

Richard didn't doubt it. "Tom, use my office and try to get hold of Mansour. Make sure those last amendments went through. Do it quickly; you know what the power's like here in good weather." In fact, he was surprised they still had the lights on. The house was missing a legitimate excuse to go dark.

"I'm on it," Tom said, and started upstairs.

"Yule, where is everyone?"

"Yer uncle's in the billiards room, yer aunt's reading in the library, Master Reginald and Miss Nyland are in their room, and Miss Sam and the new fella are still in the attic."

Reg wasn't digging up floorboards? If he'd given up looking for the damn map that would solve several problems Richard hadn't anticipated in coming to Scotland, but nothing had been simple or easy so far. There was no reason for anything to change now. He could go see what his cousin was up to, but that would have to wait until after he'd looked in on Samantha and Walter.

"I'll be in the attic," he said aloud. "Have they eaten lunch?"

"Aye, m'laird. Miss Sam brought up a tray of sandwiches an hour or so ago. I *was* about to inquire if they wanted more sodas. I'm glad ye called ahead to have us stock 'em; Miss Sam seems very partial to diet Cokes."

"That, she is," Rick returned, angling for the kitchen. "I'll bring some up there."

He pulled three from the large refrigerator even if that definitely felt like one too many. For as long as he needed Tom about, though, he would be reasonably welcoming to Walter Barstone.

The attic door was closed when he reached it, and he pushed down the handle with one elbow. "Any leaks up here?" he called, raising his voice over the roar of rain hitting the roof just a few feet above his head.

"Just the same one in the corner so far," Samantha returned. They sat in mismatched dining room chairs, Samantha with her feet up on an old gaming table, her ankles crossed. Walter wore headphones, while Samantha's hung down from her neck.

"Still listening to last night's recordings?" he asked, handing out the soda cans before he settled one hip on a mahogany credenza.

She was right about the roof; despite the noise, the only water visible came from the near corner and plopped into a quarter-full metal bucket. Samantha popped her soda top, toasted him, and took a long couple of swallows. "Yep, still listening. You're not gonna believe some of the stuff we found."

"That's true. I very likely will not believe it." He looked over at Barstone. "Did she even give you a chance to unpack?"

"Nope." The fence – or "broker", as he referred to himself – gestured at the duffle bag resting against the stair railing.

Ah. No doubt that would be his so-called "go-bag", like the one Samantha had kept beneath their bed until a few weeks ago. Something always ready, filled with cash, a change of clothes, and whatever else thieves and thief-adjacent people required if they needed to flee quickly.

It did make him wonder what Samantha had told Walter to get him there so quickly and with nothing but his go-bag. "There are some spare clothes and dress jackets in the dressing room at the top of the main stairs, if you get tired of what you're wearing. My relations like to dress for dinner on occasion – which generally means when it's the least convenient for everyone else."

"You're kidding me, right?" the broad-shouldered cross between Hulk Hogan and Diana Ross said, holding one side of the headphones away from his left ear. "I'm not doing formal dining with your relatives just so you can scare their conservative little hides with the big black man."

"That's a bit hostile and Anglophobic, isn't it?" Richard countered, unsurprised. "Whatever their conservative little hides might think, *my* only concern about your presence is that *you* haven't given up the business from which *Samantha* has recently retired."

"Yeah, like I'm the one who's nearly gotten her killed twenty times over the past year."

"It hasn't been more than three or four times," Samantha butted in. "And most of 'em had more to do with my past than Rick's. Or with his present. I know you both adore me, but I'm a bad influence on myself. Stop trying to give the credit to each other."

Richard didn't like giving up the argument, mostly because it was one he would win. Samantha's life might not be as exciting as it was a year ago, but it did have its moments. And she was much, much safer these days. He inclined his head. "Fine. Join us if you like, Walter, and dress as you like. I trust you will be leaving when Tom Donner departs."

"I'll give you one thing. You Brits have the nicest way of telling someone to beat it."

"Yes, we do. I *am* being nice. Remember that." He straightened. "How much longer will you be up here today?"

"Another hour or so. Then we have to go through the stationary camera footage. I figure we'll have something for you guys after dinner. And it's kind of spooky. You should probably tell Norway to take a Xanax."

"And miss out on another stunning performance of abject fear and helplessness? I wouldn't dream of it."

Samantha tilted her head. "You know she's faking it, then?"

He started down the staircase. "Of course I do. Your former line of business isn't the only one where it's useful to be able to decipher people. If she's auditioning for a reality show, she's wasting her time here. You and I have this one covered."

16

Sunday, 2:31 p.m.

S amantha hoped Rick wasn't spending too much time trying to decipher her today, because he would probably be really disappointed. Once the door at the foot of the stairs clicked shut, she stood and pulled the highwayman book from under her bottom. Sitting again, she opened it across her knees to the place she'd marked.

"I am not going down to dinner with you people," Stoney stated, sitting back to finish up the last recording.

"What do you mean 'you people', kemosabe?" she retorted. "I'm pretty sure I stole a diamond tiara from Aunt Mercia's jewelry safe three years ago."

Stoney snorted. "Maybe so, but you marry him and you *are* one of those people. Don't be surprised when someone comes through your window to take *your* nice jewelry."

"They can fucking give it a try. The last guy to break into Rick's house took a Samurai sword to the shoulder." That hadn't been her doing, but she and Rick made pretty good partners. She'd gotten in a couple of good punches, too. Plus, the bad guy's house had inexplicably burned down right after the fight, and even if she hadn't done it, it sent a really strong message to not mess with the Jellicoe-Addison team. Yay, team.

"What's that saying you like so much? 'The good guys have to win every battle. The bad guy only needs one good day—'"

"'As long as it's the right day,'" she finished. "And here's me, still willing to risk it."

He looked at her, a hundred different things – about fifty of which she could decipher – going across his face. "If he can't make you safe, he'd better make you happy," he finally grunted.

"You know he does." However thrilling her old life had been, and it definitely had its moments, this new one seemed much more…open-ended. With a lot less thinking about possible escape routes. And six-foot two-inches of good-looking, well-endowed, sharp as shit Brit to keep her company for the rest of her life – which would last much longer with her not hanging off eaves by her fingertips and dodging Interpol.

"Okay, honey. I get it." Stoney finished off the old can of diet Coke and opened the new one. "But once in a while a really interesting bit of information comes to my attention, and you aren't married yet."

"Stoney, I work with museums now, to find things other people have taken. I get reward money for it. You find me some interesting bits of information about those things, and I'll cut you in."

"Mm hm. You don't want to know anything else, Sam? Not even a rumor about a privately-owned Rembrandt living with the descendants of a Nazi officer, and the other guy who might pay two million to get his hands on it?"

Well, that pulled at something deep in her chest. "I always like hearing interesting things. Especially things about removing ill-gotten possessions from former Nazi households. But that doesn't mean I'll do anything with that information."

"I'm always happy to share a little gossip with my girl."

He looked kind of smug, but since she'd dragged him all the way to Scotland she figured she could afford to give him a little hope. But taking on a job with or through Stoney would entail breaking laws and adding time to her statute of limitations counter. It would also mean the end of her and Rick. There would be no way she would risk involving him, and no way she would risk losing him.

The thing she was doing right now, though, didn't count. If there was a highwayman's treasure the original statute of limitations on the thefts had run out a long time ago, and at this moment she was just unraveling strings of a big knot. She hadn't decided what to do it she *did* figure it out, and if there *was* treasure.

She finished going through the book and then the last two she'd recovered. Now she had some good, multi-sourced info that would help her shrink those circles on her map. Old tales, told and retold until they finally ended up in a couple of different local lore books. Little bits picked up or left out according to the author's preferences. Taken all together, they told the semi-factual tale of a guy's life. For her they also told where Will Dawkin hadn't been, which roads he didn't lie in wait along, which places he was more frequently and most rarely seen. Those holes, the places avoided, meant different things to her than to most other people. The tale between the lines, she'd always called it. They told their own story, and it was the kind of tale she really liked reading.

Once she got the books back into their moldy hat box, it would be time for boots on the ground. Given the sound of Noah's flood currently pounding the roof just above her head, that could take a few days, but at least now she had a pretty good idea that this treasure was real – whatever Rick wanted her to think.

Reggie and Norway were still fixated on finding the old map that had somehow ended up in Rick's possession. Since she'd made her own map, that put her several days ahead of the amateurs. Hell, she would have been embarrassed otherwise. Even if she usually knew an item's location and only needed to figure out a way to get to it and out again, this whole thing was kind of her area of expertise. Rick should have realized that. Then maybe he would have decided just to tell her what was going on. Well, if finding out on her own was the only way to solve the puzzle, she was well on her way.

"Since you won't eat with the group," she said aloud, bundling the highwayman books in a jacket so she could smuggle them back to her room, "will you come down to the dining room about eight so we can premiere the spook show?"

"I'd be more inclined if you would tell me why you're trying so hard to impress them."

Impress them? That was so far from her thinking that it took her a second to catch up. "I asked for this gear so I could do some digging into some dark holes. I *used* it to spy on Rick's cousin about a treasure. I *told* them it was for ghost hunting, so I need to show them ghost stuff. Plus, maybe the things we found will scare the piss out of Reggie and the Viking and make them hesitate to go exploring, so I can maybe figure out where the loot is before they do. Really, Stoney. Sometimes you just don't get me at all."

He grimaced. "I started not getting you a year ago. And no, I don't think staying in our business is the best way for you to stay alive. I also don't think trading it all in for a rich, high-profile guy who collects the same kind of things you steal is—"

"Used to steal," she corrected.

"Fine, 'used to steal', is the best way for you to live a long, healthy, and jail-free life." Stoney paused to wind up the headphone cord. "I do, however, kind of like the plan to slow these guys down. Who knows, after tonight they might just run away back to their own castles and leave you and Addison alone."

There seemed to be more than just a general dislike of snobbery going on here, but then Stoney had to have seen the part of the recording where Reggie and Norway called her rude. Since he'd been the one to help teach her to fit in to whichever social circle got between her and her target, that probably hadn't gone over very well.

As they left the attic she heard Rick's voice in the library. Perfect. "Okay, you go down and tell the butler, Yule, that you need a room," she said to Stoney. "I'll go and put these back." She hefted the bundle of books.

"'The butler'. Okay Lady Rawley."

Cripes. That was – would be – her. "Not yet," she countered. "And don't pretend that you wouldn't totally have a butler if you had room for one. Get going."

Once Stoney headed toward the front stairs, Samantha turned the other direction. Sneaking books back into a room – her room – seemed silly, but Rick had started this game. So yeah, she kind of wanted to find the treasure without him being able to figure out how she'd done it.

At least this time she could just pick up the hat boxes instead of dumping them over. They all still stank of mildew, but hopefully Rick wouldn't leave the books hidden there long enough to let them get ruined. Once she'd stacked the boxes back in their original, semi-precarious position, she closed the dressing room door and returned to the main part of the bedchamber.

She went into the little bathroom with the broken shower and washed the mildew smell off her hands, then nearly peed her pants as she left the loo and looked up to see two figures standing just inside the bedroom door. "I'm glad we're getting along and all," she said, putting her hands on her hips, "but you really should knock first."

"We did," Norway stated, flipping her Scandinavian locks back over one shoulder. "We wanted a word with you. I mean, Reginald wanted a word with you."

Yeah, because Reggie was so clearly the brains of the outfit. "Okay, what is it, then?"

Reggie cleared his throat. "You said your expertise – your job, as it were – is finding valuable stolen or misplaced items."

"That's true. For museums and galleries, usually. Why?"

"I, um, don't know if Ricky's said anything to you about a disagreement we're having, but the crux of it is there's a legend that a highwayman, Will Dawkin, lived in this area, and that he hid a substantial amount of – what do you Americans call it? – loot, nearby. Ricky says it's fiction, but I disagree. I'd like to hire you to help me – us – find it."

Well, shit. Now she would look like a total bitch when she came up with the loot on her own. Or she could team up with them, which would be stupid if for no other reason than that they didn't have a clue, plus Rick would feel betrayed, and he would be right. So bitch column A it was. "I've overheard enough to know that whatever's going on with this, Rick thinks it's a bad idea to look for it. I'm engaged to Rick. So my answer is no."

"You're not interested in taking his royal highness down a peg or two *and* earning ten thousand pounds in the process?" Reggie insisted, his face getting red in the cheeks and earlobes.

It was true that museums didn't pay as well as most of her old clients, but in her heyday ten thousand bucks wouldn't have been enough to get her up in the morning. Yeah, once she'd gone looking for an anatomical dummy on behalf of a sixth grader for a *lot* less, but that had been both a worthy cause and Donner's daughter who'd done the asking. These two weren't nearly as compelling. Or as cute.

"Seriously?" she said aloud. "I don't know about you, but I don't agree to marry someone because I think he's too stuffy and needs to be taught a lesson. No, I'm not going to help you embarrass Rick. Not for any amount of money."

"That's fine," Eerika said, taking Reggie's arm. "Don't get in our way when we find the treasure, then. And don't expect that we'll include you in any publicity, either."

"I have no problem with that. I'll even wish you luck. Now if you'll excuse me, I need to change my shirt. I got kind of dirty." Not really, but it was the politest way to get rid of them that she could think of.

Norway shot a look at Reggie. "Let's go, then. There's no sense in trying to reason with her."

Oh, Samantha recognized that look. The Scandinavian wench couldn't conceive of anybody turning down money, so she'd concluded that Sam knew something already – and that it must be close by and well-protected, because no one in their right mind would risk losing it. "Go ahead and tear through the attic, guys," she said. "Just keep in mind that some of the stuff I'm cataloguing is really old and delicate and valuable, and that it *all* belongs to Rick."

Her maps were up there, too, but she seriously doubted either of the Inspector Clouseaus here would be able to locate them. They scampered out anyway, and she pulled off her top to trade it for her pink Godzilla T-shirt. As she pulled it over her head, the door shoved open again. *Man, when had she suddenly become so popular?* Samantha peered through one armhole to see Rick glaring at her.

"What now?" she asked, finding the second arm and pulling Godzilla down over her chest.

"What did Reg want in here?"

"First, none of your business. Second, rude much? And third, they wanted to hire me to find your stupid highwayman treasure. I said no, and now I probably won't be invited to Christmas dinner at their place. Have fun without me."

Caribbean blue eyes narrowed as he processed all that. As she expected, it only took him a couple of seconds. "How much did he offer you?"

"Ten thousand pounds."

His mouth twitched. "That must have felt a bit insulting."

And the room began to fill with air again. Whoosh. She flashed a smile. "You know it."

He walked over to the bed and flopped onto his back, laughing. "I've been considering gifting him with a million or so, just because he's my cousin and I can afford it." He flung his arms up over his head. "And in exchange for him leaving the local scenery in peace. I'm rather fond of it."

"Except if you give him a million that'll probably convince him that you're hoarding a treasure worth ten times that amount." She wasn't so sure this was about money, anyway. Eerika wanted the fame and publicity, but Reggie... That was more complicated.

Richard lifted his head, looked at her, then let it fall back again. "Do you think I'm hoarding a ten-million-dollar treasure?"

She'd been running that scenario through her head for the last few days. "No. But I think you know way more than you're letting on. I don't care what you do or don't tell Reggie, but I'm giving you fair warning that I mean to put you in a position where you have to tell *me*."

"And what position is that?"

With his arms extended above his head like that, the dark gray sweatshirt he'd donned had lifted to expose his stomach and half of his six-pack. He looked totally edible, and he knew it. And there she stood, wearing Spanx beneath her jeans and still a little chafed between the thighs. "Is this just to distract me so I'll stop bugging you for answers?"

"In a word, yes."

"Ah." That annoyed her. She wasn't supposed to keep any secrets from him, but he was okay with keeping stuff from her even when she asked. She took another nice, long view of him stretched out on the thick quilt, then turned around. "Okay. I'll see you at dinner."

"Sam."

Before she could change her mind, she rampaged out the door and closed it firmly behind her. Then she headed up the hallway. She'd probably pay for that later, but she liked doing that. For now, she had a couple of things to do, and sex with Rick would mess up her schedule.

The door opened behind her. "Samantha."

"Forget it, Romeo. You can't orgasm me into forgetting that you're the one who's keeping secrets when I'm not allowed to have a single conversation without you jumping in like Tarzan."

His hand clamped down on her shoulder. He was frustrated too, then. Good. She lifted her chin as she faced him, meeting his narrowed gaze and making it clear as she could that she was not the party that needed to apologize here.

"I've just spent two days in a Scottish pub arguing with a Japanese ex-Yakuza about a game where kids play hockey to earn points to purchase ladder rungs. You're still more difficult to untangle."

"Yeah, well, thanks for saying so." Samantha gestured up the hallway toward the attic stairs. "Things to do. That way."

Rick grimaced. "Clearly I've gone about this the wrong way." Shifting his grip to her hand, he towed her toward the old conservatory at the end of the hall. "Come with me."

It had once been full of tropical plants, or so she assumed from the number of parrot statues and paintings that were scattered across pedestals and around the walls, but now it was just those and empty pots placed around the floor, and a stone bench with a view of both the room and the storm outside.

"Okay, we're private," she stated, jerking free of his grip. "But if you're going to tell me you have another wife locked up in a room somewhere, I'm jumping out the window."

He paused, taking a belated look around the room. "This place is rather Jane Eyre, isn't it? I hadn't thought of it that way before. But no, no wives but Patricia."

"She's more than enough, thanks."

Rick rubbed his hands together, a surprising show of hesitation for him. "Okay. If there was something to the highwayman legend, which I'm not saying there is, it wouldn't be my secret to

222

tell. I *would*, however, very much prefer that Reg not find anything – if there is anything to find."

"And me?"

"I trust you. I don't trust Walter or anyone who might be following whatever path you are or aren't digging into."

That sounded nice, but it wasn't very helpful. "I have this weird feeling that you want me to figure out what's going on so I'll know without you having to tell me."

His frown eased a little. "My biggest preference would be for everyone to stay well clear of things which could potentially be extremely inconvenient and troublesome. If there was anything going on."

"Yeah, good luck with that. Why don't you just cancel vacation and send everyone home?"

"I thought about it. But I'd forgotten how much I like it here. If I'm not mistaken, you like it here, too. Even if I did abandon it again, I doubt Reg will give this up. It's remote, but there are a plentitude of ways onto the property." He sighed. "It would have been smarter never to come back in the first place, but I had no idea Reg had been stewing about that damned map for eighteen years."

"I could figure it out without Reggie being any the wiser, but that won't stop him from trying. You'd still be stuck."

"But you'd be on my team."

"I *am* on your team."

Rick tilted his head, his dark hair drifting across his temple in that way that made her want to run her fingers through it. "If there was anything over which we might need to form a team."

"Man, I'm gonna need some drinks."

Rick smiled that loose grin that made her feel all soft and gooey inside. With a sigh she slid her arms up over his shoulders and leaned up for a slow, deep kiss. A little tension between Rick and her was good once in a while, because man, did she like making up.

He put his hands around her waist and lifted her onto the deep window sill. Still kissing, Rick pushed her knees apart and stepped between them. When his big palms slid up the insides of her thighs, though, she winced. "Hold up there, Mr. Bond. Ouch."

"We'll just turn you around, then."

Samantha snorted. "You're so practical. I say you can have me every which way, but you're going to have to do a little work with some aloe lotion, first. Tonight. Because you're gonna be so scared after you hear the stuff on those recordings, you'll do anything I want just so you don't have to sleep alone."

"Oh, I am, am I?" he asked, amusement rumbling in his chest.

She kissed him again, hot and openmouthed. "Yeah. You betcha."

"Okay, then." With a last kiss, Rick set her back on her feet. "Be extremely cautious, Samantha, but go find out what you can, if there's anything to find. I could use the help."

And just like that, she felt...unleashed. A weight lifted off her shoulders. The green Godzilla on her chest might as well have roared. She was still going behind Rick's back, but he wanted her to. Whatever this thing was, yeah, he could just tell her about it, but given how fiercely he protected her, she couldn't fault him for reacting the same way to something else just because she wasn't part of it. Yet.

Of course now she didn't just want to know the what. Now the why and the how got added to her list. Figuring them out would give her another clue or two toward figuring out Rick himself. For every day of the past year, that had been priority number one. It probably always would be. For a puzzle-solver like she was, that was pretty damn cool.

17

Sunday, 8:50 p.m.

As Walter hooked cables into the large monitor at the end of the dining room table, Samantha knelt in front of Aunt Mercia and took both the older woman's hands in hers. "You didn't want to go creeping around the house last night," she said with a half smile. "Are you sure you want to see the results?"

Richard's aunt squeezed Samantha's fingers. "That's it, exactly. I'm too old and dignified to go ghost hunting. But I certainly enjoy a good scare. Don't forget, I've spent time here, too. I'm already fairly certain we're not alone."

"Rick, will you hand me that cable?" Walter asked, and Richard shook himself as he handed another USB cord to Samantha's fence. He never tired of watching Sam charm people, but it felt especially satisfying this time.

His aunt and uncle had arrived at Canniebrae already convinced that Samantha was a gauche American grifter leading him around by the cock as she merrily bilked him of everything he was worth. His defense of her hadn't convinced them otherwise, but with her humor and her genuine interest in...everything, her thoughtfulness and her knowledge of the old objects and customs they found important and precious, she'd begun winning them over. Unless he was greatly mistaken, which he didn't think he was, they even preferred her to the well-groomed phony presently hanging onto Reg's arm and pretending to be nervous about the coming spook show, as Samantha had termed it.

Hopefully Eerika Nyland wasn't aware of just where she ranked in the popularity hierarchy, because rank seemed to matter a great deal to her. He could almost feel sorry for her, except he remembered the chaos and embarrassment Patricia had brought into his life when she'd realized that all the money and attention and privilege in the world couldn't fill an empty soul. He didn't wish a sub-human like that on anyone – even Reg, and even if it seemed rather fitting and inevitable.

He was somewhat surprised the Viking hadn't strapped a camera rig to herself so she could record her own reactions to the ghost show. Or perhaps that was Reg's job – sex partner and reality show cameraman.

Samantha straightened. "Okay. I don't want to oversell this, but hang on to your arses. To be fair there's a thing called matrixing; it's human nature to try to make sense out of random sounds or objects. So this could be that, but it might not be." She took the seat beside him, reaching for his hand. Since she had dug through ancient things for half her life and never flinched that he knew of, he presumed the handholding was for his sake. He had no objection to that.

"All ready," Walter said. "Yule?"

With a nod the butler lowered the lights. Richard was somewhat surprised the power was still on, since the weather continued to rage outside. Previously a slight breeze or a falling leaf had knocked them back into the literal Dark Ages. Perhaps the house wanted everyone to witness the evidence Samantha and Walter had found.

"Let's start with the audio from Rick and Donner's EVP session," Samantha said.

A wiggly line went across the screen, bouncing in time with Tom's recorded voice. "Did you ever wear this armor? Or was it just for show?"

A low whisper trailed his question.

"Goodness," Aunt Mercia exclaimed, putting a hand to her ample bosom. "What did it say?"

"Turn up the volume, Stoney."

Walter replayed the question, then the quieter response. This time Richard could make it out – or at least he could put words to the sounds, matrixing or not. "'For Bonny Prince Charlie'?" he quoted aloud. "Is that what you heard?"

"You mean your mother's family were Jacobites?" Reg cleared his throat. "I don't know how I feel about that."

"That's what I heard, m'laird," Yule put in, crossing himself.

"King James and Prince Charles were after the shining armor period," Samantha put in. "It could be a soldier, just not the one who wore the armor."

"Oh, it's terrifying anyway. Is there anything else?" Eerika hid her face against Reg's shoulder.

The next two pieces were both sounds that might have been speech, but no one could agree what they said. They might also have been a jacket rustling, but given the audience, Richard kept that thought to himself. Then he heard his own voice. "What say we go get a beer?" followed immediately by a very clear, "thirsty".

"Good God, I heard that," his uncle announced

"I did, as well," his wife seconded. "'Thirsty'. I have the shivers!"

"Wait till you see the next one, then," Samantha said. The monitor flickered on, showing two brightly-colored figures to one side, and misshapen purple and black shadows around them. "This is the thermal camera," she explained. "The more heat some-thing has to it, the more red and white you'll see. The colder colors are purple and black. That's Reggie and Eerika there, doing an EVP session."

"Yes or no, is it hidden in a cave?" Eerika's slightly distorted voice said. "In a—"

"I don't hear anything," Norway broke in, as if everybody didn't already know what she and Reggie were digging after.

"Shh," Tom interrupted.

"—a house somewhere? A cellar?"

As Miss Nyland asked her questions, the image flickered, a dark…fuzz blanking the image from left to right and then clearing again. "Leave me alone," hissed out of the speaker, as Aunt Mercia shrieked. "Not for you."

"Holy crap!" Tom exclaimed, lurching backward and then sitting quickly forward. "Play it again!"

Walter did so. Looking more carefully this time, knowing what was coming, Richard noted the shape could have been a drift of cold air, or it could have been what he'd felt walking through the portrait gallery. If so, he had a dead highwayman loitering there.

"Do you think that could be Will Dawkin?" Uncle Rowland asked, the older man's voice not quite steady. "Telling everyone to leave his treasure alone? That's what Reg has been barking about for the past month, anyway."

"Which means there *is* a treasure," Reg said, sending Richard a hostile glance.

"Or there was," Samantha countered. "I don't think the passage of time means much in ghost land."

Richard took a slow breath, the highly logical part of his brain going through possibilities like stray drafts, creaking floors, anything that might have caused that sight and sound. On the other hand, a few months ago he and Sam had unearthed a supposedly cursed diamond – and had suffered through several supremely odd circumstances. "That was impressive," he said. "I'm not convinced it wasn't a draft and the sound of the wind, but it definitely gives me something to think about. And to sleep on." He tightened his fingers around Samantha's.

"I don't think I'll sleep ever again!" Aunt Mercia exclaimed.

"Is there any more?" Tom asked, downing the rest of his glass of whisky. "Because my pants are nearly scared off."

"That was it," Samantha returned. "We found a few more 'maybe' sections, but it could have been somebody breathing or walking. Eerika, did you or Reggie find anything on your EMF recorder?"

"No." Reg straightened a little. "Not even that bit about leaving whoever it was alone." Eerika leaned her head close to his and muttered something. Immediately Reg stood, pulling her up beside him. "I think Eerika's a bit wobbly. We'll say goodnight now."

As they left the room and Yule turned the lights up again, Samantha leaned against Richard's shoulder. "Any bets they're gonna go listen to their recording again? And probably go stake out the portrait gallery with some more questions?"

"I am not taking that bet," he returned. "I am, however, ready to retire for the evening." He'd been ready to give her that aloe lotion massage for a couple of hours, now, and if they didn't get on with it soon he was going to have to go massage himself. And that seemed a damned waste.

"Will you join us in the library?" Aunt Mercia asked on the tail of that thought. "I need some brandy and some conversation if I'm ever going to be able to close my eyes tonight." She smiled at Walter. "And I should very much like to get to know you, Mr. Barstone. Sam credits you with raising her."

Walter paused in his disassembly of the spook equipment. "She does?" he said, lifting an eyebrow that sent creases halfway up his scalp.

"Yes, she does," Samantha put in with a slight, fond grin that made Richard a little jealous despite how well he knew that

Walter was a father figure, and nothing else. A much better father figure than her actual father had ever been.

"Well, I do like a good brandy," Walter admitted, turning off the monitor.

Uncle Rowland chuckled. "Ah ha. Very good, then. You as well, Tom. We're all family here. I'm certain you have some stories to tell."

Tom sent Samantha a lifted eyebrow of his own. "Oh, that I do."

Now even if he and Samantha could make themselves scarce, Richard wasn't going anywhere. Not while Walter and Tom were being questioned about Sam. Especially if they were going to be drinking.

"We're not retiring now?" Sam breathed, somehow still managing to sound amused.

"Nope."

"Okay. But what did you think of the video?" Tugging him to his feet, she slid an arm warmly around his waist and fell in as they led the way to the library. "Really? Not the cynical, for public consumption stuff."

"Since I met you," he returned, drawing her more closely against his side, "I've realized there are more things in heaven and earth than my philosophy covers."

"Way to plagiarize *Hamlet*. Do you mean it?"

"I'm not certain what that was, my lass. Just like I didn't know exactly what to make of that supposedly bad-luck necklace you found." He took a slow breath. "This is an old, old place. I'm actually glad you seem to have found a soldier and a highwayman. I imagine there have been much worse hereabouts."

He glanced at Yule, who finished lighting a fire in the hearth and then went to bring in some brandy snifters. With the butler as a witness to the ghost reveal, he imagined that the second the weather cleared half the village would know that Will Dawkin had made an appearance, that he'd asked to be left alone, and that he'd declared his treasure didn't belong to the Addisons. Which was fine with him, because he happened to agree with that sentiment.

The part that bothered him was how the suspicious and superstitious locals would view this. They were already extremely nervous about anyone caught digging where they shouldn't be. Of course, his own interpretation of Will Dawkin's supposed message didn't quite match the one the villagers would likely have. In his opinion the "not for you" referred to Reg. Not to Sam. Who else would a highwayman want to find his treasure but his modern counterpart?

He stayed remarkably pleasant for the next three hours if he said so himself, until with a flash and boom the lights finally did go out. For once he was glad for the iffy power, and as soon as he'd handed torches to everyone not already equipped with one, he dragged Samantha out of the library.

"Don't run me into a wall," she said, chuckling.

"We're getting out of here before the lights come back on. I thought I was going to have to put a stack of books in my lap."

"You say the sexiest things."

She'd probably learned the floorplan of Canniebrae five minutes after they'd arrived and could get to any room even in the pitch dark, but she seemed content to hold his hand and let him lead the way with the torch he carried in his free hand. At least Yule hadn't skimped on batteries for the house.

He half expected to see marching suits of armor and floating candles now – the things he'd heard and seen tonight had pushed up against some very deeply-ingrained beliefs, and explaining them all away to his own satisfaction would take some time. A life that had been exceedingly well-ordered up until a year ago now orbited around a thief who broke into his house when she got bored. Now he stabbed people with antique swords, and other people shot at them and tried to blow them up every other week.

Why not ghosts who delivered warnings and yearned for glasses of beer?

No one hurled anything at them as they wound through the maze of corridors, and he released her hand to push open their bedchamber door. One of the maids had lit the fire in the large fireplace, and he flicked off the torch in the warm orange glow.

"It's still pouring," Samantha noted, tilting her head to listen. "I hope the hole those guys dug for the wiring doesn't turn into a swimming pool."

"Or an ice skating rink," he added. "I really don't want the cellar foundation cracking." Richard sat on the chair by the fire and pulled off his shoes.

Samantha dropped into the chair opposite him and removed her own tennies. "I'm glad we're kind of on the same team again, even if you still won't tell me what's going on."

"I ca—"

"I get it," she cut in, standing again and walking over to sit on the arm of his chair. "But I also feel better about finding the books you hid in the hatbox. They were pretty helpful."

She'd found them. Of course she'd found them. The part of him that wanted to know if she'd actually had to search was immediately shouted into submission by the part that wondered if it had even taken her five minutes to track them down. "Is that your way of telling me you'd be running circles around me if we *weren't* on the same side?" he asked instead, pulling her down across his thighs.

"There might be some pride involved," she admitted, running her fingers through his dark hair and then pulling his face closer for a kiss. She wiggled her bottom against him. "You weren't kidding about needing a dictionary to hold down Captain Stiffy, were you?"

Richard shut his eyes for a moment, enjoying the sensation of her moving against him. "We are not calling it that."

"No?"

When she began bouncing, he scooped her up in his arms and carried her over to the waist-high bed. He'd always enjoyed sex, but God, she excited him. Every time with her reminded him of the first time, when they'd gone out to dinner and then hadn't even made it home. The blue Bentley Continental was one car he would be holding onto, just because that was where he'd confirmed that she hadn't just been teasing or flirting to get something from him. She'd wanted *him*, as much as he'd wanted her. As much as he still wanted her.

"Where's the aloe?" he asked, jumping onto the bed and attacking her jeans zipper amid the loud metal squeaking of the frame.

"I am honestly worried that once you get started with that, I'll end up so slippery I'll slide off the bed," she returned with a laugh, lifting her hips as he yanked her pants down.

The sight before him stopped him for a moment. "So those are Spanx," he mused, sliding a finger beneath the elastic waist and tugging on it.

"Suddenly I feel all Bridget Jones," she commented, eyeing him. "Do I look sexy?"

"How in God's name am I supposed to answer that?"

She snorted. "At least help me roll them off. They're tighter than a wet suit."

Between the two of them they managed to remove them, and he tossed them over the side of the bed. Her bright pink bikini underwear followed them a second later. The insides of her thighs were a little pink still, and he imagined a day or two ago they must indeed have chaffed. "I'm still willing to lotion you," he commented, pulling his shirt off over his head. "Extremely willing."

"Well, if you insist," she murmured, reaching over her head for a plastic bottle on the nightstand and handing it down to him.

While she pulled off her shirt and pink bra that matched her underwear, Richard shed his own jeans and put a careful amount of aloe lotion on one palm. It smelled pleasantly of coconut, but he didn't want either of them slathered in it, particularly since it wasn't edible. Sliding down onto his stomach, he started at her knee, working his way up in small, slow circles. She sighed happily, then jumped when he extended his thumb to brush it along her folds as he massaged high up on her inner thigh.

"I think that's cheating," she gasped, arching her hips.

"I do not." He did the same thing up her other thigh, and by the time he'd finished she was writhing on the bed with enough enthusiasm that any other foreplay had left his thoughts. Sliding up between her tropical-smelling thighs, he licked the lovely apex between them. The taste of her excitement was intoxicating.

"Dammit, Rick, you know the damn aloe was just a ploy. Do it right."

By "it" he assumed she meant sex, but since she'd been driving him mad practically since they'd arrived at Canniebrae, a little payback seemed fair enough. Especially this kind of payback. "I didn't quite hear you," he said, sliding a finger inside her. "Were you begging for something?"

She slid away from him, sitting up. "Me?" she asked, an excited grin on her face. "I don't beg."

"Sam—"

Samantha slowly rolled onto her stomach and hitched her arse up in the air. "You, on the other h—"

Oh, fuck the foreplay. Richard pushed up onto his knees, grabbed her by the hips, and pulled her backward as he moved forward, entering her deeply from behind. With a shivery sigh she arched her back, and he bent forward to cup her breasts as he thrust into her.

He couldn't have summoned a clever reply if he'd wanted to, but from the keening sounds of pleasure she was making and the loud, rhythmic squeaking of the bed, she probably wouldn't have heard him anyway. Richard pinched her nipples, pulling lightly, and with an abrupt shudder she came, shivering and tight, around him.

It became all sensation, him thrusting in hard and fast, pushing as deeply as he could, her lowering her head, gripping her hands into the sheets. Yes, they might have begun as a loose-cannon adrenaline junkie and a buttoned-up businessman, but they'd always, always fit here.

Closing his eyes, he came, shoving hard into her and keeping himself there as she met him just as solidly from the other side. Reaching around, he grabbed her left knee and pulled it to the right, collapsing them onto the bed sideways with him still inside her.

"How are your thighs?" he asked, panting.

"Nicely unchaffed." With a breathy chuckle she snuggled back closer against his chest. "I think two days without having you may be my tolerance limit."

And thank God for that, because even after a year, even when they argued, he wanted her. All the time. This was where he didn't have to worry about her past, their present, or their future. This was literally just them, together. Richard drew the hair away from her face and kissed her throat. "Likewise."

"Oh, good. I'm glad it's not just me."

"Mm hm. Don't get too cozy. We're going to be here for a while."

"I AM THINKING," Reginald snapped, pacing to the window and back. Sometime during the night, the rain had turned to snow and then stopped. It left behind a white blanket that looked fetching but that would probably be a muddy mess by midday. It was rather emblematic of this entire bloody holiday, really.

"Think harder, then. All of the other valuables from the west wing ended up in the attic, because the household had ample warning that it was falling into disrepair. There's no reason to believe the map would have been left behind."

He glared toward the well-covered lump on the bed. "Not if Ricky hid it first. At the same time, it would have been lovely if you'd come up with this theory four days ago."

The blanket lowered, revealing disheveled blonde hair, followed by a pair of blue eyes with smeared mascara. Ah, the perils of not removing one's make-up before bed.

"It would have been even more lovely if you ever thought of anything," she returned, her tone sharp enough to cut glass.

"I think," he retorted, "he'd forgotten all about the map and the treasure. He's rolling in money; something he stumbled over when he was fifteen, especially since he found out about Aunt Rachel's cancer at the same time, probably went right out of his head. If he thought about hiding it at all, he only did it after I went looking for it in the old library." As he considered it, Ricky had more money than Midas. An old treasure map and the prize it represented would have slipped his mind until the moment someone else expressed an interest.

"There aren't that many places it could be then, are there?" Eerika sat up, one blue strap of her nightgown sliding to her elbow.

God, she looked fetching. Reginald started toward the bed, loosening the belt of his dressing robe as he approached. "You know what would help me think better?" he murmured.

"Oh, please. It's morning. I think perhaps I'm too distracting for you, Reginald." She pulled up her sleeve. "Think of me as your reward for a job well done. *When* you do as you promised me."

Fuck. "The treasure is enough incentive, don't you think?"

"As we've been here for nearly a week and you've made precisely zed in the way of progress, I would have to say no, the treasure doesn't seem to be enough incentive for you." She lowered her head, regarding him with china-blue eyes through her long, dark lashes. It was effective, and might have been more so without the smears of black around her eyes. "So now *I'm* your incentive. I want to be famous, Reginald."

"Fine." Grabbing the ends of the belt, he pulled his dressing robe closed again. "Get dressed, Incentive. I can't search the attic and twenty-seven other rooms on my own."

With his new insight, he wouldn't be looking for cleverly-hidden as much as hastily put in the most out-of-the-way, inconspicuous place possible. Attic first, then, followed by everywhere they hadn't been searching for the past six days. Then he and Eerika would have a little chat about incentive while he rained down gold coins and precious gems on her tits. They might not be able to televise that, but he bloody well wouldn't mind doing the re-enactment. *Booty Queen*, indeed.

Now *that* image was incentive.

18

"**A** day and a half ago I was in Palm Beach," Stoney said, holding the heavy blue blanket close around him. With the huge parka he wore beneath that, he looked like a giant, grouchy grizzly bear. "There is snow outside, Sam. Snow."

She grinned at him before she went back to studying her map. "Just think of it as solid water."

"That's stupid. *This* is stupid. Addison wants you to go after Will Dawkin's stash, except he won't help, he won't admit it's real, and he would actually prefer if nobody did anything but go bird hunting and help him count up his Picassos."

"It's complicated. And he promised me he wouldn't shoot any birds." Looking at the map in light of the new stuff she'd read about Will Dawkin yesterday, she could immediately eliminate two of the possible locations she'd marked. "But at least I'm not going behind his back anymore."

"Oh, yay. What are you supposed to do when – if – you find the damn thing, then? Go tell Addison you figured out his stupid challenge so he can pat you on the head and decide you're trust-worthy enough to marry?"

"This is not a game show," she retorted. "And I haven't decided what I'll do when – *when* – I figure it out. Yoda knows there's no ifs and tries allowed." She traced the old road with one finger, winding in and out of the hills and valleys, touching villages and curving close to the handful of massive estates, including Canniebrae, that dotted the area.

Will Dawkin had been a commoner, the bastard son of a tanner and a priest's daughter. The Church – and her dad – had not been kind to her. The locals, though, had taken her in because she'd apparently been much nicer and more charitable than her father. She'd taken a position at The Bonny Lass back when it had been a traditional coaching inn. Will Dawkin had spent most of his evenings there growing up.

His life of crime had begun when several of the local lords, in the wake of the Battle of Culloden, had begun throwing nearby tenants and cotters off their rented lands in an effort to keep their own prop-erties solvent. Having more sheep equaled allowing fewer people to clutter up their grazing land. The Highland Clearances was when Will Dawkin had started holding up coaches and riders and robbing them. Despite the turmoil, the village of Orrisey had remained intact. Hell, from what she could tell, it had thrived, even back then.

Now it had that old Highlands charm with a second place award to prove it, *and* wi-fi and internet despite nearby Balmoral. It had both a quaint bakery and a high-end dress shop where even a professional shopper like Eerika had found something worthy of purchase.

"You figured it out, didn't you?" Stoney said into the quiet attic.

Samantha blinked, lifting her head. "What?"

"I recognize that look on your face, honey. You and your maps – you figured it out. You know where the loot is."

"I know where I think it is." She tapped the outline she'd made of The Bonny Lass. "Finding out for sure will take some finesse."

Stoney made his way over to where she sat. "Isn't that the pub?"

"It is now. Two hundred fifty years ago it was an inn where Will Dawkin's mother worked in the kitchen."

"That's a little obvious, don't you think? Wouldn't the Redcoats or whoever would have known that and stomped through there a long time ago?"

"You would think so, wouldn't you?" She looked at the map again. "Somewhere really close to The Bonny Lass, but not obvious. Somewhere that could be protected." She folded the map, old, familiar tension and anticipation pulling at her. Adrenaline was a hell of a drug, and she was definitely still addicted. "Wanna go for a drive?"

He shook his head. "I find the jobs. I don't go on the jobs. Plus, snow."

She could have used another pair of savvy, cynical eyes who knew what to look for. At the same time, Stoney's people didn't exactly hail from the Highlands. Him poking around would be even more noticeable than her doing it – and she had a lot more practice at blending in and being unnoticed, anyway. "Are you going to stay up here, then? The notebook I'm using for cataloguing is on the gaming table."

"Addison's not worried I'll pilfer something and sell it to one of my contacts?" He picked up the notebook and flipped it open.

"*I'm* not worried."

"Maybe, then. Or Mercia invited me to the library for cocoa at eleven o'clock. The library has a fire. Plus, cocoa."

Samantha laughed. "The great Walter Barstone, tamed by a cold day." She offered him a fist, which he bumped with his own. "Mercia likes old timey card games. So do you. Play one with her. I'll be back soon."

"Take a walkie-talkie."

"Roger that."

Rick had vacated the house hours ago to head back down to The Bonny Lass with Donner. That Japanese guy deserved all the trouble Rick decided to send in his direction. On top of the trouble he was making for Addisco, Mr. Kigomo was also making things more difficult for her, because she would have preferred being able to visit The Bonny Lass without Rick and Donner glowering at her.

Stomping into her heavy hiking boots, she tucked her jeans into the tops to help keep her feet warm and dry. A heavy sweater of nondescript olive went over her black Godzilla T-shirt, and a gray, fleece-lined coat over that. Lined leather gloves and a wool hat later, and she looked ready for either the Iditarod or an REI commercial – anything but a joint casing expedition and a possible B and E.

Maybe that was a good thing, though. The village was on Canniebrae land – Rick's land. A snatch and grab followed by a quick getaway wouldn't work, and she had the feeling that what she might find would be way more complicated than any of her previous jobs, anyway. Whatever she decided, she was going to have to be able to stand by it. And to live with it.

Yule arrived at the front door as she trotted down the last flight of the main staircase. She had no idea how the butler knew when to be where, especially with the power still out and a lot of dark, murky hallways to contend with, but he was really good at it. "If anybody asks," she said, adjusting the black wool cap to cover her ears, "I'm heading down to the village for a while. One of those pairs of shoes I saw is calling to me."

"The jeep's already gone down," Yule returned, "and the truck won't start again. Shall I have Briggs saddle Lily for ye?"

"No," she blurted, probably with too much volume. "Don't worry about it," she continued. "I go running all the time. A walk'll be nice."

He freed a sturdy, straight stick from the umbrella stand. "The snow's beginning to melt. Take a walking stick to help ye with yer footing, and dunnae stray from the road, Miss Sam."

Straying from the road was exactly what she meant to do. "Thanks, Yule. I'll be careful. I've got a walkie-talkie with me, just in case." She patted her right pocket.

Nodding, he pulled open the door. "I'll tell Mrs. Yule to have a nice hot soup ready for ye when ye get back. I reckon ye'll need it."

She stepped outside and headed down the drive, the thin layer of snow there not so much crunching as collapsing into a slick, icy mud under her feet. Well, this was going to be fun. The walking stick was going to be a lot handier than she'd expected, even if it did kind of make her feel like Gandalf the Grey.

Her breath clouded when she exhaled, but so far, the inhale still felt refreshing. A mile down the road she might be ready to go Donner party (the cannibal one, not the dinners at the lawyer's house), but so far so good. This road merged into the old one at the foot of the hill where Canniebrae perched, but today seemed like a bad day to try a shortcut. She stuck to the winding road.

Without the confining car or the horror of horseback riding, she felt more of a sense of place. Clumps of snow plopped down from the branches above her, where somewhere up ahead a fox yapped and a crow cawed in response. The late summer birds had probably been stunned by the early snow, but the year-round animals had to be more used to this kind of weather.

As for her, she'd done a job in Paris in January that had nearly frozen off her fingers, and one in Helsinki where staying still enough to fool the motion sensors had been almost impossible because she'd been shivering so badly. Both of those gigs had involved climbing up the outside of a building, which had meant no parka, thin gloves, and the only good part of it – a full face mask.

Now her cheeks were cold, but the rest of her felt downright toasty. If this was how the semi-honest life was going to treat her, so far it was pretty nice. Especially the nights. Last night she hadn't been hanging onto a ledge by her fingertips; she'd been hanging onto Rick. Nothing could beat that ride.

Aside from all the other thoughts traipsing through her mind as she turned up the old road to head toward the village, the Scottish Highlands were really pretty, and ancient, and not quite peaceful as much as biding its time, and she liked it here. Sure, she'd go stir crazy after a couple of weeks, but right now she was still discovering – or rediscovering – priceless works of art in the attic and elsewhere.

It took nearly half an hour, but the village finally came into sight through the trees. Samantha stopped to pull out the second and third pages of her map. The landscape looked a little different in the snow, but as long as there were no open holes she didn't know about, tracking down her X-marks shouldn't be too difficult.

Unfortunately, MacGyver the jeep was still parked at The Bonny Lass, which eliminated any plans of wandering in to ask to see how they stored their whisky in hopes of seeing the cellar. She could wait out in the cold for Rick and the lawyer to leave, skip the pub, or invent another reason for snooping around, or start with theory number two about the nearby hiding place. She clapped her gloved hands together. Number two it was, then.

Sighting the shallow ravine just west of the village, she lined her map up with the village's main street and then trekked around through the deeper snow until she came up on the far side. She stabbed through the white stuff with the walking stick, using it as a solid ground detector, and followed the trail she made down to the ravine's floor.

Back in Jacobite times, which would have been just prior to Will Dawkin's appearance on the local roadways, churches frequently had hidey holes and escape tunnels. Those had been mostly for Catholics when Henry the Eighth had gone Protestant, but later they'd come in handy for anti-British agitators and supporters of old King James the Second and bonnie Prince Charlie. Those holes and tunnels would also have been useful for any thieves and smugglers looking to keep stolen goods somewhere safe.

The question was, had The Bonny Lass once had an escape tunnel, and did it still have one? She crouched, digging the stick into the side of the ravine. With the snow this wasn't going to be easy, damn it. She would have to hope the warming trend continued so she could take another look tomorrow or the next day. If an opening *was* down here, it would be well hidden even under optimal conditions; anything obvious would have been found a long time ago.

She searched for twenty minutes, until the cold began sinking into her fingers despite the thick gloves. Tucking her hands beneath her armpits, Samantha straightened – then ducked again as a pair of heads came into view on the higher ground beside the ravine above her. Villagers on their way to lunch or not, she did not want to have to make up a story about why the future Lady Rawley was sneaking around in a ravine.

"Nae, I dunnae see anything," a male voice said. "Are ye certain she didnae decide it was too cold and turn back?"

"I sent Freddie up to the widow's walk," Yule's slightly distorted, mechanical-sounding voice came. "She's nae come back up the hill."

"Why do the bloody tourists think this is Disneyland?" the nearer voice returned. "We dunnae have animatronic deer, and the trails dunnae have railings or loos."

The radio crackled again. "Miss Sam's a clever lass. Keep yer eyes open. If ye're listening, Jamie, dunnae tell his lordship. Nae until Rob makes his way along her trail to the village to see if he comes across her. And ye keep looking, Duncan."

"Aye. I meant to spend the day drinking, but tramping through slush is just as fine, I reckon," the close-by voice took up again.

"Thank ye, Duncan."

"And what aboot the cousin, Yule?" Duncan returned. "He still looking for trouble?"

"Aye. But be patient. They'll nae be here much longer."

"He needs to go back to selling cars. It's nae wise for a man to be so greedy."

"He's still hunting about the house, Duncan. I doubt he has the smarts to move past pulling up floorboards."

"Ye'd best be right about that, Yule."

Samantha stayed where she was until the footsteps and voices above faded. That was how Yule always knew where to be, even in a sprawling house with iffy electricity. That was how the villagers kept in contact with each other and with Canniebrae, even with intermittent cell service and one wi-fi hot spot for miles around. They'd probably come up with the walkie-talkie solution years ago, and she'd thought she was so clever to have Stoney send a box of them up for the Canniebrae guests.

"Turtles are faster than you are, Sam," she muttered to herself, too annoyed for a minute to even acknowledge that Yule and the Duncan guy had just confirmed that she was right. The entire village was part of this. Everybody knew about the treasure except for her, Reg, and the Viking. Well, just Reg and the Viking now, because she'd figured it out now – in theory, even if she hadn't set eyeballs on anybody's gold yet.

Taking out her own radio and plugging her earphones into it, she tapped the talk button twice, paused, then tapped it three more times. She counted to five, and the earbuds crackled twice. Letting out her breath, she switched to the channel two above three, which all the guests were using. She pressed the talk button again. "Stoney?" she whispered.

"I'm glad you haven't forgotten everything," his voice came back.

"I don't forget anything."

"Okay, okay. What's up? And why are you whispering?"

"The villagers think I'm lost in a snow drift. They're looking for me, and I don't want to be discovered digging through mud looking for their gold."

"*Their* gold?" he repeated, instantly picking up on that, as she'd known he would.

"Later. They have their own walkie network. See if you can find the channel they're using. Be discreet. Yule's in on it, too. I don't know who else might be."

"Roger that. What are you going to do?"

"Get found."

That done, she moved back to channel three, pocketed the headphones and the walkie-talkie in separate pockets, and scooted along the ravine until it shallowed out beyond the village. This puzzle had just gotten a lot more complicated. From what she could piece together, it wasn't just the owner of The Bonny Lass who knew where Will Dawkin's loot was and had also been benefitting from it. It was probably the entire village and everyone between there and Canniebrae. If she knew one thing, people hiding treasure didn't want it discovered, they didn't want it taken away, and they really didn't want publicity about it.

Even if Rick knew some of this, which she assumed he did, he hadn't known about the communication going on between his home and the village. If he had, he would have used it. And if he didn't know just how many of his own employees were involved, then he couldn't know all the facts. Yule knew Reggie and Eerika were looking for the treasure, which meant the entire village knew. A couple of those villagers might feel more threatened than others. This was all suddenly more serious than tracking down a long-forgotten sack of gold coins.

Another trio of men rounded a hill beyond her, and she side-stepped deeper into the trees. The good thing about the rapidly-melting slush was that tracks distorted and disappeared almost instantly. The bad thing about this was that the locals knew the area a lot better than she did.

Scrambling up the muddy, brush-tangled hill, she kept low and angled back east in the direction of Canniebrae. As soon as she cleared the village she found a sheltered, northern-facing slope, rolled down it to cover herself in snow and mud, and then hiked back onto the road.

She spied a couple of people eyeing her as she trudged past the jeep and up to The Bonny Lass's door, but she busied herself with shaking off muck and pretended not to notice. With a last breath she pulled open the pub's door and stomped inside.

"Oh, good," she panted, as Rick saw her and practically leaped out of a booth to his feet. "You're still here. I thought I was going to have to move in to The Bonny Lass, because I am *not* walking back up that hill."

Rick reached her and caught her arm, and she leaned harder against him than she needed to. "What the hell happened?" he asked, the worry on his face making her feel a little guilty. But this was for his benefit, as much as it was for hers.

"I'll fetch some hot cider, m'laird," Jamie MacCafferty called, digging beneath the counter.

"Cocoa, if you have any," she countered, letting Rick help unzip her heavy coat. "Yule warned me to stay on the road, but I saw a stag and decided to get closer so I could take some pictures, and then I tripped and rolled halfway down the mountain. The deer took off to go have a laugh with his deer friends, and it took me like half an hour to climb back up to the road."

"I'm glad ye found it, lass," The Bonny Lass's owner said. "People do get lost out here permanently even on fine days. I'll get ye yer cocoa." He vanished into the kitchen, no doubt to announce on his own walkie that the idiot Yank had turned up on her own. That suited her just fine.

"He's right, you know." Rick hung up her coat by the door and then pulled off her wet gloves, taking her cold hands in his warm ones. "What were you thinking?"

"I had my walkie-talkie," she returned, no longer having to

fake her teeth chattering. "I wasn't ready to give up and call 'dumbass' on myself yet."

"Is it bad that I'm kinda happy you aren't good at everything?" Donner said, pulling off the light jacket he wore and actually draping it over her shoulders.

"Wow. You *do* care," she noted.

"No, I don't. I just don't want my wife hearing that I wasn't being a gentleman."

"I'm telling anyway. You gave me your jacket."

"Good," he retorted. "I'll get extra credit points for this. And I'm *loaning* you my jacket."

"Children," Rick broke in, urging her into the booth and then sliding in next to her. "What actually happened?" he murmured, wrapping her into his arms and giving her a kiss on the temple to disguise the question.

"Exactly what I said," she returned. "For all our sakes." Two men and a woman sat at one of the other booths, just within earshot of any normal-voiced conversation. Until she knew differently, every person who lived in the village was part of some sort of treasure conspiracy.

"Great," Donner muttered. "If you get me in troub—"

"Seriously, Tom," she whispered, knowing that her using his first name would catch his attention. "Shut the fuck up."

The attorney blinked. "Okay."

"Until I fell down, it was actually a really nice walk," she said in her normal tone as MacCafferty reappeared, a steaming mug in hand. "Thank you so much, Mr. MacCafferty. I think my bones may be frozen."

He chuckled. "It's Jamie to all, Miss Sam. Take small sips, or ye'll burn yer mouth. I hope our scenery was worth it."

"It is stunning out there. And I thought it was gorgeous even without the snow."

"Ye should see it here when we've a blanket of the stuff and nae just a wee dusting."

Samantha laughed. "That was quite a wee dusting."

"Och. Nae for the Highlands."

He offered to dish her up a bowl of soup, and she accepted with a grateful nod. "You are a kind man."

"Feeling any warmer?" Rick asked, still holding her close.

"Starting to." Her left side, pressed against him, felt definitely warmer than the right. Her fingers, wrapped around the warm mug, began to tingle as feeling thawed into them. "Did I interrupt the Japan thing?"

"No," Rick answered. "I think we've got it straightened out. We're just waiting for a confirmation email."

"Did we win?"

He shrugged. "We're happier than they are, I imagine."

"That's a win in my book."

"Yes. Which means weather permitting, Tom will be leaving in the morning." Rick lifted an eyebrow, clearly inviting her to respond in kind.

Dammit. She needed Stoney right now. Especially if what she'd just figured out was true. There was a big difference between a hidden treasure and a protected treasure. After some of the conversation she'd overheard earlier, the villagers were really concerned with keeping their stash secret. Considering that Rick was being all, "figure things out, if you please, but I won't help you do it," an actual ally like Stoney was pretty valuable.

"Samantha?"

"Yeah, yeah. I know what it means. Stoney hitched a ride in. Are you going to make him hike out?"

"He'll fly out."

She frowned. "Technically Donner was here a full day before Stoney showed up."

"I came on business, you know," the lawyer protested. "Not to earn you groupie points."

"Stoney is not a groupie. And here is here, whatever the reason. I want fair time."

Now Rick was frowning, too. "This is supposed to be our holiday. Anything else you may be up to is between you and me."

"And Reggie," she added. "But we can talk about that later."

"Mm hm. Tom, refresh your email, if you please. I'd like to get back to Canniebrae."

From Rick's tone he was annoyed, and while she got why, there were also a couple of things he didn't know yet. "Me, too," she seconded aloud, taking another sip of the near-scalding cocoa. "I'm deliriously imagining a nice, hot shower."

Donner hit a couple of keys on his laptop. "And...confirmed," he said, then punched a fist into the air. "You got 'em."

"We got 'em," Rick countered, his expression easing into a smile.

Because he'd gone to the trouble of making it for her, Samantha downed half of Jamie's really tasty chicken and potato soup. She hadn't felt nearly as cold as she'd looked, but she knew how important it was to play the game well. Finally Donner gathered his things, and Rick helped her back into her damp coat.

"You should wear mine," he rumbled. "It's dry."

She put a hand against his chest. "Thanks, tough guy, but I'm not that delicate."

Rick tilted her chin up with his fingers and kissed her mouth. "But you are that precious."

That warmed her up very nicely. "You've already got me, Brit," she said, zipping up his coat before he could take it off and give it to her. "You don't need to make me all swoony."

"As my youngest would say," Donner commented, holding the door open for them, "'Ew. Get a room.'"

That was probably what Olivia would say, but then she'd just turned ten and hadn't discovered boys yet. Olivia was a normal kid, as were Mike and Chris, Donner and Katie's other two kids, and all of them still fascinated Samantha. By the time she'd turned Olivia's age she'd acquired Rolexes, rings, bracelets, and necklaces right off of people while she smiled at them and asked for directions, or help finding a parent, or cab fare, or anything to get them distracted. "Ew, get a room" was normal kid vocabulary, and she'd never been a normal kid.

Donner actually climbed into the Jeep's back seat without her having to challenge him to an arm-wrestling contest for the shotgun position. Maybe the "Tom" thing had freaked him out more than he wanted to let on. But hey, the front seat was the front seat, even if the steering wheel was on the wrong side.

"Okay, what's going on?" Rick asked, glancing at her as he backed MacGyver out of its parking spot.

"That depends on whether you want onner-Day to know about the reasure-tay and the ighwayman-hay," she answered.

"Jesus, what are you, twelve?" the attorney grumbled.

"You implied this was a matter of safety," Rick cut in, before she could give Donner a few more choice words in pig-Latin. "I'm afraid your safety trumps my sense of honor. Spill."

Well, now she was going to feel really crappy if she was wrong about this. "Yeah. Okay. I don't have any proof, but here goes my theory. If you know I'm on the wrong track, say something."

"I—"

"Not you," she aimed at the back seat.

Samantha shook out her hands. She liked figuring things out. She was good at it. Usually, though, the problem was how to get into somewhere unseen, grab a thing that wasn't hers, and get out again. She might ask Stoney to round up some mirrors or a hand-held EMP device or something, but generally she kept her solutions to herself. Gabbing about them made things more dangerous for her. But she wasn't a solo act any longer. She had to be a team player.

"Okay," she repeated. "Will Dawkin hid his stash somewhere in or under The Bonny Lass, because he was comfortable there. He knew the people, and he knew the area. More importantly, the villagers took in his mom when her dad threw her out for being pregnant. So, when he started getting too famous and too hunted he took what he needed and got out of Dodge before he could get the people he cared about in trouble."

No interruptions so far, but she hadn't gotten to the tricky stuff. "When he left, he told his mom where he'd hidden the rest of his booty. I assume one of them drew a map. Then, because she felt grateful to the villagers and couldn't risk her own safety by suddenly going from cook to rich lady, she told them where the cache was hidden. All of them."

"How much loot are we talking about?" Donner asked.

"A lot. Will Dawkin really didn't like the upper classes, and he had a long career as far as highwaymen go. Anyway, at first the villagers had to be really careful, because it was a tough time to be a Highlander. They used just enough to keep the village intact, the rents paid, and everybody fed and housed. After all, cash on the laird's land belongs to the laird – or he could use the excuse of finding the stolen loot to have everybody arrested and use the village land for sheep like most of his neighbors were forced to do."

"But the statute of limitations expired a long time ago," the lawyer countered.

"And as long as nobody blabs, it's still free money. No taxes, no keeping a portion while the rest goes to the government because it's not just gold but antiquities. It's been keeping the village going for over two hundred years, and they've been smart enough about it to slide into the Second Quaintest Village position instead of going all the way to the top." She grimaced. "It probably scared the shit out of them when you found their stash," she said, looking over at Rick. "But you were a kid with a sick mom, and so when you promised never to say a word about any of it, they trusted you."

"After they impressed upon me how important it was to keep their secret," he said, the first time he'd interjected anything during her entire recital.

She nodded. "They were taking a chance. You were the future laird, after all."

"We came to an agreement. I still think it took them years to relax again." Rick blew out his breath. "I didn't come back because of...because of my mum, but they wouldn't know that. Who knows what they expected, and how long they've been waiting for disaster."

"You didn't realize that." Pulling off a glove, she ran her fingers along his cheek. "But now Reggie's shouting to everyone that he wants to find the treasure. And Eerika wants a reality show where finding the loot would probably be her hook."

"He hasn't gone down to the village since he got here."

Oh, boy. "I wasn't the first one to come up with the walkie-talkie idea."

Rick slammed on the brakes, nearly sending them skidding off the road. "Someone in my house is feeding information to the village?" he snapped, the leather covering the steering wheel creaking as he clenched it through his gloves.

"I only figured that out this morning when I heard Yule on a radio asking if anybody had stumbled across me. I think he was worried I'd gotten lost."

"Yule. My own bloody butler. He is so—"

"Two hundred fifty years, Rick," she interrupted. "It's the reason they have nice shops, quaint houses and B and B's, and a good school. They've used that money way more wisely than most people would. Nobody's driving Aston-Martin's but you."

He snapped his jaw closed again. "That was a little uncalled for."

"I know. Just making a point here."

Rick slammed his hand on the gear shift, then shoved it into reverse to back onto the road again. "I get it. I'll ask you to stop digging, then."

"Done," she returned promptly. "But I'm not the problem. They don't know that I know stuff. Reggie and the blonde leading him around by the dick are the problem."

"Then I'll close the house this afternoon."

"If Reggie's serious about this, which he seems to be, he'll be up here again as soon as your back's turned, and you know it."

"I know it. I was hoping you'd come to a different conclusion." The swearing Rick started after that was pretty impressive, even for him. She sat back and waited until he started forming regular words again. "I just finished dealing with another man whose greed outweighed his common sense," he snapped. "It...irks me to have to buy off my own cousin for the same reason."

"Then talk to him. He's not stupid. Do you really think he'd be willing to risk a relationship with you for some trinkets? I mean, why not just tell him that most of the money is probably gone?"

"Eighteen years ago, the crates still looked pretty substantial," Rick rumbled.

"Reggie doesn't need to know that." She scowled. "I mean, come on. These people are just trying to make their lives a little easier. It's not like they're Wakanda, hiding the real, ultra-sophisticated village under an invisibility shield. They're looking out for their families. *I* wouldn't take this gig."

"Well, that would make *me* back off," Donner commented.

"I can't pass that on to Reg though, can I?" Rick said, his tone still curt.

His tone hurt a little. She knew he didn't like her past, but now she couldn't decide if he was ashamed of her, or if he disliked having to keep her secret from his family. Neither choice made her feel any better about any of it. "Gee, no. You'll have to come up with another reason he shouldn't pilfer your tenants' nest egg. Pull over. I'm walking."

"Your coat's wet."

"My cold, evil heart will protect me. And it's only a quarter mile. Stop the jeep."

"We're nearly back. Stomp off once we get up the hill."

Samantha opened the jeep's door. With a curse, Rick slammed on MacGyver's brakes. As soon as she stepped the rest of the way out, Samantha slammed the door shut again. The jeep paused for a second, then continued up the road toward the house.

She let out her breath, fogging the air around her head. If Donner hadn't been in the car, she had the feeling that wouldn't have gone quite as smoothly. None of this – the highwayman treasure, Rick's cousin, the villagers – had anything to do with her. All the same, her past seemed to be jumping into the middle of everything they did or said about any of it.

Maybe because of who she'd been, who she mostly still was except for the stealing part, she didn't think Reggie would convince very easily. Like Rick had said, any offer of money to dissuade Reggie would probably just convince him that his take from the loot would be worth more, and that Rick viewed him as nothing but a greedy road bump.

Looking over the rise in the direction of the vanished jeep she crouched, pulling the map from her jacket pocket and balancing her elbows on her knees. The loot had been at The Bonny Lass. She was certain of that. Rick had found it there eighteen years ago – which also meant that was where the famous missing map had indicated the treasure lay.

The villagers knew Rick still had the map, and even if they trusted their laird that meant two things outside their control pointed to the pub. If it had been up to her, she would definitely have moved the stash, and she would have done it the minute Rick and the Addisons had left the Highlands eighteen years ago. It still presented some problems, though.

First of all, the loot needed to be safe, protected, and somewhere strangers wouldn't just stumble across it. Second, it had to be someplace where everybody could gather to either count the gold or get their share of it or vote on the money's use without the scores of tourists who visited the Highlands' Second Quaintest Village during the summer would think something weird and cultish was going on. The villagers couldn't do all their business with walkie-talkies, after all. Third, it probably needed a secondary way in or out in case of emergency, and because traditionally it had had all that.

She tapped her gloved finger on the rectangle with the cross in the middle. The church. It met all the requirements, plus that choice had some irony attached to it. After all, Will Dawkin's grandfather had been a pastor. Yep, her money was on Saint Andrew's. Of course since she'd just agreed to give up the hunt it didn't matter, but it would have been like putting together a puzzle except for the very last piece. At least now she felt like she could declare the mystery solved, with or without a hundred percent proof.

Well, mostly solved, anyway.

19

Monday, 2:23 p.m.

As Richard crested the hill in the jeep, he caught sight of Samantha straightening from a crouch, a large sheet of paper in her hands. He saw her grimace, swiftly wiped away, and he kept his own expression neutral as he stopped beside her.

Leaving a business rival to sweat didn't trouble him in the least, whatever the stakes, but just the idea of not settling an argument with Samantha left him queasy. She'd said she was with him to stay, but he'd messed up a marriage once before. In addition, Sam could just vanish, in an efficient-enough way that he, even with his money and means, might not be able to find her. But they had to remain equal partners. It was, he was discovering, a tricky balancing act. "Need a lift?"

"I'm still cooling off," she returned, folding the paper and shoving it into her pocket.

Dammit all, what was she up to, now? "Rob, take the jeep back," he said, and the driver popped up from the back seat.

Richard climbed out, watching as Rob clambered into the front seat. The jeep did a four- or five-point turn, then vanished over the rise. "There," he said, crossing the road to where Samantha stood gazing at him.

"Cooling off because I'm mad at you. Did I not clarify?"

"Yes, well, Tom said if I couldn't live with the first part of your life, I shouldn't have suggested I share the second part."

"Donner said that?" She adjusted the wool cap on her head, the auburn hair sticking out from beneath it adorably disheveled. He was glad she'd been letting her hair grow out; he loved the color of it, the way it couldn't quite decide whether it wanted to be red or brown or gold and so had just gone with all three.

"I think he meant to imply that I shouldn't have proposed, but I chose not to interpret it that way."

"Mm hm. In my opinion you can ask your cousin not to steal things even if I used to steal things. It's not really hypocrisy, because you kind of expect me to toe the line now."

"Yes, I know. I was…frustrated. I enjoy philanthropy. I do not enjoy having to buy people off, especially when it's saving them from themselves."

She continued looking at him, green eyes almost hazel in the waning daylight. "And?" she finally prompted.

Ah. "I'm not apologizing. Your former career *does* on occasion complicate things."

With a slight nod, as if she wasn't surprised, she started up the road, thankfully in the direction of the house. "Okay. Don't expect me to tell you what the paper I put in my pocket is, then."

He caught up to her. *How the devil…* "What paper?"

"The one you saw me put away. Don't deny it, because you glanced at my pocket like twelve times while you were talking."

"It was three times at most. But don't tell me. You already gave your word you'd stop pursuing the treasure."

Samantha kept walking, her gloved hands in her pockets – no doubt so he wouldn't be able to hold her hand. Or get to that paper. Their arguing had actually improved quite a bit, since now she was more likely to stand her ground as opposed to disappearing – or threatening to disappear – into the night. Neither of them had to hunt so diligently for the correct words to use or not to use, and while her…confidence in the staying power of the two of them meant that he lost more often, he couldn't bring himself to believe that was a bad thing. Few people in the world argued with him, and even fewer about something other than money.

"What you found about Will Dawkin and his cache, especially given your limited time and resources, was remarkable," he said, since she continued to be the Great Wall of China.

"We criminals all think alike, don't you know."

He glanced sideways at her. "I never said or implied anything of the sort. At fifteen when I figured it out, I'd already been working on it for three years. With the map and all those books, plus my mother's knowledge of the area to assist me."

"How did you end up with the map, anyway? And why didn't the villagers take it from you?"

That was a positive sign; questions rather than pointed quips and sarcasm. "Reg and I were digging through the wreck of the old library one dreary day, and I spotted it behind a broken book-case. It was framed, so I traced it. The original never left the house. I have no idea how long it might have been there; the estate came from my mother's side of the family, and she claimed to have never seen it before." Richard smiled a little as he recalled the conversation. "For a time, I thought she might have drawn it up and planted it there herself, to give us something less destructive to do with ourselves."

"That's the first time I've heard you talk about your mom without wincing." She sidestepped a little, nudging his shoulder with hers.

And *that* made him wince. "I didn't handle her illness well. But you know, I was fifteen. The world was supposed to be about me. No one knew more or felt things more deeply. Then cancer mucked everything up, made it about her, and then took her away from my happy little world."

"I remember being fifteen. Everybody was a sucker, and if I could take something from them, it was because they deserved it."

Christ, what different lives they'd led. It was something of a miracle, or fate, that their paths had ever crossed at all. No wonder literal explosions had been involved.

But the point was she'd been raised first by a self-absorbed cat burglar, and then by a fence. They'd set the direction of her life – an eight-year-old did as her elders dictated and accepted that was simply the way things were. It was adult Samantha who'd risked her life to save his, risked her freedom to prove that while she was an exceptional thief, she wasn't a killer. And it was that Sam who'd given up everything she knew so she could remain in his world. "I changed my mind," he said. "I apologize. Your past has nothing to do with Reg and his sudden, selfish greed."

She kicked an exposed pebble. "It hit close to home, though, didn't it? You not being a hypocrite and all."

For a moment he flashed back to an argument he'd had with his ex-wife. Patricia had wanted them to host a Christmas party in London, with all the guests requested to wear red, gold, or green. Reg had shown up in a bright yellow jumper, and when Richard had suggested there was nothing wrong with wearing a nearly gold color, Patricia had stopped speaking to him for a week. It had seemed petty at the time, and it had left him angry. Compared to the daily challenges of his life now, it would have been laughable.

He linked his arm with Samantha's and stuffed his hand back into his own pocket. "I imagine we'll have more arguments," he said, shortening his stride to match hers. "Just promise me that we won't stop talking."

"Okay," she said without hesitation. "I'm not really a stew-in-silence gal, anyway."

"Good." He stopped, their linked arms forcing her to halt beside him. "Want to come up to my place and take a look at a really old map?"

Samantha pulled her hands from her pockets and slid them

around his chest in a bear hug. "You are so boss. Will you be my boyfriend?"

"Well, I'm already engaged to someone, but very well." Leaning his head down, he caught her mouth in a kiss.

That kiss warmed him to his toes. She'd instigated it, and she'd suggested a connection between them. They already had one, yes, but he was the one generally pushing to move forward. It was a boost to his ego and a boon to his heart when Samantha Jellicoe made it clear that she wanted him as much as he wanted her.

She backed off a little. "You're still going to have to have a chat with Reggie," she pointed out.

Richard sighed. "Yes. Map first. As far as I know he's still digging through the ruins for it, but I think I'd feel better if I handed the map over to you for safekeeping."

"Wow. You *do* trust me." She kissed him again, softly. "Thanks."

With a chuckle he took her hand and continued on to Canniebrae with her. "Of course I trust you. You being sneaky is just a bonus."

"Cool."

In the foyer they shed their coats and hats and gloves. Feeling five pounds lighter inside and out, he led the way upstairs to the library. His aunt snoozed in the chair nearest the fireplace, but the room was otherwise empty of houseguests.

"You hid it in here?" Samantha whispered.

"I like irony," he said, shrugging. "And Reg announced that I'd kept the map secret and hidden it from him out of spite." Richard moved over to the bookcase nearest the window, shifted an antique globe and its pedestal out of the way, and stuck his fingers behind the bookcase. Heavy oak, wall plaster – and nothing in between.

Stretching, he reached in as far as he could. There should have been a thin wooden frame covered by glass. Instead he touched nothing but air. *Fuck.*

From somewhere close behind him, Samantha cleared her

throat. "If it helps, the first place I looked for those books you hid was other shelves in the library."

He jabbed a finger at her. "That does not help."

"It was clever to put it there, actually," she went on anyway. "I would guess Reggie got so frustrated with not finding the map in the old library where he thought it should be, that he gave up and went to the new library for clues."

"My plan was too clever, then," he said, eyeing her and torn between feeling mollified and even more annoyed.

"Yep. Which leaves you with a problem."

"Yes. Reg has the damned map." Straightening, he shoved the globe back into its place with less care than it deserved.

His aunt snorted and sat upright. "I'm sorry, my dear, what did you say? I must have drifted off."

"I was just wondering if you happen to know where Reg is," Richard improvised, when he would much rather have been swearing and throwing things.

"Oh. He and Eerika were in here earlier. I'm not certain where they went. The attic, perhaps?"

"Thank you, Aunt Mercia." He kissed her on the cheek, because God knew none of this was her fault – except for her reservations about Samantha, which Sam seemed to have managed all on her own – then headed out and up the hallway toward the attic stairs.

"Rick."

Richard stopped, looking behind him at Samantha. "I need to talk to him before he does something we'll all regret."

"Yeah. But *you* should talk to him. Without me, and without Norway."

Sighing, he nodded. "Where will you be?"

"In the kitchen. I was promised more soup. I do not turn down soup."

While he appreciated the attempt at humor – and the advice – it didn't help. This was not a conversation he wanted to have.

Hell, he'd hidden things and lied about their existence just to avoid it.

Of course only Walter was in the attic, a magnifying glass in his hand and one enormous brown eye fixed on the brass pull of a mahogany wardrobe. "It's brass; not gold," Richard informed him, leaning against the simple wooden bannister at the top of the stairs.

"Furniture's below my pay grade," Barstone returned, straightening. "I thought the knob would be hand-shaped. It's from a mold, though. Explains the uniformity."

"I thought you knew every salable point about everything."

"Nah. Seventy-five percent of everything, at best. Sam's not up here. I think she went for a walk."

If Richard hadn't known that Walter and Samantha had conversed via walkie-talkie, he would have believed the old fence wasn't sure of her whereabouts. "I gave her a ride back here. I'm actually looking for my cousin. Yule thought he might be up here."

"Just me. I'm helping with inventory."

"And you're leaving tomorrow."

Walter tilted his bald head. "You win Japan, then?"

"Nearly enough."

With a nod, Walter half turned to make a notation in the notebook Samantha had been using for her attic inventory. "You know, eventually you're going to have to ask yourself why you think keeping Sam away from me is the key to keeping her honest. By the time I first met her she was pulling jobs guys three times her age couldn't manage. All I do is try to keep her safe. Because I've for damn sure never been able to make her do anything she didn't want to do."

The idea that no one could influence Samantha but Samantha was one Richard didn't want to contemplate, especially at the moment. "And yet, you're still leaving tomorrow."

"I'm not going to complain about being somewhere with electricity and sunshine." He glanced up. "Your cousin and the blonde were up here earlier. They saw me and retreated. Said something about one of them forgetting gloves. That was about an hour ago."

"Thank you." With a curt nod he headed back into the main part of the house. The memory of the last time he'd interrupted Reg and Miss Nyland still scarred into his brain, he made a fist and rapped on the door of the bedchamber they shared.

"Enter," Eerika called, with that high-pitched trill that made his teeth clench.

Taking a deep breath, he pushed down the old brass handle and stepped into the room. The two of them sat on the bed, the framed map between them. *Fuck.* "A word, Reg?"

His cousin stood, shoulders squared as if he expected a fight. Richard would give it to him, though he preferred a more reasonable and logical resolution. "What?"

"In the hallway, if you please."

If he'd needed any more proof about which of the two of them led the team, the way Reg glanced at Eerika and only moved after she offered a slight nod would have provided it. In a business negotiation he would have sat Reg aside to speak directly with the woman making the decisions. As usual, family made things more complicated.

When Reg joined him, Richard pulled the door closed and moved down to one of the upstairs sitting rooms. "So you want to chat now that I have proof you're a liar?" his cousin said stiffly. "That doesn't precisely leave you standing on the high moral ground, does it?"

"That depends on what you mean to do next, I suppose. Care to enlighten me?" He shut the door, closing them into the sitting room.

Reg looked at him. "Why hide the bloody map?"

Perhaps this wasn't as dire as he'd thought. "Because what it represents isn't mine."

"The treasure, you mean? That's the beauty of it, Ricky. Every bit of that treasure is statute free. It belongs to whomever gets hold of it."

"As a collector of antiquities, I can tell you it's not quite that straightforward. The government likes to know when old things get found, so they can tax them and collect a share of the rarest bits. In addition, if it's on Calliebrae land, it's mine."

"Disputably. There is still treasure, then. Why?"

"I didn't say there was treasure. I said finding and claiming treasure isn't as simple as you seem to think it is."

"Fine. You've given me a piece of your boundless wisdom. Was there something else?" Reg folded his arms over his chest, clearly assuming there *was* something else.

And he was correct about that. "For my own set of reasons, I would like to gift you with a sum of money. In exchange, I will require your word that you will leave off treasure hunting. In writing."

"I'm one of those sticky problems you buy off, then. How much money?"

Richard clenched his jaw. It wasn't that... Unless that was what it had become. "First I'd like to be certain this isn't going to become our new way of relating – you throwing tantrums until I throw money at you to shut you up."

His arms still folded, Reg turned his back and stalked over to the sitting room's window. "For argument's sake let's say there is a highwayman's stash of gold and jewels at the end of that map. When you say things like you feel the need to throw money at me so you can exert some kind of control over a situation, or of me, it makes me want to punch you in the face."

"While you act like a greedy infant despite having the money to do just about whatever you want," Richard retorted, warming to the argument, "do not attempt to claim that moral high ground you seem to cherish so much."

"I think we're finished here."

As Reg stomped for the door, Richard sidestepped to block the exit. "How much do you want? Name the amount that would cause you to let go of this snipe hunt."

"How much are you willing to part with, Ricky? I'd prefer not to be the next relations to cross you, as we all remember what you did to Patricia, but the fact is that whether you have a claim on Will Dawkin's gold or not, this is the kind of publicity you can't buy. Yet you seem as determined to steer clear of it as I am to find it."

"Half a million." He didn't like putting a figure in the air first, damn it all, but this argument was beginning to circle back on itself.

"Pounds, Euros, or American dollars?"

"American dollars."

"Hmm."

Richard rolled his shoulders. "That's not precisely an answer."

To his surprise, Reg chuckled. "This must be driving you mad. You, unable to solve a problem by buying it off."

"That remains to be seen. Half a million, Reg. How much higher do you need me to go?"

"How much is in the cache? Because honestly a season or two of a reality show based on us recovering a treasure and becoming unexpected celebrities is worth more than that. We even have a name for the series. *Booty Queen.*"

Just when had he and Reg grown so far apart? It couldn't come down to one of them having access to more money than the other. That was too simple. Nor did it speak very well for Reginald Clarke Addison. "If there is a cache, I have no idea how much might still be in it after two hundred years. *I* don't want the publicity, not here and not now. I don't want Orrisey turned into a tourist dumping ground with everyone digging up the country-side – my countryside – looking for scraps, filing lawsuits, and destroying their way of life and this entire part of the Highlands. You're not the only one to take into consideration here. For God's sake, Reg." He blew out his breath. "A million. American."

"A mill…" Reg trailed off. "Well, now I'm surprised. That might just do it. But I need to speak with Eerika, first. She's part of this, too."

"You have twelve hours. After that, the amount I'm willing to give you drops by a hundred thousand dollars an hour. And I'll want the map back in exchange for the money."

Richard reached behind himself to open the sitting room door, then backed into the hallway. That hadn't gone particularly well. Hopefully the money would prove more persuasive than his oral arguments. He glanced at his watch. When had it gotten so late? Reg's twelve-hour deadline would hit at three-thirty tomorrow morning. Of course that was only for the million; he hadn't managed any sort of moratorium on the treasure hunting. He needed to have Tom write up an agreement. Something he could force Reg and Norway to abide by.

The rear stairs took him down to just outside the kitchen, and he walked into the loud, bright room to see Samantha seated at the large table there, three of the maids, two footmen, and Mrs. Yule the cook seated around her and all of them talking about traditional Highlands meals.

"It's not so much the contents of haggis as it is the consistency that grosses people out, I think," Samantha was saying, an empty bowl in front of her.

"From the way I've seen some of ye Yanks react, ye'd think we were forcing ye to eat live scorpions," Mrs. Yule said with a laugh.

Richard stepped into their line of sight. "I was always rather partial to haggis," he stated.

"M'laird!"

"No, no, sit. As you were," he commanded, as the room erupted into standing, bowing, and curtsying chaos. In the middle sat Samantha, grinning at him and no doubt thinking how very Downton Abbey he was while she had every one of his employees wrapped around her little finger. "Do you have a moment, Samantha?"

"Aye, I do," she returned, pushing to her feet. "Thank you for the soup, Mrs. Yule," she went on, giving the stout woman a hug. "And I will owe you forever if you put haggis on the table tonight for Donner and Stoney."

"I'll see what I can do, Miss Sam."

Richard took his cat burglar's hand, pulling her into the hallway. "Haggis?"

"I know! Donner will totally barf. Stoney might, too."

"At least you're an equal opportunity tormentor."

Her grin deepened. "When you walked in there and everybody stood up I thought I was in the Downton Abbey kitchen for a minute."

Ha! He *was* beginning to figure out how her mind worked. "I knew you'd say something about that. But I'll have you know that my title outranks the Earl of Grantham," he countered, trying to shove his concerns over Reg to one side for a damned minute.

"Oh, that's right! I've hooked the Marquis of Rawley. Ha! I'm out-marrying Mary Crawley. And I'm a rude, gauche American. Hey, I'm Lady Grantham, only more so."

"Good God. No more Masterpiece Theater for you."

She bumped her hip against his. "You talked to Reggie?"

"I did."

"How bad is it?"

Of course she would have deciphered his expression, probably from the moment he walked into the kitchen. "I'm not entirely certain. We traded barbs, I went from offering five hundred thousand to a million, and gave him twelve hours to swear that he's finished with the highwayman nonsense before I start dropping the price by a hundred thousand an hour."

She pulled out her phone and checked the time. "You threw money at him?"

That sounded unpleasantly familiar. "I offered him money in exchange for his leaving the map and treasure alone."

Samantha moved closer, putting her hands on both his shoulders. "You bought off your cousin. Is that what you want?"

Richard glared at her. "I told you what I want."

"Yes, I know. For the village to remain safe and protected. I meant, is that what you want your relationship with Reggie to be? Just money?"

Richard scowled, a hundred arguments and counter arguments fighting it out in his mind. Not many of them ended with him coming out unscathed. "Why didn't you mention this earlier?"

"Because you guys are cousins. You're family. I thought...I figured you'd work something out." She shrugged. "Maybe you did. Obviously I don't know shit about family."

"You have incomparable instincts," he returned, disliking that fleeting look of – what was it? – regret, he supposed, that he saw on her face when she talked about the past she *hadn't* had. He didn't see that from her often. "Since I've put nothing between us but money, what do you think will happen over the next twelve hours, say? Especially given that Miss Nyland has designed an entire reality series around their discovery and spending of the treasure? They're calling it *Booty Queen.*"

"Well, that's an amazingly horrible name."

"I am in agreement about that."

She walked up the stairs beside him in silence. However little she might know about family dynamics, she did have a good idea about what made people tick, what made them covet what other people owned. She could write a study on greed and desire and the lengths to which people would go to fill the holes in their souls.

"It's not good," she said quietly, as they turned up the hallway toward the billiards room. "If it was just Reggie, I think he'd take the money. Eerika, though, wants to be famous. The money isn't enough. It's important, but it's only fifty percent of her equation."

"What if I do close the house tonight? Pay Reg off and then send everyone packing?"

"As long as they think there's a treasure waiting at the end of their rainbow, I doubt she'll let Reggie forget it's up here. You might be able to keep them out of Canniebrae, but you can't keep them from driving up to the village and staying at one of the bed and breakfast places. Since the entire village knows what they're after, something bad might happen. Somebody *will* get hurt, Rick."

Something about the way she worded all that caught his attention. "As long as they're convinced I've been concealing a treasure, they won't stop looking for it," he mused.

Abruptly Samantha grabbed him by both shoulders, shoving him backward into one of the spare sitting rooms. "Richard William Addison," she breathed, her chin lifted so she could look him directly in the eyes, "are you thinking of doing something nefarious?"

"I'm considering," he admitted.

She continued gazing at him intently. "I am so turned on right now."

Sometimes even his good luck was abysmal. "Hold onto that thought, because I'd say we have a little less than twelve hours to resolve this."

"'We'?" She leaned up and kissed him. "I think I just had an orgasm."

"All right, all right. I get it. I'm willing to do something out of my comfort zone to solve this…dilemma so that no one gets hurt. Do you happen to have any ideas?"

"I might have one or two." She tugged his hand until he followed her back into the hallway and toward the billiards room again. "I need to throw some darts while we discuss, so I'm not tempted to puncture Donner when he hears about this and puts in his two cents."

20

Monday, 3:50 p.m.

"Samantha."

"I'm still up here," her voice came immediately. "Plotting."

Rick topped the attic stairs, the framed map in his arms. "I think," he said slowly, turning the frame to face her, "it worked."

Standing from the little office area she'd dug out for herself in the attic, she moved around a stack of antiques. "So this is the pesky little map that's caused so much trouble," she mused, swiping her hair behind an ear as she bent down. "Can I get a better look at it?"

He put it front side up over a chest of drawers. "Yes, but didn't you hear the part where I said it worked? They went for the money."

"I did." Samantha pulled that large, folded paper from her pocket and laid it down next to the old piece. She'd drawn her own map, he realized. Apparently from the clues she'd picked up from a dozen different sources. Was it necessary to see if her version was accurate? No, not really. But she more than likely wanted to know how close she'd been to the original.

"Do keep in mind that this old thing is costing me a million dollars," he returned, a bit miffed.

"Yeah."

Given that the maps had been drawn nearly two-hundred-fifty years apart, she'd been pretty much spot on. The old map was actually a little rougher than hers and not quite to scale, but that had probably been intentional. As he looked at the old map now, he was surprised it had taken him as long as it had to figure it out. If he hadn't grown up knowing the legends and the countryside, it would have been much more difficult. She'd managed it, though, and in a fraction of the time it had taken him at fifteen.

"How good a look did Reggie get at this when you were kids?" she asked.

"A pretty good look. We had it turned upside down, though. I happened to look at my tracing of it the right way up while I was out walking around the village, and it just kind of…made sense."

She nodded. "You're a good chess player, too. You see patterns."

"Thank you." He felt a little like he was being placated, but he could live with that. Lowering the frame to rest it against the bureau, he eyed his cat burglar. "There is a chance they've sincerely given up the hunt, you know."

That made her look up. "They're just spending the afternoon rolling around on all their cash, then?"

"I wrote them a check. Probably not quite as fun, but I suppose they could be rolling on it."

"Did you give 'em the speech? And have 'em sign the paper?"

Richard frowned. "I'm not an amateur, you know. I hit all the highlights: that I don't want all that publicity up here; that the past should remain in the past; that even if there was something to find, they were in way beyond their depth; that a million would more than likely put any so-called treasure to shame, that by signing their names they were agreeing to take the money in

272

exchange for the treasure. Everything but double-dog daring them to go behind my back. I'm not sure it wasn't entrapment."

"Better they decide to go behind your back now than in six months."

"True enough." It hadn't been pleasant, though. "If Reg doesn't take that bait, I suppose we can be fairly sure the treasure is safe." Reg used to have a modicum of common sense. It would be a pleasant surprise if his cousin used it today.

"Mm hm." Samantha picked up her walkie-talkie. "Stoney, anything?"

"I was just about to call you," her fence's voice came back immediately. "The cousin and the Viking just left the house. Told Yule it was to take a walk and see the snow before it melts. The village knows. They're keeping an eye on them."

"Did they tell you they were heading out?" she asked Rick.

"No, they did not." *Dammit.* "How is it you were so certain?"

Samantha shrugged. "I've spent lots of time with people who're never satisfied with what they have and who always think they can get a better deal. And no, I don't mean you."

"I should hope not."

"Nope. You drive a hard bargain, but you stick with the decision. That's why when guys like Kigomo cheat, it ticks you off."

That actually made him sound rather upstanding. He could live with that. "What's next, then?"

"Plan A. Or A point five, because I was hoping the weather would keep them inside until tomorrow. You go catch up to them, be in a good mood because you won, and keep them away from the village for at least an hour."

"And what will you be doing, pray tell?"

Half turning, she kicked her heel into the framed map, breaking the glass. "Me?" she said, her mind clearly already spinning different scenarios. "I'll be negotiating."

He caught her arm as she retrieved the map, folding it along its old creases. "You're the one who pointed out how seriously the villagers will see this."

"This is what I'm good at, Rick. Let me do it. Just keep them off the road long enough that I can get past them."

"Not alone." His grip on her arm tightened. "I'd risk bringing the eyes of the world up here before I'd risk you."

She blinked as if she'd needed the reminder that the risks she took affected him. "I'll take Stoney."

"And Tom."

"I am n—"

"And Tom," he stated again. On that point, he had no intention of budging. She might know how to deal with people who had things to hide, people who'd stepped across the street to the wrong side of the law, but Tom knew about negotiation and legality. He also had a hell of a right hook if it came down to that.

She blew out her breath. "Fine. Get going. Do you have your walkie?" She pulled it from his pocket and handed it to him. "Channel five. That's just you, me, and Stoney. The village is on seven, and everybody in the house is on three."

Reluctantly he released her arm. "Be careful."

With a swift kiss she grabbed up all the maps and headed downstairs. "You, too."

He didn't have much to be careful about, since he had the boring, pedestrian task of getting in the way of Reg and Miss Nyland, but he understood why it needed to be him. His coat and gloves waited in the foyer, and he pulled them on as Yule found him a scarf.

"It's a bit late for ye to be going out, m'laird," the butler observed.

"I'm trying to track down my cousin," Richard returned, very conscious of the fact that whatever he told Yule would make its way down to the village. "I wanted his opinion on upgrading the stable and making it a bit more useful."

"Ah. Last I saw, he and his lass were headed along the road

down to the village. They left but five minutes ago. I'd imagine ye can catch 'em up without much trouble."

"Thank you, Yule."

It had definitely gotten colder as the sun drifted lower in the sky. Whatever half-melted snow still lay on the ground would freeze into ice overnight. That would make driving a problem, but the helicopter shouldn't have any difficulty when it arrived at noon. He wouldn't have minded Tom remaining longer, but Walter Barstone needed to go.

Settling into a slow jog along the road, he caught up to Reg and Eerika just past the third curve. "There you are," he said, slowing as he reached them.

He caught the end of Reg's stifled frown as his cousin turned around. "What, am I to sign a promise to leave Scotland now? Couldn't that wait until we returned to the house?"

"The equipment drivers will be back tomorrow," he returned, biting down against his immediate urge to return sarcasm with even more blistering sarcasm. "I wanted your opinion on something before they got started. Come take a look at the stable with me before it gets dark."

Richard intentionally worded his statement as a demand rather than a request, but even so he wasn't certain whether it would work or not. He caught Eerika elbowing Reg, but pretended not to notice since his cousin fell into step beside him.

"This is not good timing," Reg muttered. "We're trying to figure out how to use an extra million dollars when we're not permitted to name the source."

"You're sharing it with her, then?" Richard returned in the same tone, as he left the road to take the more direct route back to the house. Samantha and her two-man crew needed to get past them down to the village. "You're that certain she'll stick around even without *Booty Queen*? That she's a...keeper? That's how you worded it with Samantha, isn't it?"

"I'm sharing it in the sense that I'll do some traveling and maybe fuck her on half a dozen different continents. Maybe she can turn that into a show."

Richard caught a whisper of movement off to his right, but he kept his attention on Reg and their whispered conversation. Samantha hadn't wasted any time. He assumed she meant to move the loot before Reg and Eerika could discover it, but he wasn't certain how or why that would discourage them from searching further. But he trusted her, and so he would go along with it. For now. "That's your plan, then?" he said aloud. "Take the funds you could be investing and waste them on mojitos and vibrating beds?"

"I haven't decided yet. What do you want to do with the bloody stable?"

"It's a stable." Richard paused, trying to decide what the hell he did want to do with the building. They hadn't planned out this part. He could improvise, he supposed. "I'll likely be spending more time here at Canniebrae. That means vehicles *and* horses. I want a building that will fit with the house, but also does everything a stable, garage, planting shed, and storage shed does, and also has at least temporary space for a construction overseer and whatever supplies we'll need for restoring the west wing that can't be exposed to a Highlands winter."

"You're going to have to make it a great deal larger than it is now," Reg commented, actually taking a look at the building in question.

For the next forty minutes they discussed building materials, how to separate the animals safely from the machinery, windows, heating systems, and paving the old carriage way. It almost felt like the old days, before he'd informed Uncle Rowland that while he didn't mind suggestions, he would not tolerate being "managed". Back when he and Reg had still been close.

He'd missed this, he realized, even knowing now that his cousin more than likely meant to go behind his back the second he turned around, and that he wasn't having a genuine conversation as much as he was stalling for time. Eerika didn't seem interested in any of it, instead hanging well behind them and checking her watch or her phone every two minutes. Part of him hoped he actually had just interrupted a stroll through the woods. Even that part of him, though, wasn't willing to bet on it.

At the same time, Samantha's assessment that he'd monetized his relationship with his only cousin continued to push at him. Richard took a breath. "Do you like selling cars?"

"What the bloody hell do you care?" Reg shot back at him, defensive all over again.

"Because you're very good at reading between the lines. I could use you, I think, if you want to give it a try. I need a scout in London, someone to keep an eye on up-and-coming businesses and those that aren't being utilized to their full potential. Lots of chatting people up and being charming, dinners, drinks, that sort of thing."

Reg tilted his head. "Are you serious? Why bother? You've already bought me off."

"It's not charity," Richard cut in. "This is my business, and I think you know by now how seriously I view it. I think you'd be good at it. If it...improves our relationship, I will consider that a bonus."

The younger man actually looked down at his shoes. Was it guilt over what was he and the Viking were in the midst of plotting? A genuine thoughtful moment? Richard kept a close eye on him. If this actually stopped the treasure nonsense, that would be a second additional bonus. Mostly, though, Samantha had been correct. He needed to stop looking back at who'd wronged him or thought differently than he did and start looking forward at what he wanted for his life. In his life.

"I...might consider it, Rick. I'd like to think about it, first."

Richard nodded. "I'm on holiday, anyway. We can talk before you leave."

"Certainly."

Finally, the Viking moved forward. "Reginald, I'm getting cold. And you promised me dinner in the village."

"My apologies," Reg said immediately, stepping away from the rear of the stable. "I lost track of time."

"It's getting dark," Richard put in, making one last move to keep them close by, or to maybe convince them to change their minds. "Wouldn't you rather I have Rob bring the jeep around for you?"

"No," Miss Nyland countered. "We prefer to walk."

"You know, the jeep might be a good idea, my dear. Otherwise we'll have to walk back up the hill in the dark."

She stomped one foot, and it nearly went out from under her. "Fine. Yes, we'll take the jeep. Let's be off, then."

"I hope there are no hard feelings, Eerika." Richard started around the side of the stable, whistling for Rob as he went. "No doubt Reg filled your head with fanciful tales of jewels and gold. It's far more likely, if there *was* a cache somewhere, that it would have been silks and sweets and the occasional reticule. People riding in carriages to parties didn't exactly carry all their riches with them."

"Then why is this non-existent cache worth a million dollars?" she returned. "You being a sharp-eyed businessman and all."

The gloves seemed to be coming off. That was fine with him. He'd put up with far too much shit from his relations over the past few days than he would have ever done before Samantha. Before he answered her, Rob appeared and Richard sent him to fetch the jeep.

Then he faced Miss Nyland again. "It's not worth it. By my way of thinking, my cousin has for no apparent reason become obsessed with a treasure map from when he was fourteen. I've therefore given him a sum hopefully large enough to assist him in whatever it was that sent him looking for the treasure in the first place. And you might consider the downward path of Geraldo Rivera's career after he opened an empty treasure vault, then maybe be a little more grateful to me for saving the two of you from that. Any other questions?"

"No," Reg broke in, frowning. "No more questions."

"I still want to go to dinner in the village," Miss Nyland said stiffly, her chin lifted. "Let's go now, Reginald."

For a bare second Richard thought his cousin might resist, might grow a conscience or a spine, as Sam would say. With a twitch of his cheek, though, Reg nodded. "Thanks for the loan of the jeep. We'll be back later."

"I'm not your nanny. Watch the first turn. It's slippery."

They rounded the corner, heading for the wide stable door at the front of the building. Richard stayed where he was, swearing a nearly soundless, cloudy blast of warm air. The two of them weren't just going for dinner at The Bonny Lass. He'd be a fool to believe otherwise.

He pulled the walkie-talkie from his pocket and switched it to channel three. "They're getting in the jeep now," he said quietly. "Where do you want me?"

"In the house, where we all are," Samantha returned immediately, sounding a little breathless. "Yule knows what's up. We're all there, and we're having dinner as usual. Got it?"

Richard frowned at the black box in his hand. "Yes, dear," he returned.

"Sorry. In a hurry. You'll have to stall your aunt and uncle now, so they don't start wondering where we are. Love you."

Well, at least she had time to say that. At the sound of a vehicle starting and then heading down the drive, he returned to the front of the stable. With every fiber of his being he wanted to charge down to the village and help. Instead he'd been elected to be the "everything's normal" guy. He couldn't see what was happening, didn't know what was going on, and if/when everyone returned he would have to play along and hope for the best.

This was one gig, as Samantha called it, that he really wanted to be a part of. On the other hand, if anything went wrong he was precisely the person he wanted available to swoop in and perform a rescue.

○

WHILE RICK WENT to delay his cousin, Samantha ran downstairs. "Stoney," she said into the radio, gathering up a couple of flashlights, "get your coat. I need you downstairs. Now."

"Roger that," his voice returned briskly.

She skidded into the old portrait gallery. "Grab a trowel or shovel if you can find one, too."

"Ten-four."

"Is this an all-thieves-on-deck drill?" Donner asked, turning from his perusal of a suit of armor.

"Thieves and lawyers," she countered. "Rick wants you to help me. It's not a drill. Meet me in the foyer. Dress warm."

She really could have used a little more time to finesse this plan, but it was what it was. Tactical supply-wise she didn't have much that would be useful, but most of this was going to depend on other people, anyway.

"I need Yule in the foyer," she yelled to no one in particular, hoping the house's secret walkie-talkie network would come through for her.

The butler reached the foot of the stairs just as she did. "Did you need me, Miss Sam?"

"Yes. Okay, here goes. There's a ninety-nine percent probability right now that Reg and Eerika are going after Will Dawkin's treasure horde. They've seen the old map. They think it's somewhere in a cave behind The Bonny Lass, and if they don't find it there, they'll never give up." Stoney and then Donner arrived behind her, but she kept talking.

"The three of us here are heading down to St. Andrew's, and I need you to trust me. We're on your side. I need a look at the treasure, and I'll need some help getting a few crappy pieces back into the original cave and making it look undisturbed. We have about an hour. Got it?"

Yule's craggy face had gone more gray than usual, and he kind of looked like a magician whose secret-hiding curtain had just fallen down. "I...I'm nae certain why ye've told me all this, lass."

"Because I need you to radio whoever's in charge at the village and let them know we're on our way. Your secret is safe with us, Yule. Let me help you keep it that way." She pulled open the door herself, shrugging into her coat as she did so.

"The...radio? I dunnae ken what—"

"I know how you're talking to each other and to the village, Yule. It's genius. But this is important. We're going down there whether you help us or not. Rick feels like part of this is his fault, and so we're helping make it right. Come on, guys."

"I – I'll see to it, Miss Sam."

It didn't surprise her that Stoney fell in right behind her, because whether he approved of her becoming a goody two-shoes or not, he was family. She had to give the lawyer some credit, too, because he didn't hesitate either.

"If Yule can't convince the village guys, they may just be waiting for us with torches and pitchforks," Stoney noted.

Rick's voice drifted to her from somewhere just ahead, and she veered left into the trees. "Keep low, and no talking," she whispered.

Hosting a "how to be a thief" seminar hadn't been on her agenda for today, but this would be for nothing if Reggie and Norway realized what was going on. Donner was nearly Rick's height and wasn't crouched nearly low enough, but on the other hand Stoney was wearing a bright blue coat. So far they were both in the C-minus range.

When they'd put a couple of dips and rises between them and Rick, she straightened again, accelerating into a fast trot. "Let's hoof it, team."

"How far is...the village?" Stoney panted.

"About a mile. I told you to get more exercise."

"At least it's downhill most of the way," Donner put in.

"You got the gist of what I was telling Yule, didn't you?" she asked both of them.

"Yep," Stoney said. That made sense; he was pretty familiar with her methods even if this was a rescue rather than a grab.

"I think so. Not quite sure I…get it all, though."

Great. The lawyer was running out of steam, too. This was definitely the D-Team. But Rick was busy keeping Boris and Natasha off her back. "We'll have to play it by ear. I don't know how cooperative they're willing to be. It would be easier if I just slipped in and did this on my own, but I don't know how the village will react to those two snooping around, especially when their goal is to make a really big deal out of it."

Just threatening Reggie and Norway might be easier still, but all it would take would be a phone call to the authorities, or to the Viking's producer friend about locals hiding a national treasure, and everything would change – and not for the better. Hopefully the villagers would realize that as well.

Yule had definitely communicated something, because a dozen big-ass Highlanders stood in front of the church when she and her panting cohorts slipped out of the woods. "Hi," she said. "I'm Sam, that's Donner, and this is Stoney. What did Yule tell you?"

"I'm Father Michael," the smallest of the big men offered. "What Yule said didnae make much sense, so ye'll have to tell us directly, I'm afraid."

She nodded. "I can do that. Can we head into the church while I'm talking? We don't have much time."

Jamie MacCafferty, the owner of The Bonny Lass, stepped in front of her. "I reckon we'll talk right here. Because I'm nae in favor of letting that rich fancy man take what's ours. Or letting ye get a look at it, for that matter. We had a deal with Addison."

And this was why she preferred to work alone. "Over the past month Reggie Addison has convinced himself that his cousin Rick found Will Dawkin's treasure map, and that finding the treasure will make him and his girlfriend rich and famous. He got his hands on the map even after Rick hid it from him, and in an hour or so he'll be down here to claim it all for himself."

"He'll nae find it."

"I know. Because you moved it to the church after Rick tracked it down. But there've been too many arguments and lies. If he doesn't find what he expects, he may just call the authorities out of spite and let them see what they can turn up. I think you know what that'll mean."

That caused some grumbling, most of it in Gaelic – one of the languages she didn't speak. If she and Rick ended up spending more time here, she would have to remedy that.

"What's yer idea then, lass? Just hand it all over and hope he keeps his gobber shut about where it came from? I'm nae willing to give our future over to some pretty London boy who already has gold coming out of his arse."

"I'm not willing to have you give it up, either. Let me look at the stash. While I'm doing that, some of you will need to open up the old cave behind The Bonny Lass. We'll move a few of the worst pieces back in and close it up again – just well enough that it's not obvious but a couple of amateurs could find it fairly easily. It's sealed up on the pub end, I assume?"

"Aye. For eighteen years. The ravine side's been closed for longer than that."

"We need to open the ravine side, because that's the one on the map." She pulled the original map and her version from her pocket. "I put this map together by reading up on Will Dawkin and taking a ride around the countryside. That means someone else could find it, too. Someone other than Reggie Addison. You need a decoy treasure there to keep the real one safe."

"And who are ye, that we should be trusting ye with anything, Yank?"

Lifting her chin, Samantha met Jamie MacCafferty's glare. "I'm the one who on a lark figured out where your damn treasure is and decided to help you keep it instead of calling *National Geographic* and getting a TV show out of the deal. Will Dawkin left this for you. Don't mess it up now."

He drew in a breath, his nose flaring. "If ye lot hadnae come up here, we wouldnae be in this mess."

Men. "And if William Wallace had had a six-gun and some extra ammo, Scotland would never have gone back to English rule." She checked the time on her phone. They were already cutting this far too close. "So do you want to play 'what if', or do you want to take care of what is?"

He blinked. "What is," he conceded.

Father Michael gathered up both maps. "We can debate the rest of this later. Clive, Jamie, take the other lads and start digging up the ravine, and remember ye'll have to make it look good and easy to open when we close it up again. Miss Sam, ye come with me."

Finally. "Stoney, go with the cave guys. You know what it needs to look like. Donner, you're with me."

The pastor and two other men led the way into the church, through a well-hidden door in one of the vestibules, and down into the cellar. From there they opened yet another door, this one hidden behind a bookcase. Man, she loved this kind of stuff. It was a shame the village would probably want to move the loot again after this, because this was a really good hiding place.

She pulled a flashlight from her pocket and turned it on. A dark hole became a stone-walled cave lined with heavy wooden shelves. On the shelves were metal and wooden boxes of varying sizes, together with seven silver candlesticks, a dozen old dueling-style pistols, what looked like an old saddle, and a fair-sized amount of snuff boxes.

"Wow." She couldn't help it. Right there in front of her, things that had been owned, treasured, and used by aristocrats two hundred fifty years ago. From the number of boxes still here after all this time, Will Dawkin had been one hell of a thief.

"Time limit, Jellicoe," Donner commented from behind her.

Samantha shook herself. "Right. Do you have any original chests or boxes or satchels?"

Father Michael pointed at a lower shelf. "All those there." As she took a closer look, he dug into the back corner and produced a moldy-looking lump. "We've kept most everything, just in case. Will a saddlebag work for ye? And that crate there."

"Yes. Perfect."

They began opening boxes. Most of it was jewelry and old coins, and given that the village had already been selling off things for better than two centuries, the original horde must have been massive. She selected some yucky-looking bolts of silk, a couple of broken tea cups and saucers, one gold and two silver coins that looked worn enough to pass for being buried in the dirt since the mid seventeen hundreds, one paste pearl necklace, and a pretty gold necklace from which she reluctantly pried out the ruby in the setting.

"There. Does that look like stuff scavengers would have left behind a long time ago?

"Aye," the priest returned. "Ye've a good eye for antiquities."

"They're a hobby of mine," she said, ignoring Donner's throat clearing. "Let's stuff most of it in the saddlebag, grab that wooden box and the saddle, and head over to the ravine."

Far too many people had emerged from their homes and shops to watch the goings-on. She couldn't blame them, given the significance of the treasure to Orrisey, but it looked damned suspicious. When she mentioned that to Father Michael, the pastor produced a walkie-talkie and spoke a few words in Gaelic. Almost immediately the crowd began thinning.

"I would have thought having wealth like that hidden away would have you at each other's throats," she said, as they hurried along the bottom of the ravine. "There must have been villagers who thought it belonged to them more than anyone else, or who disagreed with the speed at which you were using the funds."

"One or two, aye," the priest returned. "But when Will Dawkin left for the American Colonies he made it clear that his gift was for the village, so that we would survive whatever the Sassenach – the English bastards – tried to do to us. The whole village submits requests or suggestions, and a council of seven meets to vote on the next purchase or improvement."

"That's impressive," Donner said, thankfully not pointing out that selling off antiquities without registering them first was also illegal. Because she really didn't want to have to deal with that mess right now.

"It helps that we can be charming and persuasive, I reckon."

"I hear that," Samantha commented, stepping over an old fallen pine tree. They climbed down another dip, approaching the area she'd searched... Crap, had it just been this morning?

And she'd been dead on target, too. If she'd factored in that they'd moved the treasure because of Rick stumbling across it as a kid, she would have started this morning's search at the church, but this was where it had been for the previous two hundred plus years. Right here.

Stoney emerged from the manhole-sized opening in the side of the ravine. "It's small and rough, but we'd need way more time to open it up more. We also found a nice boulder to roll over the opening here."

"Excellent. I'll go in and place everything if you guys will hand it in to me."

Putting her flashlight between her teeth, she dove in head-first. The ground was cold and damp, but it hadn't frozen yet, thankfully. In another couple of weeks this would have been a very different operation. She picked up a fist-sized rock and scraped and punched it into the wall a couple of times where the shovel marks were too obvious, going in about a dozen feet before a higher, wider chamber opened up. At the back, crumbling dirt revealed part of a brick wall – The Bonny Lass's cellar.

Settling the flashlight into the dirt wall, she heaped up some loose soil. When the box arrived, she flipped it on its side and half buried it. The saddle went into the opposite wall as if over time the sides had caved in over it a little, while she squished the sheets of silk into the edge of the box and the dirt around it. When she got hold of the satchel she took out one of the necklaces and dropped it behind the saddle, clumping more dirt over most of it.

Digging a little wedge into the bottom of the wall, she spread the dirt around to soften the floor. The saddlebag had to appear overlooked, but not so well-hidden Reg and Norway wouldn't find it.

"They're getting in the jeep now," Rick's voice came from her pocket, making her jump. "Where do you want me?"

If they were driving down, her team had like ten minutes left. She pulled out the radio. "In the house, where we all are," she returned, digging out a little more dirt with her free hand. "Yule knows what's up. We're all there, and we're having dinner as usual. Got it?" Reaching over, she shoved the saddlebag into the space she'd made, reaching into it for a coin she could put just at its mouth so light would reflect against it. Hopefully.

"Yes, dear," Rick said, English affront nearly dripping from the speaker.

She started out again on her hands and knees; using one elbow to brace herself, she lifted the walkie-talkie again. "Sorry. In a hurry. You'll have to stall your aunt and uncle now, so they don't start wondering where we are. Love you." Once her head poked out of the hole Stoney grabbed her arm and pulled her to her feet. "We have ten minutes, max. Let's get some dirt shoved in right at the end and put the stone in front of that. We," and she gestured at herself, Stoney, and Donner, "need to get out of sight. I'm thinking The Bonny Lass cellar, so we can listen in and make sure this is working."

"Aye," Jamie said, handing a shovel to the large man Father Michael had called Clive. "Get to it, lads. Come in for a beer on the house when ye've finished, but clean yerselves up first. I have standards to maintain. This way, Miss Sam."

"Is this how you become a crime boss?" Donner whispered, leaning closer to her as they moved past where amateurs would look for footprints and climbed the steep hill.

"You'd better hope not, Guido," she returned, reaching back a hand to haul the rounder Stoney up behind her.

21

Monday, 4:58 p.m.

The walk to The Bonny Lass was much quicker, Samantha noted, when she didn't have to detour into the wilderness to avoid being seen. It would have been much easier just to have Rick just threaten Reggie and Norway into going away and keeping their yaps shut. But Rick and Reggie were family, when he didn't have much in the way of kin, and she had even less than that. She was willing to bank on a little bit of crazy as a plan, and he was willing to trust her on it. That was both gratifying and terrifying.

The Bonny Lass had already begun filling up, which didn't surprise her. For her this was a Hail Mary to save a treasure and Rick's relationship with his cousin. For the villagers of Orrisey, this was their future – and they were trusting her, too. Cripes.

Jamie pulled open the trap door behind the bar and led the way downstairs. In the chilly air the damp and mud on her jeans and coat and gloves started to feel even ickier, but for now she ignored it. When the pub owner hit the light switch she crossed the room to the far wall beside the row of beer kegs and tubes leading to the taps above.

The wall was old quarry stone and mortar, but because she was looking for it, the rough circle of newer cement and newer stones was fairly easy to make out. "Is the wall just these stones?" she asked running her gloved palm over them. "No insulation?"

"Nae. We like the cold, for the beer. The cave's just on the other side."

"Do you have a nail or a spike and a hammer?"

"I have a spike for tapping the kegs." He picked up the old, sharp metal spike and a hammer and brought them over. "If ye break down the wall I reckon that ruins yer plan, though."

She took the tools. "I'm not breaking down the wall. I just want to listen." Picking a spot at the bottom right corner of the newer section, she set the spike between two stones and struck it, hard. It barely made a dent. "Huh."

"Let me," Donner said, taking the hammer and giving the spike a wack.

"The hole has to be small, Thor," Samantha admonished. "Maybe not even all the way through."

"I got it."

"Here's a nail," Stoney said, straightening from the pile of junk in the corner. "Smaller hole."

At least her team was trying to be helpful. Donner hadn't mentioned calling the cops or getting arrested even once. That didn't mean she liked him now, but the next time they clashed she would cut him a little slack. Maybe.

"Okay, that's good," she said, when the spike was about six inches in. "We're out of time, anyway. Jamie, head upstairs and remind everybody this is just an ordinary evening."

"And if this doesnae work?" he asked.

"We go to plan B."

"Is that the plan where we give them a lesson or two so they understand we protect what's ours? Laird Rawley may not like that." The barkeep tilted his head. "Ye ken ye're only here because the laird kept his word to us all those years ago."

Great. "Beating them up is plan C. Plan B is where Lord Rawley kicks their asses and tells them to get the hell off his land."

He sniffed, nodding. "I hope yer plan A works. I'm glad to know ye've a B and a C ready to hand, though." He climbed the steep ladder. "Lights on or off?"

"Off, just in case. But normal noise upstairs."

"Aye. We've played this game before. Well, not us, but our greats and great-greats."

In a second, they were surrounded by blackness. She turned on the flashlight she still had, and used it to find a seat against the wall right beside the hole.

Stoney plunked down beside her, then patted the floor on his other side. "Come on, lawyer. Don't be shy."

Grumbling, Donner sat as well. "This is *not* going in my memoirs," he grunted, as Samantha flicked off the flashlight again.

After a minute of rustling they settled, and she put her head back to listen. Through the closed trap door above the pub was still a little too quiet, but the sound mostly wouldn't carry through the stone wall anyway. Beyond the wall, silence. It would stay that way until Reg and his greedy girlfriend shoved that stone out of the way. If they realized the stone marked the entrance to the old treasure vault.

With a few days she could have turned that cave into a ruin that would have fooled an archaeologist. Even with just fifteen minutes, it wasn't too shabby. Thanks to the slush slowly freezing all along the floor of the ravine, the entrance looked pretty well, but not too well, concealed. She hoped. It was, after all, the first time she'd laid out treasure for somebody else – somebody way less skilled than she was – to find.

"So, you do a lot of this sitting in the dark shit?" Donner whispered.

"No, she waits in the dark for saps like you to fall asleep and then she takes your best stuff," Stoney hissed back.

"That's enough, boys," she snapped, as loudly as she dared. Her father had always called the subject of a theft either saps or marks, and she'd never liked it. Cat burglary had been a challenge for her – her skill versus someone else's paranoia – and her win didn't mean she thought the other guy was stupid. Just less lucky. "I'm retired. This is a favor. Shut up."

They sat there in annoyed silence for what felt like an hour, until she risked checking her phone for the time. Forty-seven minutes they'd been waiting there. Oh, for crying out loud. For the first time it dawned on her that Reggie and Eerika might be too crap at treasure hunting to find the cave. Or what if they were less crap than she'd realized, and they'd figured, like she had, that the loot was in the church? Even she would have had to do some searching to find that hidden door, though.

"Is it here?" she heard faintly, in Norway's voice. She twisted to put her ear closer to the hole. Stoney tapped his finger against her hand, so she knew he'd heard it, too.

"There's a cave opening up," Reggie's voice returned. "Don't shove me."

"Well, hurry! We don't have much time. You don't want your cousin to come looking for us. He can still cancel a stupid check."

"If you don't want to risk it, Ree, we don't have to be here. I could be happy with the million and the job offer."

"As long as no one misses us, we're not risking anything. If we find what we expect, you can tear up that check and throw it back in his face," the Viking hissed back. "Do you see anything?"

"I dropped the torch." A pause. "I see a box!"

"Move! I want to see!"

The hushed, excited tones almost – *almost* – made Samantha feel guilty. She lived for that feeling of anticipation, of reward at the end of a complicated hunt. But there was a reason she'd never hit a museum and she'd only taken from those for whom treasures were about dollar value. The village of Orrisey needed that stash far more than Reggie or Eerika ever would. It had been left for them, for exactly the purpose they'd been putting it to.

"It looks like really old satin," Reggie said, to the accompanying sound of the box being dragged across the dirt floor.

"Silks," Norway corrected a couple of seconds later. "They're... ew, moldy. Completely rubbish. Oh, what's that? Pearls?"

So far, so good. Now *Boot Queen* just had to recognize why the pearls had been left behind.

"What... Give me the torch, Reginald. Oh, fuck. They're paste! Everything here is worthless!"

"It looks like the valuable things were taken or sold off a long time ago, darling. I'm sorry."

"Sorry? You're sorry? This would have made us famous. Now it's just...nothing. We have nothing!" Eerika's voice rose higher and higher in pitch. Great. Hysteria. They hadn't planned for that. If she started flinging the box and rocks around, the cave could collapse on them. That would mean having to dig them out, which would take more fancy footwork to avoid giving away that the treasure crap had been planted.

"Here's a saddle, Ree. And...look, a satchel. Perhaps—"

"Give me that. A coin! And a...necklace." Silence. "The stone's gone. Two – no, three coins, an old silver chain, and mold and paste." More silence. "If your cousin found this, why didn't he just tell us?"

"Maybe there was more here eighteen years ago. Or maybe he never got this far, and just assumed?"

Yes, go with that, Samantha urged silently. Don't ask the sticky questions they hadn't had time to plan for.

"I can't bel..." Norway trailed off.

"What, love? We still have the check. That's more than enough compensation for this mess."

"Yes. Come on. We have to get out of here before somebody

notices that hole is open. I'm definitely not risking that check now."

"We said we were supping at The Bonny Lass."

"I am not going in there looking like this, Reginald."

"We can't go back to Canniebrae looking like this, either. What if… We'll go into the pub and say you took a tumble in the mud, and I rescued you. We'll clean up there, and then head back."

"Yes, yes. For once you've thought of something clever. Let's go."

Crap. Samantha put the flashlight beneath her shirt and turned it on, giving them a dim glow to see by. "Let's go," she breathed, standing and hauling Stoney up beside her. "They have the jeep. If they keep us pinned down here, we'll never get back to the house before they do."

She got them to the ladder and led the way up. As she shouldered the trap door open it yanked up over her head, nearly sending her down backward off the ladder again.

"Well?" Jamie MacCafferty demanded, the pub around them immediately going silent again.

"Be loud," she ordered, hopping up to the bar's wooden floor. "They're on their way here. We need to go."

"Did it work, lass?"

"Yes, it did. So keep in mind that you don't know why the silly English are down here in the village." She jabbed a finger into his wide chest. "You didn't know what they were up to, and you have nothing to hide. Got it?" Samantha enunciated.

The big man tilted his head a little. "Aye. So don't take it wrong when I tell ye to get the devil out of here. And keep what ye saw and heard to yerselves. All of ye."

"Yeah. We were never here." She backhanded Donner in the chest and headed for the door. After she stuck her head out to make sure it was still clear, she sent her team out ahead of her. "We take the road, hurry, clean up, and sit down to dinner."

"You're bossy," Donner noted.

"Go."

As she started out after them, Jamie caught her arm. "We want ye to know, if this doesn't work, we'll be blaming ye for stepping in where ye're nae wanted."

"Okay. If this does work, your council can vote on giving me a fucking parade for me sticking my neck out this far."

He grinned, releasing her. "Ye're a bit mad, aren't ye? I like it. Ye've a deal, lass."

As she sprinted into the cold twilight, a bouncing flashlight and a pair of bodies appeared around the corner. Reversing course with a silent curse, Samantha dove back inside the pub. "They're right behind me," she muttered, as she dodged Jamie, jumped the bar, and half slid down the ladder, pulling the trap door down over her as the front door jingled and opened.

"Well, shit," she breathed, freeing her flashlight and turning it on again as she stepped onto the cellar floor. If she didn't get back to Canniebrae and take a seat at the dinner table before the treasure hunters returned, this whole gig would be blown.

She looked at the repaired wall. If the treasure hunters stuck to the tumble-and-rescue story they'd concocted in the cave, at best she probably had twenty minutes before they left to get the jeep and drove back up the hill. While she *could* get the wall down in that time, doing it quietly was something else altogether.

"Okay, Sam. Think." Flashing the light toward the junky corner, she dug past a bucket, an empty, broken keg, some cleaning supplies, bits of brick and stone, some rope, and three beer mugs. Even MacGyver would have had trouble with this one.

She picked up the rope, then squatted by the small hole Donner had made. With the spike and quiet taps on the hammer she chipped bits of it away, making the hole big enough to fit the spike all the way through.

The radio in her pocket clicked three times. Cursing, she pulled it free. "I'm here," she whispered.

"What happened?" Stoney whispered back.

"Too much gabbing. Keep heading to the house. I'll meet you there."

Pocketing the radio again, she knotted the rope around the middle of the spike and pushed it through the hole in the wall. She had to use the nail to poke it all the way into the cave, then fed through a little more rope to give the spike room to settle on the ground. Then, wrapping both hands around the rope, she pulled. Hard.

The spike stopped crosswise against the hole, which she'd wanted. The wall around it, though, didn't budge. "Dammit."

She fed rope through again, then stood, bracing one foot on the floor and the other against the bottom of the wall, and hauled backward with all her strength and weight. One golf-ball sized stone popped out of the wall and clacked to the floor in front of her.

Well, that was a start, anyway. Shifting the spike with her hand, she did it again. Five minutes later three stones sat at her feet, and she had a hole too large for the spike to work efficiently, but too small for more than one leg to fit through.

"Come on, stupid wall," she grunted, shoving her arm in and going after the next stone.

"Samantha, what's going on?"

Rick's voice on the radio was quiet, so at least he was trying to be cautious. It would take Stoney and Tom another ten minutes at least to get back up the winding hill to the house, so he was probably totally in the dark. "You've been more patient than I expected," she returned quietly.

"I just hit my limit on patience. Words, please."

"I can't right now. Reggie and Norway bought the story, Donner and Stoney are on the way back to the house, and once your cousin cleans up at The Bonny Lass so he doesn't look like he rolled in the mud, they'll be back up, too. Talk soon."

"And where are you?" he insisted, keeping his voice down. "You left that part out."

"I'm in The Bonny Lass's cellar," she finally whispered. "They haven't seen me, and I want to keep it that way."

She could almost hear him come to attention. "You need to be back here before the jeep is."

"I know. I'm working on it. Hence the wanting to stop talking."

"You opened the cave, yes?"

"Yes."

"I'm coming to get you."

"No, you're not. *You* have to be there when they get back." She shoved again with all her weight, but nothing budged. Apparently she'd found the one weak spot in the wall already.

"Yule's telling Jamie to offer Reg dinner at The Bonny Lass. That should give you another half hour or more."

"Thanks. Keep everything on schedule, Rick, or this is for nothing. Your aunt and uncle can't think anything's weird, either. Ever. If they say something to Reggie, this could start all over again."

She was not going to be the weakest link here. Rick had given in, which surprised her, but he'd also hopefully bought her a few more minutes – at least for polite British refusals if Reggie and Norway decided not to eat at the pub. That was all she could count on timewise, until or unless she heard differently.

Reggie and Eerika must have put the stone back in place at the far end of the tunnel, because she didn't feel a draft even with the hole slowly growing in size. That was good; she didn't look forward to freezing to death in the already chilly cellar of a Scottish pub.

Pulling the spike back in, she returned to prying at the concrete between the stones. Hammering was out, because that would immediately draw attention to the cellar. This was stupid. They'd gathered an entire village together and concocted a plan to save the treasury, all in less than an hour. It wasn't supposed to all fall apart because she couldn't get out of a six-hundred-year-old cellar. For most of her twenty-five years she'd done this kind of thing for a damned living.

"You know, Will Dawkin, from one thief to another, I could use some help," she muttered. "I am keeping your stash safe, after all."

More pushing and pulling wrenched another stone loose, but it was taking too long. Plus, she was going to end up with bruises all up and down her arms. No sleeveless ball gowns for her.

A wisp of cold air, really cold air, slid up her fingers through her glove and all the way up her left arm as she reached through the wall for another stone to grip. She jerked backward, and two more stones dropped to the floor.

That was wind. Spooky wind. But she could probably get everything but her shoulders through the hole now. One or two more. And an extra ten minutes. Was that too much to ask? Samantha shook out her arms and reached in again.

A hand grabbed her wrist. Barely stifling a yelp, she yanked backward again – and black-gloved fingers reached into the flash-light-lit cellar. "I told you I was coming for you," soft, smooth Brit drifted into her.

Grabbing up the flashlight, she pointed it at the hole – illuminating a frowning pair of deep blue eyes crouched low to look back at her. "You gave me a heart attack," she whispered fiercely, something deeper than relief sinking through her. "Push here and I'll pry at the mortar," she said, indicating her target rock.

"On three," Rick said, digging his fingers around the stone.

He counted down, and she pried as he shoved. With a shower of cement chips, the stone came loose. She caught it in her hands and set it aside. "What do you think?" she asked, eyeing the irregular opening.

"Give it a try. I'll pull."

Samantha handed through her walkie-talkie and the flashlight, then took off her coat and gave it to Rick, too. "Okay, ready or not."

Going down on her hands and knees then lowering onto her stomach, she stuck her head through, then squeezed her right arm followed by her shoulder. On her own she wouldn't have risked trapping one arm up and one down, but with Rick there she could attempt it. Lowering her left shoulder as much as she could, she gripped Rick's wrist and pulled as he shifted backward. "Slower," she grunted. "My boobs are getting squished."

Immediately he eased up by about half. "Well, protect your boobs," he returned. "I'm quite fond of them."

"Dammit, don't make me laugh. Pull right a little more." He did so, and her left sleeve tore as her shoulder came free. "Hallelujah. Now more left. My left!"

Her left arm came completely free, and she scooted forward on her hands and toes. After what felt like an hour of butt wiggling she edged onto one side and curled her legs into the cave with the rest of her. Whoosh. She sat up, and Rick helped her pull on her coat again.

"Well done, my lass," he said. "You'd never have gotten Tom or Walter out that way."

"Thanks, but it's not over yet. Plus now you look as dirty as I do."

He ran his flashlight over her. "I doubt that. I'll lead, shall I?"

"Sure. I like looking at your butt."

"Don't I know it." Crawling, his wildly-swinging light in one hand, he headed out through the narrow tunnel.

She would have admired his rear more if she hadn't been pouring logic all over that sudden cold breeze and the stones falling out of the wall. It had to have been the draft from Rick pulling the cover stone aside, and the change in air pressure. Unless that hadn't been it at all. As she left the main part of the cave, she turned her head to look back. "Thank you," she breathed.

Outside she straightened, taking a deep breath of the fresh, cold air. Man, she didn't like being trapped somewhere. While she was pretty sure she was going to have some sore arm muscles tomorrow, she would have risked losing a limb entirely if that had been what it took to escape. Then she turned around to look at Rick, and realized it might get even worse than that. "You *rode* here?" she hissed.

"It was faster than running." He swung into the saddle and freed his left foot from the stirrup before he reached a hand down. "You did say we're in a hurry."

So she had. Clenching her jaw, she took his hand and climbed up on Major General Llewelyn Alberic Emilius Price-Davies – Major for short – behind Rick, and slid both arms around his waist. "Punch it, Chewie."

22

Monday, 6:37 p.m.

Richard sent Major pounding up the hill. The road would have been faster, if less straightforward, but after all this he wasn't about to risk them being overtaken by the jeep.

A quarter mile above the village Samantha's walkie-talkie beeped, and with a curse she freed one hand from her vise-like grip around his middle and retrieved it from her pocket. "I'm here," she said, nearly taking his ear off with the thing as she tried to talk and hold onto him at the same time.

"Miss Sam," Jamie's voice came back. "Yule said ye'd be on this channel. They've just left. I came down to fetch ye from the cellar, but all I found was a hole and a gold coin."

"A coin?" Richard repeated.

"I didn't put it there," she said, and lifted the radio again. "I'll pay you back for the wall."

"If ye've convinced them to stay away, I'll pay for it myself. I'm putting together a parade committee. Dunnae make me call it off."

"I'll let you know. Thanks."

She pocketed the radio and grabbed Richard again, tightly enough to restrict his breathing. She definitely hadn't been faking her uneasiness about horseback riding, then. "Parade?"

"Later. Right now I'm hanging on for dear life."

He swore he could hear the jeep off to the right, but in the dark and with Samantha up behind him he refused to risk going any faster. At the same time, he couldn't help feeling a little like a romance hero, the lord rescuing his damsel and setting off to protect the village and the castle. Samantha wasn't precisely the damsel type, but she *was* his, and he *had* rescued her. She would never have made it back to Canniebrae in time on her own.

Headlights flashed into view on the right and slightly down the hill from where they rode. *Damn.* If Reg or Eerika caught even a whiff that someone from the house had been down in the village, they would assume there'd been meddling and that the treasure had been moved. Even worse, they would realize, and correctly, that they were being made to look foolish.

"It gets steep up here," he said, ducking lower along Major's withers. "Hold on."

"I am so not a frontier woman," she returned, her voice muffled and breathless against his back.

It would never do for him to admit he was a bit relieved to find there was something in the world at which she didn't excel. "You could always have robbed trains," he pointed out.

"Or river boats."

They charged over the lip of the hill and stopped just on the far side of the stable. He whistled for Briggs as Samantha staggered to the ground. Leaving Major to wait for the groom, Richard dismounted and grabbed Samantha's hand. Keeping low, they made it through the kitchen door just as the jeep pulled up to the front of stable.

"Upstairs," she panted, as they raced through the kitchen and the servants' quarters and up the back staircase.

At the door just before their bedchamber he let her go. "The blue dress?"

"Yes, please," she returned, shoving into the spare room and shutting the door behind herself.

He was getting their damned shower fixed tomorrow, if that was the last thing he did. Shedding his coat and gloves and shoes, he scooped up her blue Vera Wang dress and matching pumps, then a dark blue suit with a gray tie for himself.

As he rushed back to the next-door room he could hear Yule down below, informing Reg that the household was just sitting down for dinner. Samantha was already out of the shower, and from the goosebumps covering her bare skin she hadn't bothered waiting for the water to get warm. She dressed as he stepped into the tiny shower and washed dirt and grime from his hair and face, refusing to wince at the shock of the icy water running down his legs.

"We're going to be late," he said, as she finished toweling off her hair and then went to work on his.

"It's because we were having shower sex," she announced, putting on her lipstick, rubbing some off, and then deliberately kissing his jaw.

He kissed her back on the mouth before she could straighten. "Thank you for this. Have I mentioned that you're remarkable?"

Smiling, she helped him knot his tie. "You're not so bad, your-self. I know you're not big on public displays of affection, but it was really good shower sex. With soap." With that she ran back into the bathroom and turned the water on again.

"What are you doing?"

"Ambiance."

That didn't make sense, but given the excuse she'd thought up for them, the slightly rumpled look they'd managed actually fit rather well. They headed downstairs and stopped just outside the dining room as inside Eerika described how quaint The Bonny Lass was, and how much they'd enjoyed their meal.

Richard slid his hand around Samantha's waist and strolled into the room beside her. Tom and Walter were there already, looking very clean and neatly-pressed, as did his aunt and uncle. Reg and Miss Nyland stood to one side of the table, chatting with the four of them.

"My apologies," Richard said, turning Samantha in a circle and then holding her chair out for her. "We…lost track of time."

"And you may want to wait until morning to take a shower," Samantha added, smiling up over her shoulder at him. "I don't think there's any hot water left."

"Well, how thoughtful of you, telling us," Eerika returned.

So that was why she'd turned the water back on. If Samantha ever decided to go back to the dark side, he was going to be in a great deal of trouble. "A shame you've already eaten, Reg," he said aloud, as footmen marched in with soup and buttered rolls. "Mrs. Yule promised fresh pan-fried bass and wild rice." He took his seat at the head of the table, intentionally not inviting them to join in, anyway. Yes, he could be that petty when it suited him. He was permitting Reg to get away with a million dollars and a job offer even though his cousin had broken his word, after all. "And some haggis for Tom and Walter to try."

"Great," Tom muttered, looking dubiously at the bowl.

Reg looked rather mournfully at the rolls, but Miss Nyland wrapped her arms around one of his. "I am too stuffed to eat a single thing," she purred. "Perhaps we should retire early tonight, Reginald."

"Yes, fine. Good night, all."

"Good night, my dear," Aunt Mercia said.

They'd done it. They'd saved the treasure, the village, and enabled him to keep the promise he'd made eighteen years ago. He looked up to see Samantha grinning at him, but then she side-eyed toward his aunt and uncle. Right. It would be very like his aunt to comment to her son in the morning about how all the young people had spent dinner in exceptionally high spirits and kept toasting each other.

"Tom and Walter are leaving tomorrow," he said instead. "Do you have anything to put on the helicopter to London, Uncle Rowland?"

"Must you go?" Aunt Mercia asked, reaching over to cover Walter's hand with her pale, plump one. "It's been delightful having you both here." She smiled. "And Walter here is quite the rummy player."

"Walter," Samantha said, her eyes widening. "You didn't wager anything, did you?"

"We all have our secrets," Barstone drawled, glancing at Richard.

What did that mean? That they'd landed closer on the morality scale because they'd worked together? Because he'd concealed a theft that had been ongoing for two and a half centuries? The next time Barstone chose to do something that benefitted other than himself or Sam, then Richard would re-evaluate the score in their competition.

After dinner they moved to the formal drawing room and sat to chat well past when his aunt and uncle generally retired for the evening. Even with the benefit of years of practice at being charming, he was impatient and hard-pressed to hide that fact. He wanted to know everything Sam and her unlikely team had done, what Reg and Eerika had said, how the entire plan had gone off. Because after two weeks of tension and stress, he felt…relieved.

Finally, his uncle rose and helped his aunt to her feet. "If we don't see you before you leave tomorrow," he said in his usual grand tone, "have a safe journey. I'm certain we'll meet again at the wedding, whenever that may be, if not before."

"You'll know the date as soon as we set one," Richard contributed, rising to walk them to the door. "Uncle Rowland, would you mind sending your leatherworks portfolio to me in London?"

His uncle's cheeks flushed, a smile pulling at his heavy jowls. "I'd be happy to, Richard. What are you thinking?"

"I'm thinking New York could use a high-quality leatherworks shop that's not tied to west coast chains."

His aunt took her husband's hand and squeezed. "We'll see that you get that portfolio, Richard."

Once they were gone he headed for the side table where a dozen various bottles of liquor, glasses, and a bucket of ice sat. "Champagne would be more appropriate, but will you settle for a Scotch whisky?" He lifted a single aluminum can from the table. "And a diet Coke for milady?"

Samantha laughed. "I'll take a tiny drop of whisky. The soda would keep me awake."

"Nothing would keep me awake," Tom countered. "Anti-thieving is hard work."

"It would've seemed like less work if there'd been more profit in it," Walter said, accepting a glass. "But it gave Sam a couple of points in her 'good guy' column, so I'll drink to that."

"Thanks, Stoney."

Richard raised his glass. "Thanks to all three of you. It wasn't what any of us were expecting when we arrived, but admirably done. To us."

"To us," the other three echoed, and drank. Samantha made her usual "I hate alcohol" face, but she finished off her finger-width of whisky.

"Your ride will be here promptly at ten o'clock," Richard said, polishing off his own glass. "And it's not leaving without both of you on board."

"Thank God," Walter commented. "This place nearly froze my ass off."

"Bed now," Samantha said, yawning. "See you guys in the morning."

They all parted at the top of the stairs, and Richard followed Samantha into the spare bedchamber to turn off the trickle of now-cold water. "I thought I might have melted off the wallpaper," she commented, yawning again. "I should have realized we'd run out of hot way before that could happen."

"That was a clever touch. And I have no problem at all with Reg and Norway going to bed without supper or a hot shower."

Once they were in their own room he slipped off his jacket and hung it over a chair before he stepped out of his shoes. Sam headed into the bathroom, emerging a few minutes later in an oversized T-shirt and sweat pants. "What?" she asked, looking at his lifted eyebrow. "More for you to strip off me. Plus it's comfy."

Putting his hands on her hips, he lowered his head and kissed her. She tasted of fresh mint. "You look good in comfy."

She ran her palm along his cheek. "Are you and Reggie going to be okay?"

"I think so. I hope so. I offered him a job with Addisco. It seemed to alter things. Though he did go behind my back after he gave his word he was finished with treasure hunting."

"Yeah, but as far as you're supposed to know, he didn't go behind your back. On his own I don't think he would have gone looking for the cave, anyway. He definitely didn't want to be there. If you want to keep a relationship with your cousin, you're going to have to let this whole episode go."

Sighing, he touched his forehead to hers. "When did you become so wise?"

"I've always been wise, dude. I just try not to overwhelm you with it. You totally made your uncle's week, too, you know."

"I'm trying to let the past go. I may not need his business advice, but he is my family."

"I'm going to brag about you to Katie Donner. You have so many more awesome points than Donner does."

"Mm hm. Keep talking, Yank. But don't start without me."

Figuring that what worked for her would do for him, he settled for a pair of sweat pants, himself. They *were* comfortable, and it had been a bloody long day. After he brushed his teeth he left the bathroom, then paused as a soft snore came from the bed.

If this was what married life with Sam Jellicoe was going to be like, he looked forward to it. With a slow grin he slid beneath the covers and put his arm over her waist, tucking her back against his chest. She never fell asleep before he did. He didn't know if it was about her still being semi-nocturnal, or her level of trust, or how difficult it was for her to relax, but she'd never fallen asleep before him. Until tonight.

Whatever else had happened here, now or in the past, he was doubly glad they'd made the trip. He wouldn't be avoiding Canniebrae any longer, because Samantha had made it magical to him again.

The dim light shining beneath the door from the hallway flickered and went out, followed immediately by distant shouts of "power's oot". Richard grinned, softly kissed Samantha's cheek, and shut his eyes.

○

"IT'S NOT FOR YOU."

Samantha opened her eyes. She wasn't sure if someone had spoken, or if she'd hung onto the tail end of a dream. Rick breathed softly against the back of her neck, so it hadn't been him talking.

The fire past the foot of the bed had been roaring when she'd climbed beneath the blankets; now it was a guttering red glow. Man, she'd slept hard. But hey, she'd helped save a village and a cousinly relationship, plus dug her way through a stone wall. And earned a parade, whether Jamie MacCafferty would follow through with that or not.

She settled her head back down, then lifted it again. Two walkie-talkies lay on the floor, side by side, both of them pointing toward the door. Okay. They'd both been really tired when they'd gotten ready for bed, but that seemed...oddly symmetrical.

Scooting carefully from beneath Rick's arm, she stood. Something had made her wake up, and it hadn't been a fear thing. She had a really strong instinct for self-preservation, after all. Grimacing, she padded barefoot to the door, stepping over the radios, and slipped into the hallway.

Man, the floor was cold, but going back for shoes or socks might wake up Rick. On the other hand, what the hell was she doing out of bed at zero-dark-whatever? Taking a breath she turned around again – and heard something.

It was an old house, yeah, but that had been a creaking floorboard sound, accompanied by a footstep sound. Changing course, she headed for the main staircase and descended, as usual staying close to the bannister where the steps were sturdier and less likely to make noise.

On the first landing she paused. Dark movement down in the foyer, a human shape – with light-colored hair pulled back in a ponytail. *Norway?* That didn't bode well. Nor did the satchel the wannabe reality star carried over one arm, or the night vision camera she held in the other.

Samantha crouched, watching as Eerika put the camera in the bag, pulled on a dark coat, and turned on her phone to look at a photo. A photo of the old highwayman map.

Crap. Norway had figured it out, then, just as Samantha had. The treasure being moved after Rick had discovered it, the likeliest new hiding place, everything. And she hadn't told Reggie about it, because she was definitely alone. She'd probably figured it out down in the cave, and had kept it to herself.

"Going somewhere?" Samantha asked.

Eerika jumped, putting a hand to her chest. "What? Oh! You frightened me."

"I asked if you were going somewhere," Samantha repeated.

"Oh. Well, I was restless. Just going for a walk."

Sam had a couple of responses ready for that, but she went with the one that was the least self-incriminating. "You know I find lost treasures for a living, right? Try again."

Brushing her hair back from her face, Eerika straightened. "I don't know what you're implying, but I'm going for a walk. Excuse me."

"Rick was willing to overlook you and Reggie digging through that old cave earlier. Maybe you should check with Reggie, though, before you decide to throw his million bucks and his new job away."

Abruptly Norway's shoulders lifted. "Will Dawkin's treasure isn't protected by any law. Aside from that, it's not *my* money I'm risking. Do you not understand? A two-hundred-fifty-year-old highwayman's treasure? Not only will it make me rich even after I turn a percentage over to the government, but highwaymen are romantic. I'll be in *National Geographic*, *Vogue*, *Elle*, *People* – all of them. And I'll spend the next three to five years on the telly sharing my story of how the treasure changed my life."

Hmm. So, she did know something about popular culture in this century. Appealing to Eerika's sense of fairness or asking her to have some compassion for the villagers, would obviously be a waste of breath. Eerika Nyland had one person in her mind, and nobody else – including Reggie – mattered to her.

"Nothing's going to stop you from being the *Booty Queen*, right?" Samantha murmured, easing forward to sit on the step just below the landing.

"Correct." Norway picked up the satchel again.

"Except me."

Eerika snorted. "You? I take kick boxing, my dear, and you're well, tiny."

Five foot four-and-a-half was *not* tiny. It was petite. "One time," she said, knowing she was edging closer to trouble and deciding it was worth it, "I needed to get into a safe closed by a combination lock and a double key mechanism. The safe was on the twenty-third floor of a pretty secure office building."

"I don't care what artifact retrievals you've made, dear."

"I'm not finished," Samantha cut in, more sharply. "I went into the safe owner's house, past his three dogs, his alarm system, and his cameras, and I took the key off his neck. While he slept. Then I climbed the outside of his office building, cut through a window, cracked his safe, and retrieved the statue I'd been sent after."

That last part wasn't quite true, except that Stoney had found a buyer who wanted a particular Rodin sculpture and had paid them a million cash for it. She *had* retrieved it for someone, and that was what counted for this conversation.

"And I'm supposed to be impressed?" Norway said, just a little shrilly.

"Yeah, you should be. Firstly, there's no way you make it down to the village before I do. Secondly, even if you did manage to grab a couple of things, I would get them back. Thirdly, if you tried to get some publicity for this, I'd see to it that you look like a liar and an idiot." She sat forward, elbows on her knees. "I know where you live, I know where you work, and I know where you go. I'm one of those specially-trained people who's found legit employment in the private sector. I have connections and people who owe me favors. Get it?"

"I—"

"And I'm only bothering to give you this speech because Reggie likes you, and he's family. To put it bluntly, Eerika, don't fuck with me, and I won't ruin your life. Go back to bed and get Reggie to take you somewhere exotic and expensive, and then break up with him. And don't ever come back to this part of Scotland. I don't think you're a good fit for this family."

"And you *are* a good fit? Some ex-CIA spy?"

"Who else could keep Rick Addison safe?" Samantha stood, fluidly and in a single motion, and Eerika backed up a step. "Do we have an agreement? Or do I start pushing buttons that cost you your reputation and your job?"

"What do you care about that bloody treasure? It's my entire future!"

"I care that it's where it should be. That has nothing to do with either of us. Pitch your producer friend that series about how you hook rich guys. You could still call it *Booty Queen*, only it would be about your sex life."

"You're a bitch," Norway exclaimed, her hand going up to her chest again.

"Yes, I am. But all you have to do is go back to bed and forget all your theories about some old shit buried in a village, give me back my camera, and delete any map photos still on your phone. So, for the last time. Do we have an agreement, Eerika?"

The tall blonde stomped one foot. "You haven't left me much choice, have you?"

"No, I haven't. If we have any part of this conversation again, you'll be sewing dresses instead of buying them."

"Fine, then. You win. I do hope you're happy." With an obvious hesitation Eerika headed toward her up the stairs.

Samantha snagged the satchel from her as she reached the landing and pulled the camera out of it. "I'll take that. And the bag. It's a good size for my shoes. Now let's see those photos go away."

"The... Fine."

As Samantha watched, Norway opened her phone, called up photos, and deleted the ones she'd clearly taken of the map while it had been in its frame. Samantha pointed at one of the paste pearl necklace, held in a dirty gloved hand. "That one, too."

She followed Eerika up the stairs and waited there until she heard a door open and close down the hallway. Only then did she relax. That had been too freaking close. Whatever had made her get up, ghost or dream or flying walkie-talkies, she owed a drink and a couple of ginormous thank yous.

As she started back to the master bedchamber the floor

popped softly behind her. Samantha whipped around, ready to drop damn Eerika. Enough was enough. But the shadow that separated from one of the suits of armor was taller than Norway and wore a T-shirt over a pair of dark sweat pants. "You are definitely getting stealthier," she whispered.

Rick walked up to her and didn't stop until he'd wrapped her in his arms. He felt warm and solid in the cold dark. "How did you know she was about to leave the house?"

"My Spidey-senses started tingling." That was about as accurate as she could be.

She felt his breath in her hair as he lowered his head. "Thank you," he murmured. "Again." Shifting his grip to an arm across her shoulders, he headed them back to their bedroom.

"You're my guy." It didn't sound like enough, because it was beginning to scare her how vital he was to her, and just how far she was willing to go to protect him, and to stay in his life. "I like spring. It's a good time for a wedding."

He hesitated for a bare moment before he pushed open the door with his free hand. "Good. I like spring, as well." Rick cleared his throat. "That speech of yours was very Liam Neeson, by the way."

Samantha grinned. "Well, I do have a particular set of skills." She scooted back beneath the covers. "And very cold feet. So cold you may decide this whole marriage thing isn't worth it."

Rick pulled off his shirt and dropped it beside the bed. "You just saved a village for the second time in one night. I think I can tolerate your cold feet. As long as they're literal cold feet and not the figurative ones."

"No, they're literal." As soon as he slid beneath the covers behind her, she curled up to press them against his stomach.

"Y – *Christ!*" With a laughing yelp he rolled, clearly trying to escape.

Samantha straddled him, pinning his hands beneath hers and

gazing down at those Caribbean blue eyes. "Not so fast, Brit. Warm me up."

In a breathless second she was on her back, with him pinning her. "That I can do, cat burglar."

She grinned. "Meow."

THE END

DISCOVER MORE BY SUZANNE ENOCH

Traditional Regencies
The Black Duke's Prize
Angel's Devil

Regency Historicals
Lady Rogue
Stolen Kisses

The Bancroft Brothers
By Love Undone
Taming Rafe

With This Ring
Reforming a Rake
Meet Me at Midnight
A Matter of Scandal

Lessons in Love
The Rake
London's Perfect Scoundrel

England's Perfect Hero

Anthologies
One True Love (from The Further Observations of Lady
Whistledown)
A Touch of Scandal (from Lady Whistledown Strikes Back)

The Griffin Family
Sin and Sensibility
An Invitation to Sin
Something Sinful
Sins of a Duke

Contemporary Romantic Suspense
Flirting with Danger
Don't Look Down
Billionaires Prefer Blondes
Twice the Temptation (half historical, half contemporary)
A Touch of Minx
Barefoot in the Dark

The Notorious Gentlemen
After the Kiss
Before the Scandal
Always a Scoundrel

The Adventurers' Club
The Care and Taming of a Rogue
A Lady's Guide to Improper Behavior
Rules of an Engagement

The Scandalous Brides
A Beginner's Guide to Rakes
Taming an Impossible Rogue

Rules to Catch a Devilish Duke
The Handbook to Handling His Lordship

Standalone Short Stories
Good Earl Hunting

The Scandalous Highlanders
One Hot Scot (a short story)
The Devil Wears Kilts
Rogue with a Brogue
Mad, Bad and Dangerous in Plaid
Some Like it Scot

No Ordinary Hero
Hero in the Highlands
My One True Highlander
A Devil in Scotland

ABOUT THE AUTHOR

A lifelong lover of books, Suzanne Enoch has been writing them since she learned to read. She is the author of two well-received traditional Regencies, 24 and counting England-set Historical Romances, four contemporary Romantic Suspense novels, and a growing number of Scottish Highlands Historical Romances including the October 2016 release of HERO IN THE HIGH-LANDS (Book One in the No Ordinary Hero trilogy).

A native and current resident of Southern California, Suzanne lives with a green parakeet named Kermit, some very chirpy finches, and a small army of Star Wars figures (including a life-size Yoda). Her books regularly appear on the *New York Times* and *USA Today* bestseller lists, and when she's not busily working on her next book or staging fights with action figures, she likes to read, play video games, and go to the movies with her large and supportive village.

Website: http://www.suzanneenoch.com

Twitter: @SuzieEnoch
Facebook: https://www.facebook.com/SuzanneEnoch/

CPSIA information can be obtained
at www.ICGtesting.com
Printed in the USA
LVHW010515160622
721366LV00013B/405